AN INTRODUCTION TO PARANORMAL DIPLOMACY

VAMPIRE INNOCENT BOOK 9

MATTHEW S. COX

DIVISION ZERO PRESS

An Introduction to Paranormal Diplomacy
Vampire Innocent Book 9
© 2019 Matthew S. Cox
All Rights Reserved

Cover & interior art by: Alexandria Thompson

ISBN (eBook): 978-1-950738-18-2

ISBN (paperback): 978-1-950738-19-9

CONTENTS

DON'T PANIC, THE KITTEN IS SUPPOSED TO BE GLOWING

Chaos is a lie made up by those who cannot comprehend the infinitely complex threads linking the universe.

Or so says Professor Heath.

My theory is simpler: college students can suffer serious brain injury in various ways.

Overdosing on drugs, drunk driving, suffering too many hits in football, telling a vegan 'oops, actually this *does* have meat in it' after they start eating, or taking a philosophy class taught by a professor who isn't merely there for the paycheck—and who happens to be a vampire.

Guess which careless thing I did? So, Professor Heath stuck us with the kind of assignment high-school-me would have ignored and spent the rest of the day eating half a box of double chocolate ice cream fudge, wrapping myself in a blanket, and binge-watching *Friends* or 90210.

Sometimes, the F really is better for mental health.

Anyway, last week's philosophy class set a record for being simultaneously simple and frustrating. Professor Heath wrote the line about chaos on the whiteboard, then announced we all had to write a 2,500 word essay expounding on our feelings regarding his statement.

We could agree and support the idea the universe was run by some kind of grand architect and everything, no matter how seemingly chaotic, happened according to some plan. Or, we could dispute it and defend the notion of chaos—not 'chaos theory' though, that's a whole other bucket of head exploding WTF I'm not prepared to think about now. He also gave us a third option: simply write based on our reaction to the statement neither defending nor discrediting chaos.

He gave us the entire class period to work on it and announced he'd dedicate the next class period to discussing everyone's thoughts. Of course, he couldn't resist being a showman. Professor Heath further said he'd predict, based on what he's observed about us, how we'd respond. I'm sure he intends to blow everyone away in the manner of a stage magician. Only, in this case, he's not using sleight-of-hand but mind-reading. He gave the class time to start their essays so he could eavesdrop on our thoughts, possibly except mine. I didn't feel anything weird in my head. Not sure how big the age gap needs to be before a vampire can read the thoughts of a younger vampire.

My prediction for next philosophy class is a whole bunch of grown adults being mystified and baffled how he successfully 'predicted' them defending or disputing chaos. He did chuckle to himself once or twice during class, so I'm guessing at least one person is going to write an essay about how philosophy is total BS or do something literally chaotic and analyze the cheeseburger skit from *Saturday Night Live*.

Pepsi… no Coke.

You know, because turning in an essay entirely unrelated to the assignment would be chaotic.

I considered something along those lines and writing an erotic fanfiction involving the Smurfs and Pokémon, but the idea never made it past the tip of my brain before I blushed too hard to keep thinking about it. How chaotic would that be, right? *Me* writing something bawdy. Of course, it wouldn't have been sexy as much as completely absurd.

My initial idea to fill my essay with randomness came from having no damn idea how I felt regarding chaos and not really wanting to waste time thinking about it. Even if there *is* some grand architect, god, sentient cosmic energy, or even a burdensome bureaucratic organization run by drunk ill-tempered faeries in too-tight underwear deciding how everything happens, what good would it do for us to be aware of it? Not like said 'thing in control' would change what it's doing because we think it or they exist.

It's a real pain in the ass trying to wrap my brain around heady crap like chaos when I'm all wound up over politics. And no, not the kind of politics responsible for ruining Facebook and family dinners. I mean vampire, prima-donna bullshit type politics. Somewhere, my mother's spidey-sense is tingling because I thought a nasty word. She's probably going to go give Sierra a hard time even though the word formed in my head. Swear the girl curses more in a week than I did in eighteen years. How she gets so upset over video games is a mystery to me. Sure, some games piss me off, but when they get me seriously ticked off, I walk away. Sierra's got way more of a competitive streak than me, I guess. She can't let it go.

It's also a fairly safe bet more swear words have flown out of my mouth in the past six months than the rest of my life. By no means has my language ever been Sophia pure, though. My youngest sister only rarely uses words as harsh as 'damn.' Honestly, it wouldn't be a false statement to say I went through my life without really swearing much at all. Everything after late June is technically *not* happening within my life—since Scott murdered me. But, tragedy is managed. No, the Seahawks didn't lose the Super Bowl to the Browns. I meant less anguishing tragedies. Namely, my death. I'm over it. Mostly. My worries now consist of other stuff. Like vampire politics. And besides, the Seahawks would never lose to the Browns in the Super Bowl because the Browns would never make it there in the first place.

After the dreaded meeting with Arthur Wolent in regard to the events of one Damarco Miller, vampire hunter, I went to Aurélie's apartment to relax. She explained a little about vampire power structures. You know, stuff a *sire* really ought to do within the first couple weeks. Thanks, Dalton. In the US, we don't have much of an official political structure overseeing the undead. As she put it, the country is divided into a bunch of simple territories in a manner similar to wolf packs. Each group tends to stick to its area. There aren't any issues moving from one to another as long as a vampire doesn't cause trouble. Permanent 'moves' generally require inserting oneself into the local society and being there long enough, but it's more of a 'best practices' thing, like how society expects people not to wear socks with sandals. Not technically illegal, but few dare.

In Europe, it's entirely different. Everything is meticulous and overdone with 'melodramatic ceremony' as she put it. They, too, have territories, but also a whole bunch of traditions and weird laws or some such thing. She called it tedious and pointless—and to hear Aurélie call something tedious and pointless means quite a lot. This is a woman who spends two hours getting into her dress and would gasp at a person for not using the right utensil for the right course at a meal where everyone gets like five forks, three knives, a bunch of spoons and... yeah, way over my head.

Never in my life did I realize oysters had specific forks, or eating salad with the dinner fork could send a viscount into convulsions. European vampires are heavy on the tradition and pointless laws. Apparently, she grew tired of it and came to the US, where it's far more lax. Go figure, around here, she's considered the one who's obsessed with formality and such. But she doesn't miss the burdensome politics and the insufferable jackasses who adore it.

Speaking of, there's this major douchebag named Paolo Cabrini. He's one of the older vampires in the area and part of the power structure. I'd almost say political parties, but they don't really have anything so official... or corrupt. The best way for me to describe it— and bear in mind my exposure is fairly limited—is vampires around here fall into one of four groups.

The first are, I guess what one would call 'traditionalists.' They've kinda gathered around Arthur Wolent as a 'leader' of sorts. He's an old Fury who, for reasons beyond my knowing, is basically treated like the area's big boss for vampire kind. No, he's not like a king or anything. Or even president. Picture a neighborhood from a hundred years ago with a Mafia don living there. He's not technically or legally in control of anything, but everyone more or less does whatever he wants. No idea if the man has or had any ties to legit organized crime in life, but something about him gives off the vibe. Maybe the suits?

Second, there's Paolo's group. They, too, are traditionalists... but taken to the extreme. If vampirism were religion, he'd want to burn people at the stake for eating meat on Friday. Or stake vampires on Friday for burning meat. Okay, maybe I'm exaggerating a touch. But, yeah. He's a complete prick. The man threw a complete wobbly—as my sire Dalton would say—over me breaking ages and ages of tradition by not reinventing myself away from my mortal life. To hear him ramble on, me living at home with my parents is as horrific as, oh, I dunno... going to a Michelin-starred restaurant and being served instant mashed potatoes from a box.

Not that I've ever been to such a fancy place. Mom likes watching Gordon Ramsay on TV.

Group three are the vampires who don't really care who's in power or who thinks they're in power. They hang around mostly to have a good time and catch juicy gossip. Aurélie, my mentor, falls into this group, as do most of the socialites. They couldn't care less about me, my family, or which vampire's in charge. It would upset them more to hear about a surprise elimination on *Dancing With the Stars* than if, say, Wolent destroyed Paolo with his bare hands in the middle of one of those soirees they love so much.

No, I don't think it'll happen, but hey a girl can dream, right?

In the fourth group are the vampires who largely ignore politics. Lost Ones mostly. Though, to be fair, the Shadows don't *ignore* the politics as much as stay out of it and watch from the... well... shadows. The Lost Ones actively reject any notion of laws or organization among vampire kind, feeling superior to the 'old stuffy sods' who want to recreate the very same mortal power structures undeath is supposed to free us from.

Oops, there I go ranting like Dalton again.

Then, there's me.

I'm in like a fifth group, which isn't really a fifth group as much as its occupying the line between groups three and four. Aurélie insists on me attending those soirees, which puts me in group three since, okay, I'll tolerate the costume ball thing but the whole political scene is of less interest to me than whatever remains of the bugs my brother feeds his pet frogs. Group four might be a contender, too, since if not for Aurélie, I'd remain completely clueless about the existence of other vampires in the area.

But, as the old saying goes, ignorance is *not* bliss. One of Paolo's friends would have eventually gotten wind of me living with my mortal family and caused trouble. Having Aurélie's protection keeps him at arm's length.

But back to my other worries.

See, the thing about having the protection of an old, powerful vampire is, any other vampire who gives even one micro-crap about undead society is unable to start shit with me directly unless I do something deserving of retaliation. Not this girl. My plan is—was—to simply try to exist in as close to a mortal way as possible. Since Paolo would stir up a whole boatload of mess if he sent someone to kick my ass or hurt my family, he's trying his best to get at me politically.

Sigh.

So, when I happened to be the first vampire in the area to become aware of a hunter roaming around, and didn't run right away to ring the proverbial fire alarm, it gave the bastard an opening. I had two major problems, not the least of which was a vampire hunter trying to kill Professor Heath. Paolo managed to get Wolent to basically order me to kill the hunter. Any vampires Damarco killed while here would have been viewed the same as if I'd done it. Worse, in the course of me looking for a way to get him out of Seattle without hurting him—he seemed like a nice guy for a vampire hunter—an outsider decided to make a meal of my best friend, Ashley.

Yeah, that didn't go over well with me.

Like, seriously not well. Long story short, he ended up dead by Damarco's crossbow. Though, I *had* been trying to kill him myself at the time. So, yeah, I spent a good few days shitting bricks over how Wolent would react to the mess. Not the best time to be trying to figure out a philosophy essay capable of giving Carl Sagan brain freeze.

Okay, more like it would give brain freeze to Carl Sagan's somewhat less intelligent second cousin who had only a passing interest in astrophysics. Mr. Sagan would've probably written 50,000 words about chaos by now.

Anyway, I finally met with Wolent after several nail-biting nights. To absolutely no one's shock, Paolo wasn't happy Damarco walked out of Seattle alive. Wolent didn't seem too pleased about it either, until I explained how Damarco had no affiliation to any order, unspoken or otherwise. Apparently, an organized ancient society of vampire hunters exists—The Unspoken Order. However, the group didn't back him and likely doesn't even know about him. Damarco lost his parents to a careless vampire, decided he'd start trying to kill us all, and merely ran into an 'official' vampire hunter by chance around the time the old man died from something like cancer. Also, my giving him a mental compulsion to stay away from Seattle satisfied the 'get rid of him' requirement.

If I hadn't been as nervous as a kid being arrested for the first time standing in front of all those elders, I'd *so* have taken a picture of Paolo's face when Wolent told me he'd accept what I did, then made a remark about how having an overly soft-hearted vampire around would pose less future problems than if I'd been bloodthirsty.

For a little while, Paolo's head seemed ready to explode. It reddened more when Aurélie dug into him with a passing remark about how much time he wastes plotting against a harmless little girl. Coming from anyone else, being called a little girl would've bothered me, but I know exactly why she said it. The woman didn't insult me as much as exaggerate to make him seem even lamer. Besides, she uttered a comparatively true statement. A six-year-old would have better odds winning a fist fight against a Navy SEAL than I'd have against Paolo. Maybe someday when I'm a century or so into this undeath thing, it won't be so lopsided.

Honestly, it doesn't bother me being weak compared to the other vamps. I have no desire to start messes. Now if I could only get the

Universe to stop dicking with me. Not to complain—yes, I know every sentence starting with 'not to...' is always the exact opposite— okay, so to complain, it's driving me crazy how it seems the harder I try to keep my head down and stay normal, the more weird crap finds me.

If I start dressing up like Elvira and doing a bad Transylvanian accent, will crap leave me alone?

A glowing blue light fills the room behind me, casting the shadow of my head and my computer monitor on the wall. I peer back over my shoulder at Klepto—Sophia's kitten—or at least a three-dimensional blue ghost of said kitten—floating near my ceiling, little paws flapping as though she swam in water.

"Either someone's messing around with holograms, or something weird is going on."

"Mew," says Klepto in a bizarre, unnatural voice. Like someone plugged a kitten into a guitar amp with maximum distortion.

Okay, whatever. Yeah, pretty sure the answer to 'will the universe leave me alone' is a giant no. Probably a double middle finger right in my face.

Whatever. I turn back to the computer and stare at my half-started essay.

Regarding the destruction of Ruben, the elders didn't care as much as I thought they would. He'd been an outsider new to the area. Worse, he made a habit of killing while he fed, which tended to attract hunters. Odds are high he would've been destroyed or run out of town before long anyway. Even Paolo had little to say about Damarco finishing Ruben off—at least, after he tried to blame me for the destruction of a vampire. I found a backbone then and explained he'd nearly killed Ashley and *I* had been in the process of trying to destroy Ruben when Damarco interrupted us.

Oh, yeah... apparently, Ashley is now 'legally' considered my thrall.

I kinda had to claim her to justify attempting to destroy Ruben. Vampires don't have mortal friends. They have pets, employees, or helpers. No, I haven't told Ashley yet. And no, I am not planning to literally make her into my thrall. For one thing, she's my best friend and I can't do anything to her resulting in any of her free will being removed. Second, keeping a thrall—at least a supernatural one—requires a vampire loan them some power. Whatever power is loaned, the vampire loses until the thrall is destroyed. I don't have much to begin with. The look Paolo gave me made it clear he knew Ashley's 'thralldom' existed only on paper. Ask me if I care. The only real effect it has is me not being able to officially claim any other thralls until or unless Ashley is killed. Even the sticklers don't really care if I empower her or not. Sure, they think I'm a fool for not doing it, since it makes her 'useless and short lived.' But joke's on them. She's not my thrall to do anything for me. It's only 'paperwork' to keep other vampires off her.

Unfortunately, it leaves Michelle vulnerable, but if I don't talk about her, maybe they won't notice she exists. And it's *really* crappy of me to think, but Ashley's been my friend since preschool, basically another sister. Enough guilt. I didn't sit there contemplating which of my friends I love more, it all happened in a spur of the moment 'agree to this on the spot in two seconds or bad shit happens' kind of way.

Point being, *this* girl walked away from a potential category five hurricane of poop without a scratch. Sure, most of vampire society in the area now thinks of me as a harmless kid, and probably will for a *loooong* time, but—*thbtbtbt!* I don't care. Years from now after my parents are gone, my sibs are elderly, my friends dead, and it's only me left... *then* I might care what other vampires think of me.

My immediate plans include finishing this chaos essay, spending a quality hour with a peaches & cream bath bomb, and enjoying the time I've got left to be with family and friends. Yanno, maybe chaos really *is* a lie. Any number of things could have contributed to Dalton being in the woods the night Scott stabbed me. Things he thought or did a hundred years ago *might* have made the difference in his being there. Sierra—well, both my sisters—are terrified of school shooters. What if the Universe turned me into a vampire to protect them? Though, honestly, it would've been far simpler to cause the crazy guy to have a heart attack than set in motion a chain of events a million steps long.

And only a little arrogant on my part to think the Universe arranged all this stuff starting thousands of years ago to protect *my* sister.

Hmm. Maybe there isn't a grand architect. Stuff might simply happen… because.

Like kittens transubstantiating into an energy form capable of flight.

I look back at Klepto. She's 'swimming' around near my ceiling like a serious clipping error from a video game. Great, Sophia got her cat from Bethesda. What's next, a horse standing on the wall? Shouldn't even joke about horses. If Sophia got one, she'd squee with delight so loud, every window in Cottage Lake would shatter.

"Having fun?" I ask.

"Mew."

She doesn't appear distressed, so… I mean, what exactly counts as abnormal for a kitten who can teleport and appears capable of understanding human speech? Figuring out the answer would probably hurt less than this darn philosophy essay. Hmm. Couple weeks ago, I said something in class about things happening simply because. People have been trying to find a reason for the way stuff goes down since we started walking on two legs. Okay, maybe not *quite* so far back. Asking 'the big question' probably started around the time of cave paintings.

A butterfly farting in Istanbul doesn't make a little kid in San Francisco drop his ice cream on a hot sidewalk—and I proceed to waste ten minutes trying to figure out if butterflies *can* fart. Right, Sarah. Focus.

Why does stuff happen? Because it does. Chaos is real.

Maybe a grand architect *does* exist and he or she is a random sort of being like Salvador Dali on a major acid trip. Oh, there we go. I'll argue chaos simultaneously exists and doesn't. We're following the *chaotic* plan of an architect who designed everything to be random.

Who cares if it's right or not? This is philosophy class. I'm not searching for the right answer.

I'm searching for the *write* answer.

Meaning, whatever eats up 2,500 words and sounds more coherent than Randy Wilson trying to recite Hamlet's soliloquy at our high school graduation party after too many beers. No, not the official party. The one at Tiffany's place later the same night where I ended up in a clothes hamper. Imagine if glowing-Klepto swam through the room there. Wow. Follows-Rules Girl—that's me—didn't touch any of the 'fun' stuff, but a handful of kids hit acid. More than a handful smoked weed. Some did both. The kitten would've been a legend.

Or turned the party into an utter madhouse.

I get two pages into the essay before another sort of existential crisis invades my head.

No, not moping about the future. More about wasting the present. The pile of textbooks beside my computer screen mocks me for my undeath. What sort of vampire in their right mind goes to freakin' college? I smirk at myself. The kind of vampire who lives in her parents' basement, that's who.

Is it really worth the time? Yeah, having to attend classes shaves a couple hours off each weekday potentially spent with my siblings or parents. Before my death, I didn't go out of my way to hang out with them. In fact, I kinda tried to avoid them. Like, really. What seventeen-year-old wants to hang out with three little kids when they have friends their own age? I wasn't mean to them, just... didn't pay attention. Death put family in hyperfocus.

Really, they have friends and lives, too. Even Sam, the youngest, is nine now. They don't need or want to cling to me constantly—Sophia notwithstanding. No reason to feel guilty about two hours a night. Grr. I'm using my sibs as scapegoats to deflect my attention away from questioning my major: computer programming. I thought, hey, what's a job a person can do from home—read: vampire lair—and wouldn't be a problem? My father's a programmer. He works from home. Sounded like a perfect fit.

Only, I'm not the nerd Sophia is. She's good at math, loves schoolwork, and wants to become a professional make-up artist for like film studios. Maybe she'll change her mind as she grows up and become a scientist, doctor, or veterinarian. Sierra wants to make video games as a career but she's not exactly on the same plateau of nerdvana as Soph. Sierra's not dumb, not by a long shot. She could get straight A's and take advanced classes if she wanted to, but she's lazy and would rather sit around playing video games all the time than worry about schoolwork.

I'm kinda halfway between nerd and lazy. I don't *love* programming the way Sierra would if she could get past her laziness. Granted, I don't hate it either. It's kinda like the cheeseburger at my old school cafeteria. A comfortable choice without risk but not particularly exciting. My mind wanders. For the unlife of me, I can't figure out what my major would've been if I'd *not* been killed and turned into a vampire. Whether or not homesickness made me wimp out and come home from USC after one semester, I'd still have needed to pick a major at some point.

I'm more than a little jealous of Ashley and Michelle. Both of them knew for most of senior year where they wanted to go in life. Michelle's got her target set on law school after she finishes up a criminal justice degree. She wants to be a prosecutor someday, maybe DA, so she can clean the system up from the inside. Ashley's aiming for veterinarian. Oh, the injured dog we transported, Hershey? Yeah, he's doing great.

My problem at the moment is feeling guilty for draining my parents' money on college when it won't do me any good. Am I, as a vampire, *really* going to make a career out of programming? It would be one thing if I adored doing it and wanted to learn for the fun of it… but, meh. As for what I'd major in without undeath, no freakin' idea. I'd probably have finished with some generic arts degree if nothing leapt out at me as a good idea. About the only thing for sure is I wouldn't have majored in anthropology or English. Why get a degree if I'd end up waiting tables anyway?

Ugh. Dad's joke makes me feel even worse.

I don't want to become a lawyer like my mother. At least, I *was* exceedingly conflict-averse before death. It would've went way beyond my ability to cope having to stand up in front of people and argue a case. For heck's sake, it took me months—and a lot of encouragement from my friends—to dump Scott. I'd been afraid of that conversation for weeks, and not at all because I expected him to do anything as volatile as stab me.

Now? Yeah, I've ripped people apart with my bare hands. Pretty sure I could rip them apart verbally if I had to. Going lawyer like Mom isn't a bad idea except for the small problem of my having a severe sun allergy. No job as 'outsidey' as an attorney is a good fit for me. Judges really hate it when counsel doesn't show up on time. No way could I possibly be in court at 8:00 a.m., ever. No matter how gloomy the day.

Hmm, maybe I could study cinematography or journalism and work as a movie reviewer? Sit in my basement all day watching movies and writing about them? Totally my speed. Or do copywriting. Maybe having an English degree *won't* be as useless as my father thinks. Especially since I could mind-control my way into whatever job I wanted.

Of course, if I can't deal with a 2,500 word essay on chaos, how the heck am I going to write movie reviews—or anything—as a job? For a vampire, any official job is going to be more like a hobby. I'm not going to *need* a career. It'll be something I do for fun and a little extra cash. Kind of like how my Aunt Jody does tarot readings and such for clients.

Right. Back to work.

Apparently, thinking of changing majors away from programming makes me happy. So much so, I breeze through the rest of my partially coherent musing on chaos. Wonder if anyone else in my class is going to answer an A or B question with 'both.' Here I am feeling clever, and in all probability, Professor Heath has seen this exact argument a thousand times before. Then again, he has been teaching for a *long* time.

I'm halfway done re-reading it when a ping comes from the computer. Neither Ashley nor Michelle usually send me Facebook messages, so it's probably someone from our old high school who *just* got the memo about me 'not really being killed.' Probably a good idea for me to keep up the story about my life being normal, so I click over to the web browser… and see two new friend requests from Cody and Ben Peters.

Wow… after the craziness we experienced at the Lewis & Clark Caverns, I figured the brothers wanted to forget any of it happened. Cody has—well, fingers crossed it's *had*—more than a little crush on me. Hopefully, finding out I'm really eighteen, not to mention a vampire, helped him get past it.

Ehh, why not?

I accept the friend requests and within five seconds, a group chat pops open. 'Hey, long time, what's up?' turns into a fairly routine catch-up session. They don't need to know about any of the oddities going on here or in my vampiric life, so they get a 'not much, just dealing with college' type version of my life since the summer.

Ben: ‹Hey, we think there's a v in the area.›

Cody: ‹Yeah, Mom's getting major bad vibes from this house two blocks away. No one seems to be there during the day, but lights are on at night.›

I laugh, despite them being unable to hear me. ‹Chill out. It's just the Klopeks.›

Ben: ‹Is that bad?›

Cody: ‹LOL! Sounds like a weird monster.›

Two important pieces of information hit me. One: these two are younger than me, fourteen and fifteen. Two: they don't have a father obsessed with Eighties movies. Good chance they missed my joke.

‹Guess you guys never saw *The Burbs*?›

Ben: ‹Huh?›

‹Old movie. Weird neighbors. Umm, even if it is what you think it might be, you guys should keep your distance and not get involved. Stay safe. You're not old enough to mess with this stuff for real. And most of them don't kill, remember?›

Cody: ‹Yeah, I know. But it's super eerie. If stuff goes FUBAR, can you help?›

Klepto continues flying in circles around my ceiling like a tiny Goodyear Blimp. She's still glowing bright blue, her entire body made of energy. Oh, wow. I hope she's not destabilizing and about to melt back into a pile of mushroom dust. Sophia would be devastated.

Not wanting to tell the boys things are already FUBAR, I end up sending: ‹Yeah, sure. Be careful. Hey, need to check on something here real quick. BRB.›

Both of them reply with 'K.'

"Something wrong?" I ask, staring up at the kitten.

"Mew," says Klepto, then glides like a ghost up through the ceiling.

My room looks weird without the blue light, back to an almost black-and-white world of drab half colors. Maybe I should turn on a light? Ugh, guess I'd gotten used to it. Equal parts worried and curious, I head upstairs. It's past the Littles' bedtime, but not by a ton. They can usually get away with staying up too late as long as they're quiet. Mom goes to bed early most nights and Dad will only investigate potential breaches of bedtime if he notices a light on or hears noise.

I head upstairs, quiet as a ninja without consciously trying to be due to the combination of bare feet, carpeting, and superhuman vampire reflexes. The only way I could possibly be any quieter is flying. But, I'm not *trying* to ambush any prey, merely not wake sleeping Littles.

Scintillating blue light shines out from under Sophia's bedroom door, flashing and pulsing like she's invited a bunch of mimes over to have a rave. Considering the amount of light Klepto threw off, it's not proof my sister is awake, but I'm still worried enough to check in on her.

The sight waiting for me when I open the door is enough to derp-slap me right across the face.

Sophia, in her nightgown, floats cross-legged a few inches off the floor above a 'circle of power' made by her crayons and markers laid end to end on the carpet. She's got four extra—ghostly—arms, all six of her hands holding various small objects like feathers, bowls, a candle (not lit), and either dice or tiny bones. She legit looks like Shiva or something.

Klepto's hovering in front of her, staring. The kitten's eyes have become as big as hen's eggs, white, and filled with spirals. Pretty sure my sister's eyes are glowing, but it's hard to tell. The kitten's too bright.

I'm not sure who's trying to mesmerize who.

This is like an episode of Looney Tunes written by HP Lovecraft. Wait, no. There aren't any tentacles and no one's gone insane—yet. Let's go with Looney Tunes written by Poe.

"Uhh, Soph?" I whisper. "Everything okay?"

"Yep," she says, normal as anything.

"You're floating and you have six arms."

She grins. "I don't. It's just a helping hand spell. The arms are illusions. I've been practicing making illusions with the book Mr. Anderson let me borrow."

"Why is your kitten glowing?" Right, I'll take 'questions no one has ever asked before' for $400.

"Umm. Not sure exactly." Sophia sets down the feather and bowl. The other four arms each place their respective objects on the rug around her, then fade away. "She started glowing when I tried to figure out the spell to make light, then started flying around when I did the levitation spell. I think it's normal."

"Mew."

"It's past your bedtime, kiddo. If Mom or Dad catch you doing sorcery at this hour, you're gonna get grounded." 'Things no one ever expected to say' for $600.

"Yeah, I know. I'm already shutting down the spell." She brings her hands together in front of herself and closes her eyes.

"Trying to make teachers forget about homework again?"

"No. Trying to ward the school. So, like, if anyone evil tries to find it, they'll get lost."

Speechless. I have no idea who—if anyone—to become furious with over my little siblings being traumatized at possible violence at their school. With a sigh, I hang my head. Yeah, there definitely are more difficult questions than trying to figure out if chaos is real.

"Don't cry," whispers Sophia. "I think it worked."

"Good." I exhale my anxiety, anger, and grief out my nose.

Klepto dims back to a normal, fuzzy grey kitten with bright teal eyes… and drops to the rug on her paws. "Mew."

"Any idea why she glowed?"

Sophia shakes her head, making her long blonde hair wave back and forth. "Not exactly. This book doesn't have anything in it about familiars. I'll ask next time we visit the mystics."

"Okay. I hope your kitten isn't the harbinger of the end times."

Klepto sits back on her haunches, head cocked, giving me this 'that's right. I could end the world if I wanted to' look.

"Hah. No." Sophia scoops the kitten up and hugs her. "Gotta go to the bathroom. I swear I'll go to sleep right after."

"Okay."

She walks out into the hall carrying the kitten.

The little fuzzball keeps looking at me with the same expression as if to say the world only continued to exist because the kitten permitted it to.

Ugh. My unlife is weird.

2

FAIRY TALES AND CRIME DRAMAS

Wednesday's aren't usually known as big 'go out and have fun' nights.

Restaurant crowds—I'd say bar crowds, but neither Hunter nor I are old enough—are pretty light in the middle of the week. He's got the night off from waiting tables at Mi Tierra and claims to be all caught up with his classwork, so he picks me up from school after my calculus class lets out at 9:30 ish for a date night.

Since I don't really eat anymore, at least not out of necessity, he's been trying to come up with other things to do than take me out for dinner. Like tonight, for example. We're going to a live theater performance, or some such thing, downtown.

He opens the passenger door window to say something, but I surprise him by jumping in *Dukes of Hazzard* style. Being able to fly makes it way easier. My butt hits the seat the same time my lips crash against his.

"Hey," I say after we lean back from a long kiss. "As much as I'd love to just sit here and make out with you, we're gonna be late."

Hunter smiles at me in a 'show? What show?' kind of way. "Yeah, I guess."

"Hah." I chuck my backpack into the rear seat. "So what is this thing you're taking me to, anyway?'

"Oh, umm… about that." He drops the car in gear and pulls out. "I thought I got a good deal on a symphony concert, but I didn't read the tickets right. It's not the Seattle Philharmonic. It's some guy named Phil with a harmonica, doing stand-up comedy. Probably why the tickets were only $28."

I stare at him. "Sounds ridiculous… and probably funny."

He manages to last a whole fourteen seconds before he laughs. "I'm teasing. It's a small theater house doing a reimagining of *A Midsummer Night's Dream*, only they've turned it into a heavy metal musical."

"Okay, now we're talking weirder than a dude with a harmonica." I tap my foot. "But, I'm curious."

"Ever listen to Nightwish or Epica?" asks Hunter.

"I've never even heard of them. Bands?"

"Yeah. This is kinda like them. Basically, an opera singer fronting a metal band."

I give him major side eye. "Ooo… kay."

"If you hate it, we don't have to stay the whole time."

"Aww, it can't be *too* bad. It only sounds like a strange idea to me. See, if you ask my dad what heavy metal is, he'll say Metallica or Guns 'N Roses."

"Nah, those bands are classic rock."

I chuckle. "Don't let my dad hear you call them classic rock. He'll age away into a mummy right before our eyes."

"How's Coralie doing?"

"Huh? Where'd that come from?" I blink at him.

"Mummy?"

"Oh…" I cringe. Looking at the woman's ghost is *way* more pleasant than seeing her physical remains. "As far as I know, safe. She hasn't popped in since she warned me about Ashley. Probably good not to hear from an oracle. Means nothing crazy dangerous is going to happen soon."

Hunter looks over at me after stopping at a red light. "How's Ash?"

I wave randomly. "You know how she is. Totally freaked out for like a day, now she acts like she didn't almost die. The girl is abnormally cheerful and optimistic. Mrs. Carter made her take a week off work to rest, but Ash refused to miss school."

"A sunny disposition ought'a help her with the bad parts of being a vet." He squeezes my hand.

"I hope so. She was a mess for months when Bonkers died."

"Bonkers?"

A sad sigh escapes me. "We were like eleven or so. Bonkers was her mother's old orange tabby cat. Big ol' fluffy thing. Had to be sixteen pounds. He got the zooms all the time. Would race around the house, stop short, give you a weird look, then take off running like you pointed a gun at him."

Hunter laughs. "Cats… poor guy. So what happened to him?"

"Nothing crazy. Only age. Of course, it hit her worse because Ashley found him dead when she got home from school. Bonkers had curled up on her bed. She felt *so* guilty for not being home for his last minutes."

"Aww." Hunter slows, and pulls in behind a few cars waiting to enter a parking garage. "Way harder to deal with losing *your* cat than helping other people cope with losing their pet."

"True. I think she'll be okay. She's squishy on the outside, but tougher than she looks inside. When those idiot wanna-be hunters attacked me, she went all lioness on them."

He makes a silly face at me. "No wonder you two are such close friends. You're a lot alike."

"Hah."

"I'm serious. Most people in your situation would lose their minds."

I overact a nutty smile. "You're so sure I haven't."

"Positive." He leans in and sneaks a quick kiss since the cars aren't moving. "You're still the same girl I fell in love with four years ago."

"Yeah, no kidding. I look like a freshman again."

He chuckles. "You don't look like you're fourteen."

"Thanks."

"More like fifteen," he says, deadpan.

I gasp, feigning shock like Aurélie if someone spilled wine on her fancy dress.

"Sixteen?" He grins.

We're quiet for a moment, then both break into laughter.

"So other than having the face of a kid, you really think I'm the same person?"

"Mostly." He peels his gaze off me when the car in front of us advances into the garage. "You do seem more confident."

"Well, yeah. I guess. Being immortal does take the fear out of some things. Like going outside alone at night, talking to strange people... getting into a sword fight with a six ton wasp-tarantula."

He starts to laugh again, then gives me this 'whoa, you're not kidding, are you?' stare.

Of course, he's pulling my leg as he already got the story in vivid detail.

On the way to find a parking spot inside the garage, and the walk to the theater, we swap daily update stories. For once, mine are as mundane as his... except for Sophia's glowing kitten.

"Hah."

"What?"

"Sophia's Glowing Kitten... sounds like the name of a band."

I snicker. "Yeah, one of those groups full of tween girls doing cute covers of death metal."

"Maybe they could open for this show?" He hands me my ticket and threads his arm through mine.

"Heh, right?"

My brain keeps me laughing by forcing me to imagine the Littles plus Nicole and Megan on stage in over-the-top cute-but-creepy costumes. I imagine Sophia as the singer belting out something so adorable and sweet it gives half the audience diabetes, like the opening songs to one of those cutesy Japanese cartoons she likes. Only, Sophia would *never* front a band. She's way too shy about performing in public. Being one of twenty-something girls on stage in a dance recital is about the limit of her tolerance for stage fright. Sierra would totally do it, though. Her, I could see belching into the mic and flipping off hecklers. Sam would end up on drums, possibly also wearing a dress for the lols.

"I've never been to a live theater before, unless grade school talent shows count. Are the performances better when the actors aren't being forced to participate?" I whisper as we enter the theater.

Hunter stifles a laugh. "Pretty sure this is a little higher budget than a school talent show."

"Whoa… is this the place where they shot Lincoln?"

The room seriously looks like it came out of the early 1900s. Lots of maroon with gold trim. They've got a couple of elevated box seats —and one of them has a pair of puppets in it, the two old critics from *The Muppet Show*.

"Look!" I point. "Totally hilarious."

"Huh?" He glances around. When he finally notices the two Muppets up in their box seat, he chuckles. "Wow. Do you think they have someone talk for them or did someone pose them up there purely as an homage?"

"You said this is metal, right? Not like we'd hear them."

"Yeah, true."

We take our seats. Fortunately, the chairs are more like a modern movie theater—comfortable—and not relics from a century past. Can't tell if this place *is* as old as it looks or if it had been made on purpose to look old but isn't. Oh well. Not really worth thinking about. Sophia would want to know. Sierra wouldn't have even thought to wonder about it. Sam would be bouncing in the seat because the cushion is springy.

Though we want to keep talking, being in this room has a presence similar to a librarian shushing everyone. Even though the show hasn't started yet, it feels wrong to make too much noise. We cut the timing close, which ends up being a good thing as the lights go down within only a few minutes of us arriving.

The show is both weird as hell and awesome. According to the program booklet they handed us on the way in, four local bands are collaborating with a theater troupe. Their lead singers and backup vocalists also play 'speaking' parts, and most of the band members are up on stage except for the drummers. Having four drum sets would take up too much room, so they're down in the orchestra pit.

Being a vampire with highly keen senses is usually a benefit. Tonight, not so much. Fortunately, the same way I can 'turn off' my night vision to avoid causing a serious accident while driving at night —headlights are *super* bright to vampire eyes—I can mute my ears. Not in the sense of shutting off all sound, but there's no need for me to hear a housefly burp at thirty feet when we're surrounded by casket-sized speakers.

It's totally surreal to see people dressed up as various fey creatures while shredding on electric guitars. The singers, four women and two guys, have so much power in their voices I seriously get tingles. This music is a lot 'harder' than what I normally listen to, but the combination of it plus operatic singing really *does* work. And the music isn't all pounding heavy. Some parts are orchestral and epic, like straight off the soundtrack of a fantasy movie. Honestly, when Hunter first said 'heavy metal,' my first thought was something like what the metalheads at school listened to, where it sounded as if the singer—using the term loosely—had swallowed the microphone halfway into his throat and gagged on it.

Going to a movie on a date, especially if the film is kinda boring, is really an excuse to make out in public. A live show? Especially one with such loud music and energy... demands my attention. We hold hands, kiss occasionally, but mostly sit there enthralled by the performance. So weird to think how none of the performers are legit famous. They don't sound at all like new bands starting out.

Much to my surprise, nothing weird happens the whole time.

Holy crap! I managed to sit through an entire event feeling like a normal person.

Were I a superstitious sort, such a thing would have certainly convinced me fate had a doozy in store for me. But, chaos, right? There's no correlation between unconnected events going on in two different places. Some idiot running a red light in Brisbane, Australia doesn't cause the local Starbucks to run out of diet mocha syrup.

Still, I can't help but feel like it's about time for me to have a triple-scoop cone of weirdberry ice cream with extra WTF sauce. Sophia's cat glowed yesterday. She's messing around with magic more and more. *Something* is going to blow up in my face. Or her face. Suppose it could be worse. Sierra having magic would scare me far more. Not to say she's evil, or violent, or even prone to destructive impulses. But she lacks Sophia's extreme niceness. If someone did something mean to both of them, Sophia would feel bad about it and walk away with her head down. Magic-Sierra would light the offending party on fire.

Sam would be in the middle somewhere. He'd only light someone on fire if they hurt one of his sisters—me included—or our parents. Mostly, he'd use magic to turn his PlayStation 4 into full-immersion virtual reality. The boy just wants to have fun.

Dammit. Now I have Cyndi Lauper stuck in my head.

Not her. That would hurt. I mean her song.

Once the crowd—surprisingly there is one—thins, we head outside and walk to the parking garage. It's a bit past midnight, so most of the people around us are on edge. Seattle isn't a particularly dangerous city, but it's still a big city and there's always the risk of someone desperate trying to do something stupid. It's awesome not having to be afraid of muggers. I'm still cautious, since Hunter isn't immortal. However, barring the extremely unlikely situation of a sniper in the distance trying to assassinate him, I should be able to take care of any problems. As far as I know, my boyfriend doesn't secretly work for Mossad or the Kremlin or some other lesser-known spy agency, so he should be safe from long distance rifle fire.

Though, he does have this one jackass who keeps giving him a hard time at the restaurant.

The woman goes there twice a week and almost always bitches about everything. Hunter made the mistake of pointing out he caught her in a lie regarding some complaint about her food. Since then, she complains about him even if he isn't her waiter. Fortunately, the management knows the woman is lying. She might be lurking in wait to ambush him, but I doubt she'd try stabbing him to death with a negative feedback card. I really ought to track her down and convince her to chill.

Hunter has class in the morning, so our mission is on a tight schedule.

We hop in his car and head back to his house. Half the roof is covered in blue plastic. His mother has hired contractors to repair it due to her receiving a nice little sign-on bonus for her new job. She doesn't actually start until January, but the boss was... umm, 'really generous' to her. No, I don't feel guilty about it. First of all, squeezing a little money out of a corporation is like a totally Robin Hood thing to do. Second, it's only stealing if *I* get the money. Michelle—and my mother—would disagree, but this is me mentally sticking my tongue out at them. What's the point of being an immortal with powers if I don't use them sometimes, right?

It has to be a good sign.

No, not the tarp.

I mean, how I scurry upstairs with Hunter, the two of us acting like a pair of horny rabbits. Not once in the time I spent with Scott did sex ever feel like an 'ooh, I can't wait.' Okay, it had a few moments of pleasure, but more often than not, it ended up being a 'get it over with' situation. At the time, it never occurred to me, but in hindsight, more often than not, I only agreed to do it with him because I was afraid of how he'd react if I refused. Yeah, I know. Big red flag. Sigh.

Anyway, another bonus of having powers of mental influence: Hunter and I don't need to sneak off to weird out-of-the-way places to get romantic. So what if his mother or little brother walks in on us?

What they don't remember won't hurt them.

It's better than getting bedbugs from a shady motel. Though, after watching a play about half-naked faeries dancing in the woods... I'm sorta tempted to suggest we slip off to a private bit of forest sometime. Again, so what if someone catches us? I have powers of mind control. Wow, wanting to go have sex outside in the trees is totally and completely not like me. Thinking about it makes me blush, but not change my mind. Am I getting bolder in my undeath or is there something about vampires?

My luck, trying to have a romantic night in the woods with

Hunter would turn into a Ben Stiller movie... *There's Something About Vampires.*

We sneak inside and go up to his room. As soon as the door's shut, we fling off our clothes and leap onto the bed—and the urge to rush stops. We lay there, our noses nearly touching, for a while, basking in each other's presence. Hunter's thoughts have finally evolved past the 'I can't believe she's with me' to being thoroughly in love.

This relationship of ours still makes me feel a little guilty. How different would things be if I'd not brushed him off the first time he tried to talk to me? Honestly, my intent wasn't at all like 'go away, loser,' but at fourteen, I'd been freaked out at having a boy walk up to me and awkwardly stammer. Maybe my appearance didn't give it away, but I'd been as nervous as he sounded. If we'd started dating then, Scott wouldn't have killed me. Hunter and I could've been like kids in movies who fall in love in ninth grade and marry right after college graduation.

Yeah, as if those stories happen in real life.

Alas, someone stepped on a rotten turnip in Oklahoma, so Hunter never tried talking to me again. Chaos, right?

He knows how I feel about 'stealing' him from a living girl who could give him all the normal stuff involved with a long-term commitment. Beyond not being able to have kids, the whole 'being ordinary' thing doesn't work with me. Going out in the bright daylight, standard job, social life... none of it is plausible for me. Sure, we could be night owls and have a social life after dark, but, yeah.

Neither one of us is really so extroverted.

It baffles me how he totally doesn't care about any of it. Maybe this is true love.

"What's wrong?" whispers Hunter.

The taste of his breath on my lips annoyingly reminds me I need blood, but at least it's not an emergency. "You know, the usual guilt."

He kisses me. "No need to be guilty. Mom's new job is like winning the lottery. The tickets weren't expensive. Besides, starting next year, she's going to cover my tuition and school costs, so spending money on fun stuff now and then isn't a big deal."

"Your mom's job thing, umm, isn't what I felt guilty about. The usual."

"Oh. The usual." He brushes a hand over my head. "Well, don't feel guilty about that either. I've been totally in love with you since the first moment I saw you."

I grin, stretching my arms out to grasp the back of his neck. "Yeah, thinking about you dreaming of me every night for four years is only a little bit creepy. Love at first sight only happens in faerie tales and crime dramas."

Hunter's attempt to kiss me again stumbles into chuckling. "Which one are we living in?"

"Hmm..." I roll on top of him. "Let me think..."

He runs his hands down my sides and cradles my butt. "You're sexy when you think."

"We're in a faerie tale crime scene." I glance down at his chest, breaking eye contact. "One of those stories kids get nightmares from."

"Please tell me the look you're giving me doesn't mean you're about to break my heart." He slides his hands up off my ass, wrapping around my middle. "I'm way too happy with you. So, naturally, I worry it's all going to fall apart at any minute."

"We're not in a movie. And no, I'm not going to break your heart... even though I know you're going to break mine someday."

He starts to open his mouth to protest how he'd never cheat or leave me, but realizes my meaning before any words jump off his tongue. Even without being able to read minds, his thoughts of 'well, you have a way to keep me from growing old on you' are obvious. Only, he knows I couldn't do it to him unless something else happened. It would feel too much like murder otherwise. Doesn't make sense, I know. My family has never been religious, but it bothers me to think about giving him the Transference, ending his mortal life without an extreme situation going on. Sorta like how it might feel for a person in a sci-fi story with a completely healthy leg to cut it off so they can get a cyborg replacement part.

Yeah, I know. Too sensitive of me. But, it's who I am. Nature exists for a reason, and she probably doesn't like too many people messing with her too often. Aurélie's a believer in reincarnation. She thinks our souls go on various journeys to grow over the course of multiple lifetimes. Each time, once they've learned or evolved as much as necessary for a given lifetime, they die and go back into the machinery to get spat out from some random uterus for another ride. When I asked her about vampires, she said 'we're slow learners.' It's kinda reassuring to think about going back around after this vampiric existence of mine ends, not being in a 'dead end' so to speak facing final, total destruction. Even if I'm not a hundred percent convinced of it, it's a warm thought.

"I don't want to break your heart, Sarah."

I lay flat on top of him, cheek to his shoulder, adoring the sense of warmth in his skin. "Too late. All roads now lead to heartbreak. I'm in too deep. We break up, guilty ouch. You grow old, painful ouch. I turn you... it'll eat me up inside for the rest of eternity. The best I can hope for is to have the broken heart without the guilt. So, let's have as much fun as we can with the time we have."

"Okay. If you want to just lay here holding each other all night, we can."

"Oh, heck no. Been looking forward to this for days." I push myself up and grin down at him. "Well, we can do the holding each other thing after."

"You still look guilty."

"Totally normal for me. I have resting guilt face. It's the big eyes."

He chuckles. "Your eyes aren't too big."

"Thanks, but I know I look like the sad little orphan girl from *Les Mis*, only with brown hair."

"You don't look anywhere near as tragic. And you're way prettier." Hunter smiles.

"I need to stop being an idiot. This guilt is all on me and it's kinda stupid. I can feel how happy you are when we're together. Where does this belief come from how everyone has to grow up, get married, have kids, a house, a career good enough where people neither laugh at you nor pity you?"

"No idea." He shrugs. "Guess it's what society expects."

"No one expects the Spanish Inquisition," I mutter.

"Huh?" He blinks at me, then chuckles. "Where did that come from? One of your dad's movies?"

"Yeah."

"Society doesn't expect vampires."

I shake my head. "Nope. I sure didn't expect them either. Being anti-mainstream wasn't my idea. Do you think I'm taking the goth thing too far? I mean, they only *pretend* to die."

"Sarah, being with you is all I've ever wanted. I couldn't be happier."

Too choked up to speak, I bite my lip. In theory, setting aside the dread of his imminent old age and death, I really *am* happy with him. Sure, Michelle thinks he's a little boring and the awkward shyness wore on her already... but considering how effing crazy the rest of my life is, I don't need to date Buckaroo Banzai.

He's a much needed dose of the real world.

"C'mere." I lean down and kiss him full on the lips.

Yeah, I may not have the powers of an oracle, but my vision tells me he will be staying up past his bedtime.

3

BEYOND NORMAL PICKPOCKETING

I used to consider my first night as a vampire the most embarrassing thing to ever happen to me.

Honestly, how many people end up stranded outside naked for twenty-four hours? Even if I did spend eight or nine of those hours hiding in a mausoleum unconscious, still. And I'm not talking about the people on *Naked and Afraid*. They knew what they signed up for. It's not as mortifying when you're taking your clothes off willingly. Come to think of it, somewhere out there is a medical technician, doctor, and maybe a cop or two who stood around looking at me on a slab for a while.

Still don't know if they did an autopsy on me or not. Something tells me it would have taken me longer than three days to wake up if major organs had been removed. For once, short staffing and bureaucratic delays ended up being a good thing.

Anyway, the night I spent streaking Woodinville had been the formerly most embarrassing thing to happen to me. Tonight beat it. Apparently, Hunter and I got so into it, his little brother woke up and thought we were watching a horror movie about a team of carpenters fighting zombies—hammering and moaning. We didn't notice him at first. The poor kid stood there stunned, watching us for a full minute before he whispered 'whoa' and I realized we had an audience.

No, Ronan doesn't remember a damn thing. The problem is, I can't memory-wipe myself. His 'what the heck are you guys doing' stare is going to haunt me for years. Maybe it'll become funny to me eventually. Hunter sure thought it hilarious—but only because Ronan doesn't remember catching us, or even waking up thinking the roofers decided to come back in the middle of the night.

With any luck, by the time I wake up tomorrow afternoon, my face will no longer be bright red.

I let myself out and fly off toward Seattle in search of someone to eat. It takes me a few minutes to find a person who isn't wasted drunk or high, and also isolated enough to be vulnerable to ambush feeding. It's become my habit to avoid feeding from cops whenever possible. At this hour, there aren't too many other people out and about, but leaving a police officer dazed from blood loss could get them killed.

And yeah, after running into this one guy who abused his daughter, I cringe a little every time before going into a prospective meal's head. People are freaking scary enough. Why did humanity have to invent monsters like vampires and trolls? Oh, wait... people didn't make them up; they exist. Never mind.

Being easily mistaken for anywhere from thirteen to sixteen depending on what I'm wearing and how I carry myself does open some opportunities for feeding. Almost no one, especially guys, is the least bit worried about little old me giving them a pathetic stare from a dark alley. I imagine a vampire version of Sophia would be ridiculous. She'd just sit out in public somewhere acting sad and she'd have food lining up.

And I really, *really* need to stop thinking about my siblings as undead. In my former life, my biggest fear had been a toss-up between being in a car going off a bridge into water and having some creep grab me at night. Neither of those situations scare me at all now. My new biggest fear is something happening to my family. Yes, I would absolutely give the Transference to them if not to do so would mean they died. But it doesn't mean I'd like it. Also, pretty sure vampire society as a whole severely frowns on immortal kids.

According to Aurélie, it's physically possible, but results in an awkward, tragic situation. Brain development stalls, leaving them incapable of mentally progressing out of childhood, and no one in the vampire community wants *more* overly opinionated Star Wars fans around. But seriously, they'd remain mentally stuck at whatever age, probably incapable of looking after themselves, and having weak or no impulse control… a sure recipe for attracting too much attention.

The 'looking after themselves' issue wouldn't be a problem for any of my siblings. I'd happily play guardian for eternity. But my unlife is a special case. Few vampires want a dependent. I'm sure some day even Aurélie will think I'm ready to stretch my wings and stop basically coddling me so much. Guess I'm immature still since I don't mind the coddling. I also won't throw a fit when it stops either. Becoming a vampire was such a weird upheaval in my life, any help is appreciated.

Anyway, I don't need to play the innocent lost girl tonight. A transient rummaging trash cans in an alley all alone makes for a perfect—if aromatic—target. I need to shower anyway after making love with Hunter.

As usual for feeding, I dive into the man's thoughts to administer the 'derp slap' as Sierra calls it. My brief invasion of his mind reveals no horrifying secrets, merely a guy suffering from a more-than-moderate case of paranoia preventing him from keeping a job. He always ends up thinking his co-workers or boss are part of a conspiracy of trans-dimensional beings trying to invade Earth.

After the stuff I've seen, who knows. Maybe the guy's not crazy as much as aware. My kid brother's known for collecting offbeat pets like frogs. Now he's got an imp. Though, to be fair, Blix is more of a friend than a pet. So, yeah. Alternate dimensions aren't entirely ludicrous to me.

His blood tastes like the unidentifiable 'casserole' my high school cafeteria used to serve on Friday sometimes. All the students thought they made it from the leftovers of everything else thrown together into a bizarre goulash since the contents varied. It couldn't possibly be random leftovers or it would've been horrible. Probably a 'screw it, it's Friday' throw-together of whatever pasta, tomato sauce, and meat-like substance they had on hand.

Nature is full of symbiotes. Vampirism makes me basically a parasite, even more so than my simply being a live-at-home teenager, but not the kind of one that burrows inside its host. Ick. Then we'd be talking some *way* creepy Clive Barker situation and I'm totally not going there. Some parasites, like tarantula hawk wasps, have no regard for their hosts and kill them. Others try a little harder not to harm the host out of a need for mutual preservation. Finally, there are some parasitic organisms (symbiotes) capable of providing benefits to the host.

Tonight, I'm going to try being one of those.

After feeding, it's back into this guy's brain. Since I'm not a medical doctor or a psychologist, it's beyond me to understand if the man's mental illness is a product of physical brain damage, chemical imbalance, or a result of trauma. Like, it might be in his DNA to be nuts. Or, maybe something happened to him. Whatever the cause, no point spending an hour digging proverbial tunnels into his memories.

Something tells me trying to 'cure' his paranoia won't work. It might hide it for a while, but eventually, the mental implant will erode. Not wanting to set the guy up for a huge crash later, I play *to* his paranoia by making him think he saw a story on the news announcing the Lamphyls—don't ask me, it's his word for them—ended up being exposed and defeated, so they've all gone back to their home dimension, never to return.

Hopefully, implanting the belief he has nothing to fear might help him get his life back in order. Though, if his brain is wired to be paranoid, he's probably going to come up with some other thing to freak out over. Best I can do for now though. Almost. While he's still caught in my mental fog, I tuck all the cash I have on me at the moment into his pocket—not a fortune, only $52—and follow up by implanting a quick memory of some random, nondescript young woman giving it to him so he can eat.

My symbiote duties fulfilled, I leap back into the air.

"Okay, listen up, Universe. If I run into an actual Lamphyl, I'm gonna kick something's ass."

NO DIMENSION HOPPING ALIENS ATTACK ME ON MY WAY HOME.

It's maybe forty minutes before sunrise when I land in the cul-de-sac by my house. Neighbors are quiet. Things with the curmudgeonly Mr. Neidermayer have mostly settled down for now. Demonic pranks aren't keeping him up at night, and he's been leaving us alone. Maybe Sophia's offer of Thanksgiving pie *did* help. Swear, my kid sister thinks life is a Disney cartoon. I guess sometimes it has moments like that, but there's nowhere near as much singing in real life. People who burst into random musical numbers about cleaning their house tend to get a visit from men in white coats.

I head inside and make my way toward the kitchen, and the basement stairs. Teeny snores draw my attention to the sofa as I go by. Blix and Klepto are curled up with each other in the corner by the armrest. Aww. If not for the little imp's somewhat demonic appearance, it would be an adorable sight. Oh, hell. It's adorable anyway.

Not wanting to disturb them, I lift off and hover to the stairs, then down to my room, After peeling off my clothes, I grab a clean towel and scurry to the downstairs bathroom. Sunrise is coming up, but there's plenty of time for a shower first.

THURSDAY AFTERNOON, I WAKE FROM ONE OF THE MOST BIZARRE dreams ever.

It started off with Hunter and I chasing each other naked through the woods like faeries or elves. We had a moment at a beautiful waterfall with singing blue jays and woodland creatures—think Disney doing an R-rated romance. Pretty cool... right up until

Hunter's you-know-what started singing like the candlestick from *Beauty and the Beast.*

There's a mental image I never wanted.

And it got weirder from there. Dimensional beings invaded the woods. Hunter and I ran, hooked up with a resistance led by a guy I can only describe as a metrosexual Johnny Depp playing an Alice-in-Wonderland version of Dalton, and ended up in an Ewok village. Only, it hadn't been full of Ewoks, but imps like Blix… and they worshiped a god-kitten bearing a surprisingly strong resemblance to Klepto. Finally, the imp army got into a war with giant robots spilling in from an interdimensional portal, trying to kill them by throwing millions of itty bitty rocks. Yeah, it worked about as well as one would expect throwing small rocks at high tech killing machines would work.

"What the hell did I just dream?" I whisper at my ceiling, still hearing the continuous pelting of tiny stones for some reason. "Is this what I get for drinking the blood of a crazy homeless guy? Or is this weirdness all me?"

To no one's surprise, the ceiling doesn't respond.

I'm grateful.

Consciousness comes with a bizarre craving for cereal. Talk about not making sense. But, whatever. Eating won't make me fat. I get up, pull on some sweat pants and a T-shirt, then check my phone for the weather. It's only 2:33 p.m., so sun angriness must be determined before this door opens.

Usually, girls my age who adore rainy days are considered emo. I have a good damn reason to prefer gloom, and it's unrelated to an unhealthy obsession with Peter Murphy or black lipstick. Goths are a lifestyle choice. The sun can legit kill me. Hey, just because I've come to prefer dark, gloomy days doesn't mean I'm not still sunny on the inside.

I've got one of those snarky weather apps on my phone. Today's caption is 'bring a boat.'

Sounds like we're getting a wee bit of rain. Unusual for December, but we've had a couple of unseasonably warm days. And I mean literally, *sounds like*. The noise in my dream hadn't been thousands of small rocks bouncing off battle mecha. The rainstorm hitting the roof invaded my dream. Hooray for vampire ears. I head out into the basement to find a bunch of laundry baskets standing in formation by the machines. The one closest to my door has a 'please' card on it.

Sure, Mom. No problem.

Cereal can wait a minute.

Down in the basement behind heavily tinted windows on a gloomy day, I'm online. It doesn't take me long to sort the clothes with my accelerated reflexes. Once I've got the first load in the machine, it's time for some... whatever cereal we have upstairs. I head up to the kitchen and stop short, gawking at the sliding glass doors.

Wow, it's freakin' monsooning out there. Our back deck is awash from a pelting of rain so heavy people could legit shower in it, except for the water being like thirty-eight degrees. The cabinet contains a few boxes of cereal: Corn Pops, Captain Crunch, Cheerios, and some kind of muesli. I might be a vampire with superhuman strength, but I still don't have the jaw power for muesli... so I grab the Captain Crunch.

The roof of my mouth will heal rapidly thanks to undeath.

I plop on the living room sofa with my cereal and start flipping channels, hunting for something to watch. Alas, late afternoon television sucks. I settle on some old Seventies-looking western. No idea who any of the actors are or what the movie is, but it's the first thing to come up and not cause an immediate 'nah.'

Before too long, the rapid clomping of small shoes rushes up to the door. Sam and Sierra barge in and do the child version of dogs shimmying off all the water. Shoes and umbrellas go in their respective storage bins, and the kids run upstairs to change out of their wet clothes.

I'm about to ask 'where's Sophia' when she creeps inside. She's shivering and her face is the color of a fire extinguisher, but no source of embarrassment is obvious from looking at her. Soph collapses her frilly pink umbrella, tosses it in the bucket, and goes upstairs without taking her shoes off. Ballet flats or not, Mom would throw a fit.

Something is *definitely* wrong with youngest sis.

"Soph? What's wrong?"

"Not now," replies my kid sister without slowing down.

I debate for only like thirty seconds before setting my cereal bowl on the coffee table and hurrying up to her room. When I walk in, she whirls on me with a gasp, jumping back and nearly reaching for the winter coat on her bed as if to hide herself with it. Her face gets even redder.

"Soph? What's up? Why are you acting like I barged in on you while you were in the tub?"

She cringes, whispering, "'Cause I'm naked."

I blink at her pink dress, a white kitten applique on the chest, black leggings, ballet flats. "Umm… say what? You are not."

"Look closer. This outfit still appears dry, right?"

"Yeah, so? You have magic. Figured you made yourself immune to rain. And you had a coat on plus an umbrella."

Sophia walks over and sticks one shoulder forward. "Feel."

I rest a hand on her… and whoa. My eyes are telling me there's a dress under my hand, but my nerves say skin. "Umm?"

"Yeah. Umm," says Sophia. "Sec."

She walks past me, hurrying to the hall closet for a towel, then back to her room. She rushes in, closes the door almost hard enough to slam it, then begins drying herself off. And yeah, since she still appears to be dressed for school, it's a weird sight.

"Any particular reason you went to school today wearing… nothing?"

Her face reddens. "I did *not* go to school like this."

"Experiment go wrong?"

"No!" She stares at me, still blushing, but also frightened. "I went to the bathroom, and like, right when I shut the stall door, a bright flash happened… and all my clothes disappeared. Except for my coat, since it was back in the classroom on a hook."

I stifle a chuckle. "Usually, pickpockets steal what's *in* the pockets, not the pockets themselves."

"Not funny." She resumes drying herself. "I got stuck in the bathroom for so long I almost got in trouble."

"You just stayed in the bathroom?"

She stares at me. "Umm. *Yeah*. What was I supposed to do, make a dress out of TP? No one would ever believe the truth. They'd think I'd gone crazy and threw my clothes out a window. Or they'd think I got attacked by bullies and grill me about who did it." She tosses the towel aside, then rummages a long-sleeve pink sweatshirt, underwear, and jeans from her dresser, pulling them all on directly over her false outfit. "I dunno what happened. It sorta felt like two giant hands grabbed me and tried to pull me somewhere. Started to lift off my feet, but I fought it and slipped loose… only the energy grabbing me stole my outfit. Even got my earrings and my anklet!"

"Whoa."

Once dressed for real, she kinda looks like a video game glitch where two characters in different outfits are standing on top of each other. She snaps her fingers and dispels the fake clothes, then runs into a hug, still shaking. "I stood on the toilet for like ever so no one would see me in there. *So* embarrassing. I was so mortified I couldn't even think. Eventually, I figured standing there doing nothing would definitely get me caught. I tried a couple things, but couldn't magically create anything real. Been practicing illusions, so I made fake clothes."

"Awesome illusion. I couldn't tell."

"Yeah, but still an illusion. School desk seats are *really* cold. I tried to come up with an excuse to go home early, but they made me stay."

"Seriously?"

"Yeah. I mean, my excuse about feeling sick was super lame. But I couldn't exactly tell them about magic stuff, or what really happened. I thought about stopping time so I could go home and change, but it's too far to walk in the cold with no shoes. And I don't think I could pause time over such a big area."

I pat her back. "I can sympathize with how awkward it must've been."

She gasps at me. "You have no—wait… you do. Yeah, but still. All you did was run around outside for a couple minutes. Not the same as having to sit there in school!" She lets go and paces, making random hand gestures.

"I spent an entire night locked in a mausoleum. Was more than 'a few minutes.'" I shrug one shoulder. "But no one noticed, so I'm over it."

"I can't go back. Nope. Can't."

"Back? What?"

"To school." She stops, spinning to stare at me. "Three class periods, lunch, and recess wearing illusions! Well, I had my coat on for recess, but still. I couldn't let anyone touch me or they'd find out. Everything I bumped into made me squeak because it was so cold. And it's like everyone knew. They all kept looking at me weird."

"Probably wondering why you were blushing and acting strange. Trust me. No one knew. I have superhuman eyesight and your illusionary outfit totally fooled me."

She fidgets, head down.

"Really, no one noticed."

"*I* noticed," yells Sophia, flailing her arms.

"Aww. I know exactly how you feel. Happened to me too, though not for the same reasons. At least you didn't spend two days having a bunch of people hover over you on a slab studying every inch."

She shivers.

"Trust me, there are worse things than being stranded outside with nothing on. At least you could make the illusion."

"I can't erase memories," mumbles Sophia.

"You don't have to. No one realized. I only needed to erase memories because people noticed me and stared. They don't remember seeing me, and no one saw you. Two different ways to do the same thing. Besides, you didn't have to ride in a police car naked."

"You had a blanket." She smirks.

"Heh. Yeah. Just trying to help you feel better."

"Thanks, but what if someone bumped me in the hallway and figured it out but didn't say anything?"

I shake my head. "There is no way anyone would've noticed and *not* said anything."

"Yeah, they'd have laughed. Everyone would make fun of me for the rest of time." She folds her arms. "That's why I can't go back. And I'd get in *so* much trouble. The teachers would think I did it on purpose. They'd never believe someone could steal *all* my clothes in the bathroom right off me. And they wouldn't believe something magic happened."

"Did you somehow tick off a faerie who pranked you for revenge?"

"Umm." She makes a series of deep thought faces. "No. If a faerie was mad at me, they'd have zapped me right in the middle of class when everyone could see me right away."

"Oof." I wince… and feel awful for a second. I miss the days when the worst thing a kid had to fear at school was unexpected embarrassment.

"No oof." She shakes her head. "Because if a faerie stole my clothes right in the middle of class, you would have erased everyone's memory of it… including mine."

I chuckle. "True. But… if a faerie didn't do it as a prank, we have a bigger problem than you being embarrassed. Someone or something tried to abduct you, and missed."

Sophia gawks at me, the color draining from her face. "Umm."

"Any idea who'd want to do grab you? Tick off any elder gods lately?"

"No. How should I know?" She crosses her arms, nervously rubbing her hands up and down from shoulder to elbow.

"You're a wizard, Sophia," I say, poorly imitating Hagrid.

"Not funny."

"Seriously, you're the one with magic. I just bite people and move real fast."

She runs over and clings to me. "I'm scared. Do you really think someone tried to kidnap me?"

"You said it felt like a force tried to grab you, but slipped off?"

"Kinda. I dunno. What do you think? Look into my head."

I gaze into her deep blue eyes. Since she's thinking about the moment in question, it's easy to find. She's scurrying down the hall to the bathroom after getting permission to leave class. Goes in, heads to a stall, shuts the door… and a flash goes off. A feeling washes over her as if she'd fallen onto a giant slab of room temperature Jell-O, which absorbed her… but it's only two feet thick and she falls out the other side. In two seconds, everything she had on her is gone, and her hair's suspended in the air behind her, drawn back into nothingness. Definitely looks like a portal tried to swallow her. No tugging or tearing happened. An invisible force didn't rip her outfit off; all inanimate objects on her person merely stopped existing. She pulls her hair free of the tiny hole in space, realizes her clothes are gone, and bites her arm so she doesn't scream. As the reality of being stranded in a school bathroom sinks in, she begins to freak out in a major way.

"Hmm. It *does* kinda feel like a gateway opened right on top of you and basically vacuumed your stuff right off. Question is, did someone or some*thing* do it intentionally? Did it happen as a backlash from some magic you messed around with? Or maybe you randomly stumbled across a dimensional doorway."

She smooths her hands down the front of her sweatshirt, as if to reassure herself it's solid and real. "Umm, I dunno. Guess if someone tried to kidnap me, they would have tried again by now. Don't think I did anything unstable enough for it to zap me in the bathroom. Wouldn't a side effect happen right here, where I did the spells?"

"No idea. You're the magic person. Do the, umm, crystal ball thing."

"Scrying?" Sophia blinks. Her demeanor shifts from fearful to curious. "Hmm. Maybe. Never did it before, but I can try."

I pat her on the head. "Okay. Just don't blow up the house. Mom and Dad will be upset."

She grins. "I won't. Promise."

4

RED WINE AND OTHER CURATIVES

My cereal is still where I left it when I go downstairs.

The milk, however, is gone. Ahh, Klepto strikes again. After adding more milk, I flop on the couch again and look at the TV. I'm not 'watching' it, merely happening to stare forward in its general direction while my mind wanders in search of what bizarre oddity is affecting my family now. Things have been too sane and normal since the issue with Damarco ended. Here comes the Universe with my monthly ration of insanity.

Daryl and Jordan—Sam's friends—arrive and go upstairs, both waving and yelling 'Hi, Sarah' as they thunder over carpeted steps. I honestly have no damn idea how a pair of boys can make more noise than Dad on the stairs. The time Ashley and I fell down her steps with the steamer trunk had to be quieter than these two. And, ow. Thinking about the giant trunk makes my front teeth hurt.

Hmm. Who or what might be after Sophia? She hasn't exactly done anything out in the world capable of making enemies. Most likely, it's Eleanor St. Ives trying to mess with me. No, she doesn't have magic as far as I know. If any vampires would, bet it's Academics. But she's into science. As crazy as it is to think, it's more likely she'd invent some kind of mad scientist remote teleportation ray gun than conjure a magical portal. And I'm not saying the ray gun thing is possible. I'm a vampire who knows magic is real, not a crazy person.

Sierra soon shows up eager to hop on the PlayStation once her homework's done. I'm not really watching the TV, so I wave her to proceed. She's over the creep from *Call of Duty* screaming at her and hops right into another match. Even though I'm young, it boggles my mind how she still has any interest whatsoever in it. She plays it to death. Guess she really loves the competitiveness. While I'm nowhere near as into video games as she is, I still enjoy them—but for the story. Mindlessly shooting each other over and over again doesn't do it for me.

Dad finally realizes the Littles are home and emerges from his office. He spends about five minutes attempting to ask Sierra how her day was, but she's so focused on the game, her answers are monosyllabic. She's not deliberately ignoring him, more trying not to die. Pretty sure magical forces could yoink all of her clothes at the moment and she wouldn't even notice. At least, not until the match ended. He pats her on the head, chuckles at me, and heads for the stairs to check on Sophia and Sam.

"Oh, did I hear thunder before?" he asks, pausing at the bottom of the steps.

"Nope. Daryl and Jordan came over. You heard them impersonating a herd of breakdancing elephants."

"Ahh. All right. Everything good in Sarah world?"

Now there's a trick question if ever one existed. No way in hell am I going to tell my dad about the dream I had. Also, no reason to worry him about Sophia when I have no proof anyone tried to attack her, even if I suspect it. Sure, it might've been a random magical anomaly, but the odds are low. My gut tells me someone actively attacked her. "So far, so good. Soph had a weird day, she might want to talk."

"Okay." He heads upstairs.

I get up and go to the kitchen to rinse out the cereal bowl. Really not sure what made me want cereal so bad. Oh, wait... the transient guy's blood tasted like the Friday mystery food. Probably got me remembering Saturday morning, having cereal while watching cartoons. My brain is weird.

Mom arrives home around 4:30 p.m., way earlier than usual. She's outwardly in a good mood, so I don't question it. Nice to see her when she's not running on eleven so to speak. By quarter to five, she's changed into sweats and a T-shirt (I get my fondness for them from somewhere, right) and heads to the kitchen. Dad took on the bulk of dinner prep while her big case had been kicking her ass, so Mom's dealing with it now.

Not wanting to be too much of a parasite, I hop up off the couch and follow, intent on helping her make dinner. Once sure Dad is nowhere in earshot, I tell Mom about the crazy dream while we're preparing a baking dish of chicken tenders, a pasta side, and some veggies. The 'singing candlestick' part gets her laughing so hard she's in tears. Seriously, it might be time to call in Aurélie to erase the dream from my head. Next time Hunter and I are about to get romantic, I'm going to imagine it singing and die laughing.

There's not going to be a smooth way to recover, either.

"Think it's from the crazy blood?" I ask.

"I wouldn't know. Sometimes, crazy dreams happen for no reason at all. The brain does bizarre things. I had a professor back in college who compared dreaming to a computer disk running a de-fragmentation process. Basically, the brain's sorting out everything it recorded during the day and the crosstalk in the nerves makes random images and stuff happen."

"No kidding about random." I set the chicken in the oven.

Mom pauses stirring the pasta seasoning packet in to glance over at me. "You know, Christmas is coming up. It'll be here before we know it."

"Yeah…" I cringe internally, thinking about the nightmare of being a ghost watching my family have a shitty Christmas after my death.

"Hope you're planning to set Hank on safe mode if he shows up again," says Mom.

"If?"

She nods, resuming stirring. "Yes. Mom and Dad weren't sure how to process him being quiet and going red in the face so much during Thanksgiving."

I snicker.

"They think he got so upset at your brother wearing the dress and Sierra's attitude, he had a mild stroke." Mom dumps the last of the premixed seasoning packet in.

"Sierra didn't have an attitude. Hank was being a jerk."

"Oh, I know. Your grandparents meant attitude as in Uncle Hank's opinion of her."

"Ahh. So they understand he's unreasonable?"

"Dear," says Mom. "My parents have known he's unreasonable longer than you've been alive. Be glad you weren't around to hear his opinions on me being a lawyer."

"Ack. Let me guess, he thought you should've been a waitress?"

"Nope. He doesn't think women should work at all. Just stay home, barefoot and pregnant in the kitchen."

I glance down at my toes. Mom's not wearing socks either. "Well, two out of three."

"What?" She sets the lid on the pasta.

"We're barefoot in the kitchen. Just not pregnant."

Mom throws an oven mitt at me, but laughs. "Bite your tongue. Four is enough."

"Heh."

She goes from laughing to serious. "Are you and Hunter using protection?"

"Yeah. Infallible protection." I smirk.

"Oh. Duh. Sorry."

I hug her. "It's fine. You've got three other chances for grandkids and I'm not upset about it. Besides, there might be a really outside chance."

"Outside chance?"

"Well, more like an 'in China' chance."

She blinks. "What does China have to do with it?"

"No, I mean, like if a normal outside chance is our backyard, this is so far outside it's in China." I lean against the counter. "Aurélie said it's not unheard of for an Innocent to have certain interior parts remain working, mostly to keep up the lifelike illusion. However, having a baby can't just happen at random. Needs deliberate intent, some kind of potion, and elaborate rituals."

"Oh, you've gone Amish?"

I blink. "What?"

Mom dies laughing. I follow suit, but mostly because she's laughing.

Once we recover our breath—metaphorically in my case—Mom sighs. "Yes, so… my parents informed me Uncle Hank may request to remain at the home for Christmas dinner, as he doesn't think he can 'take it' again."

"Oh, the horror. Not being able to insult everyone around you incessantly." I roll my eyes.

"Truly."

I grab a cold iced tea from the fridge. Old habits die hard. And the kitchen is kinda warm. "You know he's going to change his mind again and be here. Deep down, he hates being alone. I'd almost feel sorry for him being stuck in the old people's home if he wasn't such an asshole."

Mom prods the pasta around the pan. "You know he grew up in a different era."

"Not an excuse to *still* be a dick to people. If his generation could handle going from riding horses to driving cars and telephones evolving into the internet, he can understand jeans do not turn a girl into a lesbian any more than a pink dress worn in protest means Sam is gay."

Mom chuckles. "I agree. But not everyone can evolve their thinking. In some cases, mind control is much more realistic."

"It's good to see you smiling. Last case really kicked your ass."

Mom leans against the counter. "Yeah. Being a lawyer is a lot like being a parent. Sometimes, no matter how hard I work, poop ends up smeared on the walls. I love both to death, but every now and then, they're enough to drive me into drinking an entire bottle of wine and sparking up an epic bong."

"Hah. Nice try, but you don't smoke."

She wags her eyebrows at me. "Not when you've seen."

I fake gasp.

"Honestly, I haven't indulged since college. But after this last litigation… ugh. It's so tempting. Wine isn't enough for some forms of stress."

"Yeah, you need something stronger. Like a vacation."

Mom perks up. "You know… that's not a bad idea."

"You and Dad could slip off somewhere after the holidays. I'm a legal adult now and none of the others are super little. Pretty sure I could keep a lid on things here provided I don't end up embroiled in an undead war for control of the Pacific Northwest."

"I didn't think you cared for politics."

"I don't."

She smiles. "Then there shouldn't be anything to worry about. Now, you've got me thinking."

"Uh, oh. Last time you 'got to thinking' I ended up with *three* siblings."

Mom throws the other oven mitt at me. "Oh, where's your father?"

"He went up to check on… shit."

"Daryl's here?"

"Huh?"

"You said 'check on shit'. I assume the boy stopped up the drain again."

"No, not literal shit. The pause clearly indicated I meant it as a 'derailed in mid thought, then had a bad thought' shit of worry. Be right back." I start for the door.

"Don't say you're worried about something and leave me hanging. What is your father up to this time?"

Skidding to a halt in the archway out of the kitchen, I glance back at her. "Sophia had an awkward, embarrassing problem at school. He went to talk to her."

"Already?" Mom blinks. "Maybe they *are* putting too many hormones in food."

I sigh. "Not the red faerie. Something weird and magical happened."

"I could take 'weird and magical' in many different ways." Mom pauses to stare at me. "Did a boy say he likes her?"

"No. Take it literally. *Magical.* Tell you about it when I come back down."

"Ahh."

I give her a 'yeah, it's like that' look, then hurry upstairs.

Flickering purple light stretches out on the beige hallway rug from Sophia's room. Explosions and gunfire fill the air—but they're coming from Sam's room. Gingerly, I nudge Sophia's door open. The light's coming from Klepto, who has again become a being of pure energy. This time, the kitten's purple. She cruises around in a circle near the ceiling like a tiny dirigible, her eyes huge in the expression of a pothead contemplating why air exists.

Sophia sits cross-legged on the floor in front of a yellow plastic pail full of water. Two lit candles stand on either side of it. Sophia's holding her hands out over the water, staring into the surface as intently as Sierra gets into video games when the score's close.

Dad's sitting across the bucket from her, cross-legged as well, hands on his knees, touching his thumbs to the tips of his middle fingers. Yeah, he's got a necktie on like a headband. It's simultaneously bizarre and cute. Like a dad making time to play dolls or tea party with his young daughter... only it's taken a Wednesday Addams turn. Okay, not the best metaphor. Sophia's nowhere near as dark. Still, it's almost enough to get me to back quietly out of the room and forget I saw anything.

Dad looks over at me. "Hey, Sarah. It's fine. Not like Soph's scrying over spilled milk."

"Ugh. Bad, Dad. Bad."

"Seriously, though. She's fine. Now she's trying to find out why it happened."

"Any luck?" I creep closer.

"Don't know yet. She hasn't said anything. You get worried about me disappearing upstairs?"

"A little. Dinner's almost ready."

He smiles. "Excellent."

Sophia looks up. "Okay. We should go downstairs. I don't think this is working."

Klepto stops glowing, and drops to land on Dad's head like a too-small hat. "Mew."

He collects the kitten, pets her a bit, then hands her to Sophia. "Go on. Wash your hands."

I duck out and stick my head into Sam's room.

My brother and Jordan are playing a racing game on the PlayStation while Blix and Ronan play fight with toy lightsabers. Daryl appears to be waiting his turn on the game, watching it.

"Hah!" Ronan jumps up to stand on the bed and points his red saber at Blix. "You've lost. I have the high ground."

Blix emits an unintelligible warble and makes a shoving gesture with his left hand.

Ronan falls over backward, and the little squeak he makes tells me he didn't pretend.

Wow. Playing Jedi with *actual* sorta force powers being used. Neat.

"Sam, dinner's almost ready," I say.

"Okay," replies my brother, still staring at the screen while he guides his race car. "Lap's got another minute and forty seconds left. Can I finish?"

"Sure."

Daryl sighs. "Darn. I should probably head home. Gonna be dinner time for me, too."

"Yeah." Jordan nods once. "My phone's been ringing for the past like six minutes."

Not my place to yell at him for ignoring his parents, so I don't.

Blix slow-mo jumps into the air, bringing his toy lightsaber over his head in an overacted two-handed chop. Ronan blocks, growling from the 'effort' it took to stop the attack. He, too, makes a pushing gesture. Blix obligingly flings himself across the room, bounces off the wall, and plays dead on the desk.

Ronan hops up and runs over to check on him, looking worried. Blix sits up grinning.

Yeah, we're far too happy right now. Something bad's on the way.

5

LIGHT ANOMALIES

My class on Thursday doesn't start until eight, so I have time to hang with the family for dinner.

Ronan's eating here tonight for reasons. Nothing bad. He just likes hanging out with Sam. Given the sign-on bonus his mother got at her new job, she already put in and finished her two weeks' notice at the old place. You know her former boss pretended to be shocked she left for better pay. Pretty sure he only tried to guilt her into staying.

After dinner, Dad whips out *Dragonslayer,* another Eighties movie.

I've got about an hour left before its time for me to head to school. At least I finished that essay on chaos, even if I waited for the day before it's due to start on it. Professor Heath gave us the whole class period last week to work on it, but all I'd managed to come up with in the room was two dozen horrible opening lines, all of which I crossed out.

Ronan and Sam flop on the floor. Sophia wedges herself between me and Mom on the sofa. Blix sits on the sofa arm closer to the recliner, Klepto draped over his head like a kitten mohawk. Sierra joins Dad in his recliner... and we all bask in another session of Eighties cheese. Dad puts on *Dragonslayer.* Though, this one doesn't look bad. Merely dated. As soon as the movie opens with villagers chaining a young woman to a post for a sacrifice, Sierra begins glaring. It's really an amazing bit of self-control on her part not to yell about movies never having young men being fed to dragons.

The Littles all emit a hopeful gasp when the woman slips out of the manacles… and groan when the dragon gets her anyway.

It's a bit much for Sierra.

"Why do they *always* have girls act so stupid? Run in circles, trip, stand there looking clueless. Cower in front of a giant rock right in plain sight?" Sierra rolls her eyes. "This is stupid."

"Yeah," says Sam. "She could'a got away. And why do they always have to make dragons look dumb and evil?"

"Stop making fun of me." Sierra scowls. "I'm serious."

"Not making fun of you. Dragons are supposed to be super smart. Why would it just breathe fire on a lady and kill her? Now he's still gonna be lonely. How come they never have a movie where a dragon takes the princess and, like, they become friends or something?"

Sierra stares at him like she can't quite figure out if he's serious or mocking her for complaining about the treatment of women in fiction.

I gesture at the screen. "She did kinda stand there like an idiot. Thought they were going to subvert the trope when they had her escape the manacles and save herself… but foom."

"People don't think right when they're terrified." Mom sips her chamomile tea.

My mother's not an alcoholic, but when work is stressing her out, she has a glass of red wine after dinner. Tea means she's in a good mood.

"We saw a giant multi-headed nope monster," says Sierra, "and Sarah didn't lose her mind."

Dad pauses the movie.

"Princesses aren't vampires." Sophia shrugs. "Not every girl's a badass."

"Says the girl who screamed her head off when the nope monster came after us," mumbles Sierra.

Sophia shoots her a 'give me a break' stare. "You screamed, too."

"I'm a kid. Huge monsters aren't supposed to exist." Sierra gestures at the screen. "The woman in the movie lives in a world where people know about dragons. She shouldn't be freaked out when she sees one."

"Hmm." Dad pats her on the shoulder. "If someone handcuffed you to a pole to feed a tiger, and the tiger showed up, how calm would you be? We know about tigers. They're not supernatural."

Sierra huffs.

"But, I get what you're saying." Dad smiles. "Hollywood does tend to overuse the damsel in distress thing."

"At least this princess had a real dress on." Sierra folds her arms.

"I don't think she's supposed to be a princess. Just a village lady." Sam jumps up. "Popcorn?"

"We *just* ate dinner." Mom gawks at him.

"So?" Sam blinks. "It's movie time. Tradition."

"Boys… where does he put it all?" Mom sighs. "All right."

Grinning, my brother dashes off to the kitchen, throws popcorn in the microwave, and runs back. Dad unpauses the movie. Two-ish minutes later, the microwave beeps.

"Don't gotta pause it," yells Sam while running to collect the popcorn.

I keep checking my phone to avoid being late. At 7:22 p.m., a flicker of soft blue-white light catches my eye over by our living room window. A transparent orb about the size of an orange floats near the ceiling. Okay, odd. Another one appears hovering over the linoleum square by the front door—the only spot in the house approved for shoes. Three fade into existence in the dining room.

"What the heck? Sophia? Are you making these?" I ask.

"No," replies my sister. "Not doing anything."

"Whoa." Sierra points. "You didn't summon them?"

Sophia looks where she pointed. "Eep! No. I have no idea what they are."

"Mew," says Klepto.

Blix babbles.

Sam jumps to his feet. "They're trying to get Soph! Look out!"

Dad lifts Sierra off his lap to sit on the recliner arm and stands. "How do you know that? They're just kinda hanging there glowing."

"Klepto said." Sam gestures at the kitten.

"The cat talks?" Mom eyes her tea as if regretting it not being wine.

"Sorta. Blix can understand her," says Sam. "And I can understand Blix."

Sophia looks over at the kitten. "Oh, I get it."

"What?" yells everyone else.

"Those lights feel scary, like I should run away from them. But it's kinda stupid to be scared of lights. Kinda like how it's lame to have a giant pom-pom as a nightmare. I think Klepto's trying to warn me by feels."

"Mew," says the kitten.

Blix babbles.

"Yeah." Sam nods at her. "Klepto can't talk to you, but she can send feelings."

"Hmm, really?" Dad scratches his chin. "Wizard's familiars can speak."

I stand. "Dad, you're forgetting a couple things. One, we're not in a roleplaying game. Two, Sophia's not a wizard. She's a... something else."

"Truth." Sierra laughs.

More orbs appear, bringing the total up to about twenty-five. They all hang still, not pulsating, not drifting. Their presence doesn't make me feel 'watched' like ghosts do, but the air does seem charged. A taste like licking pennies settles on my tongue. Ugh, this is going to get complicated, isn't it? At least tonight's class is Professor Heath's. He'll accept weird paranormal things as an excuse for lateness. No way can I leave in the middle of something like this.

"Wow. I haven't seen a light show like this since the Pink Floyd concert in '89," says Dad.

Mom scrunches her face in thought. "I don't remember there being a light show there."

"There was for me." Dad winks.

"You've taken LSD?" whispers Mom, sounding scandalized.

Whoa. Have my parents been replaced by pod people?

Dad chuckles. "Nah, just pulling your leg."

"They look like the glowy things from those ghost hunter shows." Sierra turns in place, looking at them. "So many."

Sam carefully places the popcorn bowl on the coffee table. "Light anomalies aren't this bright or this large, and they don't sit still."

"Dear," says Mom. "Did you annoy a faerie?"

I almost laugh. "Already asked her that. Not as far as she knows."

"Since when do you believe in faeries?" whispers Dad.

"Right around the time I witnessed a teleporting kitten." Mom gets up. "Suppose I should get the frying pan."

Blix gasps, feigning fear.

Two orbs launch themselves at Sophia. They're fast, but I'm faster. Unfortunately, getting to her before them requires a flying tackle. My sister collapses over me like a cloth bag full of broken broom handles, limp and bony. We land on the floor behind the couch, the light smears whizzing over us. A dining room orb hanging in midair in front of us zips for her while she's pinned under me.

So, I do the first logical thing to come to mind… roll over and throw her upward. My reflexes in 'combat mode' make the world feel like it's slowed down. It's totally a cheat code for getting into fights with normal people… or playing video games. Sophia, spinning horizontally, rises over the attacking orb. My aim is slightly off. The girl's a touch lighter than I give her credit for, so she hits the ceiling— which I hadn't intended. Not too bad though. She makes contact flat on her back, facing down at the floor, but not hard enough to hurt her or even dent the drywall.

Sam manages to jump in front of another orb going for where Sophia no longer is. The light ball hits him and vanishes, apparently doing nothing. Fearing it might've possessed him, I keep my attention on him as Sophia peels off the ceiling and falls. Dad yells 'be right back,' his voice dragged down to demonic tones in my accelerated perception. He slow-mo runs to the stairs. My little brother squirms, making a face like he soiled his pants. The light ball zooms out his back and resumes circling.

Mom puts herself in the path of another orb racing to crash into Sophia, who's still falling.

I catch and gently redirect my kid sister to the sofa. She bounces off the cushions, pops up to her feet, and runs like hell. Orbs chase her while she races in circles around the living room screaming 'go away.' Having no better ideas, I extend my claws and rake at one. My fingers get a brief, irritating shock, but my attack has no apparent effect on the orb.

A group of three go for Sophia from the side.

Again, I launch myself like Supergirl over the couch and fly into her from behind, scooping her up out of the way. Quarters are a bit cramped, but I can zoom around in here faster than she can run. The orbs don't appear capable of keeping up with me.

Dad returns wearing a red tie headband and carrying his ren-fest sword. No idea what he hopes to accomplish with it. The blade isn't even close to sharp, nor is it magical.

"Cutting them won't do anything!" I wiggle my claws at him.

Undeterred, my father rushes into battle like Conan of Suburbia. He slices wildly at the dancing orbs. I'm about to shake my head at him, but he finally hits one—and the orb dissipates in a flash of sparks. A tiny lightning bolt runs up the sword into his hand, making his hair frizz up. He goes wide eyed as if he'd snorted an entire pound of cocaine.

"Oh, boy… Yes!" Dad laughs maniacally, then yells, "I like it!"

I'm sure he's doing an impression of something from a movie I haven't seen.

"How the heck did you kill one?" I yell, while flying in a tight orbit around the living room.

"Stop!" yells Sophia. "I'm gonna puke!"

Three orbs coming at us from the left miss by inches and end up hitting Sierra—who vanishes.

Mom screams.

"Metal! Grounds them. Warning. Tingles a little," yells Dad, right before slicing another one and doing a *Woooo* worthy of Ric Flair. Sparks dance up his hair.

"Sierra!" shouts Mom.

Sam and Ronan run upstairs.

A bizarre noise I can only describe as listening to a stomach gurgle in slow motion comes from near the front window. Sierra reappears, spit out of a hole in reality, sliding on her chest across the carpet. The breach closes as abruptly as it appeared, gone in less than a second. I didn't see much but grey on the other side, like stone.

Mom rushes to pick Sierra up, but the girl's too fast for her and sprints to the kitchen. The boys come back downstairs carrying metal baseball bats.

Sophia heaves.

Oops. Guess she didn't say 'I'm gonna puke' for dramatic effect. Repeated, tight, forty-mile-an-hour circles has upset her stomach. I slow and set her on the sofa. She swoons, inches from throwing up. Mom finally gives in and runs to the kitchen to grab the iron skillet. Dad hits a third orb, cackling like an insane man. What the hell? Are these things made from highly concentrated energy drink?

Sierra runs in carrying my katana. The one I brought back from LA. Merely looking at it makes my shoulder twinge.

Mom stops short, looking at all the Littles plus Dad and Ronan running around the living room waving dangerous metal weapons. Sierra tries a few times to tag the fast-moving lights, but can't seem to make contact. Dad has no skill whatsoever with a sword, but he fully acknowledges it. The man's not at all *trying* to slice orbs. He's merely waving the sword around like an idiot hoping one of the orbs crashes into it. Sierra, on the other hand, is trying to play samurai and be all cool about it.

Ronan attempts Dad's 'flail randomly' tactic. Sam's taking a Sierra-like approach and having similar—lack of—results. Dad and Ronan hit orbs at about the same time. The boy shrieks, tiny lightning bolts dancing over his hair. He hits the floor on his back, his long hair fluffed out into a huge ball, smoke coming out of his mouth.

"Ow…"

"Yes!" bellows dad, in his best impression of *The Tick*. "This is the pain I remembered so fondly."

Mom shakes her head.

I glance at her. "Don't judge. *You* married him."

She *pffs* at me.

"Stop!" roars Sierra, thrusting her hands up.

Well, roars like Klepto's 'mew' is a roar.

A few of the orbs flicker, and slow down enough for Sam and Sierra to score hits.

My brother's hair bursts upward into a koosh of tiny lightning arcs. He blinks, eyes wide in an expression of 'hmm, perhaps I have committed an error.'

Sierra's hair fluffs up a little. Thin sparks run down her arms and across her chest. She blurts something that starts with 'sheep' and ends with trucker… actually a word rhyming with 'trucker.'

"What did you say!?" bellows Mom.

"Uhh, sheepfluffer," mutters Sierra, twitching, sparks dancing over her teeth.

Dad cackles. "Go easy on her, dear. These little bastards have a bit of a sting to them. Let her slide once."

Sierra thrusts her arm toward me, offering the sword.

Okay, these zaps can't hurt as much as having a katana rammed through most of my entire body, or being broken in half by a troll. I grab it. For me, hitting them isn't *too* difficult. About as challenging as an ordinary person attempting to whack a softball out of the air when a pair of kids are lazily playing catch. The first one I hit sends a shock down my arm into my chest. Dad used to play World of Warcraft. They had some main villain dude who always said 'you are not prepared.' Yeah, I'm totally not prepared.

Imagine sticking a fork into an electrical outlet, but the voltage went straight to the skeleton, heating it up. Compared to other crap done to me since becoming a vampire, the amount of pain is fairly trivial. It's merely hitting in a weird, sensitive place not normally exposed to pain. Like having a careless younger brother throw a dart and hit me in the arm is not too big a deal. But if the dart nailed a nipple? Yeah… I clench my jaw and power past it, continuing to offer myself up as a walking grounding rod to get rid of the remaining orbs.

Ronan's had enough. He doesn't bother trying to stand up. Sam's lost interest in hunting orbs, but he does play goalie in front of Sophia. He'll take another shock to protect her, but isn't gonna go looking for any since I'm on cleanup detail. Dad keeps trying. Alas, since the orbs' numbers have thinned out, he's not having any luck hitting them.

The light balls circle around, angling for a clear shot at Sophia, but with both parents, Sierra, and Sam surrounding her, none make it to her by the time I get the last one. Holy crap this is *not* comfortable. My bones are on fire.

Dad, his lips peeled back in a rictus grin, faces me with an expression of shared pain for a good cause. "Well, that's certainly a new one."

Sam snickers at me.

Okay, I have long hair. Not quite Sophia long. I can't sit on it like she can, but the ends are right about the level of my belt. And... it's all standing out straight.

"Whoa. Sare's a Spaceball," says Sam.

"Those helmets aren't big enough for her." Sierra grins at me. "If I didn't know how much getting zapped by those things hurt, I'd laugh."

"What happened to you?" Mom grabs Sierra by the shoulders.

"I feel like the fish who got tossed back for being too small." Sierra frowns.

"I'm smaller than you," says Sophia.

Blix appears on my shoulder. He pokes me in the forehead and my hair drops, no longer electrified.

"Thanks."

He flashes a toothy grin.

"Fish thrown back?" Mom looks Sierra over. "What do you mean?"

"It felt like someone grabbed me from behind and yanked me through a hole. I went from being here to this giant room like a castle dungeon. A bunch of people in creepy black robes were all around me. One of them said 'wrong kid,' and waved at me." She does this 'begone, peasant' gesture. "And I went flying back here."

Mom rubs her forehead. "Portals? Seriously?"

I poke her in the arm. "Vampire. Imp. Girl with magic. Kitten who teleports. Boy who routinely takes a shortcut through a mirrorverse to get here. Are you honestly questioning portals?"

"No, not so much for existing. Mostly, I'm questioning how or why someone is using them against us." Mom sinks back into the sofa.

"Hmm." Dad rubs his chin. "Perhaps I shouldn't have picked a movie about magic and dragons."

Everyone chuckles, though enthusiasm levels vary.

"You should probably get going, hon." Dad taps his watch.

"Are you serious? After what just happened? I can miss a class once or twice."

"What are the odds of a second unexplained magical attack occurring tonight?" asks Mom.

I slouch. "Good point."

"No, I'm seriously asking."

"Umm…" I fidget. "Maybe I *should* stay home."

"It's not likely they'll do anything again tonight," says Sam. "They'll wait until we're not expecting it. Probably a few days."

Blix babbles.

Sam smiles at the imp. "He'll watch her 'til you get home."

"Okay, maybe Professor Heath will know something about this. He's old." I glance at Sophia. "Up to you. I'll stay home if you want me to."

She gulps. "Yeah, don't miss school. It's really bad. Sam's right. Doing magic makes people tired. Even if they wanted to try again, they probably can't."

"Okay. Call me if anything happens." I hurry downstairs to grab my stuff.

6

THE GRAND SCHEME

Flying in the snow is annoying.

Wearing soaked, half-frozen clothes is even worse—so I took the bikini express to school. The unusual wave of warmth is gone. No rain for us today. Hopefully, the bathing suit and towel stuffed in my backpack inside a plastic trash bag won't leak all over the place. Philosophy class would be kinda interesting tonight if my mind didn't keep wandering back to the Sophia situation. As expected, Heath's predictions for each student agreeing with chaos as a concept, disagreeing with it, or writing something random have been accurate with only two exceptions. Both of those students admitted to starting off doing one thing, but changing their mind after thinking about it during the week.

Everyone has to read their paper to the class, then we spend about ten minutes discussing any points made in the essay, assuming they haven't already been brought up by someone else. As usual for me during these kinds of exercises, dread sits on my shoulders as if I'm waiting my turn for the electric chair. Part of me secretly hopes he'll forget to call on me. At least considering my last name of Wright, I'll probably be the last person called. I don't think this class has anyone named Yankovic or Zelensky.

Fingers crossed discussion time eats the entire class period before my turn. Then again, this is philosophy. Heath isn't exactly following a lesson plan chasing specific points. Sure, we go over some of the great philosophers of history and their contributions, but a lot of the time, he runs class like Socrates throwing an idea to his students like a bit of meat to wild dogs and seeing how much we chew it. This means, of course, if I don't read my essay tonight, I'll end up reading it next Thursday.

The anxiety leading up to doing it is way worse than doing it.

Anyway, back to the ordinarily interesting thing. Discussions about the nature of randomness versus predestination would normally intrigue me, but I'm too worried about Sophia and what sort of new paranormal weirdness is messing with my family to focus on it. She's probably not going to sleep tonight, or she's going to want to sleep in my room. If it helps her rest, I'll totally watch over her all night. Even if I wanted to, my body won't fall asleep until sunrise.

Alas, with the exception of this guy Ryan—easily in his forties— who wrote an essay attempting to use a royal crapton of statistical analysis to prove the performance of the Philadelphia Eagles is directly related to the Seattle Seahawks, my fellow students don't throw any super controversial or off the wall ideas into the air. Discussion periods fly by as many of the essays cover the same sorts of arguments for or against chaos existing. Speaking in public has never been something I adored. In fact, I usually try to get out of it. But, if forced—as tends to happen when having a teacher immune to mental compulsion—it's not impossible for me to deal with it.

So, I go up there to read my essay.

"Hmm." Professor Heath gives me this little smile as I walk to the podium. "You're a difficult one to read, Miss Wright. My prediction for your essay is chaos. In the sense you have written something off script, neither arguing in support or against chaos as a concept, rather demonstrating it in action."

"Sorta like the Seahawks-Eagles theory, with less math?" I ask. "Sounds legit. Both team names involve birds, right?"

A low murmur of chuckling comes from the students.

"Am I correct?" asks the professor.

"I'm honestly not sure. I guess. Let me read this and you can tell me if you read me right."

He grins. "If you're unable to answer me, I suspect my guess is correct."

"Could be."

I let out a deep breath and present my idea of chaos existing by design. As in, we are governed neither by pure chaos nor by a grand architect following a plan, but some manner of architect who created chaos *as* the plan. Consequently, both positions are equally true as well as false. My personalization of said grand architect as a crazy old scientist throwing a bunch of cosmic gloop together to 'see what happens' gets some laughs.

Fifteen seconds into the discussion, a woman with a corporate day job—I think her name's Donna or Dina or something—makes a remark about my idea supporting the notion of a supreme being while simultaneously throwing serious shade at those who claim it has any specific wants or demands of humankind.

"I'm not claiming to know anything," I say in response. "Merely exploring the idea of chaos. Why do people take the position of absolutes for everything? Either there's a grand plan or everything's completely random. Why couldn't there be both an architect *and* chaos? Something set the universe in motion and it's sitting there clapping while random things explode, change color, take on new forms. You've got some groups who think they understand *the story* and what's going on, and they come up with this notion of what a supreme being would be like, or do, or say... yet there's so much going on in the world in defiance of those claims. If a supreme being is benevolent, why didn't it stop the Holocaust or the Black Death? If a supreme being is wrathful, where are the comets or lightning bolts smiting the bad guys?"

Things rapidly devolve into a theological debate from there, me keeping mostly quiet.

When the shouting becomes too loud, Professor Heath walks to the front of the class, arms out. Everyone shuts up at once. Pretty sure he used mental influence. "Ahh, chaos in action. One idea sets off a strong reaction. The reaction begets more strong reactions, and soon the proverbial water boils. Bear in mind, we are but simple humans attempting to create a tiny light to illuminate a darkness most vast. From time immemorial, we have wondered *why*. Why do we exist? Is there a purpose to our presence, or did we merely come into being randomly? A concept without proof cannot be correct or incorrect. It is an idea. We are just as likely to be all a daydream of some vast and terrible cyclopean nightmare beast as here in the flesh. What is our life but a flash in the instant of the cosmos? A mayfly has a lifespan of a couple days. How meaningful are any of its thoughts or deeds to the grand scheme of Earth, and the Universe at large?"

"Dunno, prof, but that mayfly's probably gonna make the Seahawks have to kick a field goal," says a thirtysomething guy in the front row.

Everyone—except Ryan—laughs.

"All right, excellent discussion tonight. I'll see you all next week. Last class before the holidays, so it'll be fairly light. Good night, all, and thank you for your time this evening." Professor Heath bows, then takes a seat behind his desk.

Students shuffle around, gathering their stuff. I'm eager to get home, but still dawdle a bit to have a moment with the professor after the room's empty.

"Something on your mind, Sarah?"

"Yeah." I approach the desk. "Can't really talk to my parents about this…"

"Uh oh, sounds bad."

"Not really. Stupid first world problems, but still gnawing at me." I explain my doubts about going to college. If it's worth doing at all, or about changing majors to something capable of grabbing my interest more than programming.

He leans back in his chair, the old springs creaking, and smiles. "In the grand scheme of things, you have all the time in the world, so don't feel like you're wasting it. If seeing you in college makes your parents happy, then it's neither a waste of their money nor a waste of your time."

"It's not really the time, in general, I'm worrying about. Just the hours I'm away from my sisters and brother. Twice a week, I have to leave when they're all sitting down for dinner. But, really, I'm still ahead. If nothing happened to me, I'd be in California now and having *zero* time with them."

"True." He nods once. "Also, you don't need to be with them every minute of every day to be close and loved."

"Yeah... mostly. I think some people are trying to grab Sophia. Should really get home to help watch over her."

He opens his eyes wider. "What? Why would anyone bother with your little sister?"

"Good question, but it's probably due to her having... unusual abilities."

"Piano prodigy?" asks Heath with a hint of a grin.

"If only she had something so normal." I give him a quick explanation of me liberating Coralie's remains from a group of mystics, them using a spell to turn Sophia into a remote-control spy by borrowing her body for a little while, and the result of it unlocking some supposed buried magical potential.

Professor Heath whistles. "Well, I've heard a few rumors in my day. Never witnessed anything of the sort in the flesh. Have you considered it may be an Academic involved in mysticism who may be an enemy of Aurélie?"

"Why would they go after my sister?"

"Why do bad guys in movies kill the wife or child of a police officer? To cause pain. Aurélie is fond of you. Some Academic uses Sophia to lure you somewhere in hopes of destroying you to inflict an emotional wound on Aurélie. Make her do something rash, expose a weakness to be exploited."

I cringe. "Umm... she never said anything about having a rival or enemy evil enough to want me dead. Yeah, there's this Fury, Vanessa Prentice, who's super jealous of Aurélie, but they feel more like debutantes trying to one-up each other with increasingly expensive dresses. Not like the sort of feud to end with killing someone's kid. And I'm not even her progeny."

"You're assuming the person behind this is rational. Or, I could be assuming the worst."

"Maybe. Sierra saw a room full of people in black robes. Didn't stay there long since they sent her back once they realized they grabbed the wrong girl. A group of people—or maybe vampires—is definitely attempting to kidnap Sophia, not just one of my siblings."

Professor Heath taps his fingers on the armrest of his chair. "These people may not be as dark as I fear. They sent Sierra back without harming her."

"True, but a hired assassin doesn't shoot anyone but the target either. Doesn't make them nice." I sigh. "Anyway, I should get home before something else strange happens. Thanks for listening to me. You're right. Going to school makes my parents happy and I don't hate it. So, yeah. I'll finish, even if I never wind up using the degree."

He chuckles. "You'll need to come back every hundred years or so to keep your knowledge fresh."

"Hah. Thanks, Professor."

"Any time you need to talk, I'll be here... until I move on to some other school. But you can fly pretty quick, so my door is still open."

Smiling, I wave and jog out.

UNTIL TALKING TO HEATH, THE IDEA OF OTHER VAMPIRES BEING involved hadn't even occurred to me.

I'm halfway home before I think to turn around and race back to the apartment complex Glim usually haunts. No idea if he sits on the roof in bad weather, but I might as well check. He wouldn't go inside his ex-wife's apartment. Too stalkery. He's not watching her, or his kids, as much as watching *over* them. Presumably, he'd get involved if for whatever reason her new boyfriend ever turned violent, or someone broke into their house, or the place caught fire.

Much to my surprise, he *is* on the roof, sitting under a giant black umbrella. The sight of an obvious vampire using such a mundane means to shield himself from the snow strikes me funny. Me wearing a lime green bikini in December hits him funny. As soon as my toes sink into the several inches of snow on the roof, he's laughing. He used his shadow abilities to keep people from noticing me change in the parking deck a while back, so he's quite aware of *why* I'm wearing a swimsuit to fly in bad weather. Without him there to cover me tonight, I changed in the bathroom after the building cleared out. Only had to poke two people in the brain on my way outside so they thought I had a normal season-appropriate outfit on.

"Not the best night for admiring the stars." Glim leans forward, peering past the rim of his umbrella. "Nature is much like people. Her rage conceals the true beauty under a cloak of darkness."

"Yeah."

"You have no rage this eve, but a cloak of worry weighs as heavy on your shoulders as the clouds hang in the sky."

I raise an eyebrow. "Have you been sitting in on a poetry analysis class at SCC?"

He chuckles. "No. Nights like this always put me in an odd mood. Give me a moment to think of a good line about undeath being unable to hide your true beauty."

"Aww, thanks, but I look like a drowned rat."

"I speak of the true beauty in your soul. Your concern for others… your innocence."

"Dad joke."

"Of course." He sits up a little taller. "So, what brings you to my roof on such a lovely night?"

"Someone's after Sophia." I explain what's happened to her so far, and Heath's suggestion it might be an Academic with mystical talents. "Do you know of any vamps in the area who use magic? Or someone who might have a serious problem with Aurélie?"

He gazes across the parking lot at the living room window where his former wife and her present boyfriend sit together on the sofa watching TV. It's amazing to me to see Glim love her so much he's happy she's moved on. I've offered to play 'medium' if he ever wanted or needed to communicate with her. He could stand right next to me and no one he didn't want to see him would be able to. We'd have an easy time pretending to be a ghost and psychic. So far, he hasn't wanted to bother her. The woman appears to be doing okay. No sense ripping open old wounds.

"Nothing stands out in my mind, but I will surely look to see if any information is floating around. As far as I am aware, no vampires in the area dabble in mysticism. Most don't even believe it's real." He glances sideways at me. "You should go home and warm up. Looking at you out here in a swimsuit is making *me* cold. And I lack body temperature."

"Thank you."

He nods.

I exhale. *Please still be home and safe.* "Night."

"Good night, Sarah."

Gripping my backpack tight to my shoulder, I leap into the air and fly home as fast as I can—meaning as fast as I can go without the wind ripping my suit off.

THE CLOSET MONSTER

A bikini might not make for the most practical flight gear, but I have reasons.

The wetsuit I bought a while ago is much better for bad-weather nights, but it's also kinda cumbersome and difficult to stuff in a backpack. Not to mention, weird. Someone too far away for me to notice sees me out in a snowstorm wearing a bathing suit, they'll think I lost a bet. Or I'm an idiot. Or one of those people in Russia who goes swimming in frozen lakes. A person running around the city in a wetsuit seems, I dunno, somehow more insane.

Anyway, I arrived home a little before 10:30 without incident. Sophia had already gone to bed. Blix and Klepto both stood guard over her. When I peeked in on her, the imp saluted me. Another totally weird thing. On Halloween, my sisters set loose a crapload of imps. They all appeared to be exact copies of each other, but now... I'm sure I'd recognize Blix apart from any other imp.

Since she looks safe, I head downstairs to my room, dry off, change into a tee and sweat pants, then unpack my still-dry clothes from the waterproof bag. Class tonight didn't give out any additional homework, so I'm still current. Yay. I sit there in my room trying to come up with an idea for something to do until sunrise. Video games, movies, or TV are the obvious choices of time kill when I have no homework. Being a vampire back in the day must have completely sucked.

Ugh. Unintentional dad joke. Bad Sarah.

Speaking of Dad... he took multiple zaps from those orbs and kept right on going. Wow. I'm pretty sure my father has never been broken in half by a troll, impaled with rebar, stabbed repeatedly by rusty rapiers, shot, sliced up, clawed to ribbons... and so on. The zap from those orbs had a surprising amount of potency. Thinking about my father continuing to go after orbs after repeated shocks makes me want to run up there and hug him. I've got no explanation for how a computer geek whose idea of a good workout is carrying groceries in from the car managed to withstand it.

Wow, dad. You rock.

Back to boredom.

What did vampires do before video games?

Oh, that's right, they impaled people like shish kebabs and decorated their castle grounds in rotting bodies, or stood like creeps in windows watching young women sleep. At least, they did those things if Hollywood is right. Maybe they read novels or lost themselves in philosophical discussions. Wait, fiction novels haven't even been around all too long.

Bleh. I have video games. Why worry about what they did in the 1400s?

I sit at the computer and fire up *Skyrim*. Yeah, it's old. So what?

Before I know it, my iPhone alarm goes off. It's set to ping fifteen minutes before sunrise. Can't help but feel like sitting in my room playing video games is wasting time even if my family and friends are all sleeping. Maybe I ought to involve myself more in vampire goings-on.

Nah.

Well, more of a not yet than a nah. Maybe I will once the Littles grow up and I stop being a wimp. If Aurélie's right about kid vampires' brains remaining the same, my personality isn't going to deviate much from where it is now. I'm always going to feel stuck halfway between an adult eager for independence and a kid afraid to go too far from home. Great. I'd almost rather be Sophia's age. At least then, no one would laugh at me for being squishy. The Portland Lost Ones kinda teased me for not wanting to destroy people's crap and play pranks. Maybe it's not so much a question of immaturity on my part but of being too much of a goody.

Bleh. Whatever. I'll worry about it in the morning.

Or afternoon.

Friday begins at 2:39 p.m.

At least, it does for me. I've mercifully avoided any significant ass-kickings for a while, so it's starting to feel routine to wake up close to 2:30 in the afternoon. Though, if past experience is any sort of teacher, this gradual buildup of weird is going to end in a painful way. If I get lucky this time, maybe the pain will hit whoever's messing with us, and not me.

No cereal craving today, and skies are clear. Wouldn't call it overly sunny, but it's enough for me to stay in bed texting Ashley, Michelle, and Hunter. None of them respond with much more than an 'in school' or 'can't talk now.' Grr.

Sometimes, it's wonderful to lie awake in bed knowing I don't have to be anywhere for hours. It's peaceful, at least until the Littles get home from school. Nothing sounds unusual about their arrival, but I still want to see them before they run off to friends' houses or get absorbed in whatever they plan to do today. After trading my long sleeping tee for a plum sweater top and comfortable jeans, I nab the phone and head upstairs.

Sam and Sierra rumble down from the second floor and raid the kitchen for snacks. I trail after them, trying to start a conversation. They had a reasonably okay day at school. Sierra goes to the living room for PlayStation time. Being it's Friday, she's going to put off doing homework until Sunday. Sam heads out the door with Ronan—who must have come through the mirror—on their way to Daryl's. It's relatively normal for Sophia not to come back downstairs right away after arriving home from school, but considering the events of the past few days, I go up to check on her anyway.

She's sprawled on her bed reading the mystic book. I sit on the edge, mostly to give her a sense of safety. My being here reassures her a great deal. Probably the exact opposite effect a vampire is supposed to have on a ten-year-old girl, right?

Nothing unusual happened to her at school.

Alas, today is one of my early two days for classes. First one being at six. At least winter plus Daylight Savings makes it dark out in time for me to fly. I spend as much time as possible with her before heading to class around when Mom summons everyone for dinner. Tonight's computer science and calculus.

Fun times.

* * *

Calc ends at 9:24 p.m., a bit early.

Guess Dr. Mercer is feeling the holiday spirit. I make my way out of the building, an innocuous young woman among many normal college students. My age makes me stand out a little. Not too many eighteen-year-olds do night school. A few people look at me and wonder if I'm some sad case like a Lifetime movie where the parents died and the oldest sister has to become mom to the rest of the siblings, work a full time job, and is still trying to get a diploma at night.

If anything ever happened to our parents and I had to take care of the Littles, one of two things would happen. I'd either beg Aurélie for enough money to see all three of them to adulthood, or I'd use my powers in every way possible to make damn sure the sibs had everything they needed. Knowing myself, I'd save begging as a last resort if I couldn't deal with stuff myself. I may *look* like a kid, but begging is still kinda pathetic. Not so pathetic I wouldn't swallow a humility pill for my siblings' benefit if I had no other choice.

I grab a quick bite on the way home—some middle-aged nerdy

looking guy driving a green Saab. For some weird reason, his blood tastes like Boston crème donuts. Great. Thanks for a craving. Grr. What am I, pregnant? No, then I'd want a donut stuffed with pickles or something.

Blech.

I arrive home around 9:30 thanks to a stop at a Dunkin Donuts for an actual donut. Sierra and Sam, in their PJs, sit at the dining room table with Dad, playing a board game. Sophia's not with them. Unusual, but no one seems upset. Dad's clearly letting them stay up a bit past their bedtime for a Friday night. Maybe Sophia was tired and went to sleep already. Curious, I step out of my shoes before leaving the permitted zone, set my school bag on the floor, and head upstairs.

Faint blue light on the carpet by her bedroom door is my first clue something's wrong. It's much dimmer than both previous times she turned Klepto into a literal ball of energy. Most kittens are balls of energy, but it's supposed to be metaphorical. They don't often glow.

"Go away!" whispers Sophia. "Leave me alone."

"Crap."

Upon pushing the door open, I realize the light isn't coming from the kitten. She's her normal fuzzy grey self, growling—as much as such a tiny critter *can* growl—at the closet, the source of the blue light. Whatever's going on there is pretty intense. The glow visible around the door is as bright as if it led to outside in the middle of a summer afternoon.

Sophia's standing by her bed, arms raised, palms pointed at the closet door. There's no wind in the room, but her hair and nightgown billow about like she's outside in the middle of a hurricane. Her expression shifts from ninety-percent fear, ten-percent confidence to about sixty-forty when she notices me.

"Sare, they're trying again... I think. Klepto started growling at the closet."

The tiny kitten emits a noise like a cell phone on vibrate sliding across a table.

I cautiously approach the closet. Something inside whispers in a language so unfamiliar I'm not even sure what to call it. "Holy crap. You really *do* have a closet monster."

"It's not stopping!" Sophia pushes at the air, stepping toward me while grunting and growling as if shoving a heavy object.

In response to her approach, the light in the closet dims. The closer she gets, the weaker the glow. By the time she's crossed the room from the bed to stand beside me, her closet once again looks normal. And the whispering stops. Pretty sure whispers in an ancient, forgotten tongue don't belong in a ten-year-old's closet. Maybe her enormous hoard of dolls finally decided to revolt against their queen. Oh, there's a horrifying thought. What is it about dolls? Why are they so damn creepy? Especially in the dark... or when they move on their own.

Sophia lowers her arms and scoots behind me. "Make sure it's gone."

Klepto squeezes between Sophia's ankles, still attempting to growl at the closet.

"Are you sure opening this door is a good idea?" I reach hesitantly for the knob.

"No. But *not* looking might be bad, too."

"Do you feel anything strange?" I shift my eyes toward her.

She stares fixedly at the door, much like a mouse waiting for the cat to make the first move. "Yeah."

I stop turning the knob. "What?"

"Something's tickling my legs."

I hang my head and sigh. "Look down. It's your cat."

"Oh. Sorry," whispers Sophia.

"Right. One dead closet monster coming up."

I open the door to reveal a rectangular wall of perfect blackness. Klepto's teeny growl cuts off to a '*mrr?*', the kitten version of WTF.

"Last time I checked, we're not in a video game. Why do you have a void of infinite darkness in your closet? Does Mom know about this?"

"It's not mine. I swear." Sophia clings to me from behind. "I don't know how it got there."

"Well, you know Mom and Dad aren't going to react well to you hiding dimensional rifts." I scratch the back of my head. Honestly? I think this will bother them less than if they find adult magazines in Sam's room when he's sixteen, even though what's going on here is far less natural.

"I didn't do it. It's not mine," whisper-whines Sophia. "Is it Narnia?"

"No. This is far too black and featureless. It's even emptier than the brain of a flat-Earther."

Sophia giggles.

"I'm not sure it's anything." I stare into the abyss, but it's not looking back at me. "Actually, I think it's *nothing*."

"Huh?" she peers up at me.

"In computer science, there's this concept called null. It's like the representative existence of nothingness somehow capable of occupying space."

"Kim Kardashian?" asks Sophia.

Right as I start to laugh, an invisible force slams into me from behind and hurls me—and Sophia—into the void. Bracing for impact with a wall of onyx glass is useless, as I go right through it, like jumping out the hatch of a starship lost in deep space. Only, no stars or anything else breaks up the endless nothingness. Strong light illuminates my body, Sophia, and Klepto, but has no apparent source.

My sister's mouth is wide open. She has to be screaming, but this place is perfect in its silence. I can't even hear myself breathing. After a moment of hanging motionless, my stomach lurches... the only clue to indicate we're moving again. Best guess, we plummet straight down for a few seconds, pull out of the dive to horizontal flight for a while longer than we fell, then swerve to rocket straight upward.

Finally, a break appears in the endless black everywhere... a round hole above us. It's as if we're riding a rocket-powered elevator going up inside an old timey water well. There's barely enough time to mentally process the opening before we reach it—and our motion stops in an instant, leaving us standing in the middle of a big, rectangular room. Large, irregular stone walls make me think castle basement. Oh, wait. They call those 'dungeons.'

Eight people surround us in a circle, all wearing black robes with voluminous hoods obscuring most of their faces. Cold under my feet confirms the floor is stone as well, probably underground. We haven't taken a step... so what had an instant before been a yawning hole into infinite nothingness has become solid. The scent of damp stone, glue, and paper lurks under an aromatic bouquet like we've landed in a specialty herbal tea shop.

Sophia clings tighter to me. Klepto vibrates, err, I mean growls.

I glance around at the people, none of whom do anything or move. The vast room we've been brought to is relatively empty. It reminds me of the stereotypical 'inn basement full of giant rats' from an old fantasy video game—except instead of torches, it's got electric lights. To our left and right, long tables against the walls hold jars of glowing substances, books on stands, candles, a few skulls, and a taxidermy raven as big as a five-year-old kid.

"Uh oh," whispers Sophia.

The robed figures exchange glances, seemingly caught off guard by me being here.

"Mew! Mrow!" says Klepto.

Got a feeling she said, 'anyone touches Sophia and I'll rip your face off.'

Agreed.

I may not strike the most imposing figure in a loose white top, jeans, barefoot, and having a childish face... but clothes don't make the vampire. Even if it hadn't been dark out, these idiots were obliging enough to drag us into an underground room with no windows. Extending my claws, I step in front of Sophia and emit a low growl, closer to an angry mountain lion than a sound produced by a human my size.

"Whoever you are, you just kidnapped the wrong little girl."

Sophia gasps.

Klepto hisses and spits. The little fuzzball glances at me with a look of 'yeah, let's kick some ass. It's claw time.'

"Might wanna close your eyes, Soph."

8

SOULBOUND

Theretisn't much in the world capable of making me want to kill complete strangers.

Kidnapping or hurting my family, however, does it. I'd say sudden exposure to bright sunlight is another, but there's no 'want' involved there. Only knowing these people sent Sierra back unhurt keeps me from having a psycho-kitty claw freakout on them. I'm still tempted, but my hesitation, hoping intimidation might work and spare me the future guilt of murdering people, gives them a chance to speak.

The man directly in front of us holds his hands up in a 'whoa, hang on a sec there' gesture. At my continued hesitation in ripping faces off, he reaches up and pulls his hood back, revealing a poofy mass of dreadlocks. He's got a fairly dark complexion and movie-star good looks. A hint of grey in his thin mustache says he's pushing forty or so, but hair dye could chop ten years off. The guy's wearing multiple rings, though none have gaudy, glowing gems. Guess magic only goes so far over the top in the real world, right? It seems I've encountered Dr. Normal.

"I am Asher Jones. Please, do not be alarmed," says the guy in an accent like Dalton's.

Wow. 'Asher.' There's a bad name for a vampire hunter. Since none of these guys have crossbows or swords on them, I'm guessing they're not hunters. The others also pull their hoods down. A pale, red-haired woman in her later thirties on Asher's left stares at Sophia, her expression pleading. An Indian dude on his right nods once at me in greeting. Beside him, a scrawny girl about my age stares at me, wide-eyed in terror. Her shoulder-length snow-white hair is clearly a dye job as her eyebrows are still dark. A Chinese man stands to the left of the redhead. He, too, looks at Sophia the way one might look at the firefighter about to drag them out of a burning house. Beside him is a tall, thin guy, mid-forties, wearing an average grey business suit under his black robe. Right of the Indian dude, a somewhat younger guy who's either Hispanic or Middle Eastern offers me a shallow bow of welcome. Behind us, stands another woman. She's thirtysomething and has this air about her like she teaches third grade.

I'm sure parents would be alarmed to learn their kid's teacher moonlights as a creepy cultist.

Okay... not expecting this. They're not giving off hostility or malice. Frustratingly, their minds are blank to me. Feels similar to my first attempt to read Damarco's thoughts, only rather than a sense of an impenetrable shield around their brains, it's more of a total absence of anything in their heads... like trying to use telepathy on a stone.

Wonderful. Anti-vaxxers.

Oh, hang on... I can see into the mind of the white-haired girl. Her thoughts are unshielded and mostly 'oh, shit. What the hell is that?' in regard to me. The girl's trying to figure out what kind of demon is impersonating a young teenager.

"I just tumbled into a limitless non-space concealed in my sister's closet, only to land in a creepy dungeon surrounded by people in creepy black robes. I'm supposed to *not* be alarmed?"

"Apologies." Asher clasps his hands in front of himself. "We are in need of your sister's assistance."

"Me?" whispers Sophia, so faintly no one notices.

"Umm." I blink, then yell, "You guys ever hear of these devices called telephones? They've been around for a couple of years. They even have this *email* thing now. What the hell is going on?"

Asher's expression shows no reaction to me shouting. "We are members of the Aurora Aurea. Please understand we did not bring the child here to harm her. We are in need of her help."

The red-haired woman leans closer to Asher and whispers, "Does the older kid have *claws*? What on Earth?"

"Looks like it," whispers the Chinese guy.

The maybe-Hispanic guy makes a 'these aren't the droids you're looking for' hand motion at me. A faint amber glow dances in his eyes and fades, though I don't notice any unusual sensations. "*Iinaha masas dmaa'un.*" His expression goes from suspicious to frightened, and a touch surprised.

It's tempting to comment how sharp my claws are and offer to give the redhead a nice close look, but it's probably better to not let them know I can hear her whispering. "Not sure what language he's speaking, but I think he's figured me out."

"What are we dealing with?" asks the redhead a little louder.

Klepto emits a tiny hiss.

Good idea, kitty. I bare my fangs. Not the most subtle way to keep secrets, but these *are* mystics after all. They are certainly aware of vampires already, and a bunch of other stuff. "An ass-kicking if someone doesn't start explaining why my sister's closet ate us."

The white-haired teen looks ready to faint. Ms. Redhead and the Chinese guy both stare at me like I'm their next greatest specimen they can't wait to put in a jar.

"Our lodge is under attack by a paranormal force we are unequipped to handle." Asher sighs inaudibly out his nose. "Already, we have lost six of our number to car accidents, falls, or strange coincidental fatalities."

I tilt my head. "Define 'strange coincidental fatality.'"

The schoolteacher-looking woman behind me makes a bird motion with her hand. "Pigeon flies into the head of a man up on a platform cleaning high-rise windows. He drops a water bucket. Forty stories below, the bucket strikes a car, causing it to swerve off the road and hit a lamp post. The post falls over, spearing into the window of a café and almost impaling an old man. The barista screams, throwing a pot of coffee into the air. The scalding coffee hits another man, sending him running out the door half-blind and screaming. He collides with Leo—who happens to be walking by at the very moment—accidentally shoving him off the sidewalk into the path of an oncoming double-decker bus. Leo was one of us."

I stare at her. "Are you messing with me?"

"No, lass. I'm afraid 'tis the all of it." The woman dabs a tear from her face. "Crushed his 'ead, it did. Right under the tire."

I've no idea how the woman got through such a story keeping a straight face. It's so ridiculous, Sophia and I are obviously the victims of some bizarre prank implemented by highly trained actors capable of spouting off the most ludicrous things without cracking up.

"So… you guys can't deal with some monster, and you think a little kid is going to help?" I go to scratch my head, but stop myself as the claws are still out. "Makes less sense than a guy getting run over by a bus because a pigeon hit some other dude in the head. Oh, wait. I get it now… None of this is really happening. I'm dreaming, and the insanity is coming from me having to write a paper on chaos. A dog farts in Munich causing a guy in Arkansas to suffer a heart attack."

The others briefly exchange glances of 'this girl is nuts' then continue giving Sophia 'please help us' stares, except the white haired teen. She's ready to scream and run the instant I twitch.

"Sophia is in a unique position to be able to remedy our situation," says Asher.

"Let me guess…" I rub my forehead. "She's some kind of untapped prodigy with magic prophesized in some obscure writing who's going to save all of wizard-kind from this great, unstoppable horror… and do it all in time for the next Quidditch match."

Sophia glances up at me with a 'you've gotta be kidding' expression.

"Oh, no." Asher chuckles. "Nothing so grand. Curses can be complicated and strange. The entity killing us off one by one is the same spirit she released from a soul jar. Her connection to the spirit trap persists, linking her essence to that of the wraith. For her, magic has fifty times the potency over the spirit than for us. The same mechanism by which it is vulnerable to her shields it from others. Believe me, we have been trying. We simply aren't powerful enough."

"Umm," says Sophia in a small voice. "You guys do realize I've only found out about magic recently, right? I don't really know how to use it to fight." She kicks her toes at the floor. "I don't like fighting."

Asher approaches us, breaking their circle formation, and smiles down at Sophia. "Your inexperience in the arts does not matter. The enchantment within the soul jar bound you to the spirit. The entity is weak to you."

"Oh." Sophia looks down. "I thought it was cruel to keep him in there. I'm sorry. He told me he wouldn't hurt anyone."

"He obviously fed you a pile of bollocks," says the Indian man.

"Whoa, hold on," I say. "You guys can't be serious. I can't let my kid sister get mixed up with a 300-year-old murderer. This is clearly a nightmare. You guys are all talking in Dalton's accent. The comi-tragic pigeon-to-bus death is totally the result of the chaos assignment priming my subconscious mind. Thanks, but I'm going to change the dream channel. We're leaving."

Asher sighs, but steps back. "We are not abducting you. You are free to leave if you so choose."

Of course we are free to leave. It's my dream, so I'm in control.

"Umm." Sophia blushes. "Why did you guys steal my clothes when I was at school the other day?"

"Please accept our apologies for that mishap. None of us had ever attempted to use magic to transport a person in such a manner before. Our aim had been bringing *you* here, not merely your apparel."

The redhead grimaces apologetically. "We waited until you were alone so no one would notice the magic."

"You watched me in the bathroom!" squeak-shouts Sophia, too mortified to really yell.

"No." Asher shakes his head. "We could not see you, merely had an awareness of how many other people were in your vicinity, as well as whether or not you were able to be seen by people nearby. Once we sensed you were alone and out of sight, we attempted to bring you here during a moment when no one could see the magic."

"Only we… missed," says the redhead.

The tall, pale guy with the long face and curly roadkill hair glances at Asher. "Seems I was right, old friend. We should 'ave reached out to them via Darren Anderson's group. Grabbin' 'em outta the blue's no way ta do things."

"They would not have sent her here based on a phone call." Asher shakes his head slightly.

"And draggin' 'er 'ere fared much better, aye?" asks the tall guy.

Whatever. Enough of this dream.

I retract my claws, grab Sophia's hand, and pull her with me to the room's only exit. The door leads to a more ordinary looking basement area full of dusty junk covered in sheets. I head left, following the faint sounds of automotive traffic down a corridor, past several small rooms, to a stairwell. Stacked plastic boxes of books clutter the landing, but we squeeze past without much difficulty. Two switchbacks later, I open a plain white door into a relatively modern room—as opposed to the castle basement.

The right side of this room has a small, round table, chairs, and kitchenette like a break area in a corporate office. On my left, long work tables hold various tools, some big hand-operated machinery I don't recognize, and books in various stages of disassembly. The glue-and-paper smell is way strong in here. Not stopping to take in the sights too much, I head for the most obvious door, and emerge at the back end of an antique bookstore, surrounded by dark hardwood shelves two stories tall. Rolling brass ladders add to the effect, as well as various carvings in the wood depicting mythical beasts.

"Whoa. Did they bring us to Diagon Alley?" whispers Sophia.

"That's not a real place, but yeah, this sure looks like it belongs there."

I lead her down the aisle to the front door. The bookstore appears closed for the night—it's dark out—no one at the counter. Door's locked, but easily enough opened from the inside. We step out onto a frigid city street where small shops fill the ground floors of six- and seven-story buildings on both sides. Black double streetlamps look nothing like anything I've ever seen in Seattle and there's this weird red thing sorta shaped like an oval trashcan, only it isn't one. The letters BR sit under a crown on the face near the bottom. Despite the archaic look of the bookstore, no dragons, wizards, or flying brooms are anywhere in sight. Cars are parked on both sides of a road too narrow for two-way traffic. A dry cleaners is directly across from us next to a wholesale jewelry place. Left of the dry cleaners is a huge grey building with no obvious signs, only three rectangular, gold bas-reliefs depicting the head and forelegs of a horse on the second, third, and fourth floor walls between windows.

"Where are we?" whispers Sophia, past chattering teeth. She bounces on her toes, arms wrapped around herself, shivering.

"Good question." I glance down at my bare feet on freezing sidewalk, over at her bare feet on the same freezing sidewalk, then up at her gossamer nightgown... outside in the middle of December.

Every retail shop around us appears to be closed as well. Weird. It's only like 9:45 or so at night. Why is everything closed? Traffic's also super light. Oh, maybe I can figure out where we are by the license plates. I try to take Sophia's hand, but she won't pull them out from under her arms, trying to keep her fingers from freezing. With a hand on her shoulder, I tug her along and approach the nearest car.

The plate's totally weird. White, black letters, half as tall as it should be but much wider. Umm...

I stand there staring at it in bewilderment, until the scuff of a shoe redirects my attention to a thirtyish man walking toward us. He's yawning, not really paying attention to us or his surroundings, and appears to be in a hurry.

"Excuse me..." I step closer, not quite blocking his path.

The man stops, looks at me, then Sophia, and back to me, seeming confused. "Aye, luv?"

"What city is this?"

He laughs.

"No, seriously... where are we?"

His mirth fades. Again, he looks at Sophia outside in a nightie.

"London… have you two been abducted?" He pulls a cell phone off a belt clip. "I can ring the police."

I stare into his eyes, forcing him to see us both properly dressed in winter coats, and not remember my question. "Thanks."

"Uh oh. We're gonna be in trouble." Sophia peers up at me, teeth chattering even louder. "We're outside after bedtime and we don't have passports."

9

CREEPING DOOM

C rap!

"Gotta be a dream," I say.

"You look like you're awake." Sophia shivers. "I'm cold."

"Dammit."

"What?" She tilts her head.

"Mew," says Klepto.

"I'm a vampire."

"But you know that already?" Sophia scrunches up her nose.

An uneasy feeling hits me while looking around. I fish my phone out of my purse, open my GPS app, and tag my current location. Apparently, the street name is both B521 and Hatton Garden. Oh, not confusing at all. Still, it would be dumb of me to forget where to find these mystics.

I hurry back into the bookstore with her, out of the freezing December night. "I didn't say dammit *because* of being a vampire. I said it because it means I can't possibly be asleep and dreaming... unless the entire day has been a dream, including going to school."

"Oh. I don't think you're dreaming. 'Cause then we'd both be having the same dream at the same time, and it's too weird to happen."

"More or less weird than us being drawn into a void in your closet?"

She gives me a super apologetic look. "I'm sorry."

"Stop... I know you didn't make it." I ruffle her hair.

"No. I didn't close it right."

Grumbling, I storm down the aisle to the rear of the store, through the back room, and take the steps to the basement, interrupting the group of mystics having a 'well, now what' sort of discussion.

"London?" I yell. "You yoinked us to freakin' London?"

The white-haired girl about screams at the sight of me, even though she's a little taller and, unlike me, *looks* eighteen. Can't fault her really. Normal-me would've reacted the same way to an angry vampire. Asher and the other mystics regard me, varying degrees of hope and worry on their faces.

"We brought you to where we are," says Asher after a pause. "You make it sound like we tossed you randomly across the globe."

"You guys grabbed a little girl out of her bedroom in the middle of the night. Only creeps and weirdos do that." I jab a finger at him. "Open the—the... whatever you did, and send us back."

"It will require time for us to make the necessary preparations," says the Chinese guy. "But since you're already here, please help us before the spirit wipes us out."

"Unbelievable," I mutter. "You don't even try to talk to us first, then somehow drag us to freakin' London in the middle of the night without warning, and you expect her, a ten-year-old who has like a month of practice using magic, to take on this entity who's killing off adult mystics?"

The group trades glances again. Ms. Redhead and the schoolteacher have a 'kid's got a point' quality to their expressions. Sophia timidly peers up at me. Ugh. She's totally going to volunteer to help them, but at least she's too shy to say anything. My sister *is* sweet and nice enough to risk herself to stop other people from dying. But she's also a child who isn't really capable of understanding what it means to risk her life. I just *can't* allow her to jump into a situation like this.

"You're phrasing it in a way to make it sound bad," says the Indian guy.

I briefly daydream about ripping his spine out and clubbing him over the head with it, but resist the temptation. "How exactly should I phrase it? Other than a ghost and magic being involved, how is this any different from a bunch of wackos grabbing a child out of her room at night, handing her a gun, and asking her to go shoot bad guys?"

Asher clears his throat. "It would not be in our interest to expedite your return to the United States. I understand your frustration, but please try to see things from our perspective. Only eight of us remain, and we will surely perish without your sister's aid. Opening the portal would be no different from committing suicide. It has become clear to us she is our only chance to stop this entity."

Sophia starts to raise her hand.

Before she can ask what she needs to do to help them, I grab her wrist and haul her back upstairs and outside, fuming. Stupid, thoughtless, entitled mystics. Where do they get off dragging us across the damn ocean to fix their problems for them? Okay, maybe the problem is one Sophia started, but she didn't mean to. She's a kid. If a child on a tour of a chemistry lab accidentally bumps something and starts a wicked fire, they're not going to hand her a hose and ask her to help put it out.

I stop short on the sidewalk, shocked out of my mental tirade at the touch of freezing concrete under my feet. Dammit. We can't stay outside for long. Sophia's nightgown isn't doing much for warmth. And double crap... we're in London. They're like... umm... eight hours in the future from Washington State. Was almost ten at night when we... oh, shit! It's gotta be creeping up on six in the morning here. Sunrise any minute. No wonder the guy looked so tired. He had to be on his way to work before dawn. Also explains why everything is closed.

Near to panicking, I hurry down the street and make a few random turns, searching for a good place to shelter from the sun. Sophia's a trooper, tolerating the freezing cold without too much protest other than a shriek when we step in a puddle crossing the street. Grr. I scoop her up and carry her up to a jog even though we're lost.

Finally, I spot a cop. No, I'm not going to tell the police what happened to us or sic them on the mystics. But, a cop ought to know the area. I rush up to him and dive straight into his head, forcing him to ignore how we're dressed. Since Sophia's with me, my standards for crash pad are higher. Need somewhere relatively child safe. No drug users, vagrants, gang punks, or whatever.

"Excuse me," I say. "Where's the nearest hotel?" Do they call them hotels here, or are they inns? Argh, don't be a dumbass. I'm in London, not medieval times.

The constable points to the left. "Go down end of the block, hang a left, then another left soon as you can. Point A'll be on yer right."

"Point A?" I blink.

"Aye. Point A Hotel. Closest one to us. Or ye kin follow Holywell Row up ta The Curtain. 'At way." He points past my shoulder.

"Okay. Thanks." I get a glimpse of the building from his memory, a tall, thin black-walled place on Paul Street.

With little time to debate, I rush to the corner, carrying Sophia, whip around the next corner, and haul ass past some kind of night club and a short, wide building named The Lycaeum to the Point A hotel.

By sheer luck, I still have my purse with me—didn't put it down with my book bag—but we don't have time for me to go through the process of filling out paperwork. Also, the clerk will probably call the police on two young girls taking out a hotel room on their own, especially when the smaller one has only a nightgown on in December.

Right. Into his brain I burrow.

He programs a room key for us at my compulsion, then forgets he ever saw us. Haze fogs my brain within seconds of us entering the stairwell. The walls shift and wobble in a blurry mess halfway between trying to escape the Titanic and overdosing on LSD. I have a vague impression of force yanking on my arm and seeing a super close-up view of Sophia's foot in my face...

And the next thing I know, I'm on the floor of a tiny bathroom.

The air smells like Sophia, faintly strawberry. I sit up, momentarily confused by the abrupt change in surroundings. It finally hits me I must've blacked out due to sunrise on the stairs. Somehow, Sophia managed to drag me to our room.

"Oh, shit. We're in London." I suppose it could be worse. London's about the only place on the planet rivalling Seattle for rain. According to my phone, it's 2:58 p.m. on Saturday. Oh, neat. It auto-switched time zones.

Cartoon sounds come from the outer room.

I pull myself upright and walk out into a small, ultra-modern hotel room. Sophia's sitting on the bed watching an unfamiliar animated show. As soon as she sees me, she springs off the bed, runs over, and clamp-hugs me.

"Can we get food? Please! I'm *soooo* hungry. I didn't call room service 'cause you didn't really get the room the normal way."

"Yeah... sure. In a bit. Need to call Mom and Dad."

"I did already. Thought it would be better to tell them right away than let them discover us missing in the morning. They want you to call home as soon as you wake up. Mom was ready to go right to the airport and come here after calling the police, but she got stuck in a logic trap. We can't really say magic kidnapped us."

"Ugh. The PIBs would straight up crap a Rubik's cube if we did."

She laughs, though sounds more nervous than amused. "I talked them into waiting for you to call. Mom still wanted to fly here, but you're eighteen and have mind-control powers."

Oh yay. Welcome to adult responsibility. "Gee... hope I'm ready for so much trust."

"It's not trust. They couldn't find a babysitter for Sam and Sierra," deadpans Sophia.

"Hah."

"Seriously, you should call them right away. Mom sounded totally calm on the phone."

"Crap."

She whistles. "Exactly."

I sit on the end of the bed, Sophia beside me, and dial home on speakerphone.

"Hello?" asks Mom, too casual to have looked at the caller ID.

"Mom. Hey, sorry. Just woke up."

"Sarah!" says Mom a little louder than normal volume. "What the heck is going on? Where are you and Sophia? Are you seriously in London? Sophia is not pulling my leg?"

"Afraid she's right."

Mom exhales hard. "This isn't funny."

"Not trying to be."

"You're not talking about London, Ohio?" asks Mom.

"Nope. England." I say. "Unless they have weird license plates and drive on the wrong side of the road in Ohio."

Sophia leans against me, cringing at Mom's groan.

Click.

"Sarah?" asks Dad, from another handset. "How's the weather over there? Did you check out Big Ben yet?"

"Jonathan!" yells Mom. "Our daughters are overseas without money or passports."

"Or clothes," says Sophia. "All I have is a nightgown."

"Easily enough fixed," I mutter. "There's shops all over the place here. We're in London, not stranded far from civilization."

"What are you going to do?" asks Mom.

"You have to try fish and chips from a legit place," says Dad.

"Jonathan! You're not helping," shouts Mom, attempting to muffle the phone.

My father either trusts me to protect Sophia, or he's not coping well with instantaneous overnight international travel. Probably trusts me. If the weird stuff was going to make him crack, he'd have snapped four months ago.

"Relax, Mom."

"Don't you tell me to relax, young lady. I am as calm as can be considering two of my daughters are in Europe for reasons I can't discuss with any sane person."

"You've got Dad to talk to," I mutter. "Oh, wait. You said sane."

Dad makes a *thbptptpt* sound.

"Tell me what, exactly, is going on," says Mom.

"So… remember the thing with the soul jar?" I explain the group of mystics trying to grab Sophia because they believe she has power over this wayward spirit, but I'm not about to let her involve herself in anything dangerous. "As soon as it gets dark enough for me to go online, we're heading right to the airport."

"You still have your authorized user card?" asks Mom.

"Yeah. Should I use it or charge the flight on *Vee*-sa."

"Umm. You don't have a Visa. When did you get a Visa?"

"Allie," says Dad. "Capital V." He makes wee-ooo noises.

"Oh…" Mom hums. "Well, an international flight ticket bought same day is going to be ridiculously expensive. And you don't have passports, so you'll need to use the special Visa card anyway."

Right, Mom's telling me 'go ahead and steal plane fare' without saying those exact words. Plausible deniability. Besides, I think she could get disbarred for inciting the commission of a crime. But… supernatural stuff. The PIBs will clean it up if I make too big a mess. Hmm. Maybe I should call them for help? Nah. Not yet. Then I'll owe them a favor.

"Okay. Will do. Please try not to panic. We're fine. This is only annoying."

"I'm mildly jealous," says Dad. "I've always wanted to visit London."

"Heh. We're not here to sightsee. Anything specific I need to know, or can I call you back if anything changes?"

"Other than my nerves going crazy, no." Mom lets out a heavy sigh. "This stuff isn't easy to get used to. I'm not sure how to process people kidnapping the two of you but *not* holding you against your will. It's almost weirder than how you got to London."

Sophia bites her lip at me.

"Yeah. Okay. The tiny one is famished. Need to figure out a way to feed her without causing a giant mess."

"Put a bib on her," says Dad.

Sophia rolls her eyes. "Not that kind of mess. Sarah's offline. She can't make people forget seeing us. It's December. People are gonna call the cops if they see me outside barefoot in a nightgown. They'll think I'm abandoned."

"The police might be of help, no?" asks Dad.

"What exactly am I supposed to tell them? We were teleported here? Or should we make up a story about guys in a black van grabbing us off the street back home, flying us to London, and dumping us in an alley?"

"Oh, good point."

Mom sighs. "I hate not being able to help more directly."

"You and me both." I frown. "Waiting for the sun to go down is a huge pain."

The scent of cooked meat reaches my nose.

"Mew," says Klepto.

I glance toward the meow. The kitten's standing on the room's tiny table, next to a plate holding a grilled chicken sandwich and fries.

"Ooh!" Sophia leaps up and runs over to eat.

Somewhere, someone's about to wonder why their late lunch vanished.

"Right. Food situation's dealt with. I'll call again once we're at the airport."

"All right. Be careful," says Mom.

"Don't mess with those guys in the big fuzzy hats." Dad chuckles. "It's illegal."

"Not on my list of stuff to do, Dad. See you guys as soon as possible."

Mom verbally worries at me for a few minutes more, but eventually, we get through the 'I love you' thing and the 'be careful' thing about ten times. Sophia's already done with her lunch before I'm off the phone.

"Damn. Battery's getting low. Better charge it." I fish the charging cable out of my purse and hunt around for an outlet.

"Wait! You'll fry it," shouts Sophia. "They have like different power here."

"Oh, crap. Yeah. Ugh. I need coffee. I'm not thinking."

"Does coffee do any good for you?" She tilts her head.

"Maybe, but only in the sense of making me think it's doing something. I need a power adapter."

"Mew," says Klepto… then vanishes.

"The cat is on it." Sophia winks, then returns to the bed to resume watching cartoons. "So, we're gonna stay here until it's dark out?"

"Yeah. As soon as I'm online, we'll go someplace and get you real clothes… then hit the airport."

She fidgets. "Do you think we should help the mystics? The ghost is gonna kill them."

Okay, maybe I'd been too pissed off at them to think about anything more than giving them the proverbial finger by storming out… but this is a centuries-old serial killer. I got a brief look at him when Soph let him out of that jar, and he did *not* strike me as a warm fuzzy sorta guy. Sure he left her be in peace, but she'd freed him. No guarantee his 'sense of honor' will stop him from harming Sophia if they meet again, especially if she's acting against him. If what Asher said is true and she is connected to this ghost somehow by the broken enchantment in the soul jar, the spirit has to know this. As soon as he perceives her as a threat, it will be her on the receiving end of some ridiculous thirty-step chain reaction 'accident.'

I don't want the mystics to die, but—sorry to be a bitch here—Sophia's life is worth way more to me than theirs. Even if she manages to save all eight of the remaining mystics, if it kills her to do it, we're way into unacceptable territory.

"It sucks what's happening to them, but I can't let you be hurt. You aren't the only one capable of stopping the bad ghost. According to them, it's only *easier* for you. But, you're a kid with no training. Those mystics opened a portal and pulled us across the planet. You can't do anything so powerful. I don't know what they're even thinking asking you to take on a wraith."

"What's a wraith?"

I shrug. "Same thing as a ghost, but sounds more evil."

Klepto reappears on the bed, a power adapter in her mouth.

"Thanks!" I pet her, then hook my phone up to charge.

So, a few hours to pass.

It takes a bit of doing, but I eventually figure out the TV controls and find *The Goonies* playing on a movie channel. Sophia leans against me on the bed with the kitten cozied between us. Yeah, my kid sister screams, scared of the Fratellis. No way is she going to end up taking on a legit dangerous spirit.

When the movie's over, Sophia scrambles off to the bathroom. I collect my phone from the charger and hunt around online for a clothes shop. Looks like a department store is fairly close, a bit south of us. Marks & Spencer, Finsbury Pavement. Hmm. Weird name for a store, but definitely sounds British.

Sophia screams.

Nothing in a bathroom should prompt slasher movie victim screams, especially when Sam and his frogs are thousands of miles away. Could the mystics be jackasses enough to try magically grabbing her again? Maybe they yoinked her nightgown. No, her scream had way too much terror and not enough anger.

Sophia backs out of the bathroom, still in her nightgown, pale-faced and trembling.

"Soph?" I drop the phone on the bed and jump to my feet. "What's wrong?"

She glances at me for an instant, then runs to the outer door, scrambling to undo the deadbolt and chain. Okay, something in the bathroom has clearly horrified her beyond reason. Did Dad forget to flush again? Wait, he's not even here.

My sister bolts out into the hallway.

I hurry after her, glancing left into the bathroom at a wall of black fur filling it entirely. "Okay, weird. This hotel has a serious mold problem."

Even without my vampiric abilities active, I overtake Sophia in the hall and grab her at the stairwell door. She's trembling as hard as if she'd witnessed a man shot in the face.

"Hey," I say in a soothing tone. "It's okay. Why are you so scared?"

She spins into me and grabs on. "Look out… he's coming."

"What?"

"Look!" She points back down the hall.

I twist to peer behind me. A ten-foot-wide sphere of black fur squeezes out the door of our hotel room. Tiny wings at the top, no bigger than Chinese take-out wings, flap furiously, but the creature drifts forward at a snail's pace.

Oh. It's only Fuzzydoom.

Wait. Fuzzydoom? I blink. We're not in the mirrorverse.

"What the heck is he doing here? How'd he get out of the mirror?"

"Umm…" Sophia fidgets. "I may have been a little mad at the mystics for what they did to me at school."

I glance back down the hall. "So, you summoned the pom-pom of annihilation?"

"No!" whines Sophia, stomping. "I didn't mean to do it. I wanted to try making a portal or something so we could go home. But *he* came out." She shivers.

"Send him back."

"I can't. I'm too scared to do magic." She pulls back, trying to get away from me and dart down the stairs.

Fortunately, Sophia is a twig. I don't need vampiric strength to hold her. "You have to send it back. If it touches anyone, it's going to kill them."

She struggles, whining out her nose. The poor kid's phobic of this monster she created despite it looking like it came from Looney Tunes. It's one thing to be ten years old and still terrified of a nightmare monster she invented at age three… but it's something else entirely for said nightmare monster to actually exist. Can't use the 'grow up, it's all in your head' tactic. I'm still not sure if Fuzzydoom *can* actually kill anyone who touches even one hair. Honestly, instant death is a bit dark for a three-year-old to come up with. She probably convinced herself touching it would do something super bad to her. When she grew up a little, and didn't outgrow the fear, the consequences of touching the pom-pom from hell changed to a more tangible 'kill' instead of an undefined, but awful, fate.

You might think it's strange of me to stand here psychoanalyzing my sister when such a dangerous monster is stalking us. But Fuzzydoom legit moves so damn slow I think a granite statue could outrun the stupid thing.

Anyway, better to assume it *is* capable of hurting people. Sophia would totally lose her mind if something she made gave someone a paper cut. If it *killed* a person? I'd have no choice but to be forced to erase the memory. Otherwise, she'd be crushed... and spend the rest of her life in therapy. Seriously, this kid is *too* nice. We get kidnapped and she feels guilty for not helping the people who kidnapped us. Between her age and optimism, I'm sure she has no real comprehension of the danger helping those mystics really puts her in.

"Soph," I say, grabbing her head in both hands and staring into her eyes. "I realize you're legit phobic of the giant fuzzball, but I also know you don't want to hurt anyone, right?"

"Mmm." She nods, tears streaming down her face.

"It's slower than the week before Christmas. It's never going to catch you. Send it back to the mirror world before it hurts someone."

Shivering, Sophia points at it... and squeaks.

I hug her from behind, resting my chin on her shoulder. "Try to sound a little more commanding. Your magic pulled it across. You can send it home. It can't hurt you."

"He," whispers Sophia. "Fuzzydoom is a boy."

"Okay. Send him home before he hurts anyone." I squeeze her. "You got this, kiddo."

"Mew," says Klepto.

Sophia wipes her face. "She thinks I can do it, too."

"Because you can. You're phobic. Can't help being scared of it, but it's nothing to be ashamed of."

"Yeah it is. Fuzzydoom's a silly giant puff ball. What kind of chicken would be afraid of him?" She takes a deep breath.

"A magic puffball with a killing touch. Sometimes it's the weird stuff that's scary. C'mon. Someone's going to walk out and try to pet him."

Sophia widens her stance, raises both arms, and stares at Fuzzydoom. She's still trembling faintly. "Go back."

"Through the portal," I add.

"Go back through the portal." Sophia leans forward, 'pushing' at the air like she did before when the mystics enchanted her closet.

Fuzzydoom stops advancing. His tiny wings beat faster, straining against some invisible force pushing him away. Sophia emits a growl only slightly more menacing than Klepto's. The giant puffball zooms off into a streak of black and zips into our hotel room. A loud *boom* follows, heavy enough to shake the entire building.

She lowers her arms. "Whew. I did it. He's gone. Guess I'm not powerful enough to teleport us yet."

I ruffle her hair. "Seems. So, umm... can we save the giant pom-pom of death for a real emergency?"

"This isn't?" She fidgets, seeming inches from running off in a panic.

"Well... a real emergency where something needs to die. Something Fuzzydoom is capable of catching, like if a ninety-nine-year-old killer using a walker limped after us."

She rolls her eyes. "He's *scary!*"

"I believe you. C'mon, let's stay out of sight. It'll be dark out soon."

"Okay."

We return to the room and shut the door. She sits on the bed, staring guiltily down at the floor, swishing her feet back and forth. Grr. She doesn't feel right about leaving the mystics to fend for themselves. Did Sophia really believe Asher's claim she could do something a whole group of practiced mystics can't?

Whatever. I'd rather have her glum for a bit than hurt or dead.

WARDROBE DYSFUNCTION

Hello, Darkness my old friend.

Red light in my eyes paints a brief glow on the hotel room ceiling as I come online. Sophia's stretched out on the bed, watching another kid's movie about cute trolls.

"Time to get going."

"'Kay," says Sophia.

I grab my phone and call the parents, again on speakerphone. "Hey. I'm finally awake. On the way to the store now."

"What about taking a mirror?" asks Mom.

"Uhh." Sophia shakes her head. "No way. We're super far. We'd definitely get lost or eaten on the way. Crossing ocean areas is like really, really bad."

"How bad?" I ask.

"Like being a level six character going right to the endgame zones in WoW bad." She shivers. "Mr. Anderson said even Blix couldn't use mirrors to cross the ocean."

"Yeah, don't do that," says Dad.

"Oh." I cringe. "Never mind. I don't feel like playing chicken with C'thulu."

"I hear he's got a lousy poker face. Third tentacle from the left twitches every time he bluffs." Dad chuckles.

I grin. "Okay. We're gonna head out. I'll call again from the airport."

"All right, dear," says Mom. "I'll try to worry only a lot instead of having a complete meltdown."

"Situation is under control, Mom." I exhale. "Talk soon."

We hang up.

"Umm…" Sophia stares at me. "I'm barefoot in a nightie. I can't get on a plane like this. Someone's going to call the cops."

"Sorry… Yeah, I meant go to the airport by way of a store. You had to be cold out there."

She hugs herself, shivering. "Freezing. Sorry."

"Why are you apologizing?"

"For not saying anything about being cold before. You looked really angry. I didn't want you to snap at me."

"Aww…" I pull her into a hug. "I'm sorry."

"What for?" wheezes Sophia.

I stop squeezing her so tight. "For the way I used to snap at you sometimes. You know a lot has, uhh, changed with me and it's put everything in a totally different perspective. I promise I'll never snap at you again."

She leans back, smiling at me, half her face hidden under a wall of hair. "I know you didn't really mean it before. Mom says mean stuff sometimes when she's upset at her job. It happens."

"Yeah, but you don't deserve to be snapped at. And I didn't even have a stressful job. Just teenage BS."

"Am I gonna have teenage BS, too?"

"Probably, but you won't suffer the same symptoms. Sierra will be more like I was. You won't snap at anyone. Probably just start crying and make everyone around you feel like an ogre for being mean."

Sophia stares at me, then bursts into tears.

Of course, she's faking it.

"Hah." I squeeze her.

"I don't cry at everything."

"No, you don't. But you're really sensitive and sweet and empathetic. When you get a little older, the world's gonna start hitting you where it hurts. If you ever get so sad you want to crawl under your bed and never come out, please talk to me, kay?"

"Umm… you're making me scared to get older."

"Don't be scared. I'll always be there to help you with anything."

"Promise?"

"Yep."

She holds up a pinky.

I hook mine through hers.

We pinky swear.

"Ready to hit the store?"

"Yeah. And can we get dinner?"

"Sure."

Again, I take hold of Sophia's hand. We leave the hotel room and go down the stairs. Poor kid is already shivering by the time we reach the lobby. Five seconds outside, her teeth start chattering. I try to move fast, following the navigation app on my phone toward Marks & Spencer. Being it's much earlier in the evening than 6:30-or-so a.m. when we arrived, there are a lot more people out and about. Everyone who notices Sophia in a nightie and me going barefoot as well on slush-coated streets stares at us. Wanting as little disruption as possible, I prod everyone I see to forget noticing us the same way I dealt with being stranded out in Woodinville naked my first full night as a vampire.

It's quite a bit easier for me here, though. Not only am I much more comfortable using my abilities, simply being barefoot in the winter isn't embarrassing at all, hence doesn't distract me. The sidewalk is mostly clear, save for some patches of slick ice. Freezing slush doesn't bother me to step on since body heat and me have a strange relationship. I do, however, pick Sophia up so she doesn't have to put her feet in snow. Frostbite bad.

By the time we reach the department store, I'm already feeling the effects of using mental powers constantly. Definitely going to need to stop for a bite on the way to the airport. This store has too many people, and probably cameras.

We go straight to the girls' clothing section, trying to avoid contact with as many people as possible. Anyone who notices Sophia gets a quick prod to see her wearing a normal outfit... and dammit. I should've suggested she use an illusion of proper clothes. Would've saved me a lot of work.

She picks out a dress, black tights, socks, and a new pack of underpants since she's been wearing the current ones for two days in a row. The stuff is a bit overpriced, but we're in a pinch. I also get Sophia a winter coat—she insists on pink—and myself a passable pair of sneakers and white socks. Also, places like this have so much security, if I gave the clerk a compulsion forcing her to give us store credit, she'd get fired or possibly prosecuted.

No big deal... I whip out my authorized user card and legit buy the clothes. While the clerk rings us up, I text Mom an explanation for the charge so she doesn't call the bank and dispute it, or answer 'no' to the 'did you make this purchase?' text she's about to receive. A sudden use in London is certainly going to trigger an alert.

Sophia runs to the dressing rooms to change.

Yeah, I've also been wearing the same clothes for two days, but considering the prices here, I'll deal with feeling a tad funky. Also, supernatural weirdness is going on. Buying new clothes would only jinx me into ending up clawed to shreds.

My sister emerges from the dressing room having changed, carrying her wadded-up nightgown. I stuff it in my purse for now and lead her outside. We still get the occasional funny look, but they're directed at me for not having a winter coat. Neither one of us looks grubby enough to appear as vagrants, probably why no one's come up to talk and check on us. Frustratingly, every time I peek at someone's thoughts, they think I'm like fourteen or fifteen and being an idiot for going outside sans coat. Swear, if I hear 'that smartass kid's gonna get sick and not feel so untouchable' one more time...

"Where are we going?" whispers Sophia.

"The airport. Gonna grab a taxi." I pick a direction at random and walk.

She hurries along beside me. "Can we get food?"

"Yeah… my plan exactly. I'm feeling a bit drained after all the mental poking. Could really use someone to eat."

Sophia giggles.

Wow… my adorable little sister laughing at the idea of me biting someone is beyond creepy.

SOMETHING WE SHOULDN'T BE DOING

Navigating an unfamiliar city while hungry, trying not to freak out, and in a hurry sucks.

Speaking of sucking, my hunt for a taxi takes a backseat to finding a meal. Sophia's hungry, too. But for one thing, she doesn't consume blood; two, most airports have a food court. Easier to get her something once we're there and I no longer need to panic about not knowing which way to go.

Also, trying to get this done as fast as possible is frustrating. Might be simpler to try the old 'pretending to make out in public' thing than go for complete privacy. I'm seconds away from pouncing on some poor slob and dragging him bodily into a secluded place when I notice a man surreptitiously slip into an alley leading a tiny dog on a leash while looking around to make sure no one noticed him.

Aha. I've located a serial dog-poo-not-picker-upper.

Sophia stops to stand watch at the alley entrance. The little dog—which might be a shih tzu cross bred with a Pomeranian—stops sniffing for a spot to let fly and stares at me as I approach. Much like the dog-walker, I'm slipping into an alley to get away with something most people would object to. At least in my case, no one is going to step in the aftereffects and ruin their carpet.

The man jumps, startled by my presence. He offers a polite nod, despite giving off the kind of awkwardness more appropriate for being caught trying to break into a place. Guess the Brits take errant dog poo seriously. He starts to tug the little dog out of the alley, but freezes the instant my mental influence seeps into his brain.

At that, the tiny dog begins to growl at me.

Klepto leaps from Sophia's arms and emits a war screech similar to a balloon with a slow leak. The poor dog takes off, paws skittering on the pavement. Klepto chases it around, keeping the little beast occupied while I make a meal of the guy.

Blood thick with the flavor of fried fish spills into my mouth. Gee, thanks, Dad. He *had* to mention fish and chips and put it in my brain. Suppose I'm technically having British food, so, whatever. I take my fill, which isn't enough to threaten the man's health, extract my fangs, and seal the bite wound. Licking the last bits of blood off someone's neck used to feel as awkward and inappropriately intimate as an unexpected butt-pat from a total stranger. Guess I'm becoming a real vampire since it no longer bothers me.

"Mmm!" Sophia's muffled scream comes from behind me.

I whirl, expecting to chase down and beat the shit out of some creep carrying her off. Instead, I find three punks—two women and a man—glaring at me as if they caught me selling drugs on their turf. The guy holding Sophia appears to be the oldest, somewhere in his later twenties. Leather jacket, short mohawk, jeans. The girl on his right is a little on the butch side, also a bit younger than him. She's rocking the jeans-and-wifebeater look, giving me a 'are you serious' sort of smirk. The other girl's the youngest by appearance, maybe eighteen or nineteen. Blonde, and too pretty for her anarchist half-tee and shredded jeans. Girl looks more like an affluent socialite dressing up as a gang thug for Halloween.

As soon as I really look at them, it's obvious they're vampires. Can't tell bloodline by sight—except for Shadows—but their outfits suggest Lost Ones. None of the three appear to be carrying weapons. Their body language puts me on edge, though. Feels like I've been caught doing something mildly illegal by a trio of questionable security guards who are about to take great delight in exerting their authority over me. I'm expecting abuse of some kind, verbal, physical, or something darker... only the blonde seems a bit too innocent in the face for this encounter to end up being twisted.

Then again, I'm basically the super-sheltered suburban girl. What the heck do I know about gangs, especially gangs in London made up of vampires? A woman who looks like a grown version of Sophia might still be a sadistic freak.

The dude with his hand over Sophia's mouth appears to be exerting zero effort holding her off the ground. Sure, she—like most of the Wright family—is skinny as heck, but she's more substantial than a styrofoam cutout. Granted, he's a vampire, so I'm not surprised he's stronger than he looks. He steps closer, giving me an up and down appraising smirk. "Well, well. What 'ave we 'ere?"

"A guy in a fake leather jacket using a line from a 1960s evil mastermind?" I ask, eyebrow up.

Both women snicker.

"Oi, luv. I'll 'ave ya know this is real leather."

"Sorry, the shininess threw me off. Mind putting her down?"

The blonde walks over. I edge back from her, trying not to let them surround me. She mostly ignores me, approaching the guy I fed from.

"Go on home," she whispers, patting him on the cheek.

The man fast-walks out of the alley, the tiny dog scurrying after him.

Klepto appears in a flash on the male vampire's arm, biting the thumb of the hand covering my sister's mouth.

"Gah, blimey!" blurts the guy. "Little blighter came outta nowhere."

"Best put her down before the kitten gets angry," I deadpan.

"You got some balls on you," says the other woman. "Waltzing into the city unannounced. What's your purpose here? Who are you spying for?"

Sophia stops struggling and dangles limp, her huge blue eyes fixed on me.

"Umm... What?" I fold my arms. "I'm not spying."

"'Ow'd ya even get inta the city wi'out bein' seen?" asks the guy. "Yer obviously not as 'armless as ya look."

I hold my hands up in a 'slow down' gesture. "Back up a bit. I'm not here to cause any trouble. First of all, we didn't ask to be here. We got kidnapped. And what do you mean by unannounced? Does London have call-ahead feeding or something?"

The blonde laughs. "She smells new. Maybe she really didn't know?"

"Wild one? From Wales maybe?" asks the brown-haired woman.

"At's not a Welsh accent, Joanie, this one's a Yank," says the blonde.

Klepto continues to furiously gnaw on the man's thumb.

"No, I'm not from Wales."

"Whatever, lass." The guy shakes his head. "Can't go just traipsin' inta' the city wi'out presentin' yerself first thing ta Mr. Corley. Ya get a one-night grace period, and ya didn't do et."

"Honestly, I have no idea who Mr. Corley even is. I'm not from around here, and we're not going to stay long. We're on our way to the airport right now."

The blonde sidles up to me. "Where ya from, luv?"

"You had it right. The US. Seattle." I look at the dude. "Would you *please* put her down already?"

He does.

Sophia runs over and clings to me.

"She is adorable," says the blonde.

"C'mon, luv." The guy steps closer, but doesn't try to grab me. "You should deal with this now. Runnin' off won't look good. Already in a bit of shite. No sense makin' it worse."

If my mother heard the number of F-bombs going off in my head at the moment, she'd faint. There's a 6000-swear per minute F-bomb rotary machine gun firing full blast in my cerebrum. All I want to do is go the heck home and we're about to get dragged into some political BS. Worse, Aurélie has no influence here at all. I have to assume even mentioning her could bite me in the ass. While she's easily flighty enough to randomly move to the United States on a whim, it's also possible she had reasons more pressing than simple distaste for overbearing rules.

"Seattle, huh?" asks Joan, the sorta-butch woman with short, brown hair.

"Yeah. I'm Sarah. This is Sophia."

"Meredith." The blonde slaps the guy on the back. "He's Kallen."

"Umm, so yeah. We ended up in London unexpectedly against our will. Could you guys maybe just tell this Mr. Corley person we made a wrong turn and are leaving?"

Kallen sighs. "You really ought'a tell 'im yerself. Looks better on ya. If yer on the level, won' take long t'all."

"Corley's fair. Entering his city and ignoring him is a real big insult, but he's not unreasonable." Joan waves at me to follow her. "He is aware things aren't the same in the US. Won't hold it against you for not knowing. But ya know now."

Damn. Ashley thought I'd be miserable in California, alone, cut off from my friends, too far away from family for the safety net of my parents to be present. She might've had a point after all. The lack of Aurélie's presence makes me feel vulnerable like I'm about to read a philosophy essay to a crowded amphitheater while naked. As vampires go, I'm still pretty new, and my bloodline isn't known for vulgar displays of badassery.

Worse, Sophia's hip-deep in this mess next to me.

I really don't have much choice other than to play meek and hope for a little sympathy. Maybe being an Innocent will help me out there. We're awesome at projecting harmlessness. Don't want to overdo it though and come off as fake.

"Okay... but I really don't have any idea where he is, what he looks like, or pretty much anything about London."

"No worries, luv." Kallen grins. "You fly?"

"Probably not, seein' as how she's on 'er way ta Heathrow," says Joan.

"I can fly, yeah... but not across the whole Atlantic Ocean with a passenger. It's almost 4,800 miles—yes, I looked it up before we left the hotel room. As fast as I can fly, it would take like thirty hours.

Sunrise would probably catch me in the air over the ocean, assuming I didn't get lost on the way. Hard to navigate when there's nothing but water to the horizon in every direction."

"Aye, pain in the arse 'tis." Kallen floats a few inches off the ground. "Follow us then."

Sophia whimpers.

"It's okay. Just a formality." I pull her on like a backpack, holding her forearms against my chest.

Meredith and Joan leap into the air. Kallen waits for me, so I launch myself after them.

Nothing about going with them feels reassuring. There's a reason I never went to certain parties during high school. These three all look like older versions of the seniors who'd be hanging out drinking, getting into fights, maybe breaking into places for the laughs. Could be, I'm judging too much by their clothes. They didn't talk like thugs.

Sigh.

Guess I'll find out soon how big a mistake following them is.

A MATTER OF INTERNATIONAL VAMPIRE ETIQUETTE

Meredith takes the lead once we've climbed up to a couple hundred feet.

Klepto's burrowed under my shirt, wedged between Sophia's chest and my back. Ouch, but no big deal. Her claws are tiny. I heal fast. Kallen flies behind and above us, probably on guard for me trying to run away. Meredith starts off pulling way ahead, notices she's losing me, and circles back, flying upside down right under me.

"Why ya goin' so slow?"

"I'm flying as fast as I can."

"Really?" She blinks. "Oy. American vamps must be diluted. Poor thing. Ahh well."

She rolls over so she's facing down at the ground again, then pulls out in front of me before I can reply, matches my speed, and keeps going. According to the GPS app on my phone, my top speed is approximately 140 miles an hour. I can squeeze out a little more in a dive or if I'm emotional enough (extreme fear, anger, or joy—for example, if Dad tells me they're making a second season of *Firefly*).

Our flight doesn't take *too* long, maybe six minutes, before she dives toward a building surrounded by manicured grass. I'm not letting go of Sophia's arms to pull my phone out and check a map. Looks like we're heading for a stuffy old four-story manor house. Ugh. I'd worry about making a bad impression due to my ordinary top, jeans, and sneakers, but my three escorts aren't exactly rocking formal wear.

Meredith lands in a paved circle by a fountain not far from the main entrance. I alight next to her and let Sophia slip down to her feet, but keep a firm grip on her hand. Kallen flies right to the door, opening it and waiting for us. Joan comes in behind me like a security guard. Yeah, this doesn't feel too welcoming.

Nothing's waving any giant red danger flags, so I follow Meredith up the steps and inside. The place feels more like a grand hotel than a private residence. Mortal servants scurry about trying not to make eye contact with us. A few give me pitying looks, their thoughts revealing they think Sophia and I are being brought here as food. They don't recognize me as a vampire and seem surprised at Sophia's presence. Good thing. Suppose it means Corley doesn't make a habit of feeding on children.

Not a bad quality to have in a vampire king.

Meredith leads us upstairs to the second floor, then strolls to the left down a large hallway carpeted in red, paintings of landscapes on both sides, stopping at an ornate pair of double doors at the end.

For some stupid reason, I'm expecting these three to bring me into a room where some big, imposing dude sits on a throne frowning at a court full of socialites. It shouldn't surprise me to *not* see such an obviously melodramatic scene, but it does anyway.

The room ahead of us reminds me of going to the Boeing Christmas party with my parents in years past, only without the festive decorations or lame karaoke turned up so loud it hurts. Somewhere between eighty and a hundred people stand or sit around in small conversation clusters. Their attire ranges from punk—like my escorts—to expensive evening gowns or suits. I'm not getting the same vibe from this as the soirees back home Aurélie brings me to. This feels more like a 'happens every night, attend as often as you wish' situation.

The sight of ninety-ish vampires in the same room gives me pause. I sincerely hope this is the majority of them in the area. Or maybe not. Fairly sure the population of London and its surroundings is a little higher than Seattle.

My new 'friends' bring me to the inner left corner of the room, where a group of well-dressed people have gathered around a pale, silver-haired man in a dark suit. His face doesn't look quite old enough for grey hair, but I'd guess him a little older than Dad, who's forty-six. The man radiates a quiet, imposing presence more like a no-nonsense CEO than a literal king. It's pretty clear he's Mr. Corley given the way everyone close to him is throwing off serious bootlicker body language. One of the women keeps calling him 'Peter,' which he doesn't appear to mind, but every time she says it, all the others cringe.

Meredith, Kallen, and Joan stand close to me, making no move to approach closer. We've stopped at an uncomfortable distance for conversation, far enough to encourage raising my voice were I to speak. The hint is obvious... stay quiet and wait to be noticed. See, being around Aurélie *has* taught me something.

Corley and those around him appear to be discussing something political about the Middle East and its effect on the stock market here. I neither understand stock markets, nor care to... and the din of other conversations provides enough interference for me to deliberately avoid eavesdropping. It's unclear if I'm being tested or simply ignored for some predetermined time all who wish to speak with Corley are forced to wait through. Either way, no point in causing a scene. I'm a foreigner here in a land basically without a consulate. Whatever happens to me—and Sophia—tonight is going to be based entirely on me, not on vampires maneuvering around Aurélie's influence or pissed off at Dalton.

Yeah. No pressure, right?

A mild eruption of laughter comes from those around Corley. Seems he cracked a joke. Hopefully not at my expense, though even if it is, I'm in no position to protest. A few minutes later, he looks at us. The man has to have some manner of radiant power like Aurélie, only it's not making me think of him as the most handsome thing on the planet... more like he's the principal and I've been caught with a locker full of weed. Hey, I haven't been out of high school for a full year yet. So what if I keep comparing stuff to school? It's my only real frame of reference. Geez. Okay, looking at him makes me feel like a level one character being brought before the archmage? There? Happy? Nothing to do with school.

Anyway, as he moves closer, I realize he's larger than I thought. Under the expensive suit is a body of a retired soldier who still hits the gym four times a week. He's no musclebound monster, but the man's definitely not a pencil-pusher.

Meredith, Kallen, and Joan all bow their heads in a brief show of respect.

I do the same.

Sophia edges behind me.

"Mew," says Klepto, thoroughly unimpressed.

The initial 'oh, there's the miscreant' expression he gives me eases off to neutral in a few seconds, then a sort of confused interest. He walks right up to me, which catches me off guard. Everything I'm reading about this place and this man so far makes it seem like he really would prefer to be on a throne up above the common vampires.

"You must be the new arrival," says Corley. "Younger than I thought. Tell me, why have you chosen to disregard our customs?"

"No disrespect intended, Mr. Corley," I say. "I'm unfamiliar with the traditions here because I'm from America. We didn't even intend to be here. Mystics ambushed us. One moment, we're at home. The next, we're in London with only a little time before sunrise. Someone I know back home did mention Europe has some differences, but being dragged across the world kinda freaked me out. Didn't think about it as much as trying to get to the airport so we could go home."

He narrows his eyes for a second or two before widening them back to normal. "Interesting. Brought here against your will and not intending to remain."

"Yes, sir. If I really understood how important it was to present myself to you, I would have."

"I see." Mr. Corley folds his arms, tapping his fingers on his elbow. "Has America descended to such depravity? Tell me, child. How old were you at the time of your Transference?"

"Eighteen."

"I find that difficult to believe, yet you do not seem to be trying to deceive me."

"I'm an Innocent. The Transference shaved a couple years off my face. Everyone mistakes me for a kid."

"Innocent, you say..." He raises both eyebrows. "And yet you do not seem... mentally affected."

Say what? I pause, looking at him for a few seconds before catching myself acting too informal. "Umm. Thanks?"

"Tell ya later," whispers Meredith.

Mr. Corley gestures at me. "I understand the reasons you did not keep the tradition, and they are understandable. The lax education in proper tradition is America's fault, not yours. Nor, did you intentionally enter my city."

Whew.

"However..."

Crap.

"While I do not consider your failure to appear an affront or insult, tradition must be maintained. As such, you will need to perform a minor service as a gesture of respect."

Oh, please be a simple fetch quest.

Mr. Corley pauses, tapping a finger to his chin.

Uh oh. He's old enough to hear my thoughts. Umm... sorry. A fetch quest is a video game thing. Means an easy 'go here and do something' job.

He chuckles. "Ahh, yes. I believe the task I had in mind for you meets the definition. There is another in the city who defies tradition wantonly. He is an annoyance who's been pestering us for some time. I charge you to eliminate the threat of the werewolf known as Ronald Haddon."

Sophia gasps.

Corley's entourage all seem to notice my sister at the same time.

About a third of them react as if they'd spotted a stray kitten on the street. A handful look at her like a fancy, expensive chocolate treat.

I gawk. "W-werewolf?"

"Yes. Is that a problem?" asks Mr. Corley.

Refusing his task feels about as smart as making fun of a Mafia don's ugly daughter, right in front of him. Sending me to kill a werewolf—holy crap, they're real, too?—sounds an awful lot like a fancy way of sentencing me to destruction for breaking rules. The guy's impossible to read... and he's probably listening in on my every thought.

"I, well... haven't been a vampire long, and never even saw a werewolf before. Wouldn't he tear me to pieces? Besides, I don't like to randomly kill people."

"Says the girl with a little kid thrall," mutters Meredith.

"Oh..." I glance at her. "Sophia's not my thrall. She's my actual sister."

Corley's expression could be 'are you bloody serious' as easily as 'hmm, interesting.'

"What?" Joan grasps Sophia's left wrist and lifts her arm up to her face.

Sophia's eyes widen into veritable platters, but she doesn't move or make a sound.

I tense. Don't care. If she bites my kid sister, I'm going to do something severely stupid.

The woman merely sniffs her hand. "This child is mortal."

"Yeah. Like I said, she's my actual sister. I've only been a vampire for six months."

"Aww, she hasn't peeled off the little sticky things yet." Meredith lets go of Sophia's wrist.

My sister's attempt to emit a 'whew' of relief too quiet to hear fails. Several vampires near us chuckle.

"What are you babbling about?" Kallen squints at her.

Meredith waves randomly. "You know how when ya get some new electronic bits, they always have them plastic films on? The ones ya try ta leave there to stop scratches, but always cave in and peel off after an hour?"

"Kinell, ya start makin' sense someday, girl." He chuckles.

"I'm sayin' she's new, ya oaf." Meredith slugs him in the shoulder.

"For what reason is your mortal sibling with you, much less aware of the existence of vampires?" asks Mr. Corley.

Uh oh. Cheesy, innocent smile time. "Do you want the long version or the short version?"

"The version which offers me enough information."

"Right..." I take an unnecessary breath in search of calm. "My ex-boyfriend stabbed me to death when I tried to break up with him, but a vampire named Dalton had been stalking me for a blood meal. He thought I was younger than I am, and didn't want to watch a kid die, so he gave me the Transference to save me. The police showed up before he finished killing my ex, so they got me to the morgue. I woke up alone, freaked out, and couldn't stand the guilt at what my death would do to my family, so I went home."

Most of the vampires in earshot laugh like they watched a two-year-old pick up a blob of mud and try to eat it. Finding me cute, moronic, and nauseating all at once. Yeah... a vampire going home to their mortal family, to them, is probably about as stupid as a toddler eating mud.

"It works. My family is on board with the whole 'don't talk about it' thing."

Mr. Corley tilts his head. "I am curious as to why these mystics would go to the trouble of bringing you here."

"It's not me they wanted. Soph broke a soul jar and let a bad ghost loose. They want her to destroy it." I grimace. "Magic doesn't make any sense to me. Somehow, because she broke it, they say she's got extra power over the spirit."

Murmurs drift among the vampires close enough to hear us.

"Mr. Corley," I say, in as respectful a tone as possible, "I'm sorry I entered your territory without announcing myself. I didn't know it was required. My sister and I were kidnapped through a magical portal. Kallen, Meredith, and Joan found me while we were on the way to the airport."

He raises a hand to stall the rest of my sad attempt to weasel out of his task.

"I understand you are new, unaccustomed to our ways, and here against your will. These are reasons I am not angry with you. But, our rules are not to be cast aside. A token gesture of atonement is needed. For this, I have decided you will deal with the werewolf Ronald Haddon. Ensure he no longer presents as a nuisance. This werewolf kills wantonly, including children."

Sophia squeezes me.

I cringe. Yeah, sure. Hit me where it hurts. "Can I ask a stupid question?"

He nods once.

"If he's such a danger or pest for so long, why haven't any of the older vampires around here dealt with him?"

"A valid question." Mr. Corley smiles. "Delicate politics. We have treaties in place with his kind. Killing him would create a disturbance in the balance more severe than his presence. You are not one of us, which affords us the necessary leeway to preserve our arrangements."

Hmm. I could always forget the werewolf and run home. Not like I ever plan on returning to London. But... agreeing to this task and skating is sure to tick Mr. Corley off *way* more than a minor faux pas of etiquette. I seriously had no idea about the show up and say hello rule. Running off would be a deliberate middle finger to the guy. Besides, they know Sophia's mortal. Easy for them to threaten her to get me to do whatever they want, and they haven't gone there. I'm much better off making allies—or at least keeping them neutral—than creating enemies. The last thing I need is another LA vampire situation. My life is complicated enough without a steady stream of London undead showing up in Cottage Lake trying to rip my head off.

How dangerous can a werewolf be?

"You will deal with this threat, then?" asks Mr. Corley.

Nice of him to wait for me to stop arguing with myself.

"Yes, sir. I'll do it."

13

WERE IN THE WORLD

Problem, thy name is little sister.

No, Sophia isn't a problem in and of herself. But I am now in a completely untenable situation. Do I bring her with me to kill a werewolf? Do I leave her here with a hundred vampires—some of whom are looking at her like a Godiva treat? The mystics wouldn't hurt her, but leaving her alone with them would certainly result in her agreeing to help them, and getting herself hurt or killed in the process. Can't leave her randomly on the street somewhere. Pretty sure no one operates boarding kennels for little siblings.

Dammit.

"So," whispers Meredith after Corley goes back to his entourage. "If you're wondering why he made the comment about mental damage... there's an Innocent here who's not right in the head."

I raise both eyebrows. "One Innocent being not right in the head makes him think we're all the same?"

"Aye, seems." Meredith shrugs. "There's only *one* of them in all o' London."

"Technically two now." Joan indicates me.

Sophia squeezes my arm. "What's gonna happen?"

"Still working things out. A werewolf can't be worse than a giant troll, can it?"

"Come again, luv?" asks Kallen. "Did you say troll?"

"Yeah. Long story. My life is weird."

Joan and Kallen go wide-eyed, staring past me.

Though their expressions say it, I'm pretty sure Freddy Krueger isn't sneaking up on me. I turn, surprised to see Mr. Corley approaching us again.

"Your sister is welcome to remain here while you attend to your task."

I glance at the woman who seemed most interested in making a snack of her. Yeah, umm… not sure about her staying here.

"Miss Wright…" Corley rests a hand on my shoulder. "Because you are so new among our kind and also not used to our customs, I shall not be angry with you for the implication your sister would be at risk after I've extended an offer of protection. She will be safe here. You have my word."

Aww, crap. I upset him. Despite his calm expression, I can't help but feel scared like nine-year-old me gave my third-grade teacher the finger in the middle of class. No way in hell would I have ever done such a thing, for fear of being looked at the way he's looking at me now. And the detention part. And the call to the parents. Slow down, Sarah. Just because this guy could order my destruction if he felt like it is no reason to be terrified. He seems like a reasonable guy. Friendly even.

"Oh. I, umm. Sorry. I didn't understand you meant it as an official offer of protection. I'm not used to speaking with… heads of state?"

He chuckles at the floor, then looks at me. "I find such a comparison more preferable to being thought of as a Mafia boss."

Oops.

Mr. Corley nods politely at my sister. "Sophia will be perfectly safe here until you return."

She stares up at me with a heartbreakingly pleading expression.

I hug her. "You'll be safe here."

"I'm not worrying about me. I don't want you to get eaten by a werewolf."

Kallen pats me on the back. "I reckon' she'll be fine, luv."

"Where is this guy, anyway? I don't know my way around here."

"Aye. We got it sorted. Meredith and I will be goin' wif yas." Kallen grins.

I don't want to let go of Sophia, but the sooner I do, the sooner we get to go home. Reluctantly, I stand and follow the two local vamps to the door. Sophia remains still, staring at me the whole time until I'm out the door. Leaving her here rubs me entirely the wrong way, but what choice do I have? It's possible Corley meant to hold onto her as a bit of silent encouragement to keep me on task, like the way the Mafia says 'nice house, shame if something happened to it.' I suppose it's also possible Corley is exactly as he seems on the surface and genuinely intending to keep her safe. Making serious decisions when knowing so little about everyone involved is nerve-wracking.

Once outside, we take flight. As casual as anything, Meredith starts up a conversation about Innocent vampires, wondering if my bloodline is responsible for my 'relatively slow' flight speed. To me, being able to clock 140 without a vehicle is pretty damn impressive. These two aren't too much faster than me. She never thought to use her phone and a GPS app to determine her actual speed. The temptation is too much for her to resist, and she ends up zipping around in a series of random aerial sprints before rejoining us.

"175!" She cheers.

Great. Get down with your bad self.

Okay, I'm in a mood. Understandable considering Sophia's situation. I'm sure all the vampires in there are deathly afraid of going against Mr. Corley, but all it would take is one idiot. Even if whatever vampire who hurt her died viciously for it, nothing would bring her back.

Worry bumps me up to maybe 160.

At least, it feels like it.

Kallen and Meredith lead me to a residential area close to the outskirts of the city in the north. We glide in to land on a quiet street lined with oldish looking lamps, dense trees, and quaint English homes.

"Wow," I mutter. "Which house are we picking the baby-who-lived up from?"

Meredith and Kallen chuckle.

He points at one, three down from the little courtyard we landed in. "There."

My stomach does a backflip so hard my voice trembles. "So, umm, how bad are weres? I've never seen one before."

"Hard ta say." Kallen puts an arm around my shoulders. "Wee ones aren't too bad. They kin range from irritating little blighters to ones what could tear Mr. Corley in half."

Gulp. "Is he like the biggest badass in London?"

"Inside the city, aye." Meredith nods. "Rumor 'as it there's a few real old blokes livin' way out in the boondocks."

"Be straight with me… did Corley send me here to get killed?"

"Nah." Kallen shakes his head. "He's not a roundabout sorta bloke. If he wanted ya ta die, he'd 'ave been up front wi' it."

"Really? Who would go somewhere knowing they'd die?" I blink.

Kallen's permanent smile flattens. "Picture it as a, go 'ere and get kilt, or die right 'ere, *after* we kill the wee one in front of ya, and hunt down everyone ya know."

"Oh." I gulp again. Wow, I want to go home *so* bad. This place is crazy. "Yeah, I can see why someone would do it then. I'm not going to start some kinda war if I kill this guy, right?"

"Well, maybe still," says Kallen. "See, we got a thousand-year-old armistice with the furry bastards. Basically, they stay outta the city, we stay outta the countryside. This were, the Haddon bloke, 'e's fairly new. Just like ya are."

"Oh. Okay. So Mr. Corley's sent a baby to get rid of an annoying baby."

Meredith laughs. "Something like that."

"Aye, but this baby's got teeth. See, the fing about weres is"—Kallen makes a pouncing gesture—"if ya get 'em when they look normal, they go down pretty easy like. Even a new one can be a right ballache if ya catch 'em full cheesed off."

"So, make it quick," I say.

"Aye." He swats me on the back again. "And painless."

"Make sure to rip the heart out." Meredith pokes me in the chest. "If ya don't, he'll get back up."

"Do I need silver?"

"Nah. Folklore nonsense." Kallen waves dismissively. "Claws or fangs work perfectly fine if you get the heart."

"Oh, wait. The girl's an Innocent. Ye 'ave claws, dear?" asks Meredith.

"Yeah. It's weird to say this, but I'm better using a sword."

"Odd for an American." Kallen grins.

"Kinda odd for anyone these days." Meredith stuffs her hands in her back pockets.

I smile at her. "I have an interesting sire. Hey, can I ask you a weird question?"

"Go for it, hon."

"You're an Old Guard, right?"

"Aye."

"Isn't that anarchy shirt a bit strange then? Like you guys are all about tradition."

"It's called irony, luv." She winks.

"Oh, right. Don't mind me. I'm stalling." I swallow. "This guy eats kids. I can do this. Hey, how is it a werewolf is running around eating children and it's not all over the news like a serial killer story?"

Kallen's lip twitches. "'E 'eads into Whitechapel, nibbles on the poor ones no one'll miss."

I narrow my eyes. This is starting to sound a bit strange.

"You guys gonna help or just watch to make sure I do it?"

"Can't get involved," says Meredith. "Treaty and all. But... we'll swoop in and grab ya if ya start losin'."

Small favors. "Right. Here I go."

Fists clenched, I approach the home of one Ronald Haddon, werewolf.

Well, this is new. First time in London. First time kicking in a door to do an assassination. Dalton said 'spend enough time in London and you'll want to kill someone.'

I figured he meant a little more than two days.

14

A HAIRY TECHNICALITY

I'm *so* not the kick down doors type.

Kallen said werewolves are easy prey when in human form, so going all Sarah Smash is a bad idea. I can't believe my brain is plotting the most effective way to ambush-kill a person, but my odds of getting out of here alive go up quite a bit if I can stay sneaky. Seriously though, if this guy does eat street kids, he doesn't count as a person.

I leap the small fence around the property, sneak around to the back, and glide up to a second story window. The house isn't big, maybe half the size of mine. This area has a lot of houses, all pretty much the same design in slightly varying sizes. Serious Monopoly house vibe going on. The third window I check is open a little. Enough for me to get my fingers under it and lift, then glide in horizontally to the messiest bedroom in the world.

A strong human scent saturates the air.

Seriously, the scale of the mess makes me think a fourteen-year-old boy lives here alone. The bed smells like it hasn't had its linens changed in months. Plastic bottles, empty chip bags, and clothes litter the floor. Band posters and topless women adorn the walls. Okay this isn't a kid's room. Or the parents are super permissive. Mom and Dad would drop dead on the spot if teenage Sam ever tried to put bare boobs up on his walls. Funny, Mom never complained about my shirtless Hugh Jackman Wolverine poster.

Sniff.

Yeah, definitely a man. Though, some of the guys I went to school with had some ripe days. I didn't have super keen senses then either. Suppose a teen boy *could* smell like a man if he had some hygiene laziness. Regardless of who is responsible for the disaster in this room, no one is here.

I slip out into the hallway and encounter a complication: multiple scents. It's difficult for me to say for sure, but at a guess, there are at least four different people living here. Damn. I broke the first rule of Assassin Club. No, not talking about it. I went into a target's residence without knowing *anything* about him other than his name. No idea what he looks like, who else might be here, and so on.

Hi. I'm Sarah, and I'm new at being a contract killer.

Grr. How did I go from the nice, normal kid no one at school really noticed to a creature of the night ready to kill a total stranger at the command of a vampire king? Yanno, if I'm really lying on the floor at Bethany Cooke's house after someone spiked my drink with LSD, haven't tried to dump Scott yet, and this entire vampire thing has been an acid dream... I'm seriously going to wound someone.

Sigh.

Nah. Bizarre drug-induced hallucinatory dreams never last this long. And other than the paranormal stuff, far too much *normal* has happened during the past six months for it to be a funky trip.

I freeze still and listen.

Faint conversation comes from down the hallway, multiple people and too quiet to be real. Gotta be someone watching television with headphones. To my left, tiny creaks and clicks sound exactly like Sophia punishing a PlayStation controller. Someone's playing a video game, also likely using headphones. I can hear the buttons, as well as the warbles of a stomach working on junk food. No other sounds of life exist in the house.

So there are two people in the place, not counting me. Since I don't have a clue what Ron Haddon looks like, I'm going to need to rely on my vampiric powers. One of two situations will occur. If I *can* read a werewolf's mind, I'll be able to figure out his name. If I bump into someone in the house whose mind is shielded, good bet he's the werewolf.

But dammit. It's going to take more than 'good bet' for me to kill a guy.

Might as well check the upstairs bedroom first.

I sneak up to the last door on the right. The scent of blood is obvious at the end of the hall. I crouch and sniff at the bottom of the door. Yep. It's coming from this room. But... it doesn't smell right. Stale. Weak, or something.

Maybe he eats sick kids. Even worse.

It takes me a few seconds forcing myself to think about innocent street kids being hunted by a furry monster to work up the nerve to grab the doorknob.

"'Mon in, luv," says a man.

Crap. How the heck? Whatever.

I open the door.

The bedroom is much neater than the first one, but still messy. A cheap particleboard computer desk stands against the wall to my right, the man seated at it looking up at me from his chair. He's shirtless, reasonably buff, wearing blue running shorts with little white stripes down the sides. Cute, but a bit old for me, mid-twenties. Short brown hair, thick eyebrows... he totally looks like how I'd imagine half the football players from my old school would turn out five or six years after graduation.

Also, the instant I make eye contact, it's obvious he's something more than human. He's not a vampire, but still radiates a strong supernatural presence. The hairs on the back of my neck would probably be standing up if he had any amount of hostility in his demeanor.

"Didn't mean to make so much noise."

"You looking for Troy?"

"No, Ron."

He tilts his head, confused. "Those bastards. Ya look a bit young ta be doin' that sorta thing."

I frown. "I'm not a hooker sent by your buddies."

"Not where I was going. Different bastards." He smiles. "Question is, did they send you here to kill me or to get rid of you?"

"Oh. Been wondering the same thing myself." I bite my lip. "Guess I'm not as quiet as I think."

"You didn't make too much noise. Smelled a girl outside."

I blush. Okay, so I've gone a day or two in the same clothes without showering. Still doesn't make it nice to hear. "What's that supposed to mean?"

"It means I smelled a girl out in the hall." He shrugs. "Guys smell different from girls. I'm not tryin' to say you stink."

I glance around the walls, plain. He didn't take any time to decorate. "Good grief. Vampire vs. werewolf. Talk about overdone."

Ron chuckles. "You're kinda young. Do we really have to do this? My roommates will be pissed if we get blood everywhere."

"Already is blood everywhere. I can smell it. Why kids?"

"Sometimes I grab one when I can't find a sheep or pig, but kids don't have much meat. Need a handful. Too much work."

"I mean children, not baby goats."

Ron starts to chuckle, but stops and stares at me a moment. "Wait, you're serious?"

Time to cheat. Or at least try. Attempting to read his thoughts takes effort, like I'm pushing my head into dense gelatin. Sights, memories, and emotions appear as indistinct flickers. Glimpses behind a pane of smudged glass or sounds from far off in a tunnel. Emotion is much easier to pick up, and he's horrified.

"They told me you ate poor street kids in Whitechapel."

Ron shakes his head. "Lass, I think you've been punked."

"So you don't kill children?"

"No way... at least, not intentionally."

Huh? "Not intentionally? How does one accidentally eat children?"

"My condition causes blackouts sometimes. I lose time."

"Full moon?"

"Nah. Thought the same at first, too. Moon's got an effect on me, but the blackouts aren't from it. If I go too long without having raw meat, the monster takes over. Ever since I figured out how it works, haven't had a blackout. Keep ta sheep an' goats mostly. One a week's enough. The blood you're smelling in here must be on me shoes, or the laundry in the bag there—but it's sheep's blood."

"You eat an entire sheep or goat at once?"

"Aye."

"How…"

He leans back, lacing his fingers behind his head, grinning. "Just talented I reckon."

"Right…" I sigh.

Ron lowers his arms, smile fading. "Look, luv. I didn't ask for this condition. Been a bit of a shock ta the system, yanno? How's a bloke supposed to deal with finding out he's a werewolf, then learnin' all the other shite what's supposed to be all mythical's all real, too?"

"I know what you mean. Same thing happened to me."

"For real?"

"Yeah."

"Figured all you lot hung out at goth clubs pretending to be vampires until you found real ones and begged 'em to do it to ya."

"Hah." I laugh. "Yeah, maybe some do."

"Try most. Your lot's in it for the power and immortality. We're all a bunch of unlucky bastards. Attacked, left for dead, but not finished off. Wake up back in one piece, then the craziness starts."

I step into the room, relaxing a bit. Ron seems to sense me lowering my guard and does the same. "Funny you should say that. I woke up in a morgue cooler with no idea what happened to me. Didn't have even the slightest clue vampires existed even though I'd become one."

"Wow. Some random bastard do it to ya for kicks? How'd ya not see it coming?"

"My ex-boyfriend stabbed me to death when I tried to break up with him. The guy who turned me was there by chance, saw it happen, tried to save me."

"Oh, aye. Rough time, lass. Fer me, I's goin' in for the early shift at Tesco. Big hairy bastard came outta nowhere. Not a bloody clue what he wanted. Grabbed me in his jaws and tossed me aside. Could'a been get outta my way or I figure he's runnin' around tryin' ta make more weres ta piss off the vamps. Like gettin' hit by a truck I didn't see coming."

"Sorry." I look around again at the room. Makes sense now why he didn't bother decorating. He's not expecting to be here long. "Guess it's hard for you to have roommates without them noticing something's strange after a while?"

"Aye."

"Okay, so you don't eat children."

He shakes his head.

"Why would the vampires want you destroyed?"

"Feck if I know. Probably your gang initiation. Kinda how the bangers in the East End have'ta kill someone ta get into the gang proper like." Ron snaps his fingers. "Oh, an' the bastard what bit me killed one of them. Could be a revenge bit, but you should know, killing me won't make him lose a moment of sleep."

I pace. "I don't want to kill you… but I can't just leave. They have my little sister."

"If you ain't got no real loyalty to them, I kin help ya get her back."

"What?" I stare at him. "If you go there, they'll totally kill you."

"Aye, likely. My life is pretty shite as is. Gettin' offed wouldn't bother me. I can't let a li'l one get hurt over me."

"No, it's not quite like you're thinking. They're not holding her prisoner, threatening her to get me to kill you. They're, umm… protecting her."

Ron stands, reaching for a shirt. "Aye, they don't usually make threats with words."

"Why did you break the treaty and come to the city?"

"Didn't. Always been here. The werewolf part is new. Bastard what bit me's the one who broke the treaty whatsit."

"So… you haven't technically broken any treaty or rules."

"Other than staying in the city after the bite, aye."

"You could go to the countryside. Corley didn't technically order me to destroy you. He said something like 'deal with the nuisance.' If you left the city, it'll probably count. If not, I can play dumb American newbie vampire."

He pulls a clingy white tank top on, then grabs a flannel. "Not so easy ta pick up and leave. Need a job at least. Place ta stay. I'm just a dim sod with unusually strong arms—stronger now. Plenty of those around for the physical jobs."

"Is this your house? Could you sell it?"

"Nah. Renting. Roommates."

"Oh, duh. Hmm."

Ron—who's a bit taller than I expected—steps close and crouches to stare into my eyes. "Are you too much of a newbie to do the thing where you can make people follow commands?"

"I can do it. Mental influence is one of the first abilities we figure out. Vampires who can't make their food forget them or who have to kill people don't last long. It's probably an evolutionary survival thing necessary for the continuation of the species, like how people just know to avoid frozen dinners from Walmart or gas station sushi."

"Brilliant." He flops back in his chair and starts clicking his computer mouse. "Maybe you can deal with the nuisance after all."

"What do you mean?"

"Well, you've been ordered to get rid of me. I could bugger off outta London for the countryside where I grew up if you mind-wank Mr. Nesbitt." He sits at the computer, minimizes the game, and pulls up a web browser. After a brief search, he gestures at a picture of a rural factory. "He owns the Crowthorne textile mill. I don't mind physical work now, seein' as how I'm so strong these days."

Gee. I have no idea what it's like 'encouraging' a boss to hire someone. So far, I've poked my mother's boss in the head, got Hunter's mom a job, and even saved Michelle's internship. Though, honestly, the Michelle situation was totally necessary. Undoing paranormal weirdness is ethically pristine. Mildly exploiting a wealthy dude to hire on another laborer at his mill is far less morally dark than murder. Since Mr. Corley basically ordered me to get rid of

Ron, I'm kinda obligated to do this. My actions will result in Ron no longer being in London. I'll be satisfying the desired result of the request if not the intent.

Mr. Corley didn't specifically command me to tear the werewolf apart and bring his still-beating heart back as a tribute.

"Sure. No problem. Want to lug crap around or be plant foreman?"

Ron laughs. "I wouldn't know what I'm doing as foreman. Laborer is fine. Better if you get him to hire me on at a decent enough rate."

"Easy. One small problem."

"What?"

I hook my thumbs in my jean pockets. "I have to visit the guy at night. My powers don't work in the daytime."

Ron gives me this look like I tried to offer a vegan a triple cheeseburger with extra murder. "Uhh, yeah. You're a vampire right? Isn't that kinda obvious. Got it sorted. Have Nesbitt's home address."

"Oh joy. More breaking and entering tonight. Let's go." I fake smile.

15

CROWTHORNE

Ron asks me to give him a minute to 'hit the bog' whatever the hell that means.

He runs to the bathroom. Ooo-kay. Not sure what bathrooms and bogs have to do with each other, but it's not worth wasting brain power on. A short while later, he returns to the bedroom and throws some clothes in a bag before breaking down his computer setup and packing it all in a cardboard box.

"I'll come back in the day for the big stuff. Your pals won't notice as long as I'm gone before sundown."

I shrug. "Sounds reasonable. Didn't expect you to move out *tonight.*"

He gathers his 'important' stuff and goes outside. I follow him to a tiny green car. It's so small it would be more accurate to say Ron 'wears' it rather than gets into it after putting his things in the back seat. Seriously, its tires are the size of Frisbees. Thicker, but about the same diameter. We bump into each other both going for the passenger side door.

He looks down at me. "You want to drive?"

"Umm. No. I have no idea where you're going."

"Other side, luv."

I stare at the car. The steering wheel is on the wrong side. "Oops. Is it obvious I'm American?"

"Aye. A touch."

"Heh."

While walking around the front to the other door, I scan the area for Kallen and Meredith. If they're still here watching me, they're hiding. Not seeing them makes me nervous. Did they see me talking to this guy instead of going all psycho-death-kitty on him? If they're on their way back to tell Mr. Corley I 'plan-B-ed' the werewolf, what is he going to do to Sophia?

Okay, bad thoughts. The guy gave me his word as undead king-emperor whatever she wouldn't be harmed. He might give off Mafia boss vibes to me, but it's the suit. And I'm not used to royalty. Actual kings and queens have a lot in common with organized crime bosses. Go back far enough in time and royalty arbitrarily ordered people killed for stupid, trivial things they considered insulting.

Ron's car is legit like a motorcycle with a cabin and seats. I've seen lawn mowers with bigger engines. Dad once told me a joke about a car company, Yugo. Something like the cars had so little power, turning on the radio made them drive slower. Pretty sure if I turned the radio on in this car, we'd lose ten miles per hour. I keep looking out the window waiting to see a four-year-old in a pedal car zoom by.

Yeah, I'm accustomed to flying at 140, so being in a car at all is going to feel slow.

Roads are for lesser mortals.

Not sure how safe I feel in a car small enough for me to lift and carry around, but other than ending up trapped in burning wreckage, a crash isn't going to cause permanent harm. Riding in the passenger seat affords me the opportunity to pull out my phone and trade texts with Ashley, Michelle, and Hunter. And yeah, I really ought to tell the parents there's been a complication of the unavoidable kind.

I'm still not fully confident big brother doesn't read every text message everyone sends. It would require a ridiculous amount of staffing, but they probably have AIs set up to filter out the boring crap. So... I don't use obvious terms in text messages. Pretty sure the

Persons In Black appreciate me making their jobs easier. Vampires don't want to go public, and the small branch of our government responsible for the 'weird stuff' doesn't want them to go public. Win-win, right?

Predictably, the parents are upset and worried at the delay. They pick up on the 'local V-ip' reference right away. Telling them I had to make nice with the 'in-laws' for using the wrong fork with my salad is hopefully enough of a clue I accidentally committed a breach of etiquette. I can fill in the details later.

I've established a code with my friends and Hunter. 'WSA' for 'weird shit alert' tells them something vampire or paranormal related happened and I can't talk about it by text. They're understandably freaking out. Ashley went to the house and learned the truth from my parents. She knows Sophia and I got dimensionally yoinked to London. Since Ashley knows, Michelle knows. Hunter got the scoop via Ronan.

Everyone back home is in a state of controlled worry. Exactly like me. I'm hopeful the lack of Coralie showing up to warn me means Sophia is going to be okay. Then again, are ghosts capable of traveling close to 5,000 miles? We could be so far away she *can't* warn me.

Ugh. Bad thoughts.

I need to focus on the task in front of me.

Ron tells me about growing up in Crowthorne and how he moved to London after his parents decided to sell their home, buy a houseboat, and 'go live the good life.' Last he heard from them was three months ago when they docked at Malta. Before that, Jamaica. He's got some friends and a grandfather out here, which is the reason he chose this town.

"Yer sure yer kid sis is all right?" asks Ron. "She's mortal, aye?"

"Sure is a strong word. Mostly sure?" I manage a weak smile. "Yeah, she's mortal. I don't think they're going to hurt her. Mr. Corley seemed angry when I worried about it."

He whistles. "Oy, right surprise, that. Never figured a vampire'd be dodgy about 'armin' wee ones."

"Not so sure he objects to the idea of hurting kids as much as me questioning his offer of protection. But he did make it a point to say you ate children. Wonder why?"

"Probably wanted ya ta throw a wobbly. Get all sorts a cheesed off and come at me right away. Er, maybe it's the folklore. All werewolves devour babies, ya know."

"Not really. Never heard much about werewolves at all except for movies, and they've got to be far from accurate." I gaze to my left out the window. Feels so bizarre to be a passenger in the 'driver's seat.' We're also driving in the wrong lane, but everyone else is, too, so no one's getting into any accidents.

We end up talking about more normal things for the remainder of the hour-long ride.

He appears to know his way around the winding rural roads, not bothering to look at his phone for directions. The countryside is beautiful, making me grateful for the ability to see in total darkness, but it's difficult to enjoy anything while worrying about my sister, or being stuck so far away from home.

Come to think of it, it's extremely weird how the mystics who abducted us simply let us leave.

I mean, why go to all the trouble of magically kidnapping Sophia in the first place? Honestly, keeping us locked up wouldn't have endeared us to their cause. Asher could be underestimating me. Perhaps he thinks I'll storm off in a huff, get all scared and confused being in a foreign country, and reluctantly go back to him.

Hah. So much for his theory.

A few minutes after we make a right turn onto a road called A322, we go past a giant textile mill surrounded by farmland. Only someone with vampire eyes could see the mill clearly at night from the road, but it totally looks like medieval peasants built it stone-by-stone in the 1200s, except for the electric lights. The *Skyrim*-playing geek inside me squeals in delight despite everything else weighing on my mind. It's a brief mental squeal. Not enough to feel guilty about while Sophia's possibly in danger and we're stranded in England.

I'm allowed small squeals, right?

Seriously, how often does one see a giant freakin' building ripped straight out of the pages of a fantasy book? Okay, it's quite a bit more boring and mundane than a Nord stronghold. This place doesn't have archers prowling the walls, but still. Pretty cool.

About a half-mile from the mill, Ron pulls over and points at a gated driveway up ahead. "Mr. Nesbitt lives here. Probably best if me an' my car aren't seen."

"Yeah. Probably. So, how should I do this? Do you have a phone number or something to stick in his head?"

Ron thinks for a moment. "Best I remember, he's usually at the mill during the week. I'll go there tomorrow. Can you make him react to my name or some such thing and agree to hire me on?"

"No problem. Be back in a few minutes."

"Thanks."

I hop out, shut the flimsy little door, and glide into the air among the trees. For no particular reason, I start humming Ozzy Osbourne's *Bark at the Moon.* Yeah, my dad listens to oldies. And who am I kidding? The song isn't in my head 'for no particular reason.' I just spent an hour in a tiny car with a werewolf. There's gotta be a parallelism somewhere between fat man in a tiny coat and furry man in a tiny car.

The driveway winds through trees for about a quarter mile before reaching a nice house. It's smaller and plainer than I expected considering how Ron described this guy. Made him sound like the rich old miser who owns the entire village of Crowthorne. Miser's probably not the right word, since Ron didn't infer he's nasty or greedy… merely well off. Anyway, it reminds me of the big houses people in movies always seem to have. Two stories, built-in two-car garage, faux brickface. Compared to the place Ron lived in, it's basically a mansion, being five times the size.

A few lit windows draw my attention first.

I peek in on a pair of boys, maybe twelve and fourteen, playing a video game in a living room already fully decorated for Christmas. No adults in the room, so I move on. The next nearest lit window, almost straight up, is a bedroom belonging to a teen girl. Posters tell me she's seriously into punk bands, but hasn't taken it far enough to do anything funky with her hair. Headphones and a book occupy her attention enough for her not to see me floating outside her window.

Again, no Mr. Nesbitt.

Another lit window around the corner on the ground floor gives me a view of a TV room. A couple in their early fifties sit in recliners on either side of a small table, watching television. Nice of them to relinquish the larger screen—and room—to the boys for video games. Presumably, the man is Mr. Nesbitt. Okay, target acquired.

The window's not budging, so I check the doors. Both front and back are locked. Again, not surprising. After flying around the entire outside of the house, checking each window, I'm still without a means of getting in. Don't want to take the chance they have a video doorbell. Unlike what some paranormal enthusiasts believe, vampires *do* show up on cameras. Hmm. I'm going to need an inside agent.

Both boys on the sofa have their backs to the window and are quite absorbed in the game. The daughter has headphones on, but a book consumes her attention. Easier to distract someone from reading than away from an X-box, but the consequences for doing so are usually more severe. Especially in like Sophia's case. If she's into a story, interrupting her at the wrong moment can result in tears or screaming.

I hover up to the girl's window and use my iPhone's flash to get her attention. The instant she looks at me, I'm in. All your brain are belong to us. Or me in this case. It's a little depressing to see her reaction to me is a desire to shriek. Suppose I shouldn't take it as a reflection on my looks. After all, I'm hovering outside a second-story window. My hair's dark brown and long. She probably mistook me for the girl from *The Ring.*

The teen, Lucy, stares blankly at me while I implant the urge for her to open the window and screen. She does, and I climb in. Ugh. Whatever 'music' she's listening to is horrendous. Some guy shouting bad poetry totally off key over guitar, drums, and bass played by people who've never touched an instrument in their life before they decided to record the track.

More motivation to get out of here fast.

Going down to the room where Mr. Nesbitt and his wife are watching TV is going to require sneaking past the kids playing X-box, and also require me to mind-tweak Mrs. Nesbitt. The more people who see me, the more risk. If they ask too many questions, it might cause the implant to unravel. He may or may not associate a strange girl in his house with the inexplicable desire to hire Ron Haddon on at the mill, but the last thing I need is to mess this up and have Mr. Corley get pissed. I'm doing this as much to satisfy my 'atonement' to him as to help Ron out.

I give Lucy a mental prod to go tell her father there's an enormous spider in her room. Wait, no. Giant spider might result in the boys coming up to check it out, too. New plan. Upstairs toilet is backed up. I program her to go fetch her father, complain about the toilet, and return to her bedroom. If all goes well, he won't make it to the bathroom and wonder why she didn't go there.

A moment later, she blinks off the mental fog, spins on her heel, and hurries out as if I'm not standing next to her. I hide against the wall by the door, waiting. Soon, the grumbles of a mildly annoyed man come up the stairs behind the soft thumps of a sock-footed teen. Lucy diverts into the bedroom and stops with an expression like she forgot why she walked in here.

Mr. Nesbitt goes by, muttering about shoddy plumbing.

I pop out into the hall. He stops short, turning to stare at me. Of course, being I'm relatively harmless looking, he doesn't immediately run off screaming. Probably mistakes me for some new friend of his daughter's. His confused 'who are you' stare gives me plenty of time to place his brain on the derp express. I drag him into Lucy's room, hit her with the same fog I use for feeding to keep her out of the way, and dive into Mr. Nesbitt's head.

Much like I did to the woman who ended up hiring Mrs. Lawrence—Hunter's mother—I implant a mental image of Ron along with a strong sense of trust and loyalty. Provided Ron doesn't do anything to actively piss him off, Mr. Nesbitt will regard him kind of like a son in law. Tomorrow, when Ron shows up at the mill, the guy will hire him for whatever job best suits a strong man, and pay him a little above average for it. Since I don't know thing one about textile mills, I leave the exact job specifics to Nesbitt. So the boys don't get in trouble, I start changing the reason Lucy called him upstairs to 'spider,' but in his head, it doesn't make sense. Lucy would've smashed a big spider herself. Damn. Screw it. The mother already heard her ask for help with a toilet anyway. I simply erase his suspicion the boys caused it, make him blame the plumbing, and also think the toilet's fixed. Finally, he gets a nudge to go back downstairs.

Once I'm done with him, I erase myself from Lucy's memory. For thoroughness, I give her a brief memory of having a problem with the toilet her father fixed. No need to go into detail about *what* sort of problem. While the two of them stand there staring into the fourth dimension, I dive out the window and fly back to the tiny car.

Ron's sitting behind the wheel, looking far too conspicuous. Any cop finding him would *know* he's doing something he shouldn't be. He practically jumps out of his clothes when I land right beside the car and open the door.

"Chill." I get in. "You should never play poker."

"What's poker have to do with anything?"

"You look like you're the getaway driver waiting for the bank robbers to come back. Acting casual isn't in your repertoire."

Look at me sounding like I'm a bad girl.

He exhales. "How'd it go?"

"Fine. Go to the mill tomorrow, ask to see Mr. Nesbitt... and you'll have a job."

"Brilliant. No more Tesco stock boy." He starts the engine. "Thanks fer not rippin' my head off."

"No problem. Thanks for not ripping *my* head off. You're my first werewolf."

Chuckling, he pulls back onto the road, the car's engine straining to accelerate. "Was it good for you?"

"Hah." I look over at him. "You're nothing like I expected. So, is it anything close to what the movies show?"

"No. It's more like being in college again. A couple times a month, I wake up naked somewhere out in the country and don't remember the day before."

"Umm… what kind of college did you go to? Must be different here than in the States."

"Nah, lass. You'll see in a couple years when ya get there."

"I'm in college now," I say, my voice—and eyebrows—flat.

He steals a quick glance at me, not wanting to take his eyes off the road for long. "Wow. Really? Are you a genius or something?"

"Well, I've never been tempted to eat a Tide pod, but no… not a genius. I've got a young face. I was eighteen when the supernatural stuff happened. It's only been six months, so I'm still technically eighteen."

"Right on."

"So you wake up randomly naked in strange places?" I gaze out at the passing trees. "Only happened to me once."

"Bad batch of E?"

"What? Oh, ecstasy? No… morgue."

He cringes. "Story behind that, I bet."

"Not really. Takes a couple days for the conversion to vampire to kick in. My sire's not the most organized person. Cops found me before he came back and… well… I woke up in a morgue cooler with no idea how I got there or why I didn't have any clothes on. Guessing the wolf takes over for you?"

"Aye. If I go too long wi'out 'avin raw meat, I'll black right the feck out an' wake up somewhere messy. Made a right hames of a sheep farm a while ago. Since I figured out it's connected ta meat, it's become manageable. Sorta like diabetes, but I don' 'ave ta wait on the NHS fer insulin. Just blag a sheep or goat when'er I need ta."

"Cool. No one likes random violent murder."

"Aye." He laughs. "Speakin' of. I appreciate ya not goin' straight ta the claws an' fangs part."

"No problem. And wow… 'dealing with the werewolf' was a lot easier than I expected. Figured it would be hairy."

"Ouch."

I snicker. "Sorry. The puns are genetic. Comes from my father."

He smiles.

"So, umm, where are we going now?"

"My grandfather's. Gonna spend the night there. He ought'a let me stay wif him 'til I get paid 'nuff times ta get me own place. Er, maybe he'll 'preciate the company an' I'll stay. We'll figure it out."

"Cool. Okay, I guess I'll call this done then."

"One werewolf dealt with."

"Yep." I roll down the window.

"I could pull over for ya if'n yer gonna leap out."

"It's fine. Kinda in a hurry to get back to my sister."

He nods, but slows anyway. "Night, luv."

"Bye!" I wave, and hurl myself out into the night.

16

HARMLESS

C heating the system doesn't bother me half as much as stealing.

Somehow, I've gone from being a reasonably ordinary girl who wouldn't even think of shoplifting to being casual about mind-controlling people for financial gain. Oh, and I've killed people, too. Not by choice, mind you. Sun panic. My victims weren't exactly innocent citizens either. Though, drug dealers don't deserve death. I'm not using their status as criminals to clear my conscience, but I'd certainly feel worse about shredding a busload of nuns. Maybe it ought to bother me more than it does, but the moment doesn't seem real. One second, I'm standing there talking to a bunch of gang members about to do a drug deal, the next thing I know, everyone's dead or injured. It's easy for my brain to think someone else did the killing.

In a bizarre way, someone else *did* do it. My primal vampiric id took over.

Giving my id direct access to my claws is about as dangerous as implanting cybernetic machine guns on a pissy housecat and taking him to the veterinarian for a deworming pill and claw trim. Of course, it's not something I *wanted* to happen, nor did the situation result from me—or Dalton—being stupid.

Killing three people should bother me more than it does. Hopefully, it's denial talking and not being an undead monster who places no value on human life. Yeah, gotta be denial. I'm a vampire, not an insurance adjuster.

It's pretty easy to spot London from the air at night. Crowthorne isn't too far away to the west, and London has a *crapload* of lights. Flying lets me cover an hour's worth of driving in a hair over fifteen minutes. Straight line, no traffic, and cruising faster than forty-five. I swear the battery-powered Barbie car my five-year-old self drove around had better acceleration than Ron's wind-up toy.

My bigger and more immediate problem than any possible guilt about manipulating Mr. Nesbitt, is—where the crap am I? London, obviously. But, where in? I stop at a hover, looking down at the sprawling lights. Everything looks the same. Best as memory serves, Mr. Crowley's mansion is north of the city center near some green spots, but nothing appears familiar.

A few minutes into me flying around like a mentally challenged pigeon, I spot Kallen and Meredith zooming toward me. Oh, whew. Finally. I stop again, hovering in place while waiting for them to glide up in front of me—and trying to come up with a good excuse for what I did. They're both smiling, Meredith on the verge of laughing at me.

"Must be sorted if you're up here swannin' around London."

"So how'd it go?" asks Kallen.

I stare at them, my thought train derailed in the middle of crafting a lame excuse to explain Ron's continued existence.

"She's adorable." Meredith grins at me. "You totally look like you're about to brick it."

"Umm, what?"

"Ya look scared, luv." She winks at me.

"Well... it didn't exactly go as Mr. Corley probably wanted it to."

Meredith folds her arms, trying—and failing—to appear displeased. "How'd it go then?"

"He smelled me coming, so I had to talk my way closer. But... he didn't break the treaty. He's been in London for a while. Some other werewolf bit him and ran off." I explain the whole Nesbitt thing and Ron's plan to relocate out to Crowthorne.

Kallen swings around and gives me a one-armed buddy hug. "Don' worry about it. We know ya didn't get into a furball wif him."

"Aye. Just takin' the piss." Meredith laughs.

I blush, reflexively looking at the ground below us. "You're what?"

The two exchange a glance, then laugh harder.

"What is it you Yanks say? Take the piss means like, erm…" Kallen strokes his short beard. "Pullin yer leg. Messin' wif ya."

Meredith play-punches my shoulder. "Aye, not lit'raly 'avin a wee. Been quite a few years since I 'ad ta do that."

Oh, geez. Duh. Is it obvious my head is spinning? Sure, *my* plumbing still works if I consume normal food and drink. These two aren't Innocents. "Right. Sorry. I'm not thinking straight. Kinda worried Mr. Corley won't be happy Ron's still alive."

"Nah, luv." Kallen squeezes me, apparently failing to realize I'm not one of his 280-pound buddies. "Corley wanted ta see how you'd react. He loaded ya up with a bit of bollocks and sat back to watch."

"Aye. Call it a temperament test." Meredith grabs Kallen's hand and frees me from the trash compactor. "He wouldn't 'ave gone spare on ya if ya killed the furry bugger, though. The way ya dealt wif 'im's like sayin' yer not a violent sort likely ta cause trouble."

"Yeah, umm… no. I really don't cause trouble… but damn if it doesn't keep finding me." I furrow my brow at her. "Where'd the whole 'eats kids' thing come from?"

"Corley probably said it ta get ya mad enough ta go werewolf huntin'." Kallen grins. "Needed a bit of a push, I reckon."

"C'mon." Meredith waves for me to follow and glides off.

I fly after her, thinking about the situation. In hindsight, Corley didn't actually order me to kill Ron, only 'deal with' him. He's obviously old enough to see my thoughts, so he had to pick up on my protectiveness toward Sophia. Maybe he wanted to see if he could get me fired up enough to strike without thinking. Admittedly, considering how wound up I am over Sophia's safety and being abducted across the planet... if I'd gotten the drop on Ron, there's a good chance blood would've gone flying. But, maybe once I got a good look at how... normal he seemed, I'd have hesitated.

Ugh. I really need to stop overanalyzing everything, but how the heck does one deal with vampire kings? Or presidents, or whatever the heck he counts as. Mr. Corley scares me more than Arthur Wolent, but not in the same way. Wolent, I'm afraid of offending because the man could twist a semi-trailer in half with his bare hands. Mr. Corley's in another league. Like, he's got the entirety of an old-world system of vampire monarchy behind him... or something. Possibly hundreds of vampires at his command.

Yeah, that's some scary stuff right there.

And no, I'm not 'scared' of him literally as much as desperately trying not to offend him. I don't want to end up being the main character in a movie who accidentally stumbles into the wrong doorway while on vacation, trips over a carpet and dumps an entire buffet table into the lap of the president of some fourth-world country... and ends up sentenced to thirty years in a labor camp.

Meredith and Kallen telling me Corley's not going to be angry with me for Ron still being alive helps calm me enough to resume thinking about going home. It might be ethically questionable to 'steal' airfare using vampire powers, but the Persons In Black will appreciate me not leaving an inexplicable paper trail. As in, how does Mom's credit card spontaneously show up in London buying one-way airfare back to the US? Or buying clothing. Oops. There's my good girl nature causing problems again. I probably shouldn't have used the card at the department store. At least clothes shopping they can more easily make look like an online purchase. Not so much for a plane ticket.

My escorts bring me back to the manor house, straight to the same room.

Plenty of people are still here. It's not a social event or even a party, more like a high-society hangout, only for vampires instead of rich people. Roughly half of the attendees are dressed like normal people—the sort of crowd you'd find at a Chili's or Bonefish Grill on a

Wednesday night. A small number *do* look like they belong to the ultra-rich jet set. An equal number dress like punks.

Mr. Corley excuses himself from the small group he'd been conversing with to approach the three of us. He's got a weird little smile like a teacher who gave the class a trick quiz and doesn't think anyone figured it out.

Walking up to the guy and falling to one knee is probably melodramatic. I'm not a messenger in *Game of Thrones*. But, he is basically a king. Am I supposed to do something? Paralyzed by dread and indecision, I stand there pulling a dumbass, probably making a face like I sat in lukewarm oatmeal.

"Miss Wright. You have returned, and do not carry the scent of blood about you." Mr. Corley regards me for a few seconds. "Yet you seem a little paler than before."

"The werewolf you sent me after isn't like people told you he is." I explain everything, more or less keeping my voice steady and not sounding like a total fool. "He's probably going to make a trip or two back into London to collect his stuff, but he'll be permanently staying in Crowthorne, out of your territory."

Mr. Crowley smiles. "Nicely handled." He leans closer, lowering his voice. "Do relax a bit, child. We may have tradition, but we are not humorless."

Now I'm certain he sent me on a trivial errand purely to satisfy the requirement I do *something* to answer for the breach of etiquette. Geez. Couldn't he have asked me to go pick up coffee? Meh. I should be glad he accepted my situation as out of my control. Pretty sure if someone deliberately ignores him out of contempt, they'd be sent after a much larger, fuzzier werewolf with a less normal disposition.

Mr. Corley gives me a tiny lift of the eyebrow I take as equivalent to a nod. He glances to the side, beckoning Joan over with a small wave. "You are welcome to stay in London as long as you like. If you happen to leave, as I'm sure you intend to, please do me the courtesy of announcing your return should you find yourself in my city again."

"I will—as soon as I can find this place. The city's sorta overwhelming."

"Make yourself at home if you care to. This chamber is always open for our kind, except when the sun is up." He glances at Joan. "Please show Sarah to her sister."

I bow gratefully at Mr. Corley. "Thanks."

Joan leads me out of the big room, down a fancy hallway of red carpet, gold-trimmed walls, and tiny marble tables set between impractically delicate chairs. "How'd it go with the wolf?"

"Found a diplomatic solution. An escape claws." I make a clawing gesture at the air. "As in, we escaped having to use claws."

She shakes her head. "Wow."

"Are you looking at me like that because I didn't kill the werewolf or for being twenty years too young to make Dad jokes?"

"Both, but mostly what you said. Americans are strange."

"Not all of us. My dad is exceptional. Both goblets were poisoned. I've spent the past eighteen years developing an immunity to puns. It has side effects."

She starts to give me a 'what are you rambling about' stare, but ends up laughing once her brain catches up.

Yeah, Joan definitely looks like a 'beat his head in, talk later' sort of woman. She leads me to the end of the corridor and pauses by a single door, also white with gold trim.

When she doesn't go in right away, I glance at her. "What?"

"Don't mind Charlotte," whispers Joan. "She's the sweetest. Would never harm anyone."

"Umm, okay."

Joan opens the door.

We enter a moderately large room decorated in mostly burgundy and dark brown wood. Tapestries, curtains, the fabric on a giant four-poster bed, and the carpet are all more or less the same shade of maroon. The décor lends the anachronistic bedroom a coziness at odds with the amount of space.

Sophia sits on the floor beside the bed, surrounded by an array of dolls, beside a woman in a dress Aurélie would love—it makes her look like a big doll. Her black hair's fluffed up into ringlet curls, falling over her shoulders to midway down her back. Rich brown skin and delicate features give her an almost Caribbean look. Despite appearing to be in her early twenties, the woman plays dolls like a child, acting and sounding younger than Sophia. Her voice isn't abnormally high; the childishness comes through in her words and mannerisms.

Something tells me the woman isn't acting childish for Sophia's amusement. My sister is ten. No need to behave like a six-year-old to play dolls and keep her occupied. In fact, watching them gives me the feeling Sophia is babysitting this woman more than the other way around.

I'm about to mistake her for a mortal until she glances in my direction and reveals striking bright gold eyes.

The instant we lock stares, a most bizarre feeling comes over me. I'm immediately drawn to her in a way... I dunno, almost like we're related. We're not, but the feeling is similar. Like when playing *Call of Duty* or some such game, how teammates' names are all in a specific color so allies are obvious? Yeah, same situation here only without the floating text. Takes me a second or two to figure out, but it's obvious to me she's an Innocent. Vampires can sense each other as fast as a glance, but reading bloodlines isn't normally possible. However, she's also the first other Innocent I've ever run into.

And she's taking 'innocent' *way* more literally than I do. Eep. Oh, crap! Please tell me I'm not destined to mentally crack like her at some point. Do they call us 'innocents' because we regress to being mental children?

"Sarah!" Sophia grins at me, then looks at the woman. "I'm sorry, but I have to go home now."

Charlotte nods, her lip quivering as if she's about to cry. "Aww. Thanks for playing with me. It was nice to finally have another little girl here. Who's she?"

"My sister, Sarah."

"Hi!" She waves at me. "I'm Charlotte."

"Hello." I smile back at her. "Nice to meet you."

The woman begins grabbing dolls one by one and introducing them to me. Joan can't look at her. Somehow, I manage to keep a straight face and roll with it, pretending I'm interacting with a kid somewhere between six and eight. My sister doesn't look the least bit freaked out at spending a few hours in the company of such a strange woman. Her being a vampire only adds to the unsettling air about her, a tangible otherworldly presence making the entire room feel heavy.

"You have so many lovely friends," I say in regard to the dolls. "I'm sorry we have to go, but we're both very far away from home and our parents are worried about us."

"I understand." Charlotte looks down. "I miss my mommy and daddy, too. The people here take care of me, but I wish they'd let me have a sister or a friend."

I slow blink.

Sophia hugs the woman, almost vanishing into the puffy dress. "Bye. Nice meeting you"

"Bye." Charlotte waves at us, then resumes playing dolls alone.

Joan is all too eager to leave, and hurries out the door. I take Sophia by the hand and follow. We're halfway down the corridor before my sister breaks the silence.

"She's nice."

"Charlotte's... special." Joan exhales. "Looks creepy, but she's more of a child than your sister."

"Mind if I ask why?" I bite my lip. Am I going to turn into her eventually?

"It's not the bloodline if that's what you're worrying about. Poor woman already had a whole bunch of bats dancing around in her upstairs before ol' Mr. Hargreaves gave her the Transference. Had ta be going on 150 years ago when he found her in the place."

"The place?" asks Sophia.

"Back in the 1890s, they tossed people with mental problems in asylums or prisons without much of a second thought. Some harmless woman like her might land in the same cell as Jack the Ripper. Didn't help her much bein' a *servant* girl."

"Why'd you say servant weird?" I ask as we enter the room where all the other vampires are hanging out.

Joan stops a few steps in and whispers, "Because the wealthy family she worked for didn't exactly pay her. Not quite the same situation you lot had over in the States, more an indenture in theory. I'm not old enough to have been around when it happened, so I've just got folklore and whispers. Some people think she killed the Lord and Lady. Some say she merely watched another killer work, and it broke her."

"She didn't hurt anyone," says Sophia.

"Nice to think she didn't." Joan sighs. "Anyway, the poor girl's lost her mind, and wherever she lost it, she ain't about to find it again."

"So sad…" I squeeze Sophia's hand.

"If ya really want to know, ya can ask ol' Mr. Hargreaves when he shows up here. They say he felt sorry for her. Got her out of the asylum before it killed her. Kinda treats 'er like a daughter. Easy to find him. Crazy old bastard still dresses like it's 1850."

I chuckle. "He'd probably get along well with someone I know. Interesting, but we're not going to be here long. What I said about our parents freaking out is true."

"You came all the way to London without them knowing?" asks Joan.

"Yeah." I pull out my phone to check the time: 10:28 p.m. Might not be too late to catch a flight.

"How'd you manage that?"

"Magic," says Sophia.

"Hah."

Klepto appears in a flash in Sophia's hands. "Mew."

"Feck!" Joan jumps back, staring at her.

"Yeah. I had the same reaction the first time, too. Umm… which way to the airport?"

Joan points. "Ya bloody well can't miss it. It's bastarding huge. Fly southwest from 'ere. Looks like a big brown rectangle from the air wif a lighter band down the middle."

"Great. Thanks!"

Sophia gives me this guilty look, but keeps quiet.

Maybe we should help the mystics, but I still can't let her get involved in something so dangerous.

THE WORST PART IS WAITING

Well, crap.

Good news: Heathrow airport is super obvious from the air. Guess being easy to spot from altitude is a good quality to have in an airport. Wouldn't want 747s randomly popping into people's backyards. Bad news: only two flights go nonstop to Seattle each day, and neither one departs this late. British Airways has one leaving at 3:40 p.m., arriving at 6:00 p.m. Seattle time (estimated). Sounds awesome, only like two hours, right?

Nope.

Time zones. It's anywhere from a nine to eleven hour flight.

The earlier flight leaves at 9:40 a.m. No way in hell am I making it on board a plane so early unless I'm packed in a trunk and have a helper. We're going to try racing to the airport to get on the later flight. If it doesn't pan out, some poor person is going to become my unwilling servant for a day. I hate the thought of mentally dominating a guy to escort Sophia and 'Sarah-in-a-box' on an international flight, but a few truths mitigate my guilt.

One: Sophia flying 'alone' with a giant piece of luggage is going to stand out and attract nosy, or simply well-intentioned people.

Two: If I'm corpse-sleeping, I can't use mind control to make sure no one interferes with Sophia.

Three: Sophia's going to freak out being on an airplane alone.

Oh, there's a four: my parents will pay the person back for the airfare.

However, taking a flight while I'm a little more than figuratively *dead* to the world is far from an ideal situation. And crap. If they x-ray my trunk, they'll discover my skeleton. Ugh. Call me a worrywart, but human 'remains' in a piece of checked luggage is probably going to get noticed. Guess I now know why vampires still use boats.

New plan: do not miss the 3:40 flight.

To help us make the time, we got a room at the Novotel London, a hotel basically right at the edge of the airport grounds. Since we'll be going back into the airport in broad—hopefully gloomy—daylight when my powers don't work, I obtained our tickets tonight, exploiting a manager override for children of British Airways employees. Courtesy of a few implanted commands, the ticket agent and manager think our dad's a pilot who works for the airline. Easy peasy as they say.

The simplest plans often fail in the biggest ways, but I'm hopeful. All I need to do is wake up as soon as I can, likely close to 2:30 in the afternoon, then rush with Sophia to the terminal and act casual. I'd feel much more comfortable on a late flight where I'm online the whole time, but a girl's gotta take risks sometimes to get things done.

"You forgot a five," says Sophia, flopping on the bed in our hotel room.

"What?"

Klepto teleports from the floor to my shoulder, rubs against my cheek, then jumps on the bed.

"You explained why turning a person into a servant wasn't bad. You missed a five." She yawns. "Wait, it's not really another reason. I'm tired. I mean, we have another option so you don't have to make someone into your vampire slave."

"I can't fly us myself. It's too far."

The kitten curls up on top of Sophia's chest.

"No." She swishes her feet back and forth. "We could help the mystics and they send us back the same way they brought us here."

"Soph…" I kick my sneakers off and lay next to her. "You're only getting started with this magic stuff. What kind of idiot would I be to let you charge into a fight with a spirit capable of killing mystics who've been doing magic for longer than you've been alive?"

"He's a ghost. And I don't gotta blow him up. Maybe. He talked to me once, right?"

"Because he needed something. He knew you could break him out of the jar, and he also knew you are way too nice for your own good. He lied to you. Pretended to be a poor, sad trapped spirit suffering in agony."

Sophia sighs at the ceiling. "He told me he did bad things and deserved to be punished, but he'd already been executed. The jar was too much. He didn't pretend to be suffering."

"He preyed on your niceness. Didn't he promise you he wouldn't hurt anyone if you let him out? He already lied."

"Sorta."

"What do you mean, sorta?"

She rolls her head to look at me. "He said he wouldn't hurt any innocent people."

"But he has."

Klepto stretches.

Sophia looks up at the ceiling again. "He doesn't think mystics are innocent people."

"Ugh. Look, I'll think about it, okay? Go to sleep."

Klepto hops off her to the bed.

"Okay." Sophia gets up, changes into her nightgown, and goes into the bathroom.

Minutes later, she returns and crawls in bed smelling of toothpaste. I sit beside her, staring at the blank TV. Hopefully, the mental command I gave the hotel manager holds and no cleaning people will barge in on us before we're gone. This room has some serious curtains. I might even be able to stay online in here during full daylight. Not surprising for an airport hotel, really. People who work nights and need to fly late sleep during the day, so a dark room helps. Good for me, too. Means I can use the bed instead of the bathtub. Perhaps an ordinary vampire would still want more protection than fabric over the windows, but as an Innocent, I should be fine.

Despite being hours away from sleep, I stretch out on the bed anyway. Damn, I'm undead and hotel beds *still* feel like stone slabs. Klepto pokes her head out from under the blanket by Sophia's chin, settling in for the night.

Does this kitten sleep?

For a while, I try to figure out if a tiny cat made from enchanted mushroom powder needs sleep. Not to be grim, but if something cut her open, would mushroom dust leak out? Is she like a stuffed animal or did Sophia somehow make an actual animal? Klepto eats food and uses a litterbox so... I'll assume she's more like a real cat than not. Guess my sister's magic literally changed one substance into another, sort of the way the Washington State Highway Department transmogrifies money into traffic delays.

Only a couple more hours and we can put this madness behind us.

SECOND TO FLYING, THE BEST PART ABOUT BECOMING A VAMPIRE IS sleep.

Not sleep per se, but how I can no longer lie awake all night while worried or excited. As soon as sunrise happens, bam. I'm out. So damn nice. My parents changed our Christmas policy due to something I did years ago. We used to wait for the morning to open presents, but the anticipation drove me nuts to the point I couldn't sleep on Christmas Eve. For no reason other than desperately wanting to sleep, nine-year-old me snuck downstairs at around one in the morning. I used a knife to surgically slice open all my presents enough to peek under the wrapping paper and see what they were, and re-sealed them all. With the suspense gone, I could sleep.

The next morning when it came time to officially open the gifts, it required a little acting on my part to seem surprised. Seriously, I hadn't wanted to break the rules or play with any toys early… only sleep. My parents still haven't admitted to catching me in the act or figuring out what happened, but the next year, they let us open our presents on Christmas Eve.

So yeah, instant sleep is one of the better perks of being a vampire.

One second, my mind is swirling with all the ways everything *could* go wrong. The next, I'm trying to figure out how it *did* go wrong. In a seeming instant, the room goes from the washed out mostly black and white view I have in total darkness to ordinary light. My world is strange in the dark. Everything *looks* to exist in various tones of grey or black, but I somehow still know what color objects are.

The dense curtains allow a small strip of sunlight in at the top, but it's on the ceiling. To any normal person, the room would appear quite dark, but that scrap of daylight, to me, is like a full size ceiling lamp being on. Back to the reason I'm trying to figure out how my plan failed: Sophia's not on the bed beside me.

I sit up fast and check my phone for the time: 2:31 p.m. Great. Woke up early. Good sign.

My sister wouldn't have hesitated to put the TV on, but it's silent. Simple sound can't wake me up before my body's ready to stir. Somehow, the vampire part of me can sense a direct threat. I could literally sack out on a concert stage in front of a sound system the size of a small house and not care, but if a hunter tiptoed into my room wanting to kill me, good chance he'd wake me up.

Or she. I shouldn't assume all vampire hunters are guys.

Considering the time, it isn't directly alarming for Sophia not to be in bed. However, her clothes—the new ones I got her the other day— are still draped on the chair by the small writing table. No sign of Klepto either. I crawl out of bed and check the bathroom. She's not there, so I stick my head out into the hallway and look both directions. Still no sign of her, only one guy in a pilot's uniform who's doing a spot-on impression of a zombie. Dude seriously looks like he needs sleep big time. He goes by, not even looking at me, and enters a room three away from ours on the opposite side.

The *slam* of his door swinging shut makes me jump.

There's no way Sophia would have left the room alone. She's far too timid. Maybe if we happened to be in Woodinville, somewhere relatively familiar, she might've gone down to the in-hotel restaurant by herself, but in a completely different country? Not happening.

Especially not in a nightgown.

I hurry downstairs to the front desk. Two dark-haired women in black blazers behind the reception counter give me curious looks as I rush toward them. It's not *too* bright out, but there's enough sunlight to stiffen my muscles and make me feel like a department store dummy brought to life. The women likely think I'm a victim of assault, on drugs, or doing an impression of teenage Darth Vader. Despite feeling like I'm made out of wood, I've *still* got more believable facial expressions than him.

Just call me Mannequin Skywalker.

"Hey…" I crash into the reception desk, grabbing the edge to keep from falling. "Did you see a little girl leave the hotel? Ten, really skinny, blonde? I can't find my sister."

The women exchange a glance.

"No," says the slightly younger one. "I've not seen any children at all today, leaving or otherwise."

Her co-worker's a few years into her thirties and rocking an 'actually, I *am* the manager' black bob 'do. "We've been on shift since five. Had a few check-ins and some people go out, but no children. If you can't locate her, we can check the cameras. Should we phone the police?"

Eep. "Uhh, not yet. Maybe she's running around upstairs and got lost." I push off the counter, trying not to act too obviously like I don't want police involved.

"Are you okay?" asks the younger woman. "Where's your mum an' dad?"

"Mom's home waiting for us. We're supposed to be on a plane in like an hour. Thanks!" I force a smile past my worry and hurry back to the elevator, hoping they don't call the police anyway.

The women murmur back and forth, but without vampiric hearing, I can't understand them. Screw it. I rush into the stairwell.

Dammit. If the cops show up, what do I tell them? In a paradoxical twist, the truth is the last thing they'd believe... and I'm a rotten liar. Crap! The police are probably going to think I'm a trafficking victim going to the US for some sick perv rich guy. I could give them real information about our parents, but we'd still be stuck for an explanation for what we're doing in London.

Hold up. I'm eighteen. Need to stop thinking like a kid. I don't *need* parental supervision—it just comes in handy to let someone else worry about crap. However, there's still the issue of me not having a passport. A Washington State driver's license isn't going to cut it, though it would verify my age. I'm not worried about being deported —going home is what I *want*, but they'd misinterpret me not wanting to talk about magic as me lying. I'm going to end up stuck at a police station until dark. As soon as my powers are online, I'll be fine... but that's a whole day wasted.

And where the hell is Sophia?

I run back and forth down the halls of all three floors, already wasting so much time we'll never make the flight. Dammit! Wait, did she crawl under the bed to hide? Anything could've happened while I lay in deathly repose. However, if someone walked in on us, they'd have freaked the hell out at the sight of me. I'd have come to in a body cooler again, most likely.

Once in our room again, I dive to the floor and peek under the bed. No kid sister. I sit back on my heels and sigh at the clothes left behind—or rather, the empty chair where they'd been a half hour ago.

Her shoes are gone, too. Both had *definitely* been here when I woke up.

Argh!

I bonk my head repeatedly against the mattress.

"Damn mystics."

BIG GIRLS DON'T SCRY

I t makes no sense for the mystics to magically kidnap my sister again.

Or maybe it does. I bet Asher let us leave because he expected we'd get lost and scared, then turn around and go back, reluctantly agreeing to help him because we had no other choice. Seeing as how we didn't, he's most likely decided to try again... this time taking only Sophia. She already wants to help them because she's too nice for her own self-preservation, and probably feeling guilty for letting the spirit out in the first place.

I can't leave her alone with them or they're going to get her killed.

At least I packed light for this abduction. The only reason I remember to bring the phone charger and power converter with me when I run out the door is they're still connected to my phone. My parents are going to lose their damn minds when they find out I lost Sophia. They'll lose their minds anyway when they don't receive a text telling them we're on the plane, but at least waiting buys me some time.

I hurry downstairs again. The women give me urgent looks, but there's no sign of cops. They'd have been here by now considering the time spent roaming the corridors looking for her. The 'manager' picks up the phone when I go right past the desk and outside, not checking out, not having a little sister with me, and not even looking at them.

Crap.

Bigger problem… I can't fly at the moment due to an acute case of daylight.

Fortunately, this *is* London after all, and it's a touch gloomy. It only feels like I'm microwaving myself on low rather than body-surfing a hibachi table. Best part: no smoke, only mild agony… like being trapped in a stuck elevator flooded with a Justin Bieber cover of Nickelback. Or would Nickelback covering Bieber be more of a crime against humanity?

Argh. Whatever. 'Crime against humanity' is a good way to describe what I'm going to do to those mystics for kidnapping Sophia… twice. I've got another minor problem though… Heathrow airport is like *all the way* across London from the mystics' bookstore. Flying has become so second nature, not being able to do it at the moment leaves me standing there feeling clueless, staring at a strange building across the street. It's four stories tall, and each successive story upward is wider than the one below it, like an upside-down ziggurat. Expecting police to show up at any minute, I hoof it to the left, heading east past a bus stop.

After passing a few large buildings, I follow the sidewalk as it curves left around a massive arrangement of bushes, and keep going into an office park or some such thing. Long, rectangular brick buildings with teal-framed windows surround me on both sides. I go right again at the first opportunity and end up stuck at a dead end due to a metal gate blocking the way into a car park.

Grr.

I head to the right, jogging across a parking lot, then slip through bushes and end up back on the same street our hotel was on, only farther down in front of a Radisson hotel. There's a Marriot then a Sheraton all in a row, then some smaller building surrounded by trees and a round Holiday Inn.

It's going to take me forever to get to the bookstore on foot. The only reason I'm not thoroughly going nuts is knowing the mystics aren't actively trying to hurt Sophia. They're not exactly protecting her either, but their goal isn't to harm her. Giving a kid the magical version of a handgun and sending them into a paranormal warzone falls somewhere between child endangerment and 'wtf is wrong with you?' Still, they don't *want* her to get hurt. I only need to find her before she makes an error, not before someone alive does something horrible to her.

If the police get me, I'll feed them a bogus story about someone grabbing me from behind with chloroform or something and waking up in London not knowing how I got here. Wait, no. They'll go all 'kicked hornet nest' trying to figure out who did it. Maybe staying silent and trying to call the Persons In Black would be my best bet.

Yeah, I'll try that if I get picked up by the cops.

Not sure why the idea of police scares me so much. I haven't done anything wrong... except enter a country without a passport.

Think, Sarah, *think*.

I'm out in the daytime and need to go all the way across London. Don't have enough cash for a taxi. Hmm. Do they have Uber in London?

Out comes my phone.

Wow, they do!

Sorry, Mom. Gotta use the account.

Hold on while I use the power of the internet to summon a total stranger, who I will then get in the car with. Should be completely safe, right? Damn. I hate being scared again. At the moment, I'm no more dangerous than a slightly undersized teenager. If the Universe decides to send me a total creep, I could be in big trouble. But Sophia's in danger. No choice but to roll those dice. My mind races over all the stuff I used to read about how to survive as a young woman alone. Scream. Make noise. Go for the eyes. Creeps are looking for easy targets. If the Uber driver does anything shady, I'll go thermonuclear.

A minute or so later, I get a pop up on my phone from the Uber app—it's a photo of a skinny blonde guy with a huge smile. Trevor. He looks maybe twenty-three, and I'd bet money he's not going to be interested in me at all. Just a feeling from looking at him.

Cool.

I hit the button to confirm I still need a ride.

Maybe fifteen minutes later, a little green car matching the photo rolls up. Trevor's behind the wheel. I run over and hop in the passenger seat—which feels like the driver's side.

"Hi, Trevor?" I show him the Uber app on my screen.

"Aye. Allison?"

"No, Sarah. Account's in my mom's name."

"You're American?"

"Yeah. Obvious, huh?"

"Little bit. Least ya didn't try to open my door. Last Yank I had got in behind the wheel while I loaded 'her bags in the back."

I chuckle.

"Only, she kept sitting there, like she didn't know what to do." He pulls out into traffic. "Had this look on 'er like, blimey, there's this giant round thing in my face, no idea what the bloody hell it is. Just ignore it."

"Hah. So what did you do?"

"Got in on your side, waited. Lady looks at me, so's I say whenever you're ready. Key's already in it. She looks at me, looks at the wheel, back at me. Then goes, 'your car's broken.'"

I laugh in spite of my worries over Sophia.

"Somethin' wrong? Ya look out of sorts."

"My story is too crazy to believe. I'm not a morning person. Real ditzy and groggy if I have to get out of bed too early. So I'm at the airport. I get on the wrong plane. Fall asleep. Wake up halfway across the ocean."

"Wow. They not scan your ticket?"

"No, I just kinda walked with the crowd. Maybe they assumed the guy next to me was my father or something. It's like a total freak series of events. My parents know the guy who owns this bookstore. I'm gonna spend the night there and fly home in the morning. Sorry if I'm a little freaked out. Not used to being so far from home."

"Gotta be rough. What're ya bout seventeen?"

I blink at him. Holy crap. He's like the first person in the world not to assume I'm fourteen-to-sixteen. Maybe because we're sitting next to each other in a car and about the same height. Or, he's not looking at me the way most guys do. He still de-aged me by a year, but *pff*. What's one year? Either way, points for Trevor.

We talk on the ride, him telling me about his post-grad studies working toward becoming a dentist. The guy's certainly personable enough. Except for the reason I'm here and all the supernatural stuff, I share some honest information about my school plans, classes, and lack of a social life.

Finally, he pulls over in a familiar street next to the dry cleaner's place. I thank him for the ride, click in a decent tip on the app, and get out of the car, standing there until he drives away. Then, I glare at the bookstore.

It's open at this hour, but doesn't appear to have any customers. Perfect.

I walk in, heading right for the back room. Asher blindsides me, seemingly appearing from thin air out of a gap between shelves on my right. His sudden appearance startles me to a halt. The look on his face says he wasn't expecting to see me either.

"Where is she?!" I yell, and attempt to slam him into the nearest shelf.

Attempt being the operative word.

Hello, Universe. I'm an ordinary person right now.

He braces a hand on the shelf, largely ignoring my two-fisted grip of his orangey-brown turtleneck. Furious, I keep trying to fling him to the floor without success while screaming various things like 'where is she,' 'what did you do with my sister,' and several other less polite phrasings. He spins me around, my back to his chest, and scoops me off my feet, pinning my arms against my chest. I grunt, straining to escape his hold as he carries me toward the back room. I haven't been manhandled like this in a while.

The last time a tall, muscular guy carried me somewhere against my will, I'd been kinda laughing about it. One of Michelle's non-romantic guy friends from high school helped her insist I join them at a party. He jokingly carried me out to the car.

Asher, however, isn't joking.

And wait... no. The last time someone carried me somewhere against my will, I ended up handcuffed in a dungeon cell under a night club. Dammit! I'm pinned too tight to bite his arm. Too close for my feet or knees to find his balls, and he's got my wrists pinned together against my chest. I keep growling and demanding to know what they did to Sophia all the way into the back room and down to the basement.

Boy, did he just screw up.

Unlike Abaddon, *this* building does not have windows in the basement.

The instant we're far enough away from daylight for me to come online, I overpower his hold on me and spin, grabbing him one-handed by the throat and shoving him against the wall. Red light from my glowing eyes tints the cinderblocks on either side of his head. While I *could* lift him off his feet, doing so would prevent him from speaking.

"Where. Is. Sophia?" His mind is still closed off from me, which only infuriates me into growling again, but now I sound like an angry mountain lion, not a harmless kid.

"She's not here."

I increase pressure on his throat. "Where did you send her?"

"We haven't done anything other than facilitate your initial arrival."

"Bullshit."

Asher closes his eyes in the expression of a resigned sigh.

The redhead woman and the Indian guy run into view at the end of the short corridor, staring at us. Both start raising their hands like wizards about to throw fireballs, but Asher waves them off.

"Sophia vanished out of a locked hotel room. She did *not* wander off in her nightgown. Like twenty minutes later, her clothes disappeared off the chair. You expect me to believe you didn't grab her again?"

Asher holds his left hand up, showing off a wide dark copper ring engraved with an intricate weave of black lines. Appropriately enough, it's on his middle finger. "Nothing I say will change your mind, so you'll need to look for yourself."

"Nice try, but you know I can't see into your head."

"A moment." He removes the ring, though it takes a bit of twisting before it slips off. "Try now."

I hang my head for a second and sigh. "Seriously. Does *everyone* have mind-shielding trinkets?"

He offers a faint smile. "Its primary purpose is not against your kind, but darker spirits. A coincidence their means of exploiting the mental faculties of mortals so mirrors yours. Many within the Aurora Aurea seek to shield themselves from such invasion."

Hmm. The guys back in Seattle don't have magic rings.

I peer into his head, this time having no difficulty. The foremost concept rattling around his prefrontal cortex is the recent death of Martin Collier—the tall guy with the tall face who'd been among the eight when they dragged us through the portal. A shawarma cart went rolling downhill out of control after its handle snapped off in the owner's grip. It managed not to strike a whole bunch of other pedestrians, bounced down a stairwell into a subway station, caromed off a wall, and crashed into Martin, hurling him forward into the path of an oncoming train.

Street meat went everywhere.

"Wow… I don't know what to say to that."

"To what exactly?" asks Asher.

The redhead and the Indian man—Anna Riordan and Keval Patel according to Asher's thoughts—walk closer, looking at me like a pair of cops about to attempt their first hostage negotiation.

"Martin…"

"Oh. Yes. You see what sort of situation we're in. Have you found anything about your sister?"

I focus again on his head. He's thoroughly convinced Sophia can destroy the spirit he calls Fletcher Maltby. He, too, is alarmed at her disappearing, and really didn't have anything to do with magical abduction number two.

"Damn…" I let go of his neck. The red light in my eyes fades along with my anger at him. "Sorry."

The face of Martin Collier hangs in my mind. Ironically, I remember him protesting their grabbing Sophia without warning or asking. The one person among them who voiced an objection to them forcibly relocating my kid sister to London is dead. Maybe he wouldn't have died if not for me dragging Sophia out of here and trying to go home. I shouldn't feel guilty about it. No reasonable person with a younger sibling to take care of would've been like, 'oh sure, let's take this child and charge head-first into a dangerous situation.'

I shouldn't feel guilty… but I kinda do.

Anna and Keval relax now that their leader's no longer in the potentially fatal grip of an angry vampire. Asher puts his ring back on.

To distract myself from Martin's death and Sophia being lost without any trace, I half-ass a humorous tone. "Great. So everyone gets a mind block item. Mystics… vampire hunters. Makes my life difficult."

"The hunter you speak of likely has a more specific artifact focused solely on your kind. Our warding magic is a general protection spell. Older vampires can often penetrate it." Asher puts a hand on my shoulder. "We are responsible for Sophia being in whatever situation she's in. I and my lodge mates will do everything we can to find her."

It's easy to think 'yeah, sure you will,' but they do have a strong motivation to locate her. I just know if they're able to find her and get her back, it's going to turn into a guilt leverage situation. Would it make me a bitch to still refuse to let her go after this spirit after they find her? *If* they find her. I'm getting ahead of myself, but I really don't want to think about any other potential ending to Sophia missing.

"If you guys didn't grab her this time, where the heck did she go?"

"We can't answer that yet." Anna nudges me with a plastic bag. "We need to locate her first."

I glance down at the bag dangling from two of her fingers. "What's this?"

"Her things."

"What?" I take the bag and peer into it. Clothes, shoes, earrings, a fabric anklet. "Oh."

Anna grimaces. "Apologies for any awkwardness it caused. We had not intended to steal all her possessions."

"I know. You wanted to steal her. She was in the bathroom at school when it happened. It took her a while to stop freaking out enough to think of creating an illusion of an outfit."

Asher blinks, looking impressed. "I take by your tone this illusion was indistinguishable from real clothing?"

"Other than it leaving her freezing all day, yeah."

"Amazing," whispers Keval. "It took me six years of study to be able to conjure illusions without them glowing or being transparent."

"Umm, yeah. Soph had some pretty strong motivation to get it right."

"Come..." Asher gestures down the hall, then walks off.

I follow them into the same room where we first appeared.

The others pause in their work at the long tables along the walls on either side to look at us. Asher introduces the white-haired teen as Mindy Carlin, the Chinese guy as Wing Tang, the man I mistook for Hispanic as Rafi Ismail, and the 'schoolteacher' woman as Leslie Elliot. Mindy's still giving off fear vibes, but also some new hostility. Since I know she doesn't have a brain condom on, we lock stares. Yeah, she blames me for Martin's death. Guess she's still an apprentice or whatever and hasn't earned her warding ring yet. Leslie also appears to blame me for Martin, but doesn't give me an accusing stare. She glances away, head bowed, trying to make my guilt worse.

Wing and Rafi, at least if I'm reading their body language right, don't hold wanting to protect Sophia against me.

"I'm sorry about Martin," I say, my voice quiet. "Sophia's only ten. She didn't even know magic existed until two months ago. Something tries to kidnap her from school, then weird light things attack us at home... then we're sucked through her closet into a ring of people in black robes. Maybe it *is* true her link to the soul jar gives her the ability to control this spirit, but I hope you can understand why I tried to protect her."

Leslie closes her eyes, sighing out her nose.

"Yes." Wing sets a beaker of green liquid on the table and walks up to me. "Martin was right. We should not have taken it upon ourselves to bring her here without asking."

"You want us to consider your reaction from your point of view…" Mandy shifts her weight back, away from me. "Think about it from ours. This thing is hunting us. We can't do anything to stop it. We've tried. Used ta be fourteen of us. Now seven. We figure out what's happening, and know the one who opened the soul jar can bugger this thing off easy as pie, what would you do in our place?"

"Maybe easy as pie for you, but she's a kid." I rake my hands up over my head, close to ripping my hair out from anxiety and frustration.

"A child who, mere weeks after discovering she has the gift, creates an illusion stable enough to fool people in close proximity—and keep it going for hours," says Asher.

"You can Obi-Wan all you like about how special she is, but she's still a child. She's never once used magic to hurt or attack anything." I flail my arms. "What is she supposed to even do?"

"We would teach her how to banish spirits. It is not terribly advanced." He exhales hard. "Alas, we must focus on finding her first."

"What?" asks Mandy. "Where'd she go?"

"Unknown." Asher glances at me.

I re-explain waking up to find her gone, searching for a while, then noticing her clothing vanished. "Someone or something took her the same way you guys tried to at the school. Only, they didn't miss."

"We will attempt to divine her location." Anna Riordan jogs over to one of the huge tables and begins collecting bowls and jars. "This will take a little while."

"Great," I whisper. "All I've got is time."

I SPEND THE NEXT FORTY MINUTES OR SO UPSTAIRS IN THE BOOKSTORE on the phone with my parents.

Dad's ready to drive Mom to Boeing, steal a plane, and head straight to London. His plan has two major problems aside from the closest he's ever come to being a pilot is playing flight simulator video games as a teenager. One, Sierra and Sam can't be left home alone. Two, if he somehow managed to steal an airplane, get it off the ground with enough fuel to make it here, and did so, he'd certainly be arrested the instant he landed.

I'm three minutes into trying to talk him out of the idea when he starts shouting over me about not being serious. Wow, I'm beside myself with anxiety. Somehow, I manage not to fall to pieces and cry. Maybe the magical element to her disappearance twists it enough not to seem as real or as serious.

While he's not going to steal an airplane, Dad does plan to go interrogate Darren Anderson and the other mystics at the Brass Tap. He might try to make contact with Glim again, too. Shadows have a way when it comes to gathering information. Mom is scarily calm. Her lack of shouting or crying when told I've lost track of Sophia tells me she's gone into focus mode. Usually when she gets like this, opposing counsel ends up with a drinking problem, insomnia, or both.

The three of us go back and forth reassuring each other. My parents keep me from giving in to feeling like a failure, and I keep them from losing their minds in worry. I'm a damn vampire. I've got tools people don't. Like Mr. Corley. And Charlotte. Joan might think the woman-child is harmless, but I sensed a shitload of bottled up… something. Don't want to call it rage, since it's not quite anger. I don't think she killed her, well, owners, nor do I think she'd arbitrarily kill people. But if someone hurt Sophia, it wouldn't surprise me to see some psychotic Alice in WTFland stuff come from her. The woman's over a hundred years old. Power from age coupled with the total lack of restraint a mental six-year-old can show when pissed off.

Eek.

I pace around the shelves.

Go into the back room.

Back out into the bookstore.

It starts to get dark out.

Once again into the store room. By chance, I spot an antique sword on a shelf. Curiosity pulls me closer. It's about forty inches long, double edged but not terribly sharp, the blade tapering to a fine point. Thanks to the little brain-zap Dalton gave me, I know it's an arming sword, common in the European Middle Ages. On a whim, I set my purse on the nearby table and pick the sword up, backing away into the middle of the store room.

Without much thought, I drop into a fighting stance and begin going through the motions of sword forms. It's absolutely bizarre to simultaneously feel like I'm doing something for the first time as well as it seeming routine. Frustration at being powerless to help Sophia adds speed and power to my strikes, making the blade whistle. Even though it's a fairly dull museum piece, I'm swinging it fast enough to do serious damage.

Bits and pieces of memories flash in my head, but they're not mine. I'm Dalton, in a tavern somewhere, jumping over a table and thrusting a blade like this into a man's chest dressed in the fashion of the 1920s. A spinning slash puts me in a cistern, surrounded by scraps. I see a two-second flicker of the past—Dalton slicing a malformed head in half at nose level.

Whoa.

I certainly don't feel like a master—or even 'good' at this—but the sword in my hand is… comfortable.

The door to the basement creaks open. I smell Asher, so I don't bother looking or stopping, leaping horizontally over an imaginary foe trying to slide into my legs. The maneuver lands me in a thrusting stab I imagine piercing the face of another make-believe adversary.

Asher clears his throat.

I stop, relax my stance, and face him, sword hanging from my hand. "Where is she?"

"You're older than you look. Don't usually see such fancy moves except on film."

"Wow. First time anyone's ever said that. Usually, it's the reverse." I set the sword back on the shelf where I found it. "A friend taught me some of what he knows. And some of those fancy moves are only possible on film without superhuman strength and agility." I walk up to him. "Did you find her?"

Asher's falling expression answers before he can open his mouth. "Not exactly. We are unable to locate her. I suspect she is either outside our dimension or in a place magic cannot penetrate."

"A place magic can't penetrate? Like what?"

He clasps his hands in front of himself. "Certain crystal caves or other geographic phenomena known to interfere. Perhaps a ward. You assume she was taken. Perhaps someone tried, and she ran off, using magic to hide herself. It is possible Fletcher Maltby went after her."

"If she ran off, I'd have gotten a message by now."

"You are making assumptions." Asher taps his fingers against the back of his hand. "You said she is inexperienced. She may have sent herself somewhere unexpectedly and cannot get a message to you."

Frustration builds to the point my hands shake. "So, what do you mean? Is she gone?"

"Merely misplaced." He offers a weak smile. "We are still working to locate her. Seeing across dimensions is far more complicated. I came up here to warn you about the time. Dawn approaches. You should probably seek out a place to shelter. Of course, you are welcome to stay here. Bear in mind Fletcher Maltby is still out there. He may attack us at any moment. You'd likely be safer spending the day elsewhere."

I pace, really wanting to smash something. "I can't just leave with Sophia missing."

"The sun will be up fairly soon. You won't do her any good as a pile of dust. It is unlikely we'll discover anything while you've enough time to do much."

"Grr." No way it's dawn already. I tromp over to my purse and pull my phone out. I'm shocked to see it's 6:18 a.m. "Umm…"

"Sun's up around eight. You'd better head down to the basement and hope Maltby doesn't flood us with gas and set off a bomb. I recommend you find a secure place where you won't be caught in whatever efforts he undertakes to harm us."

"I'll be back as soon as I can. Please find her." I'm too angry at him for doing this to us to beg, but also too worried and desperate to stop myself from sounding a little pleading.

He nods. "We all need sleep. Everyone's staying here for now, hoping our wards hold out against the spirit. He won't be far from us, which is why you should shelter somewhere else."

Unable to think of anything to say not involving a lot of swearing and threats, I stuff the phone in my purse and hurry to the front door. I'm not taking an Uber again. Hopefully, there's a basement around here I can break into. Pretty sure I saw a big apartment building a short ways down the road. Ought to be a boiler room there away from the sun.

Again, I'm really damn grateful worry won't keep me up all day.

SIMONE

The instant I walk out of the bookstore, someone grabs me from the right and shoves me against the building in a motion so fast it makes me feel mortal.

I find myself locking stares with a pale green-eyed woman. She's obviously a vampire given how fast she moved. Long, chestnut brown hair in a thick braid drapes like a boa constrictor over the shoulder of her grey skirt-suit jacket. The lady's got a 1940s sort of relationship with lipstick. Ruby red. She's somewhere between the 'dame' who walks in at the start of every private eye movie and the 'shockingly' capable woman who saves her entire archaeological team from a mummy in a middle finger to the patriarchy.

She looks me over, little clue of any emotion in her face. Something's a tiny bit familiar about her, but it's gotta be déjà vu.

Being shoved into a wall like someone who owes the bookie money puts me on edge, but oddly, I don't feel threatened. More like a piece of merchandise being appraised. Since it's doubtful Mr. Corley's suffered a massive brain fart and decided to send someone to beat me up for failing to kill the werewolf, I keep quiet and wait for her to say something—or start trying to kill me.

Last time I had a pale woman with dark hair grab me, I ended up pulling rebar out of my boob. I'm not looking forward to having rusty metal stuck in places it does not belong... again. Crap. This woman feels older than Petra. Could be worse. She doesn't give off vibes as old as Aurélie. Still, she's gotta be over 150. Doesn't really matter once the numbers get in that range. A vampire at 150 or 396 will spank me all the same.

"Hmm. Just a kid," says the woman, unsurprisingly in a British accent, though not as haughty as expected. "Must have been a pity case since you're a bit young for him."

"Excuse me?" I stare at her. I've never considered myself to be one of the hot girls, but I am no pity date. If this woman wasn't so old... Still, I gasp. "You've gotta be mixing me up with someone else."

"You are definitely the one. I can feel him all over you."

"Uhh, look here, lady, unless you're talking about Hunter, I haven't touched your man. No idea what you're smelling, but you're wrong."

"There's a hunter about?"

Despite her holding two fistfuls of my shirt, I facepalm. "No. Not *a* hunter. A boy named Hunter. He's mortal, and back in the US."

"Oh. Yes. Not my concern." She finally lets go of me. "You are Dalton's offspring."

Fire appears in my thoughts. People screaming. A tiny memory flashback replays in my head from a swordfight Dalton had been in ages ago. This woman is in the background, swinging a cutlass and dagger, cornered by multiple enemies.

"You're the woman he loves." Crap. What's her damn name? Dalton mentioned her several times, but I'm drawing a stupid blank. How embarrassing.

"Love*d*." She sets her hands on her hips. "Thought I felt him return to London, but, turns out it's only his progeny. I've no issue with you."

"Nice to hear." I smooth my shirt out where she'd grabbed me. "And he still loves you. It's pretty obvious. But, yeah, he's totally infuriating sometimes."

"Sometimes?" She stares blankly for a second, then chuckles.

"Infuriating is part of his charm. He would have been more charming if he understood the concept of loyalty. So, what brings you to London? What sort of mess did he get himself into this time he's called you in to help clean up?"

"He's got nothing to do with this." I give her a brief explanation of why I'm so far away from home.

The woman taps a finger to her chin, the blood red polish on her nail a perfect match to her lips. "Ahh, mystics. Unpredictable and dangerous. They have their uses. Pity the Church drove them underground. It would be a far more interesting world if people still practiced magic openly."

"Didn't Alastair Crowley try that not too long ago?" Could've sworn Sophia or one of the Seattle mystics mentioned something about him.

She waves dismissively. "Aye. However I am referring to a time before calendars needed four digits for the year."

"Whoa. I didn't think you've been around so long."

"I haven't. Merely heard stories." She again gives me an appraising once over. The feeling is part madam considering hiring the desperate street waif and part pirate queen trying to figure out if she's going to let me join the crew. "I suppose you have nowhere to go for sunrise then."

"Not exactly."

"Are you able to fly?"

"Yeah. Probably not as fast as you can."

"Brilliant. Follow me." She looks around. Once satisfied we're not being observed, she glides straight up.

I follow. We keep climbing vertically to roughly a thousand feet before she veers off to the northwest. She's not hauling ass or even going fast, so I pull up alongside, still trying to remember...

"Simone."

"Yes?" She glances over at me.

"Lot on my mind right now. Took me too long to remember your name."

"You think Dalton still has feelings for me, but you couldn't remember who I am?"

I gaze down to my left at the sprawl of London lights. Night flying really is beautiful. It's a shame so few people get to enjoy it. "Considering the relatively brief amount of time Dalton has spent with me, he's mentioned you quite frequently."

"Oh, why am I not surprised? He abandoned you?"

"Technically, it's probably more accurate to say I abandoned him."

"We have that in common." She laughs. "I should've been smarter and done it right away."

"I have no romantic feelings for him at all. He's more like a younger uncle who can't quite get his life in order and keeps calling my parents asking for bail money."

Simone covers her mouth to subdue her continued laughing.

"He told me about the time he ran away from the window because he was scared. Pretty sure he thinks about it every night. He's sorry." I tell her about the LA vampires kidnapping my little brother and his friends over Dalton's firebomb situation, and him going with me to get them back. She obviously knows about the firebomb, since she asked him to do it. The woman's basically an arranger of dirty deeds among vampire kind—and a broker of valuable things.

"Oh, he's certainly a good talker. I'll give him credit for it."

"I think he's sincere. The woman you caught him with, he was doing a job. Like a CIA spy trying to get information. People can make mistakes and be truly sorry for them."

Simone smiles at me, but her eyes have gone a little cold. "Perhaps, but you really ought to stop talking about him while I still somewhat like you."

I cringe. "Oops. Umm, I burned a lot of power today... do we have time to stop for a bite?"

"At this hour, it would be problematic. I've some reserves if you don't mind bottled."

"Never had bottled."

"It's not the most pleasant on the tongue. Blood is far better warm, but it is sufficient to feed."

"Thanks. Very generous of you. Bottled is fine."

She leads me to an ordinary looking house on a residential street in North London. We land in a small backyard enclosed by high white walls shrouded in ivy, and walk in via the back door. The place has a lived-in feel and I catch the scent of at least two live people, probably working for her.

A narrow doorway in the corner of the kitchen leads down to a finished basement decorated like a wealthy person's living room (lots of weird art objects) without windows. Simone opens a cabinet, takes out a twenty-ounce plastic bottle, and offers it to me. It's still got a Coca-Cola label, but contains blood. I can't help but cringe a little at it not being at least refrigerated.

"Didn't he teach you anything?" asks Simone.

"Not much, but it's not like I stayed with him. Mostly my fault."

She gives me a disapproving smirk, shakes her head, and sighs. "You don't need to keep taking the blame for his shortfalls, dear. If you have a quantity of fresh blood in a container like this bottle, adding a few drops of yours to it acts as a preservative."

Oh, maybe I have heard this before. Or am I doing the déjà vu thing again?

I nod, open the cap, and take a sip. The blood tastes like syrupy flat Coke. Not as unpleasant as she made it out to seem. I drain the bottle, shake the last few drops out, and hand the empty back to her.

"I'm impressed. You didn't cringe. I can't stand it lukewarm." She gestures at the sofa. "All yours."

"Thank you."

She nods. "You are welcome. Good morning."

I stretch out on the sofa, watching her cross the basement to another door and slip into a bedroom. Dalton's description made her out to be a black market bigwig. Doesn't seem right for her to live in such an unassuming house. Bet she's got a large manor somewhere and this is a safehouse or some such thing she keeps on the side. Certainly, a woman in her line of work wouldn't bring me directly to her primary lair the first time meeting me.

Whatever. It's a good place to stay out of the sun.

I'm not nervous. If she wanted to hurt me, it would've happened already. It's my sire she's pissed at. Me, she probably thinks of as another person affected by the disaster known as Dalton Ames. I smile at the ceiling. Nah.

Dalton didn't ruin my life. He saved it. Sure, he's not perfect, but who is?

A SLIGHTLY ELEVATED RISK OF DEATH

A most unusual sensation greets me when I return to consciousness.

Repetitive squishing in my boob, complete with tiny needles. I lift my head off the sofa cushion and peer into the eyes of Klepto, who's kneading my right breast with vengeance.

Tiny, adorable vengeance, but vengeance nonetheless.

"Klepto!" I sit upright, cradling her.

"Mew," says the kitten.

"Where'd you come from?"

"Mew."

"How'd you find me?"

"Mew."

I am an idiot. I bow my head, bonking it into Klepto's. "Can you understand me? Make the tribble noise for yes.

She tribbles.

Whoa. Okay, so the kitten *can* understand English. And aww. The noise is super cute. Kind of like a combination purr-meow. I lift my head and stare into her bright teal eyes. "Is Sophia in danger?"

No response.

"She's neither safe nor in immediate danger?"

Tribble.

I flop over on my back, relieved. Beats danger.

"Mew."

I raise my head to look at the kitten again. "Can you lead me to her?"

Tribble.

"Awesome." I fish my phone out and check the weather. Partly cloudy with some sun. Screw it. I can't make Sophia wait. I get up, Klepto perching on my shoulder. It doesn't take much searching around the place for me to score a pen and Post-It pad. I leave Simone a thank-you note for letting me sleep here and tell her I had to leave due to missing sister, apologizing for taking off before she wakes up.

No one appears to be moving around upstairs, so I tiptoe up the steps to the kitchen and gingerly crack open the door. It's almost a sauna out there, but nowhere near as bad as the time we had to drag Dalton out of a construction yard, or even the day I took Sophia to the park and the guy in the minivan thought he smelled steak grilling.

This should only be as uncomfortable as a visit to a new OB/GYN who keeps making icebreaker jokes about spelunking.

Once again, the stupid fireball in the sky is stealing my ability to fly. I don't feel like scaling the ten-foot-high walls around the backyard only to land in another backyard with ten-foot-high walls, so I rush across the house to the front door and let myself out

Klepto nibbles on my left ear.

One way to do it...

I turn left and start walking.

The kitten perches on my shoulder, occasionally head butting me to get my attention, and pointing a paw where I need to go. She's obviously following an 'as the crow flies' sense, since we hit multiple dead ends and a few wrought iron fences I end up climbing to cut across parks or people's yards.

Brightness makes it difficult to see clearly past about a hundred feet. Everything washes out to a nuclear glowing haze. It's tempting to detour to a shop and grab a hoodie, but Sophia's more important than my comfort.

I'm not prepared for the distance… it feels like we walk for hours before Klepto emits a faint growl and jabs her little paw at a gate. Jaw clenched, I look up from the sidewalk and take in my surroundings. My eyes involuntarily water at the pain of sunlight—it's like I've been given those annoying damn eye drops at the doctor's office, and my pupils have dilated all the way, making light hurt my eyes. Seems the kitten has led me to the outskirts of London, the start of open land and large estates or fields.

The gate Klepto's growling at blocks a long driveway lined with trees leading up to a sizable manor house surrounded by fields and forest. It's not *massive* but still enough land for whoever lives here to have stables and probably a few horses.

"Sophia's in there?"

Tribble.

"Okay, hang on. I'm going to have to climb this wall."

"Mew," says Klepto.

I swear her eyes light up for a second. The motorized gate kicks on, opening. Wow. I have a universal garage door kitten. She purrs when I kiss her atop the head. Once inside the gate, I head for the trees, trying to stay out of sight by hiding behind each tree in turn, looking around, and scurrying to the next one.

Eventually, I make it to the top of the driveway and lurk in the bushes, looking at four cars parked by the house. One black BMW, a silver Mercedes, and two… no ideas. Generic middle class British car, kinda small.

Klepto jumps to the ground and trots off to the right. I follow her around to the side of the house and a door intended for servants, or maybe for bringing in large shipments of foodstuffs. The kitten stares at the door for a few seconds. It shouldn't shock me to see the knob turn on its own, but it's still a 'whoa' moment.

She paws the door open and ducks inside. I hurry after her into an industrial kitchen—everything is burnished steel—pulling the door closed behind me. My attempt to lie my way out of getting caught sneaking into the Abaddon Night Club blew up spectacularly in my face. Dalton, I am not. Breaking into places is about as far as an activity can possibly be out of my skill set—and comfort zone. Oh, hell. People keep mistaking me for fifteen, or even fourteen. I could try pretending someone tried to grab me and I ran in here to hide.

Better idea. Let's not get caught.

Easier said than done. Even inside, the reasonably bright day is an inferno to my eyes. I'm doing okay, no smoke or fire, but my reaction time and vision are like an eighty-year-old's. Okay, I'm lying. I *am* normal. Just accustomed to being boosted. After spending the winter flying to school, having to drive again in the spring for my early classes is going to be tedious. Same comparison.

We leave the kitchen for an interior hallway more like a hotel than someone's actual house. I peer into various doorways we go by, checking out sitting rooms, a dining hall, more sitting rooms, a room full of armor suits on stands and paintings. This is totally like one of those houses you always see in those movies where some tween gets orphaned and forced to live with wealthy tangential relatives who honestly couldn't be bothered to take a child in but do so for mysterious reasons.

I'm either going to befriend a ghost who's not as scary as they appear, foil a murder plot, or end up with the entire Dutch East India company wanting me dead.

Klepto abruptly darts to the left, jumps at a closed door, and disappears in a brief teleport flash. I run after her without question and nearly crash into the back wall of a smaller-than-expected broom closet. Door shut.

Ahh, darkness.

Someone walks by outside. I'm guessing a woman by the sound of her footsteps and pace. I reflexively hold my breath, waiting for silence. Eventually, Klepto licks my ear.

"Yeah," I whisper. "I don't hear her anymore either."

Tribble.

I ease the door open, mentally groaning at the drag of going offline again, and slip out into the hallway.

The kitten teleport-jumps to the floor. I jog after her to a stairwell.

The polished hardwood stairs are too tall for the kitten to manage the traditional way, so she teleports onto my shoulder for a ride.

At the top, she indicates left.

We go all the way to the end of a long corridor, following it around a corner to the right, and down another stretch of corridor to a set of double doors. Something tells me Sophia's in there. A bit overcome with eagerness, I rush forward lacking due caution. Fortunately, I don't set off any traps or walk into an ambush.

Unfortunately, the room is devoid of small blonde girls.

It's a study with a huge hardwood desk, marble-inlaid fireplace, some potted plants, and obnoxiously large windows looking out over a second-floor patio big enough for a soiree. Klepto jumps down and scurries over to a closed curtain.

"Sec."

I push the double doors closed, trying to be as quiet as possible. The whole sneaking thing works much better when I don't make tons of noise or leave doors open as an obvious sign someone's invaded the place.

Squishy teal carpeting absorbs any sound from my footsteps, letting me hurry across the room to the big curtain. Pulling it open reveals a breathtaking ornate brass door with more gears, cogs, and pointlessly elaborate moving parts than a steampunk novel. Two giant gear rings, each three feet across but thin, have possibly Latin writing etched into them.

One lever-style handle of white porcelain juts out of the middle of the central gear. I grab and try to turn it, but no luck. Locked.

"Go away," says Sophia from inside.

"Soph!" I whisper-shout. "It's me."

"Sare!" A soft *thump* hits the door. "Let me out! It's really scary in here. There's all this writing on the walls like a crazy person used to be in here."

I struggle at the annoying handle. "Umm. How? Wait. Klepto, can you make this open?"

"Mew." She hangs her head.

"Are you hurt?"

"No. Little scared, but they didn't hurt me."

I study the door. So many moving parts. My eyes cross trying to make sense of it. Error. It's not going to make sense. It *has* to be magic.

"Who is they?"

"Umm. Not sure. There's a woman and a man. I didn't see them. I woke up inside this cell. They spoke to me through the door. Said I shouldn't be scared and they'll let me go once it's finished."

"Once what's finished? Are they doing something to you?"

"Umm. I dunno. I can't do any magic. Maybe they're trying to steal it."

I grab a fireplace poker and try to jam it into the gears. The tip bounces off an invisible barrier. Multiple jabs confirm the same 'glass' covers the whole front face. Damn. Probably wouldn't matter anyway. Nothing except cuckoo clocks and watches have *this* many gears. A door does not need gears. They've got to be decorative. Jamming them won't help.

Klepto hisses.

Crap.

I look behind me.

A man and woman freeze not quite halfway to me from the door, as if they'd been trying to sneak up on me. Both appear to be in their thirties and wear black—dress for her, fancy suit on him. She's rather pale, but obviously not a vampire.

"Gomez and Morticia are here," I mutter.

She almost smiles, but catches herself.

He raises his arm, pointing a small gun at me I hadn't noticed.

Ack.

I do *not* want to be shot while basking in sunlight-flavored fail.

The man glances sideways at her. "I'm confused, Katy. Didn't you say the older sister was quite dangerous? She's a kid, too."

"Vampire or something, I think."

"Clearly not." He gestures the gun at me. "She's out in the day."

Repeat: I do *not* want to be shot in sunlight. It might be final death. I may be a terrible liar, but *really* being afraid of the gun helps me act timid. I raise my hands in surrender.

"Umm, sorry for sneaking into your house, but you guys did kidnap my sister. I'm only here to get her and go home to the US."

"That's fine," says the man. "But not yet."

"What do you mean 'not yet'? Why did you take Sophia?"

He wags the gun toward the door. "Walk."

"Aww, come on. You guys caught me. This is the part of the movie where you're supposed to villain monologue and tell me all about your evil plans."

Katy snickers. "Go on, Jacob. Tell her. Not like it'll matter."

Wow. Is she running with my joke or does she not realize how she sounds exactly like a movie bad girl?

"Fine. Shall I presume you have never heard of The Serene Lodge?" asks Jacob.

"Are we standing in it now?"

He sighs. "No. It is not a place, but an order. Similar to the Aurora Aurea you've aligned yourself with."

Katy frowns at the words 'Aurora Aurea,' kind of the way Sierra does whenever anyone says 'Brussels sprouts.'

"We're not aligned with them. They kidnapped us from the US against our will."

"You spent most of last night at their sanctum." Katy folds her arms. "Rather cozy with your kidnappers."

Jacob steps toward me. "If you are no friends of theirs, then you will not mind staying with us for a few days."

"Why can't we just leave?" I ask.

"Because... we know why they brought the child here." Katy taps her foot. "The phantom running around loose and preying upon them. They believe she can stop it. We don't want this to happen. The two of you will stay here until the spirit finishes its task. Neither of you will be harmed, but we cannot let you leave until the Aurora Aurea has been wiped out to the last."

I can't help but stare at the gun. It might be one of those little James Bond 'slightly bigger than a BB gun' pistols, but a bullet is still a bullet. "We're not trying to stop it. My sister is only ten."

"She won't let me do it," yells Sophia from behind the door.

"You may well be telling the truth." Jacob flicks the gun twice toward the door, ordering me to go there. "Sorry, child. We cannot take the chance. This war is a thousand years old and could end in a mere week."

Jacob's pants vanish.

I blink.

Katy gasps.

"Wow. You didn't really strike me as the sort of guy who goes commando." I cringe.

Jacob hesitates for a second, but finally looks away from me, down at himself—rather Klepto sitting between his ankles. I swear the damn kitten grins, and launches herself straight up at the dangly bits.

He howls in pain.

A few facts stand out in glaring neon-flashing marquee style. One: I can't open the door trapping Sophia. Two: them locking me up is bad in multiple ways I don't have the time to ponder at the moment. Three: Asher and his friends are going to die. Four: Asher and his friends might be able to get Sophia out. I'm damn sure they'd try, considering she is their best ticket at living. Oh, and five: I doubt the mystics will try to follow Klepto back here to save both of us.

I'm sorry, Soph, but the only thing I can do right now is run like hell and get help.

Jacob howls, spinning in circles with a small furry critter dangling from his small furry critter. He starts to point the gun at the kitten, but hesitates. Can't blame a guy for not wanting a gun pointing there. While he's eminently distracted, I pounce at Katy, shoving her out of my way and running for the door.

Only, she doesn't go down as easy as I'd hoped.

No, she's not a vampire or super strong.

She grabs my arm as I try to barge past her, trapping my wrist and swinging me into a face-first meeting with the carpet. Before my brain can even fully process what the rug tastes like, she's got her knee in my back and my arm twisted up behind my neck.

Ow.

The bitch is like a jiu-jitsu master or some crap.

Even without the intense pain in my shoulder, elbow, and wrist, I'm not strong enough to do a one-armed push up with all 130-some-odd pounds of Katy on my back. Jacob grabs Klepto and yanks her away, doubling over and gasping. The kitten disappears from his hand. I can't see much from this angle, my face mushed into the rug, but Jacob screams in pain again.

"Katy! Get this daemon off me!"

"Little occupied. Or do you want this one telling the fools where we are?"

Jacob wails and growls, bumping into chairs and a bookshelf in his ongoing battle with the furry terror. I rock side to side, trying to throw the bitch off my back, but she twists my arm a tiny bit more—the blinding flash of agony makes me scream and stop trying to move. Dammit! I hate being offline.

Thump.

My eyes focus on a little grey furball bouncing across the rug, having been thrown. Klepto catches herself, skidding backward to a halt, claws in the carpet.

Pop!

The gun goes off, sounding more like a firecracker than a firearm—and Klepto disappears in a brief flash. Jacob spins, aiming around the room, breathing heavy.

"Did you get it?" asks Katy.

"I don't know. I hit it and it burst into loose energy."

It did kinda look like her teleportation, but I'm not completely sure.

Thirty seconds of silence becomes a minute. Klepto doesn't reappear for a counterattack.

Shit… I can't help but choke up.

Jacob hands the pistol to Katy.

She presses it against the back of my head. "Be good and don't move, all right? I promise you won't be hurt. Merely delayed."

Grumbling, Jacob retrieves his pants from the floor.

Katy holds me at gunpoint until he finishes putting them back on—he had to take his shoes off—then passes the weapon back to him.

"Stand up," says Jacob, still sounding winded.

Katy lets go of my arm and gets off me.

I push myself up, shaking from a mix of fear, sadness, and anger. Sophia's quiet. Either she felt Klepto explode and she's curled up too heartbroken to cry, or she hasn't realized what happened. Once on my feet, I fire a side-eye glare at Jacob. His hair's a bit messy, but he otherwise looks unhurt.

"Walk," says Jacob, wagging the gun at the door.

They escort me down the hall, around the corner to the left, and back to the stairwell. Since the guy shot a rolling kitten on the first try, I'm too scared to attempt running. Better I have time to figure out a way to escape or do something than take a bullet to the head and my family has to lose me a week before Christmas.

We cross the downstairs to a basement door. Ooh. The fools. As soon as I have darkness, Jacob's little gun is going to get rammed into a body cavity. Metaphorically, I mean. Not literally going to... yeah, gross.

Katy opens the door, revealing a passage with a rounded ceiling, all bricks covered in peeling white paint. A narrow wooden stairway leads to the basement... which is sunlit. Dammit! Who has sunlight in their basement?

Okay, to be fair, my house did, too, before Dad mega-tinted the windows. My new bedroom doesn't have windows. Maybe this basement has a chamber or two without them. I grab the banister and make my way down into a damp, musty former wine cellar. The basement is *massive*. Stone columns support a ceiling of filthy boards littered in dangling scraps of wire hanging on ceramic insulators. This place is old.

Katy prods me past the columns and a large stack of antique furniture piled into a veritable wall. On the other side, channels of sunlight filter in from narrow windows at the ceiling level, illuminating a row of five large cages next to a legit medieval torture rack. Various manacles hang from hooks on the wall above them, along with stuff like little whips, metal tongs, giant tweezers, and a whole bunch of other 'tools' I don't recognize. Three creepy-as-hell cages shaped like people farther away in the corner give me the chills. Someone standing in one of those things couldn't move much at all.

Oh, hell no. I've gone straight from Boris and Natasha to *The Hills Have Eyes*.

"Uhh…"

Katy steps past me, Jacob keeping me at gunpoint, and pulls one of the big cube-shaped cages open. "Go on. Crawl in."

"Why do you guys have a torture chamber in your basement?"

Jacob waves dismissively, his expression blasé. "Any self-respecting order of practitioners should have some means of containing specimens. The other implements are mostly for ambiance. We never use them for their intended purpose. These items are charged with energy we find helpful to amplify certain workings of magic."

My smarm-thrower is about to fire up, but it's a little difficult to cop an attitude with a guy pointing a gun in my face when I'm not immune to bullets. Also, playing up the harmless child angle might work better.

"Can you guys please not leave me down here in a basement? It's really scary. Couldn't you put me in the same room with my sister? Sophia's terrified. She hates being alone."

"It's an involved pain in the ass to seal the ward. We're lazy." Jacob pokes me in the sternum with the gun. "Go on and get in the cage. It's only for a few days. Less if the spirit works fast."

"But she's only ten. You don't need to put her in solitary confinement like Hannibal Lecter. What are you doing to her in there?"

Katy taps her nails on the cage door. "The girl possesses the art. We can't risk her using it. She is merely in a warded room to contain her abilities. It isn't harmful."

"Your demonic little furball from hell has left me in a rather foul mood," says Jacob. "You and your sister have stumbled into a centuries-old war. While I have no great desire to harm you, if it must be done to secure victory for The Serene Lodge, so be it. Now, crawl into the bloody cage."

"Okay… okay. Chill." I get down on all fours and crawl into the four-foot cube of metal bars. At least it's super dusty and doesn't appear to have been used recently. "You guys really aren't that serene."

Katy goes to shut the door, but pauses. She swipes my purse, then shuts the door, locks it, and drops the key into her little black handbag. My purse, she hangs on a stone column quite well out of my reach from the cage. "Relax, sweetie. We're not going to steal from you, but I'm sure you've got a telephone in there."

Smiling, Jacob lowers the gun, tilts it sideways, and flicks the safety on.

"Hey, what are you doing with a gun? This is England, right? Aren't they illegal here?"

"My dear…" He drops the small pistol in his jacket pocket. "We are mystics. We flagrantly disregard the laws of physics and reality. Why would you expect us to obey any laws?"

Katy waves at me. "Make yourself comfortable, hon. I'll bring you some food in a little while."

The pair walk off out of sight around the giant pile of old furniture, seeming pleased with themselves as if they'd already won whatever war they keep talking about. I assume they're referring to a conflict between their sect and the Aurora Aurea.

I grab the bars on the door and rattle it. They're fairly beefy, three-quarters of an inch thick. Definitely not a dog kennel. I can mule-kick this off as soon as my powers come online. Hopefully, the angle of these basement windows will hurry it up and bring on the darkness.

And dammit!

Again, I try to sneak into a place during the day, and again I get locked up.

I'm going to develop a complex.

Grr. Thinking of Sophia locked in a cell alone gets me fuming mad. To blow off steam, I give escape by brute force my best shot. Yeah, doesn't do much good at normal Sarah strength. Since I am apparently stuck, I sit cross-legged, elbows on my knees, chin in my hands, and fume.

Jacob thought Klepto's claws hurt.

Wait until he sees mine.

THE BASEMENT OF HAPPINESS

Locked in a cage in the basement of a big ol' manor house in England isn't the most uncomfortable thing.

Could be worse. I could be stuck in a living room surrounded by elderly distant relatives we see once every five years or so having my cheeks pinched every ten minutes. Compared to visiting my Aunt Jody's mother—and her side of the extended family—when I was like nine, give me the cage. At least it's quiet down here. And no claw-like fingers are trying to sneak attack my face. Sierra was two then, probably doesn't remember it well or know why the scent of 'old person' terrifies her at a subconscious level. Nothing against the elders, but bring an adorable toddler within arms' reach of attention-deprived seniors and they wind up basically playing tackle football for cuddle time.

One might think I should be having a freak out, but I'm too pissed.

A big reason my predominant emotion is anger rather than fear is knowing Sophia's not in any imminent danger. Gomez and Morticia want to keep her from helping Asher—exactly the same thing *I* tried to do, only for the opposite reason. I didn't want Sophia to get hurt. These two *want* the Aurora Aurea to go extinct. Am I a dumbass for trying to prevent my kid sister from getting into a fight with a murderous ghost?

I mean, what logical person would think sending a ten-year-old to stop a serial killer is a good idea, even if he is already dead?

The bad part about having time and silence is, it makes me think about Martin Collier. Not like I knew the guy at all. But it's surreal to be in the same room with someone, everything normal, then two days later, he's dead. No guarantee allowing Sophia to help them would have saved his life, but guilt still gnaws on me in the silence. Not to mention Klepto. The little kitten tried her damndest to give me an opening to escape and possibly paid for it with her life.

Who shoots a kitten? Seriously!

I stare at my purse, dangling six feet off the ground near the opposite wall. Every time my phone beeps with an incoming text, it drives me a little further into a pit of fury. My parents are either going utterly batshit crazy at my lack of replying, or they're assuming I had to shut the phone off for an airplane ride. No amount of sticking my arm past the bars and attempting to 'Jedi' my purse into my hand works.

Hmm. Could Sophia do it?

Probably with practice. After all, she rewound time to re-do a botched argument with Mom.

I look around at my enclosure. It's basically a tiny jail cell. A half-inch thick metal plate above and below me, and bars all around. Seems old. I kinda wonder if it might've been used to hold criminals in an era before organized police. Sitting fifteen feet away from a medieval torture rack is probably pushing my thoughts back in time. And yeah, it is kinda creepy down here. Basements tend to give off weird vibes. If not for a locked, barred door in my way, I'd totally get the hell out of here.

But, I'm stuck being stared at by who knows how many ghosts who aren't thrilled at my invasion of their territory. Yeah, same here. I'm not happy to invade it. Having dealt with a couple ghosts—and being a 'creature of the night' myself—it's not too nerve wracking to be trapped in a haunted basement. I'm definitely getting the sense something is staring at me with malicious intent, but no ability to act on it.

Kinda like the old woman who used to live across the street from my grade school. Far as I know, she hated the sound of children screaming at recess, and spent the whole time glaring at us from her porch.

Anyway. I rattle the cage door again, sigh, and shoot an uneasy look at the rack.

It's dusty enough to support the claim they really don't use it on people. If it works as a paranormal amplifier for their magic, it must mean it's been exposed to suffering and/or death. And whoa, is that an iron maiden behind it? I didn't think those things actually existed. It's gotta be a prop. Half the metal implements hanging on the wall above me, I don't want to know what they're for. Hooks, clamps, giant shears… yeah.

These people have serious issues.

Grr. Seems I've really turned into the precocious orphan sent to live with rich relatives from one of those movies. Found a nefarious plot, got caught, and ended up kidnapped. I wonder if this is how Penny from *Inspector Gadget* feels. She gets kidnapped so damn much it's gotta be merely as annoying as the bus being six minutes late for the fortieth time in a row. Then again, it's a kid's show, so they're never going to let anything truly bad happen to her. I'm also a vampire, so it's not like I can die again.

Well, technically, I can. It's merely a lot more difficult to kill me than most. Except during the day.

Cheek mushed into my fist, I dwell on my theoretical mortality. Exactly how vulnerable is my body during the 'offline' time? Aurélie sounded pretty convinced any injury I suffer while exposed to the sunlight would become permanent, and if ordinarily fatal, would destroy me. Not saying I distrust her, but she's also not an Innocent. And we are rare. I'd ask Charlotte, but she probably wouldn't know and it would be as awkward as asking a little child to contemplate mortality.

Faint jingling from behind the wall of furniture derails my train of thought.

I stare at the spot, wondering what sort of phantasmal creep show is about to jump out and ambush me. Even though I'm a vampire and have 'seen some shit,' there's something about being trapped in a cage unable to run away from creepy noises. It's probably a rat dragging a bottle opener across the floor. It can't be Katy coming downstairs to bring me a tray of food. Not unless she's put on shoes with tiny bells. She totally doesn't seem the type to wear those. Then again, Jacob did *not* strike me as the type of guy to go commando, so who knows?

The noise tracks from the left, coming closer and closer to the end of the furniture wall.

My mind races for a way out. If the thing coming for me is solid, the cage will protect me as much as trap me. But if it's not…

Anxiety builds to the point I almost scream.

… and Klepto trots into view carrying a key.

I gasp, grab the bars on the door, and try—unsuccessfully—to stick my head outside the cage. "You sneaky little…"

She drops the key on the floor in front of me, sits back on her haunches, and mews.

I scoop her up, pull her inside, and hug her. "You are awesome!"

Tribble.

"OMG, I thought you died."

The kitten gives me a look of 'bitch, please.'

I laugh, wipe away a few joy tears, and reach for the key. Considering she opens locks by staring at them and didn't simply open this cage, my guess is it has some magic in it. Enchanted mini-prisons suggest these mystics expect to keep creatures or magical beings capable of opening locks by staring at them prisoner. Yeah, my life is weird.

"Can you get the key to where Sophia is, too?"

Tribble.

Klepto disappears in a brief flash.

Might as well wait for her to return. How sick is it this cage is the *nicest* thing they could've put me in down here? I could have been stuck standing, chained to the wall. Stuffed in an iron maiden, a steel bathtub thing with only a hole for my head to poke out, the rack... and I'm pretty sure one of those giant chairs in the pile has spikes all over it.

"What the hell is wrong with these people?"

Okay... collecting macabre stuff doesn't necessarily mean someone is psychotic. They didn't use anything torturous on me. I would've rather been locked in a bedroom, but this abduction is still more comfortable than my last one.

Klepto reappears in a brief flicker, standing on top of an old-timey copper skeleton key big enough to legit beat someone to death with. She snorts and grunts, struggling to drag it toward me. Spinning gears in the handle end click on the concrete floor, and look equally as purposeless as the gears in the door.

At least these mystics are consistent with a theme, right?

Okay, screw it. Don't care if the sun is still up. We're not sitting here all day. Solitary confinement drives hardened criminals nuts. There's no way in hell I'm letting Sophia sit in the vault a minute longer.

I unlock the cage door and crawl out. Klepto, not noticing me since she's still trying to drag the mammoth key, jump-squeaks when I pick her up and hold her nose to nose. "You are the best little fuzzball ever. Can you do me one more tiny favor?"

Tribble.

"Steal Jacob's little gun and lose it somewhere outside in the back yard."

She tribbles again, and vanishes out of my hands.

Sweet. Let no one ever claim a multipurpose Swiss Army kitten is ever silly.

My skin tingles on contact with the giant key. It's kinda like licking the contacts of a nine-volt battery, only my hand instead of my tongue. I'd call it weird, but it's kinda ordinary compared to a teleporting cat. After recovering my purse and slinging it over my shoulder, I grab my phone. Hate to say it, but the parents have to wait.

I dial Asher's number, but it doesn't even ring. The heck? No signal. But text messages had been dinging in for the maybe half hour I spent sitting in the cage. Only... no. Not text messages. The dings came from network drop warnings and reconnect notifications. Basements, even giant ones like this, shouldn't cut off cell signal. Gotta be magic.

Okay, whatever. Would have been nice to have some backup for our escape, but it's not an option. Neither is staying here. As much as I really want to grab Katy and Jacob and smack their heads together, getting away is more important. Hey, if the ordinary non-vampire non-magic-using twelve-year-old from the Victorian books can bring down an international jewel-smuggling operation and two corrupt members of Parliament, I should be able to escape a manor house unnoticed with my sister while offline.

Or so I hope.

22

THE DIFFERENCE OF NIGHT
AND DAY

Jacob and Katy certainly seemed like a pair of villains from a kid's movie.

Maybe a PG-13 one, but still. Hopefully, they'll make the classic mistake of overconfidence, too. Sophia's behind a giant, enchanted vault door and 'the older kid sister' is stuck in the basement. Here's hoping they forgot about the kitten. Come to think of it, if the cage had an enchantment so Klepto couldn't zap it open, might it be able to hold me, even when I'm online?

Eek. Don't want to think about it. The belief I could kick the door off as soon as it became dark kept me from panicking. A delay comparable to feeling like I'm stuck in traffic is a lot different from a true sense of being captive. Not sure I'd have been as calm without expecting to be able to break out as soon as the sun went down.

More motivation not to get caught on the way out.

As soon as the kitten returns from disposing of Jacob's pistol, I sneak up to the top of the basement stairs and peek under the door. Two women, neither of whom are Katy, work in the kitchen, starting dinner preparations most likely. Klepto disappears off my shoulder. A moment later, a crash comes from the pantry—cans and boxes falling to the floor.

"Blimey. Damn that old haunt," mutters the older of the two women. "Makin' a mess of it again."

The women hurry to the left, disappearing through a doorway. Both scold someone named 'Murray' for knocking things over, as if a poltergeist was as routine as a mischievous cat. Wow. This house...

Anyway, opportunity has arrived.

I slip out of the basement stairs and hurry to the hall. The layout is mildly confusing, but it hadn't been *too* long ago they marched me downstairs at gunpoint. One small wrong turn later, I find the stairs and creep up to the second floor. Maybe it would be smarter of me to flee while I'm on the ground floor and near windows, but abandoning Sophia here is not happening. She might not be in imminent danger, but who knows what these kooky mystics would do if they discover me gone before I can get back here with Asher and the other mystics. So, yeah. I'm not leaving this house without my sister.

Swear on my dead hamster Wilbur, if anyone sneaks up on me, they're getting walloped over the head by a six-pound key.

The path to the large sitting room containing the warded vault is eerily clear, no sign of Katy or Jacob anywhere. Feels too easy, but maybe they really are overconfident. They sure seemed to celebrate winning that mystic 'war' of theirs as soon as they locked me in the cage.

Clinging to the huge key like a tiny club, I sneak along the corridor in a constant state of twisting side to side, watching for an ambush. The room is empty as well, so I slip in, shut the door, and run to the false window curtains, yanking them open.

The door and all its moving, spinning, whirring parts is a mesmerizing nightmare of metal. I stand there clutching the key and staring at this mess of cogs and gears, unable to find a keyhole. The key is three times the size of the handle at the center of the door. Finally, one of the larger gears, half solid, half hollow, rotates enough for the solid part to stop blocking the keyhole. It's high center on the door, right about where a peephole would normally be.

I heft the key in both hands and stuff the end in before the gear can rotate back over it.

Every mechanism in the door stops moving the instant the key hits the back end of the socket.

"Eep!" yells Sophia.

The damn key doesn't want to turn in either direction. Crap! What am I doing wrong? Wait… this is magic. Maybe the key only needs to be in the socket? After all, the gears stopped moving and something must have happened inside the cell to make my sister yelp.

I grasp the handle, and rotate it down a quarter turn.

It works!

Pulling the huge metal door open is a bit of a task. Okay, so I am on the smaller side of average—but still quite within a normal size range. No one calls me 'the short girl.' Having only my ordinary pre-vampire strength at the moment, I'm not budging this door one-armed. So, I grab the knob in both hands, brace a foot on the wall, and strain.

The four-inch-thick copper-and-brass door eases out into the room, exposing a stone-walled chamber the size of a big closet. Weird hand-brushed writing in black ink covers the interior. Sophia, dressed except for her shoes, sits on a pile of blankets, pillows, and stuffed animals. Aww, they tried to make solitary confinement in a nightmarish cell as sweet as possible.

Her nightgown lay wadded up on top of her shoes near the door.

She stares at me for two seconds, then leaps to her feet and runs into a hug. Sophia's shaking, but surprisingly, doesn't cry. She whimpers a little, but appears frightened of making too much noise.

"Shh," I whisper. "Stay quiet until we're out of here."

"'Kay."

Sophia hurriedly slips her shoes on while I stuff her nightgown into my purse.

"The words and stuff on the walls were glowing blue, but went dark."

I take her hand and lead the way to the only door. "Probably when I put the key in."

Hall's still clear, so I hurry out, a little less concerned at being quiet. Jacob's gun ought to be keeping the rose bushes out back company, so running away is now a viable option. I'm feeling pretty hopeful—until we reach the corner out in the hall.

Katy and Jacob come around the other corner at the opposite side of the house roughly the same time we do. Crap! They must have sensed the ward on the cell shut down. Jacob's a step behind Katy. She and I are equidistant from the stairs to the first floor in the middle of the house. Like a scene out of an Old West movie, we have a staredown. I could hear a pin drop on carpet. Or a tiny kitten's hiss.

Which Klepto obligingly provides.

Jacob stuffs his hand in his suit jacket pocket and makes a constipated face.

Hah. No gun for you. Step left.

Confident I can outrun a woman in high heels, I sprint for the stairs. Sophia's shorter stride isn't a noticeable problem as fear has lit a bonfire under her butt. For a second, I appear to be winning the race against Katy.

Then the bitch cheats.

She jumps forward like a bad movie edit, instantaneously going from like fifty feet away to standing at the top of the stairs ready to jiu-jitsu me into another pretzel. Annoyed at the loss of his pistol, but undeterred, Jacob stomps toward us with intent to grab.

Klepto appears in a flash, hanging on Katy's face.

She screams

I capitalize on the furry blindfold and body check her down the stairs. Klepto disappears, not wanting to go tumbling with her. The woman only falls for two seconds before swooping back up to her feet like a movie going in reverse. Crap! I dodge around her and keep running, launching myself into a fully committed knee-to-groin strike on Jacob.

"Oof." He wheezes and crumples to the floor in a ball, grabbing Sophia's ankle as we go by. She trips forward, hanging by my grip of her hand, but quickly kicks her leg free and scrambles upright.

"We're running away from the stairs," yells Sophia.

"I know." I dart around the corner the dynamic duo came from and start peeking in doors. "Maybe there's a servant's stair."

Sitting room. Bathroom. Library. Another sitting room. Study. Den. Grr!

The double doors at the end of the hallway open to a room mirroring the one where I found Sophia, only it doesn't have a warded vault cell—and has much bigger windows. Six beautiful floor-to-ceiling windows of paned glass offer a lovely view of the countryside surrounding the manor. Alas, they also let in a buttload of sunlight. It's later in the afternoon, so it doesn't make me cringe too badly. Only about as much as a Will Farrell movie.

A bell jar between two windows contains a statue of a weird little creature. It's humanoid, about the size of a toddler, with a slightly oversized head, large all-black eyes, pointed elfish ears, and androgynous childish features. The doll's outfit is part medieval peasant, part jester's costume, and part flower—like the poor kid in the school play who got stuck being a daisy. Though it's adorable, I can't help but feel an underlying malevolence behind the cuteness. Basically, it's a standard two-year-old. Probably silicon. Little guy—or girl—looks really lifelike.

"Screw it. We're only ten feet up. Let's jump." I run to the nearest window, looking for a way to open it, but stop short upon realizing the windows have bars. Seriously? What the hell is wrong with these people?

The door slaps open.

I spin, ready to go declawed wildcat all over them—but Jacob's pointing a shotgun at me.

My fault. I should have been more specific in my request of the fuzzball and asked her to remove all lethal weapons from the house. His face is beet red, and the look he's giving me says he's highly tempted to pay me back for the ball shot with buck shot.

"There's no need to make this needlessly difficult," says Katy. She plucks a pair of handcuffs out of her purse.

"It's already become so." Jacob grumbles.

Katy mumbles something in a foreign language and ninja-star throws the cuffs at Sophia, aiming low for her ankles. The restraint accelerates into a literal projectile, surrounded by an aura of white light.

"No!" yells Sophia, crossing her arms in front of her face.

The handcuff-missile bounces off something invisible a few feet in front of her, ricocheting to the side and smashing the bell jar over the weird doll before embedding in the wall, charring the wallpaper.

Sophia gasps.

Both Katy's eyebrows go up. "Little brat. That was expensive."

"So why'd you break it?" snaps Sophia in an uncharacteristically snotty voice.

Katy gasps. "Cheeky little thing, aren't ya?"

Klepto appears clinging to Jacob's backside, but only for an instant. The kitten—and his pants—vanish.

He's wearing boxers now.

"Speaking of cheeky," I say.

"Aha!" Jacob grins, aiming at me. "Your little fur demon got the trousers again, but I expected it this time. We'll not be having a repeat. The little terror comes near me one more time and your big sister's going to need a new head."

Sophia's cheeks go pale.

Klepto huffs.

"Well, I suppose we can put them both in the warded vault since we'll have to redo the damn incantations anyway," mutters Katy.

Tiny claw marks on her forehead and cheeks would've made me laugh if I didn't have a shotgun trained on me. "If it's such a pain to replace the spells after opening the door, how did you plan to feed her?"

"There's a hatch," says Jacob.

"Oh. Is that how the kitten got out last time?" I glance at Sophia.

"No. She poofed before they energized the wards."

Jacob edges closer, a manic glint in his eyes as he puts the tip of the shotgun barrel within two feet of my cheek. "Now, little girl... collect your demonic fuzzball. We're not going to hurt it, merely stick it in a jar so the three of you all stay where you're supposed to be. Katy, be a dear and fetch a warded vessel."

Umm, cat? Now would be an awesome time to steal his shotgun. Maybe she's worried he'll blow my head off if she appears on top of it. Yeah, I kind of am, too. On second thought, now is *not* a good time to steal the shotgun.

Sophia clenches her hands in fists, stomps, and lets out a shriek loud enough to make my brain vibrate inside my skull. Jacob's eyes cross and his aim falters a little—but not enough for me to risk moving.

My kid sister continues shrieking well past an ordinary ten-year-old's lung capacity.

Katy clamps her hands over her ears. Even Klepto's giving her a 'knock it off' stare.

Sophia thrusts her arms out to either side, her scream cutting off the instant her hands are as far apart as they can get. All the windows go dark.

The red light in my eyes as I come online appears as a brief flash on Jacob's face.

He glances sideways at the windows. "Remarkable…"

"Did she just turn off the sun?" asks Katy.

"It appears so." Jacob goes wide-eyed like a thrilled little boy watching a magic trick.

"To what end?" Katy scratches her head.

Sophia grins. "Oh… you'll see."

The girl's as innocent as it gets, but wow did she sound creepy as hell.

"I'm not normally a violent person," I say. "But you guys kidnapped my little sister."

Katy and Jacob stand statue still, stuck in normal human time as I accelerate myself and zip up to him. Like plucking a prop out of the hands of a mannequin, I grab the shotgun and bend it into a U shape. Some wood and plastic parts break off and fall to the rug.

He jumps back. "My dear, it appears she *is* a vampire… or something."

I toss the ruined shotgun aside. "Behold the power of a motivated Gen-Z'er."

Katy runs at me, attempting some kind of jiu-jitsu grab.

My supernatural speed makes it relatively easy to lean around her reaching arms and rabbit-punch her in the forehead. It's more difficult for me to resist hammering her with all my strength than it is to avoid her attack. Yeah, I'm pissed, but dammit, killing still feels wrong.

The woman flies over backward, the force of my punch throwing her off her feet. She hits the floor in a stupor, making fish-out-of-water expressions at the ceiling. I stalk up to her, intent on doing a little brain surgery. With telepathy, not claws. Honest.

"See," says Sophia.

Jacob grabs an amulet under his vest, raises his left hand, and starts to chant something in maybe Latin or Arabic.

My sister's 'I win' expression melts to a look of worry. She yells, "Counterspell!" and dashes at him, trying to kick his balls up into his throat.

He catches her ankle, blocking the kick, and doesn't let go. "Uh-uh-uh." He wags a finger at her. "Naughty, naughty. That's not going to work."

She balances on one foot, narrowing her eyes in defiance. "Still stopped you from doing magic, didn't I?"

Katy mumbles incoherently and grabs her forehead in both hands.

I turn toward Jacob, extending my claws and holding my hands up so he can see them. "Let go of my sister. Mine are a lot sharper than the kitten's. There's no need for this to get needlessly complicated."

"Hey, that's my line," mumbles Katy, sounding dazed.

Jacob looks at me.

The instant he makes eye contact, I dive in. Ooh! Goody. I guess The Serene Lodge doesn't believe in magic rings. He's on the express train to Derpville, staring into space while I implant a deep compulsion to leave Sophia alone. By the time I'm done with him, he'll sooner light himself on fire than inconvenience her by getting in front of her in line at Starbucks.

"Umm, Sare?" asks Sophia. "Can you please make him let go of my leg?"

204 | AN INTRODUCTION TO PARANORMAL DIPLOMACY

A small mental poke does so.

She backs away from him. "What are you gonna do to them?"

"Only make them leave you alone."

Sophia slouches in relief.

I grab Katy off the floor and throw her onto the largest of the three sofas in here. She, too gets a mental command to steer clear of my sister. Since I am resisting the urge to vent my frustrations in violent ways, the command takes on a dangerous level of potency. The woman might jump into traffic to stay away from her. I'm not too worried, though. Odds are low we'll see them again. It's tempting to do something more vengeful like stuff them in a cage downstairs, but meh. Not worth the time. Mental control is enough of a leash. They're out of my hair for good.

Damn, it's good to be a gangster. Or something.

"Umm, Sare?" asks Sophia in a timid voice.

"What? Is my fly open?"

"No."

I check my hands. Didn't forget to put my claws away. "What?"

She points. "Look."

My gaze follows her finger to the smashed bell jar. The strange little figure is missing.

"What happened to the doll?" whispers Sophia.

"No idea."

My sister creeps up to the wooden disc surrounded in bits of broken glass, careful not to step on any. "I'm feeling a *ton* of magic here." She eyes the still-smoking cuffs in the wall at her eye level. "She carries handcuffs in her purse. Who does that?"

"The same sort of people who have a full medieval torture setup in their basement."

"What?" She blinks at me. "Are you serious?"

"Yeah. But I don't think they use it on anyone. More for spiritual energy in their magic."

She hurries over to me. "Oh. Creepy. Let's get out of here."

"I couldn't agree more." I take her hand and look at the window. "Wow... you're getting scary powerful."

Sophia strolls along beside me down the corridor. "Not really. I only made a bubble of dark over the house. I didn't like change actual time or anything."

"Mew." Klepto appears on Sophia's shoulder and starts purring.

"Wait a sec. These two made me go out in the sunlight. They owe me an idiot tax."

"You're going to bite them, aren't you?" asks Sophia.

"Yep. Be right back."

23

A SQUISHY ULTIMATUM

U ber to the rescue for the second time.

Charging rides to Mom's account bothers me less than stealing a car or doing something even worse like attempting to drive in England. I'd totally get into a head-on collision within five minutes, or spend two hours trapped in a traffic circle. Exactly how are those things supposed to work anyway?

I'm not worried about Katy or Jacob coming after us, so we wait on the street outside their gate for a ride. Sophia's bit of magic isn't *too* obvious. I mean, it's perfectly reasonable to see a giant dome of blackness over an estate, right? Good thing this house is a bit removed from the city.

Another bit of good news: my phone works. Once we went outside, I got signal back. I texted the parents to let them know Sophia's okay… and admitted guilt finally got the better of me enough to possibly consider letting her help the mystics as long as it's not too dangerous.

Mom started typing a long response. Dad sent ‹wear a headband›. Mom's response stalled. I picture them arguing now.

Our Uber shows up a few minutes later, the same time Mom sends ‹Call me.›

Uh oh. If it takes her four minutes to type 'call me,' it's time to throw my iPhone into the ocean. Seriously, though. I am not the kind of girl who can blow off her parents, especially when we're stranded in a foreign country.

Hi, I'm Sarah, and I have a guilt management problem.

This Uber driver isn't a probably gay young man with a sunny disposition and a great sense of humor. We've gotten a slightly more urban version of Latrine, the witch from *Men in Tights*. I'm mostly shocked she doesn't have a six-pack of beer in the passenger seat. Seriously, this woman's like a rail-thin old babushka who's into recreational exposure to high voltage. I've never seen eyes so wide before, and her hair... all the Aquanet ever used in the 1980s couldn't tame it.

I send a quick <can't, in car. Will call asap> to Mom, and get in. Sophia takes the back seat.

We have a pleasant conversation on the ride into London.

Okay, I'm exaggerating a bit. It's not entirely pleasant, and it's not exactly a conversation.

Conversation implies more than one person talks. 'Latrine' spends the entire ride rambling—in a heavy accent—about Northern Ireland, something about Catholics, and Brexit. Apparently, the IRA is ready to go 'to the next level' and she's all for it. My sense of self-preservation keeps me nodding along. To be fair, she didn't do *all* the talking. Over the course of a forty minute ride, I did say 'not really sure, I'm from America' once. I think she's 'educating' me about the reality of the situation 'they' don't bother teaching young people over in the States. Her accent, like I said, is on the thick side. She could as easily be giving me instructions for skinning eels as outlining her political manifesto.

Fortunately, she's animated but not aggressive.

Grateful to get away from her, I jump out of the car as soon as we stop in front of the bookstore. "Thanks for the ride." I'd make a pithy comment about the IRA, but I wouldn't want my joke to bomb.

Asher's standing behind the bookstore counter like an employee. He looks up when we walk in. "Sarah! We've found—"

"Hi," says Sophia, trailing behind me.

"Your sister." Asher blinks.

I approach the counter, steel myself, and look him in the eye. "Is everyone still alive?"

"Aye. For now."

"If you can tell me honestly she's not going to be in a ridiculous amount of danger, we'll help."

Asher stands there in silent shock. A subtle shift in his posture—relaxation—along with a hard breath leaving his nostrils makes me feel like a doctor delivering good news.

Sophia sidles up beside me. "I can handle a little danger. Just not a ridiculous level. This won't involve five-headed dragon tarantulas, right?"

"Do I even want to know?" asks Asher.

"No," my sister and I reply simultaneously.

"Thank you." Asher bows. "I would not have proceeded in bringing her here if I thought stopping Fletcher Maltby presented any serious risks to her. The same enchantment fragments from the broken soul jar responsible for his being vulnerable to her work in reverse. It is difficult for him to act directly against her, verging on impossible. The act of trapping a spirit in a jar is perhaps the closest thing magically possible to complete control over another sentient being. As the original creator of the jar is long since dead, Sophia inherited its control over Maltby upon rupturing it."

"What about another pigeon-to-window-washer-to-car-to-lamppost-to-coffee burn situation? Does this jar thing protect her from crazy coincidences?"

"Unfortunately not as much. Indirect actions wouldn't be complicated by the enchantment. However, such risks can be mitigated by situational awareness. Also, someone with your reflexes would have a trivial time pulling her out of harm's way."

I fold my arms. "Provided we do this at night."

"Of course. We're aiming to confront a spirit." Asher walks out from behind the counter. He locks the door, hanging a 'ring bell for service' sign before leading us to the back room.

"Ghosts aren't vampires. Nothing forces them to hide during the day," I say, walking after him.

"Of course not. The night merely has fewer witnesses." He smiles. "Mind if I ask what happened with Sophia? Our divination sensed her as if she popped out of an alternate dimension."

"I kinda did." Sophia takes the basement stairs slow, clinging to the railing. "Warded cell."

"What?" Asher opens his mouth again, but can't think of anything else to say fast enough.

"You ever hear of The Serene Lodge?" I ask.

"Oh, those wankers," calls Keval Patel, from the other room. "Yeah. We've heard of them."

Asher suppresses an eye roll. "We are not the only order of mystics. The Aurora Aurea is but one of many. The Lodge, alas, has been in conflict with us for some years. Ever since Crowley went stark raving mad."

"Crowley or Corley?" I scratch my head.

"Crowley. As in Alastair." Asher walks into the large room where Sophia and I first appeared after being vacuumed up by her closet. "The Aurora Aurea predates his Golden Dawn sect by several centuries. We had, by and large, kept near perfect secrecy until he decided to attempt bringing magic into the public consciousness."

Anna Riordan groans. "The man was addled."

"Yeah... I've heard he basically tried to have as many women as possible in some kinda..." I'm not going to say 'orgiastic sex cult' in front of Sophia. "Cult."

"There is some truth in what you say." Asher nods once. "But he wasn't as depraved as most people believe. Mystics from multiple orders decided it best to keep the public unaware of magic. Via memory-altering spells, misinformation, and doctored documents, they created an embellished fiction to highlight his less than savory proclivities and make him sound like a lunatic. Most who witnessed his actual magic soon regarded him as a charlatan no more talented than a tarot card reader only interested in libertine debauchery."

Wing Tang hurries over. He smiles enthusiastically at Sophia before looking at me. "The daughter of a Serene Lodge stakeholder became involved with Crowley, dabbled in things best left alone, and ended up having her soul cast into the Cauldron while a demonic force took her body. She, or should I say her body, spent the rest of its life in an asylum."

"Her name wasn't Charlotte, was it?" I ask.

Sophia gasps.

"No. Olivia or something similar," says Asher. "The Serene Lodge naturally blamed Crowley, and by extension the Golden Dawn, and by further extension the Aurora Aurea—even though we had little to do with each other. Crowley was, at that point, a *former* member, having split off to form his own sect."

"The Serenes are a somewhat darker group than us." Keval cringes, shaking his head as if declining an offer of limburger cheese. "They mostly deal in summoning creatures of darkness. Demons, imps, bog faeries, undead, and so on. Our order is dedicated primarily to the search for knowledge and maintaining balance between the world of the mundane and the other."

Leslie, who still gives off schoolteacher vibes, walks over to add herself to the conversation. "Some ways back, the Serene Lodge fools got it in their 'eads we wanted to become more powerful than them outta some sense of spite. For a while, our respective houses were like a couple neighbors tryin' ta outdo each other with the grandiosity of their garden. Then the business wit' Crowley happened, an' fings got violent."

"Are there more than two of them?" I ask, then explain what happened at the house.

These guys have been wound so tight with fear so long, my description of Klepto attacking Jacob the first time after de-pantsing him has everyone in tears. Keval and Rafi hit the floor. I've never seen anyone literally 'ROFL' before, but wow.

However, when I get to the part of Sophia summoning darkness— by the way, the dome faded out before our Uber showed up—they all stop laughing and stare at her in awe. A discussion ensues. She's apparently potent, but not ridiculously so. Tweens often experience spikes in magical power, especially during moments of heightened emotion (like having an idiot point a shotgun at my face). They're more impressed by her being a 'spontaneous' invoker or 'true mystic,' able to do magic by desiring something to happen without having to follow an established tradition of occultism or complex rituals.

The Seattle mystics already explained this to us. She *can* use rituals if she learns them, but doesn't have to. Rituals are safer for the user and far less tiring, but can take hours to perform and require material components as well as the knowledge of how to do them. Any of Asher's people could have summoned a similar dome of darkness, but it would have taken them like twenty minutes—if they could find the 'spell' to do it.

My kid sister jumps into the magical discussion.

While they start formulating a plan to deal with the spirit she set loose, I wander out of the room to the area by the bottom of the steps for some privacy, and call home. Gotta keep my promise to Mom. She and Dad both hop on the line, as well as Sierra and Sam (who are sharing a phone upstairs in the parents' bedroom). I explain another group of mystics took Sophia not to hurt her, but to keep her sidelined long enough for the spectral killer to finish off the first group of mystics who originally dragged us to London. Oh, and I also mention Sophia talked me into helping them deal with the wraith.

My mother would probably be somewhat *less* upset if I said I'd sold Sophia to the circus and planned to join a group of traveling mimes to spend the rest of my life roaming across Europe. It wouldn't be accurate to categorize our resulting conversation as an argument, more me trying to convince her my initial opinion on the danger to Sophia's life was overstated.

Before Mom completely goes thermonuclear, I blurt the story of Klepto yoinking Jacob's pants and going after 'the mouse.' Dad's having trouble breathing. Mom is horrified Sophia saw a man's junk until I clarify she'd been locked in a vault at the time. Then, she's horrified those two locked Sophia in a vault.

"I'm not sure how long this is going to take. Asher believes Sophia can slap this ghost around like no big deal. Maybe another day or two," I say.

"Good grief, Sarah. Christmas is coming up. You absolutely *must* be home before the twenty-fourth," yells Mom.

"Believe me. I want to be. If, for whatever reason, we're not done by then, I'm going to demand they send us home for Christmas. They wouldn't do it before because they wanted us to help them, but if we promise to come back after..."

Mom exhales.

"You'll probably need to do some mental tinkering at the school so they forget about Sophia missing days," says Dad.

"Jonathan..." Mom pauses. "You really are spending too much time in front of your computer. The kids are on break until after New Year's."

"Oh." Dad chuckles. "Easy then."

"Sare?" yells Sophia from the other room. "C'mere."

I glance at the doorway. "Let me go. Sounds like we're ready to roll. I'll call or text as soon as I have more information."

Mom emits a strangled noise of frustration. "All right, dear. But dammit. The next time you're going to get abducted to a foreign country, you damn well better ask permission first."

"Umm, Mom? You should probably take a nap. It wouldn't be an 'abduction' if I planned to go."

Dad stifles a laugh. "Stay safe, hon."

"Doing my best. Talk to you guys soon." I sigh, hit the end call button, and head back to the ritual room, phone still in hand.

The mystics plus Sophia stand in a group, all looking at me.

"We have a slight problem," says Asher. "Sophia doesn't know how to banish a spirit."

I smirk. "You're shocked? She's ten and hasn't had any real training."

He smiles. "Yes, I understand. We have taught her the means by which she can destroy the spirit, but she refuses to eliminate this abomination despite his evil. She wants to usher him back to the Cauldron."

"The man got eviler from being in the jar," says Sophia. "He should'a gone back to the Cauldron when they hanged him."

"I'm inclined to agree with the child," says Keval. "Souls belong in continuous rotation. To disrupt the process is to defy the very workings of the Universe."

That's me. Girl Disrupted. "What about vampires? My soul's not going anywhere any time soon."

"Delays are not the same thing as destruction." Keval traces a big circle in the air with both hands. "Believe it or not, the soul jar is a more disruptive situation than your vampirism. All living—or unliving—things eventually meet their end. When they do, their souls return to the source. What my dear friend Asher is advocating is a *break* in the cycle, not merely a delay."

"As a result of her interaction with the soul jar, Sophia does have the ability to banish the spirit." Anna pats her on the head. "However, opening spirit doors is not something one often learns so soon along their path. While it might be possible she could stumble across the proper alignment of energies, the chance of her doing something accidental is too high."

I look at my sister. She's wearing the same sort of uneasy smile she did right before asking Mom if Klepto could stay. Her lack of freaking out tells me we're not looking at a 'you have no choice but to destroy him' scenario.

"What's the problem?" I ask. "I sense you're all sneaking up on me with something."

And wow, does this feel strange. It's like being Mom, right before Sophia asked if she could keep the kitten. All these mystics, grown adults except for Mandy—who's my age—are fidgeting about to ask *my* permission.

And I thought becoming a vampire odd.

"He's been punished enough." Sophia widens her cheesy smile. "I hated being locked in the vault for half a day. Even if he was a bad guy, he was stuck in a tiny space alone for hundreds of years. Can we please help him move on?"

"Assuming, of course, it is possible," says Asher.

Sophia looks down. "Yes. If there's no other choice, I'll dispel him. He's already dead. Everyone here is alive. It's wrong to let him kill you."

"Okay, so why is everyone looking at me like you're about to ask me to do something I'm going to say no to? Does this involve selling my sister to the circus?"

A few of them chuckle. Sophia furrows her brow, confused.

"No." Asher smiles. "None of us have the requisite knowledge of spirit doors to pass along to her. There is one who does, an elder mystic out in Gwynedd who should be able to help."

"Spending centuries in a jar is enough punishment," says Sophia. "Well... and being executed."

"Sophia has agreed to help stop Fletcher Maltby, but her price is we accept her decision not to destroy him entirely if at all possible." Wing fidgets. "We are not in any position to argue, so we will do whatever we can to help her accomplish her goal the way she's made up her mind to. As long as the wraith is no longer a threat to us, we don't care if he's destroyed or passed on."

Asher raises a finger. "On the condition the elder is able to give her the necessary teaching. If she does not know the means, is unable to teach her, or refuses, Sophia will do what is necessary."

My sister clasps her hands in front of herself and looks down. "They already showed me the spell to destroy a spirit. It feels icky."

"Hold on." I point at Asher. "Did you guys teach her necromancy?"

"No." Asher ruffles Sophia's hair. "Your sister is such a tender soul, the mere idea of permanent destruction bothers her."

I let a sigh of relief slide out my nostrils. "Yeah. She is a bit squishy."

24

THE OBLIGATORY HERMIT MENTOR

Great. I'm in one of my dad's Eighties movies.

You know the ones, where the hero needs to find some ancient old wizard who lives out at the butt crack end of nowhere? Yeah. It's like that. Why do the people with all the knowledge always live far away from everything? It's almost like once someone figures out how things work, they want nothing to do with other people.

Asher and the other mystics are afraid to leave their bookstore, much less drive the entire width of the British Isle. Theresa Bromfield, said reclusive elder, lives in Gwynedd, which is in Wales. It's something like 200-250 miles away as the crow flies. Only a complete fool would get into a car and attempt to drive such a long distance—much of it on winding country roads—when there's a spirit out there who can kill a person by redirecting pigeons.

I've programmed a navigation point in my phone for a seemingly random spot in the forest southwest of a town called Betwys-y-Coed (sounds like Bet-wiss a coyd) a bit west of the River Conwy. (Asher pronounced it like 'Conooie'.)

Carrying Sophia on my back while flying from dance class to home, no big deal. Going 250 miles, on the other hand, is a bit different. Wing risks his life to run out and pick up a motorcycle helmet in her size. Fortunately, no pianos fell out of the sky and crushed his car on the way. He also bought two harnesses like rock climbers wear, hooking them together with carabiners. Sophia's not only wearing a dress, but a winter coat down to her knees… awkward. However, she doesn't really need to secure the thigh straps. She won't be hanging like dead weight off me. All we need is some added protection against a slip.

As soon as it's dark enough for me to go online, we 'suit up.' I put on the larger harness. Leslie helps Sophia into hers, securing it on over her winter coat. She also gives my sister a pair of mittens and a scarf since we'll be traveling fast and high. Not sure how much help the scarf is since the motorcycle helmet squishes it all the way down off her face. I crouch so they can hook the two carabiners on, then stand.

It's not exactly comfortable on the ground, since Sophia's feet dangle a few inches off the floor. With my vampiric abilities active, her weight is as negligible as a balloon. I'm literally wearing my sister as a backpack. She reaches around and grabs the harness straps in front of me, seeming content. Klepto opts for the safety of a zippered pocket on her coat.

"Okay. Here we go. Wish us luck," I say. "Ready, Soph?"

"Can I say yes *and* no?"

"A totally valid answer." I go out the bookstore's rear door into a narrow alley containing trash cans and stray cats. The only other living things here won't care about seeing people fly. Or at least, won't be able to tell anyone they did.

I zip into the air, borrowing Simone's trick of going straight up to about 1,500 feet before veering laterally. Sophia's weight shifts from hanging to laying on top of me. She squeezes me so tight I'm glad breathing is an illusion. My purse is sitting this one out at the bookstore both to reduce drag as well as stop me from losing it.

My kid sister wearing a motorcycle helmet allows me to go as fast as I can, 143 MPH according to the navigation app on my phone, without risk of hurting her or causing facial frostbite. I'm not too worried about dropping the phone, since at this altitude, I should be able to catch it before it crashes into the ground. A hard dive and swoop might result in Sophia throwing up, but it's much easier to shower than buy a new phone.

Wind racing past us on top of the helmet muting her voice dissuades Sophia from trying to talk in the air. She clings to me, her body stiff, muscles tensed. Maybe twenty minutes into the flight, she relaxes enough to get fidgety. From then on, she keeps repositioning her legs from straight together, around me, and even sorta-riding on my back like I'm a high-end Japanese motorcycle.

A little shy of two hours later, we're above Wales. I slow to a hover when my phone tells me we've arrived at the GPS dot and gaze around at miles and miles of unbroken trees below us. Obviously, a hermetic old mystic's home isn't going to show up on Google Maps. Nothing for me to do but go down there and hunt, so I descend to a couple hundred feet and begin a spiral search pattern. I'm surprised at how close to accurate Asher's coordinates turn out to be. My hyper sensitive eyes pick up a scrap of light in the woods maybe a quarter mile away from where I start.

I stuff the phone in my pocket and head for the glow, gliding down until we're skimming above the treetops.

The light's coming from the window of a small cabin deep in the woods.

"It's so dark here," says Sophia.

"Do you see the window up there?"

"Kinda. Is that the place?"

"How many old witches could possibly live out here?"

She laughs. "Since you asked, there's gonna be a ton of them."

I slow to a hover and sink straight down into the branches until I'm on solid ground. Sophia swishes her legs back and forth, waving her arms and pretending to be stuck to me. Hah. I squat so her feet touch the dirt. She unclamps the carabiners and pulls her helmet off.

"Ack. It's cold," says Sophia, her breath fogging.

"You're just noticing now?"

"The helmet was warm. My face is freezing." She pulls the scarf up to her eyes.

"C'mon." I take her by the hand and hike through the woods toward the cabin.

When we're about a three-car-driveway length away, the door opens, revealing the silhouette of a woman with a long ponytail in a dress. It takes my eyes a second to adjust to the light behind her and lift the shadow from her form. She's gotta be in her seventies, and doesn't look happy to see me. I'm guessing the giant crossbow isn't her usual response to Jehovah's Witnesses or aggressive girl scouts trying to push Samoas and Thin Mints.

"*Mae hynny'n ddigon agos,*" says the woman.

"Uhh, bless you."

"You're close enough." She shuts her left eye, sighting over the bolt at me. "Unless ya want a witchwood quarrel in your heart, don't take another step."

"No," yells Sophia. "Don't shoot her."

The woman appears surprised to hear a child's voice. She looks back and forth around me, squinting. I get the feeling she can't see Sophia. Maybe I'm glowing to her. A flash appears atop the crossbow as Klepto teleports to stand on it, then sits back on her haunches. "Mew."

"What the...?"

Klepto—and the quarrel—vanish.

"I'm not here to harm you. We need your help," I say. "Are you Theresa Bromfield?"

"Aye, but you fiends'll find no help from me this night. Whatever foul reason you've brought a little child here, you heard wrong. I'll not be helpin' ya sacrifice a lamb."

"That's speciesist." I frown. "You're making vast generalizations about the morality and attitude of an entire class of beings."

The woman stares at me like I'm an idiot.

"And Sophia's not here to be sacrificed. I'll rip the head off anyone who tries to hurt her. We've sought you out in hopes you may be able to teach her something." Gah. I've played too much *Skyrim.*

"My sister's not a fiend," says Sophia. "I need to stop a bad spirit from killing more people. I don't want to destroy him. Asher Jones said you can show me how to open a spirit door."

"Asher sent you?" calls Theresa, a note of skepticism in her voice.

"Yes." I approach until we're both standing in the light leaking out the cabin's door. "This is my actual sister. Asher showed her a means to destroy this ghost, but she'd rather help him return to the Cauldron. If you can't or won't help, we'll be on our way."

"Please!" Sophia bounces on her toes. "I don't wanna destroy anyone, even if he is kinda bad."

Tendons in the old woman's neck twitch in response. "Wait there." She goes inside, leaving the door open. A moment later, she returns and throws a small glass bottle to/at me.

I catch it. The more or less spherical flask is about the size of a racquetball, flat on one face, a narrow neck sticking out the opposite side, plugged by a cork. It appears to hold iced tea. Or at least a liquid the same shade of brown. At least it's not whiskey. I'd smell it despite the cork.

"Drink it. Wait five seconds, then say you will not harm me." Theresa fixes me with the sort of stare a teacher would use on misbehaving students, not the least bit afraid.

"What is this? I'm not in the habit of drinking strange potions from friendly forest witches."

Theresa chuckles. "It's a kind of truth spell. Doesn't last long. One or two statements. If ya lie, yer guts'll catch fire. Ya tell the truth, nothin' happens."

Predictably, her mind is closed off to me, so I can't verify.

Sophia lets out a long sigh. "You probably shouldn't drink that. The ghost is mean and already dead. I'd rather be made to destroy him than have something happen to you."

"Relax, child." Theresa continues to stare at me, though her tone loses some hostility. "I do not deceive her as to the nature of the elixir. If she speaks truth, it's no different from water."

I pull the cork out, releasing a scent like herbal mud. Oh, lovely.

This is going to taste horrible. "If you wanted to destroy me, you'd have fired the bolt right away."

"Aye." Theresa folds her arms. "You've the right of it."

"Witchwood works?" I hesitate, the bottle near my lip. "As far as I know, stakes are just annoying."

"Then ya 'aven't been hit with a witchwood one. Got a few skulls of your kind in the cabinet."

Sophia stands protectively in front of me.

I cringe. "We're not all the same. Do you want to kill all humans because some are evil?"

"Not rightly given ta trusting things what consider me food." Theresa gestures at me. "G'won and do it, or take yer leave in peace if ya so choose."

Sophia tugs on my arm.

This woman would have tried to shoot me right away if she wanted to kill me. Maybe she didn't because of the distance, expecting to miss. However, she twitched when Sophia mentioned not wanting to destroy the ghost. Can this woman somehow sense our, umm... 'empathy?' Oh, screw it.

I swig the potion. Gah. It tastes the same as it smells: floral dirt. Blech.

A few seconds after gulping the potion down, it churns in my stomach. We had a kid in my class in high school who made a habit of chugging warm soda so he could belch super loud at pep rallies, assemblies... basically anywhere the entire school (or large crowds) could cheer him on. What's going on inside me now makes me think of how he must have felt in the seconds after downing an entire can of soda in four seconds. I'm either about to burp so loud they'll hear me back in London, or my belly's going to explode like I'm giving birth to the monster from *Alien*.

"I will not harm you," I say.

The storm in my gut lessens. In seconds, all discomfort is gone.

Theresa drops her defensiveness. "All right then, dear. Come in."

I take Sophia by the hand and approach. The place is cozy, consisting of one main room containing a fireplace and sofa on the right, a table on the left near a wood-burning cook stove. A pair of doors—one on either side of the fireplace—are both closed. A tiny hallway leads deeper into the house on the kitchenette side. The place smells of wood smoke and baking pie. I don't see a single bit of modern technology anywhere. Oil lamps as well as the fireplace provide the only light.

She waits for us to walk inside, then closes the door and ushers us over to the table. After fetching tea and some cookies for Sophia, the old one takes a seat. "So, let's hear it. What's going on?"

Between nibbles, Sophia explains how she felt sorry for the ghost, let him out of the soul jar, and now we've we ended up being brought to London against our will. Theresa is surprised to hear her say she *still* wants to help Asher and the others. Admittedly, after Martin's death, I kinda want to stop the ghost, too. Doesn't mean I'm totally cool with being kidnapped across the ocean, but maybe it's possible for me to see it more like a teacher forcing a kid to clean up a mess they made rather than leaving it for the janitor. After the explanation, Sophia demonstrates she has actual talent by summoning a small light.

Apparently trusting the old woman not to shoot me, Klepto reappears holding the witchwood crossbow bolt she stole earlier in her mouth, and drops it on the table. Other than not having a metal tip and being covered by a bunch of tiny carved symbols, the quarrel looks fairly ordinary, if medieval. It's *way* thinner than anything most reasonable people would consider a 'stake.'

"Hmm. Sounds like you've landed in quite the spot." Theresa emits a wheezy grandma-type chuckle despite not being overweight or terribly old. "It is possible to send the spirit across, and whatever justice the universe feels necessary will find him."

Sophia smiles. "Okay."

"Whoa…" I blink. "Like Hell?"

"No, child. If he is truly run afoul, he'll come back as a cockroach, dung beetle, flea… or perhaps one of those people who go door-to-door selling religion."

Sophia's eyes widen. "Or even a telemarketer?"

"I'm not sure what that is," says Theresa.

"Not worth the explanation."

"Umm." Sophia shrugs. "My parents think they're evil."

Theresa glances at me. "Forgive me for referring to you as 'child.' It's easy to forget how old you are."

"I'm not old. Haven't been a vampire a year yet. I really am the age I appear to be."

"Such a tragedy for the fiends to take a girl as young as you." Theresa sighs. "You have my sympathies."

"I'm eighteen, not fourteen." I force myself not to frown.

"Bah. Four years? Either one's a baby to me." She shifts her attention to Sophia. "Come, little one. I'll show you what you need to know."

Sophia follows Theresa over to the hearth. They sit on the floor in front of the fireplace, discussing the arrangement of the physical world to the spirit world and how magic can open pathways between them. A banishing of the type Sophia wants to perform requires a focused gateway permitting only one-way travel. Doing the magic wrong can easily result in a door any number of spirits might come flying out of. Theresa goes into an explanation of how to manipulate the energy responsible for separating the two worlds. Once their conversation passes the forty-minute mark, they both begin making strange, ghostly light orbs appear and glide around.

I stay at the table, giving them distance. All this mystical stuff goes right over my head. Even though I'm literally seeing it work, it *sounds* as out there and ridiculous as horoscopes. Considering my kid sister summoned a 1,000-foot-sphere of darkness earlier this afternoon, watching her create tiny spirit orbs shouldn't even register as odd.

Yeah... my life really has 'gone to plaid.'

STRAIGHT AS THE SISTER FLIES

A pparently, learning how to create gateways across the interstitial space between dimensions requires more than a few minutes of practice. A quick training montage set to gripping rock music won't do the trick.

Who'd have thought?

If Theresa Bromfield didn't trust me yet, she's gotta trust me the next day after I spent the morning and early afternoon helpless in her root cellar. Sleeping in someone's house—or under it—is the vampire equivalent of a cat showing you their stomach. Considering I woke up again, good chance it's safe for me to trust her. She doesn't seem like the sort of forest witch who'd want to bake Sophia into a pie.

I awake to a dirt ceiling and a spirit orb floating above me. It's pale blue, five inches around, and contains a spectral hamster. Even though he's monochromatic blue rather than brown-and-white, I recognize Wilbur.

"Willie?" I try to pet him, but he's merely an image. Unlike Klepto, he's also apparently still a hundred percent hammie and can't understand English. "What are you doing here?"

The spirit hamster sniffs at me, then perches up on his hind legs the way he used to do when begging for treats. A moment later, he fades away. Either I'm hallucinating, or there's been some mishaps with ghost doorways while I slept.

I stand, brush the dirt off my clothes, and think about taking a shower since I've been stuck in the same clothes for days. Something tells me a bath out here would involve water so cold even a vampire would shriek. I head up the little stairway to the wooden board over the hole, giving it a nudge to check the nuclear-ness of the outside world. The day is delightfully gloomy, so I push the board open the rest of the way and climb out.

Despite not really wanting to be out here in the land time forgot and worrying about Sophia chasing down a dangerous spirit, I find myself taking in the wet-earth smell of recent rain and the overwhelming presence of the forest. It makes me want to go home even more. Dad found a word online a while ago: 'petrichor.' He said it's the name of the smell left in the air after rain, and wants desperately to be able to use it in conversation.

Heh. I smile to myself, thinking this is the perfect opportunity to set him up to take the shot.

Right. Gotta get home first. Preferably *before* Christmas Eve.

Theresa and Sophia are still working on magic stuff when I walk into the cabin, though they're at the table rather than on the floor by the fireplace. Theresa is surprised to see me.

So surprised, in fact, she screams.

Sophia screams in reaction to her, much higher pitched and about a tenth the duration.

"Aaah," I deadpan.

Theresa gawks at me. Sophia presses a hand to her chest, giving the old one a 'why did you do that?' stare.

"I realize teenagers can be scary in the morning, but I've never made someone scream in terror before." Technically true. Lucy *wanted* to scream when she saw me floating outside her window, but I derp-slapped her before she could.

"Why are you awake?" rasps Theresa.

"Because it's a little after 2:30 and I'm not recovering from a brutal beating." I check my phone. Sure enough, 2:48. A little later than usual. Guess I'm tired from being out in the sun.

"But it's still daylight out…" Theresa narrows her eyes at me. "And your aura is gone."

"I have an aura?"

"Not in the traditional sense. Supernatural beings stand out to me." She gets out of her chair and tentatively approaches. "Oh, you are still alight, but much dimmer."

"Remember me saying not all vamps are the same? Yeah. Hi."

After a brief explanation of the Innocent bloodline, magic school resumes.

I sit there watching, waiting for dark while Sophia attends Hagwarts.

Nah, Theresa isn't ugly or ill-tempered. But she's an old woman teaching magic, so the pun happened. Thanks, Dad. Bad enough he passed along his stick-figure genes, I've got to deal with a predisposition to puns.

Much to my surprise, the sun goes down at 3:43 p.m. Sure it's rainy today but wow, it's early for darkness. I bet there's a boatload of vampires in an area with such long periods of darkness. No wonder she had a crossbow ready and recognized me so fast. Anyway, a couple hours later, it sounds like my sister has the hang of banishing spirits. Over the course of eavesdropping, I've learned Theresa is like her, able to use magic without the requirement of doing rituals.

No 'go seek knowledge from the wise old hermit' quest would be complete without a fetch quest. True to form, Theresa asks me to pick up some groceries for her from the nearby town, saving her the hike.

Least I can do.

At least it doesn't involve killing six-dozen kobolds.

Sophia remains at the cabin to eat dinner with Theresa while I fly northeast to the village to buy the items on her list. It's all ordinary foodstuffs, though navigating a Welsh grocery store is perhaps harder than killing a small army of kobolds. I get trapped in the aisles like the forest in the original Zelda video game where you can walk endlessly while going nowhere. Fortunately, the store doesn't have random monsters trying to kill me. Merely a creepy bearded guy who follows me around staring at my ass. Eww. He's gotta be past sixty and he thinks I'm hot.

As much as I'm afraid to, I dig into his head. If he's a threat to young girls, I can't just leave him be. Fortunately, he's content to look from afar and has no desire to assault anyone. Doesn't mean I need to put up with him stalking me either, so he gets a prod to go home.

By the time I fly back to the cabin with the groceries, dinner is finished. Sophia runs to grab her coat as I set the bags on the table.

"Thank you, child," says Theresa. "Would have taken me a whole day to run up there and back."

"No problem. Thanks for helping Sophia."

My sister hurries over to me, fumbling to start the zipper on her coat. "Yes. Thank you!"

"If you happen to find yourself in Wales again, I'd love to have you visit." She smiles at us—mostly Sophia.

"Do you use Facebook?" asks Sophia.

"No, dear. I'm not a necromancer."

I cackle.

Theresa glances at me.

"It's a website, not magic," says Sophia.

"Not a fan of spiders." Theresa winks.

Okay, now I know she's teasing us.

"If we ever do happen to be in the area again, we'll stop by."

Theresa smiles and gets started putting the groceries away. I pull on my harness, help Sophia into hers, and head outside. She clips on, stuffs the helmet down over her head, and reaches around in front of me to grab my harness straps.

"Okay. Ready."

Every vampire in Seattle would laugh at me for turning myself into a flying mount. Except Stefano. He'd call me something nasty. Whatever. We leap into the air at 5:07 p.m. and land near the bookstore at 6:52 p.m. Heck of a commute, especially considering how fast I can fly compared to cars. At least up here I don't have to deal with traffic lights or random strangers trying to wash my face if we stop. By the time we land, a thin crust of ice has formed on my chest and legs, as well as Sophia's helmet. I hurry inside, happy to find all the mystics still alive.

They help Sophia warm up with some hot cocoa and set to the task of discussing our next move. Considering we're back in civilization where cellular reception actually exists, I catch up on a bunch of texts. Ashley's pestering me to hurry up and get home because she wants me to go Christmas shopping with her. The 'rents are coping, happy to hear things here are still under control.

"Excellent," says Asher, in response to something going on in the ritual room. "Looks like everything is in place."

I hop off the chair and hurry over there.

The mystics crowd around Sophia, who's cradling a grape-sized blue light orb above her hands. A brighter spot marks the upper right side of the sphere.

"Aye, brilliant," says Mandy. "But it'll be a ballache ta drive 'round after et."

"What's up?" I ask.

"It's a pointer." Sophia grins at me. "Shows me which way to go to find the ghost."

Asher brushes some manner of silvery powder off his hands. "We came up with a means for her to sense Fletcher's presence using the link she established with him when she broke the seal of the soul jar. Think of it as a three-dimensional compass. If you imagine a line from the center of the orb out through the white spot, it points at the spirit."

"No way ta tell 'ow far, though," says Mandy. "Stickin ta' roads gonna be a right pain."

I twirl a strand of hair around my finger innocently. "Roads aren't going to be a problem."

"Aye, not fer ya." She looks around. "Yer not gonna be carryin' the lot of us on yer back, though?"

"She doesn't need to. There isn't much we'll be able to accomplish."

Asher grasps Sophia's shoulders, bowing his head. "I am sorry we brought you here without warning or even asking first. That you are still willing to help us says much of what kind of person you are. Thank you."

"It's okay. I don't want him to hurt anyone else." Sophia releases the tracking spell. The orb dissipates into a luminous blue fog, blowing around her as she walks through it to get her coat. "We'll find him."

"The best thing we can do," says Asher, "Is to go home. If we're outside the wards here, it will tempt him to show himself. Except Mandy. You stay inside the sanctum."

She nods.

Wow, no protest? The girl must be terrified. Great. Now I feel even worse for trying to drag Sophia home and leaving these mystics to their fate.

"One question." I hold up a hand. "How hard is this guy going to be to find?"

"Not hard." Sophia tugs on my harness so I crouch a little, allowing her to clip on. "They said I'll be able to see him because of the soul jar stuff. He'll probably remember me, so I'm going to talk to him. If he *wants* to go back to the Cauldron, it's gonna be real easy. All I gotta do is open a door."

"What if he doesn't want to go?" I ask.

She grimaces. "It won't be as easy."

"Obviously."

"Umm, well… if he *doesn't* want to go, I'll have'ta open the door then try to stuff him through it."

I shrug. "Doesn't sound too difficult."

"Ghosts are slippery. And while I'm trying to squeeze him into the doorway, he might do bad stuff like make cars try to hit me or throw rocks."

"Or pigeons," says Mandy.

"S'okay. I won't let anything hit you."

She reaches around and grabs my harness, then whispers, "I know.

You being here to protect me is a big reason I said yes to helping them."

"All right." I stand, lifting her off her feet. "Might as well deal with this ghost. No time like the present."

STUPID WHITE CRAP FALLING FROM THE SKY

Naturally, the weather decides to cooperate.

I'd say 'at least it's not raining,' but it's doing worse: snowing. One good thing about the proto-blizzard slamming London at the moment: it keeps people focused on the mess at ground level. Sophia and I spend the first few minutes in the air arguing over pants. As in, I think she's going to freeze flying around in a dress and we should get her jeans. She's fine with the dress and doesn't want to waste time shopping.

Given the lack of visibility in the air, I don't need to go up as high to avoid people seeing us. Sophia's more comfortable, even though a fall from 200 feet would still be deadly. This altitude makes *me* more nervous because if the harness slips off and she falls, I have less time to react and catch her than if we'd been at 1,500 feet. If she had jeans on, we could have secured the thigh straps. No chance of her slipping out then.

Grr.

Once we're cruising and I'm horizontal so she can lay on top of me, she lets go of the harness over my chest, bracing her elbows against my back and conjuring the pointer. Even wearing a puffy winter coat, her little bony elbows are like daggers.

"Turn left... bit more. Bit more. Wait. Stop. Back to the right. Stop!"

I slow to a hover.

"No, I meant stop turning, not stop flying." She points. "Go that way."

"Are you going to be able to see him from up here?"

"Not past all this snow, but the compass is a ball. When it points down, I'll know he's close." She points to the right. "Over there, now."

I turn.

We fly a few minutes before Sophia yells. "Eight o'clock. He just went way off to the side. Maybe we passed over him."

I swing a left turn.

"Straight," says Sophia. "I'm pretty sure I can convince him to move on."

"What if he doesn't want to? He didn't seem too talkative last time."

"Umm. Theresa showed me how I can push him into the gateway. It's much harder, but I can probably do it... only 'cause the jar thing. Like, any other ghost I probably couldn't since I'm too new."

I'd question why the ghost left her alone if she has so much power over him, but undead serial killers tortured for several centuries probably aren't the most rational minds. But if Asher's right, maybe he *can't* do anything to her, at least not directly. Makes sense why he'd have left her alone then.

She points again. We turn.

For the better part of an hour, I feel like a giant drunken moth chasing a candle taped to another drunken moth. We zig-zag back and forth across London. My clothes are soaked from snow and my hair's developing ice patches. Either her spell is seriously confused, or the ghost is teleporting around.

"Are you sure that compass works?" I yell over the wind.

"Yes. I think he's moving. Most of the mystics left the safety of the wards at the same time. Mr. Maltby is like a big guy with no self-control at a buffet. Doesn't know what to grab first and wants to eat everything at once."

I chuckle.

"Nine o'clock!" yells Sophia.

I veer left, pulling out of the turn when she thrusts her arm past my head, pointing.

Not sure which direction we're going. The snow makes it impossible for me to see much but a blurry glow from ground-level lights. Hope builds as we keep going straight for way longer than he stayed in one place before. I fly faster, trusting we're getting somewhere at last. Also, I'm worried. If the ghost has stopped bouncing around, he must have chosen a victim.

A few minutes later, Sophia yells, "Stop!"

I metaphorically slam on the brakes.

Sophia lurches forward. Fortunately, I have the reflexes to duck before her helmet cracks me in the back of the skull.

"Ugh. We went past. Dot's pointing down," wheezes Sophia.

"Sorry. Stopped a bit hard."

"Yeah..."

I swing around and ease into free fall. Sophia squeals in alarm, so I slow a bit, allowing her weight to settle against me.

"Keep going down. Bit to the right. More... okay, we're on top of him!"

We dive through the snow; for a brief moment, we're falling at the same speed as the flakes, which looks super bizarre. Imagine a pillow exploding into fluff in zero-G. All these little white things hanging in space around me, neither falling nor going up. The ground comes into view, so I slow, letting the suspended ice crystals pull ahead.

The ghost has gone after one of the mystics who lives outside the city. No damn idea where we are as far as a map goes, but it's a modest house with a good amount of land around it. A few lights inside give away someone being home.

I land about fifteen feet from the front porch, up to my ankles in snow. It's still coming down pretty hard. I do a slow turn, gazing around us at lots of white stuff, a fence, trees coated in ice, and a small SUV not as covered as everything else. Someone recently drove it. Sophia unclips the two carabiners joining our harnesses and drops to her feet. Klepto's little grey head pokes out the neck of her winter coat, below her chin.

My sister lifts her helmet's visor, looking around. "It's really dark."

As if on cue, three lights on the house turn on, illuminating the front yard.

The door opens.

Leslie Elliot steps out onto the porch, approaching the steps. "What're you two doin' 'ere?"

"Umm..." I say. "Following the—"

A phantasmal blur manifests in the doorway and rushes at Leslie from behind. I launch myself toward her, the world around me seeming to descend into slow motion as my reflexes speed up. The woman's feet shoot out from under her, yanked by the passing ghost. His tortured face leers at me for an instant before he swerves away and streaks off to the right. Leslie hangs in midair, creeping downward, drifting forward. I picture it happening before it does. Her head is going to hit the second step from the bottom. Icy bricks. Broken neck or cracked open skull.

I dive into flight, accelerating as much as I can in such a short distance—and cruise into the porch with a meaty *smack*.

Good news: Leslie lands on top of me, *not* bashing open her head.

Bad news: I hit the bricks so hard, *my* neck broke.

No big deal. Nothing I can't walk off.

Leslie slides off me into the snow, screaming from the fall.

No reason for me to move just yet.

"Cripes! Bugger's 'ere isn't he? Bastard came for me." Leslie grabs my arm. "Good on ya for gettin' 'ere in time." She pulls me up, notices my head swaying around like a bowling ball in a plastic shopping bag, screams, then bursts into tears.

"Chill out. I'm fine."

She screams again... and faints.

"Hey, wait!" yells Sophia. "I wanna talk!"

Rapid crunching of small feet in snow trails off into the distance.

Dammit. I grab a fistful of my hair in my left hand, holding my head upright. Seems I've suffered a pretty bad break. My neck is like jelly. Doing a kamikaze into a brick porch probably wasn't the best way to go about saving this woman's life, but it's a bit late for regrets. Flying into *her* at full speed wouldn't have ended well either. Maybe the ghost tried to trick me into doing it since he seems to like complicated deaths. Simply pushing the woman down icy stairs is awfully basic for him.

Sophia runs across the field toward the woods, shouting at the spirit to wait for her.

Leslie comes to and looks at me as if about to scream again.

"Seriously, relax. I'm fine," I wheeze.

"You don't look fine, luv. Are you… holding your head up in your hand?"

"Yeah. I'll be okay in about twenty minutes."

"Cripes. I can't even look at ya."

I extend my fangs. "Does this help?"

She glances over. "Gah! Why would you ask me if that helps? Cripes, no!"

"Oh. Sorry." I retract them. "Thought it might make me seem a bit more paranormal than a teenage girl with a broken neck, not be so disturbing."

"Cripes," wheezes Leslie. "Yer gonna give me a coronary."

"Please yell to Sophia not to run into the woods. I'm stuck rasping until my throat mends."

Leslie stands. "Oy, lass. C'mon back 'ere. Don't ya run off alone."

A moment passes.

"Don't see 'er." Leslie pauses, then yells, "Sophia? C'mon back ta the 'ouse."

I try to sigh, but produce a noise more like boiling jelly. Scott ran around after I tore his head completely off his body, and he wasn't even a full vampire. An internal decapitation shouldn't slow me down. I wobble to my feet.

"Where are you goin'? Yer head's not on straight."

"Can't leave Sophia alone."

"What are you gonna do if something's out there? Yer head'll be floppin inta yer chest. Sit tight. I'll go."

"The spirit's after you. It's a bad idea for *you* to run off into the woods at night in a snowstorm."

"Sophia?" shouts Leslie. "Oy, luv, where are ya?"

Silence worries and relieves me. If something bad happened, she'd have screamed. But, Sophia should also be answering us. Grr. I start walking, still holding my head up by hand. Leslie follows. Dumb of me to get into a fight with a Jell-O neck. Dumb of her to do anything until the ghost is dealt with. Does two people doing a half-witted thing make for a full wit, or does the multiplicative property of dumbassery mean we're only worth a quarter-wit?

The pair of us going off into the woods feels about as smart as a guy using a torch to investigate a natural gas leak at night. At least he'll be damn sure if he finds it—for a thousandth of a second. Snow might be a pain in the ass, but it does make it super easy to follow my sister. Less so once we're in the trees, but enough of a dusting reached the ground for a trail of footprints to continue.

A high-pitched scream comes from the forest up ahead.

"Oh, shit." I break into a run.

27

ELDER MAGIC

Running while supporting the weight of my head in my hand is a bizarre sensation.

All sorts of squishing goes on in places that shouldn't be squishing. I don't think about it much, too focused on getting to Sophia. Her screaming grows faint as though she rushed away at high speed.

"Where did ya go?" calls Leslie, well behind me.

"Here!"

Doubt she heard me rasping, but I keep racing along the small footprint trail—right up until Sophia's tracks abruptly cease. The last footprints are smeared, like she swerved to face something leaping at her. Her silver motorcycle helmet lays on the ground a short distance to the right and a little farther ahead. My first thought is the ghost grabbed her, but I'm not sure the spirit is even capable of doing so. She obviously didn't fly away on her own. I've heard of giant eagles ambushing small dogs or cats, even toddlers, and trying to carry them away… but Sophia's a little big for an eagle to haul off.

Also, her screaming would've gone up into the air—which it didn't do. And, if a bird, vampire, or for all I know, gargoyle, carried her into the sky, she'd *still* be shrieking. Yet, the forest is completely silent.

Color saturates the world around me, the browns and greens of the snowy forest becoming vibrant in a radiant area. Someone's got a light source. I turn my entire body around, hoping the less I move my jelly neck, the faster it will heal. Leslie walks up to me, a tennis-ball sized light orb floating above her left hand.

"She's gone," I say, in a surprisingly calm voice. Dad gave me his skinny genes. Guess Mom gave me her crisis management. "Tracks stop short here. I think something jumped out at her, but I don't see any other tracks."

Leslie stoops to examine the ground. "Aye. She twisted away from somethin'"

"Someone kidnapped my sister *again*." I growl.

The poor woman jumps. "Ya hear that?"

"What?"

"Sounded like a cougar. Ain't s'posed ta be any o' them 'round 'ere. Fink it's a werewolf?"

"Just me. I'm angry."

"Oh. 'Ang on a moment, luv."

Leslie pulls a small pouch out from under her coat on a cord around her neck. From it, she pours a bunch of little runestones into her hand. After using her foot to clear an area of snow, she crouches, holding the stones in both hands over the dirt patch. Eyes closed, she whispers a few lines in—I think—Latin while shaking the stones around like she's playing Yahtzee.

High-pitched squealing starts up inside my head. Oh, goody. My bones must be knitting. I grab my head in both hands, trying to keep it positioned in as natural an orientation as possible. A wicked itch starts *inside* my neck. It's almost enough to make me want to tear my throat open so I can scratch the deep muscles. I don't, though, and force myself to be content with snarling.

Leslie dumps the runestones on the ground and pores over them.

My neck tightens. Seconds later, a loud *crack* echoes in my head with a sensation like someone whacked me on the skull—no skin in the way—with a carpenter's hammer.

"Oy, someone's comin'," whispers Leslie.

"Nah. You didn't hear a twig snap."

"Loud as anything."

"My neck."

She blinks at me. "You takin' the Mick?"

"No idea what you just said."

"I asked if yer messin' wif me?"

"No." I blink, gasp, and let go of my hair, allowing my neck to once again support the weight of my head. "See? Back to rights."

"What on Earth happened?"

"The ghost tried to sweep you off your feet so you would fall down your porch and break your neck. I flew at like motorcycle speed into bricks. You landed on top of me instead of the stone, and didn't die."

"Fanks for that, luv."

"Welcome." I squeeze my fists tight. "Where's Sophia?"

"Magic happened here." She points at the runestones.

I gaze up. "Oh, look. Sky."

"Come again?"

I give her a flat stare. "No kidding there's magic in the area. You basically pointed out the sky exists."

She shakes her head. "No... I mean something happened right at this spot and recently."

"Are you sure you aren't sensing Sophia's presence or the magic she's using to find the ghost?"

"Quite." Leslie points at the stones as if they mean something. "The magic done here was strong. Ancient. Elder magic."

"Theresa?"

"No, lass. Stop bein' daft." She swats at me. "Not 'elder' as in old person. Elder as in magic older than human kind. Fey. Demons maybe."

"Sons of bitches." I peel off my harness and hand it to her. "Hang on to this, okay? I think I know where she is. Only thing I don't know is how they slipped my compulsion."

"All right." Leslie picks up the helmet. "I'll mind this fer her, too."

28

DARKNESS AND DOUBT

S now hits me in the face like tiny daggers.

My theory about emotion affecting my flight speed is true. According to my phone, I'm doing 174 on the way to Jacob and Katy's mansion. I don't have any idea how the hell they managed to sidestep my command to leave her alone. Maybe they summoned a demon and commanded it to make sure the spirit gets to finish murdering the rest of the Aurora Aurea mystics. Anything they summon wouldn't be subject to my mental programming.

But, if they knew for a certainty the creature they created would go after my sister, would my compulsion prevent them from summoning it in the first place? My emotion had been pretty high when I hammered the concept into their brains. Magic is involved, though, which means any rules of logic don't necessarily apply, only esoteric arcane rules so complicated they make the average online sweepstakes terms and conditions seem like two plus two.

Wonder if they realized they'd been affected by a mental command and found a way to get rid of it?

Either way… no more Ms. Nice Girl.

I dive into a hard landing right on the porch and kick the door.

It's flimsier than it looks—my foot goes through it. Standing there on one leg with one foot stuck in the door pisses me off even more. I pull my leg out and kick again, aiming for a spot above the doorknob rather than the center of the door. Aha. Bingo. The door flies open with enough force to almost come off the hinges.

I storm across the foyer, hunting for either stairs or a dumbass mystic in need of a beating.

Voices from an archway on the left draw my attention. Just so happens, I discover all three at the same time—stairs, Katy, and Jacob.

"Where is she?" I ask, my voice more snarl than voice.

"Where is who?" Jacob steps toward me, one eyebrow up.

I grab him and throw him aside. He crashes into the wallpaper above the wainscoting, his body horizontal, his head breaking an oval hole in the drywall on impact. Mostly limp, he falls straight down, crushing a small table and two little vases.

Katy backpedals, starting to scream.

I lunge, grab two fistfuls of her expensive top, and slam her against the opposite wall, holding her up off her feet. So what if I have to look up at her? I'm not tall enough to be intimidating. Her being off the ground is more effective than me looking down on her.

"Where is my sister?"

She gurgles, unable to speak or breathe due to the force I'm exerting on her chest. The woman feebly grabs at my wrists, inflicting mild scratches I barely notice.

Snap.

An irritating, stinging pain jabs me in the back. I peer over my shoulder. Jacob, still on the floor, blood gushing from his nose, struggles to keep his arm—and his small pistol—pointing up at me.

"Oh, you found it. Shoot me again, and you'll need a surgeon to remove the gun from your intestines. And I'm not going to make you swallow it."

His eyes widen.

Katy starts to go limp. I ease off on the pressure. She sucks in a huge breath.

"Where. Is. Sophia?"

"We haven't seen her," yells Jacob.

"We didn't touch the girl. We wouldn't dare!" rasps Katy.

Eyes narrow, I mentally bore into her brain. Shit! She's not lying. My compulsion is holding strong and she has no memory of doing anything more dangerous than spending the entire day in a foul mood over their 'great war' not being over any time soon.

Oops.

My anger evaporates.

I'm not *too* guilty. Didn't kill either of them, and they deserved a bit of roughing up for putting my sister in a small, windowless cell. I delete myself from Katy's memory, inserting a chaotic scene of a man dressed like Barney the Dinosaur showing up as a singing telegram, but becoming unglued and kicking in the door before charging Jacob and slamming him into the wall, then running off singing show tunes at the top of his lungs.

Jacob gets the same memory.

Yeah, it's messed up, but maybe it'll give them pause before reporting anything to the police.

Grumbling to myself, I storm outside and go back into the air.

Dammit! If those two didn't grab Sophia, who did?

I pull my phone out of my pocket and send Asher a text, warning him about Sophia disappearing and suggesting he should have his people take steps to protect themselves. I add an ‹If you can find her, please do.›

Minutes blur into meaningless time as I cruise aimlessly around over London.

Eventually, I end up on top of a huge skyscraper overlooking the Thames, curled in a ball, hugging my knees to my chest and feeling like a complete failure. How is it I can negotiate a minor issue of werewolf versus vampire treaty politics, make nice with Mr. Corley, but can't keep my sister safe?

I never should've gone home at all. How selfish could I have possibly been to inflict all this supernatural bullshit on my family? *I* couldn't bear the guilt of them thinking me dead. Going home has to be the most selfish thing I've ever done. Sure, they'd have been crushed, but Sophia wouldn't be infused with magic and currently abducted by who-knows-what. The spirit of Fletcher Maltby would still be in a jar, harmless. Christmas would come next week, and the scene I dreamed not long ago would play out. Sierra, Sam, and Sophia all miserable, not interested in any presents. My parents unable to soothe their sorrow. I'd be off with Dalton, not knowing what my family was going through, but certain they'd be having it rough. First Christmas as a vampire would have been too depressing to think about.

But the one after couldn't be so bad, right? The Littles are my siblings, not my kids. They'd get over losing me. By the time they hit their teens, they'd probably not remember having an older sister too much. Sophia wouldn't end up as messed up as the kid in *Dead Like Me*, hanging toilet seats in the tree, would she? Sierra wouldn't give up on school, fail out, wind up on the street. My death wouldn't drive my parents into arguing every night, ultimately getting a divorce?

No, probably not. I'm being melodramatic and self-pitying.

I'm not important enough to rip my entire family apart by dying. They'd deal.

Right?

Mom's voice yells at me in the back of my mind, purely a product of my imagination. *No matter what happens, you're still part of this family, young lady. Don't go running off. Don't do that to us.*

"I know, Mom. I can't run off. At least not until I find Soph. But I don't know where to start. This magic bullshit is so over the top." I wipe my face off on my sleeve.

I've never felt so alone as I do right now, 5,000 miles away from everyone who knows me, high up above a city filled with complete strangers. It's a metaphor for being vampire. I don't belong.

Oy, stop being so bloody emo, says Dalton in the back of my mind. *Ya made your choice, and, 'tis a bit unorthodox, but it works for ya.*

Yeah, sounds like something he'd say.

Because it is me sayin' it, luv. We've got a mental link, remember?

I sit up a little straighter. How long have you been watching me?

Not long. Felt you goin' off the deep end into the black abyss of despair. Or some such dark poetic nonsense. Hon, knock that shite off.

I chuckle.

Oh, how's Simone doing?

Fine.

Give 'er my regards.

Probably not a great idea. What's she doing in London? Didn't you say you did the LA job for her?

Aye. She runs a multinational organization. Don't have to be in the States ta contract out.

Oh. Umm...

No. Not the foggiest idea about how ta find Sophia. Your best bet's the mystics. Maybe ol' Hargreaves. He's old blood. Dabbles in mysticism. Part of Mr. Corley's crowd.

I met them. By the way, thanks for warning me about having to present myself to them upon entering the city.

Never imagined you'd be in London. If'n I thought you'd go there, I'd have mentioned it.

Okay. Fair. Probably wouldn't be here by choice. Nothing against the place, but I'm a 'stay close to home' kind of girl.

Obviously. That Asher bloke might be able to cook up a way to find Sophia. Same as she's usin' ta go after the wraith.

"Maybe... yeah." My eyes widen. Hope starts to lift the slab of despair off my shoulders. "I could—"

Dalton's cackling laughter fills my brain to the point I can't think about anything else.

Do you mind?

He keeps laughing, but quieter.

Don't want to know. "Okay... All I need is a magic compass to lead me to her."

"Mew," says Klepto.

I nearly jump out of my saturated clothes. It takes my heart a second to resume pretending to beat. The little kitten, also soaked in snow, sits on the roof next to where I'd been wallowing in sorrow. She looks absolutely pathetic drenched.

"Aww..." I scoop her up and cradle her in my arms.

She gnaws on my wrist. "Mew!"

Sorry, luv. Just saw the bit with the kitten dangling from that bloke's jubblies. Classic!

"You can find her!" I spin around, hugging the kitten.

You look like a bloody Disney princess about to break into song, singing at the little cat.

Bite me.

Rather not, luv. It'd be kinda awkward seein' as how you're like me little sister.

Ugh. I should know better than to say 'bite me' to a vampire.

"Mew." Klepto squirms.

I peer over the edge at the street far below. A good coating of the white stuff makes it impossible to differentiate sidewalk from paving. Only a handful of cars brave the fresh snowfall, struggling to travel at a walking pace. Yellow lights flash everywhere on road crew vehicles trying to clear the roads. Looking at the River Thames not far in front of me sends a chill down my back. The grey water laced with ice chunks is the encyclopedia photo for 'an effing cold night.'

"Should be able to get down without being noticed. Lead the way."

Klepto shakes her head. "Mew."

"You can't?"

She growls.

"What?"

The kitten stares up.

"Oh… you want me to fly? She's far away?"

Tribble.

I take off, cradling the kitten to my chest. "Okay. Show me where to go. Whatever direction you look at, I'll go."

She nods.

Having a kitten capable of understanding me is beyond strange. Okay, self-pitying dumbass mode over. There's someone out there in serious need of an ass kicking.

29

A LITTLE SUPERNATURAL WAR

The kitten uses her head as a pointer, directing me to fly.

I start worrying when we leave London behind.

Worry translates to me flying faster. After like an hour, I become even more worried.

"Did Theresa grab her?"

"Mew."

"Is Sophia far away?"

Tribble.

"I should fly as fast as possible."

Tribble.

"Are we going to make it to her before sunrise?"

Tribble.

"Okay." I pour on speed.

Eventually, we leave the snowstorm behind—and go out over ocean. Ack. I realize England is basically a giant island, but what the hell? She's outside England? I'm fairly sure we're heading west, but I'm a little fuzzy on geography.

Ireland is west of England, says Dalton. *If you're headin' due west from London, and you've hit water, yer likely past Wales and over St. George's Channel. Aye, looks like it.*

You can see what I'm seeing?

Not exactly. I can see your memory of what you saw. Little kitty is leading you to the Emerald Isle.

Anything I should know? Is there some other vampire king I'll need to show myself to?

Nah. There aren't many of us there. Mostly werewolves and other things.

Other... things?

Aye. Old critters. Fey. Dryads, leprechauns, boggarts, various beasts. If ya see a giant black dog wit' glowin' red eyes, run the feck away.

Umm...

Trust me, luv. Those blighters don't much care for undead.

Sounds like I should get the heck out of Ireland as fast as possible.

It's not too bad. There's a difference between things existing and the place bein' overrun. Unless ya go lookin' for trouble, ya should be okay.

Hah. I never go looking for trouble, but it keeps finding me! Hey, would you mind, umm, 'staying on the phone' and letting me know if something's about to ruin my day?

Sure, but I've only about two hours left before sunrise here.

Thanks. Don't roast yourself. I'll manage.

Klepto keeps me going more or less in a straight line for another hour before meowing loud.

I don't speak 'cat,' but it really sounded like she yelled, "Stop!" so I slow to a casual glide.

The kitten strains to peer down. I follow her pointing nose, heading for a forest so thick I'm sure nobody lives in it. Damn. Leslie said she sensed the presence of old Fey magic. Dalton said Ireland's full of Fey creatures. This is going to get weird.

I wriggle past dense branches of oaks or some such trees, fighting my way through to the ground. It's pretty obvious people don't come here often if ever. Dense underbrush stretches as far as I can see, undisturbed by trails. Ivy and moss cling to most of the trunks, the majority of them wider than phone booths. This is an old forest.

Klepto mews.

When I look down at her, she points her head all the way to the left. I turn until she ends up looking straight ahead.

"This way?"

Tribble.

It's annoying to walk in knee-deep brush, so I levitate a few feet off the ground and glide. Before long, Sophia's voice drifts out of the woods up ahead. She sounds more frustrated than frightened.

"... not understanding me. I don't have magic to do what you want. No, I don't know how to find people, and I can't blow up a village."

Say what?

I fly faster. A chorus of tiny voices jabbers in a rapid-fire yammering like an Alvin and the Chipmunks version of the *Jerry Springer Show*. I follow the voices to an area devoid of underbrush. Sophia's lashed to a tree by hundreds of brown roots, covering her from shoulders to shins. Fifty or sixty little creatures have gathered around her, all about two feet tall—the same type of critter the Serene Lodge idiots had in a giant bell jar. Sinister toddlers with cherubic faces, overly large eyes, and weird little suits made to look like leaves and flower petals. They're androgynous as well as ageless. None appear to be older or younger than any others.

Bugger. Dalton yawns. *Brownies. Be careful.*

Careful? They're so small...

Curses are nasty business. A .44 magnum in the hands of a six-year-old is still deadly. Don't let their size trick ya.

Dammit. I really wanted to rip someone's face off for kidnapping my sister *again*.

I'd advise against it in this case. You might get one or two, but it won't be worth it. All right, luv. About time for me to go. Sunrise and all.

Okay. Thanks for the advice.

It's borderline ridiculous to think of these little critters as remotely dangerous. Of course, they *do* have a marked sense of malevolence to them despite their creepy childishness. Sophia squirms, grumbling.

"Guys, please let me go. If I could help you, I would. But"—She finally spots me—"Sarah!"

All the brownies whirl, look at me, and lean back in unison, emitting a collective gasp.

Wow, so this is how Gru from *Despicable Me* feels, surrounded by a bunch of tiny, evil things. Maybe the brownies aren't 'evil' as much as mischievous.

"Hi. Sorry to barge in on your territory, but you guys have my sister and I really need her back."

The brownies keep staring at me, edging away as I near. None say or do anything. Okay, this could be simple. I walk right up to Sophia, the little guys clearing out of my way but filling in behind me.

"I tried to talk to the ghost, but he wouldn't stop. Sorry for running into the woods alone." Sophia huffs, blowing a lock of hair off her face—which falls right back over her eye. "Stupid of me, huh?"

I extend my claws and slash at the roots, and it's like I'm trying to cut power cables using a cheap plastic knife. "Oh, come on." I rake repeatedly at the cocoon of plant matter holding my kid sister to the tree, failing to even scratch one root. The damn things are only as big around as a pencil—and apparently made of adamantium. "What the heck?"

"The roots are magic," mutters Sophia.

"So are these!" I hold my claws up to her. "People aren't supposed to have three-inch razors for fingernails. And fingernails aren't supposed to be this tough. My nails have sliced leather biker jackets like paper and it didn't hurt me at all."

A brownie fairly close behind me murmurs in a rapid, indecipherable warble. Pretty sure he or she said 'what's this dumb bitch trying to do?' The others—I swear they've doubled in number since I landed—watch me with their cute, oversized eyes and sinister smiles. It's like someone buried a hundred medieval Teletubby dolls in *Pet Sematary*. Wait, no, those damn things are way creepy even without a cursed graveyard changing them.

Sophia squirms. She doesn't seem *too* uncomfortable. The roots aren't squeezing her overly tight, merely keeping her still. Gonna be a real problem if she has to go to the bathroom before they let her go. It's incredibly tempting to see if my claws cut brownies better than these roots. However, Dalton warned me not to piss them off. If *he* thinks something is too dangerous, I'm afraid to test it. This is a man who thought sneaking a giant incendiary device into a nest of a hundred hostile vampires was a reasonable business venture.

"So, umm... why did these little guys kidnap you?"

She huffs at the same bit of stray hair again. "They want me to blow up a village of leprechauns."

I fix her hair out of her face. "Did you just say 'leprechauns'?"

"Yeah. One of the brownies saw me at the big house do the darkness spell. They don't understand I only made a bubble of darkness. The brownies think I'm powerful enough to change day into night, so they believe I can destroy the leprechauns. They're having a war."

"Umm..." I shouldn't be hearing this. Never once in my life has LSD entered my system. The most hallucinogenic substance I've ever been exposed to is alcohol—unless Enya's music counts. "That's twice now you've said leprechauns."

Sophia shrugs. "Brownies are real. Why not leprechauns?"

The child has a point.

"Okay, so... do they realize you are the absolute worst person in the world to ask to kill something?"

"I told them I don't wanna hurt anyone, but they say they're not gonna let me go until I help them win the war."

Eyes closed, I seethe for a few seconds in silence, repeating 'Dalton is the king of reckless ideas and he's afraid to mess with brownies' a few times. "Okay, I'll bite. *Why* are brownies and leprechauns having a war?" I'm really hoping the answer to my question isn't 'Uwe Boll is filming *Leprechaun III: Brownout.*'

"Umm, they didn't say." Sophia scrunches up her face. "My nose itches."

I pull one sleeve down over my hand and fix her itchy nose problem, then face the—even larger—group of little flower-hooded psychos. "Will someone please either explain why you want my sister to attack leprechauns or let her go?"

A brownie in the front row points at her. "She go after she promise to help."

Grr. "But we helped one of you guys escape the jar."

"No. Accident." A brownie shakes their head. "You not *want* set me free. Human woman throw metal at her and she knock it away. Accident. Not do nice thing."

Sigh. Remind me to tell Dad *never* to run a D&D game for brownies. Talk about rules lawyering. "Why must the leprechauns die?"

"To stop the witches," yells another brownie.

"Leprechauns have witches?" I blink.

"Human witches," yells another tiny voice from the middle of the crowd.

I sigh at the ground. This is going to be painful. "What are the human witches doing?"

About a third of the brownies chirp, "Trying to destroy us!" at once.

Witches, I feel you. I wouldn't mind baking a few brownies myself. "Why are the witches trying to destroy you?"

The first—I think—brownie who spoke English says, "Because of the human girl."

"I didn't do it!" yells Sophia.

"No, not this human girl." A brownie points at her, then flails their little arms. "The other human girl."

I'm a millimeter from screaming 'what the F does this have to do with leprechauns,' but I manage to find Zen. Of course, I sound like Mom when she's super pissed off. You know the tone of voice parents use where they sound superficially calm, but everyone knows shit's about to get real if small butts don't kick into gear and do whatever immediately? Yeah, that's me right now.

"How are the leprechauns responsible for the human girl being responsible for the witches trying to destroy you guys?"

"They're not," chirps one.

Damn good thing I'm undead, or I'd have just died to a massive aneurysm. Daydreaming about punting a brownie or four into the sun keeps me from shouting an F-bomb in front of Sophia. Instead, I just let out an, "Aaaargh!" I breathe hard in and out my nose for a few seconds, trying to calm down. Then ask, "Mmm mmm mm mmmm?"

What the hell?

Did a random piece of duct tape appear over my mouth?

I grab my face and... don't have lips. When I shoot a 'what the hell?' look to Sophia, she screams—and her mouth abruptly vanishes.

I glare at the brownies, trying to ask WTF with my eyeballs.

"Loud noises bad. No yelling," says one.

Sophia wriggles, failing to scream or move much, while I go off on an epic rant. In the span of forty seconds, I use more swear words than in all the hours of my life leading up to this moment combined. The brownies find my mumbling to be quite funny. After I manage— somehow—to calm myself, I stare at them while trying to do Superman's laser beam eye thing.

Doesn't work.

"No yelling," says another brownie.

Fine. Whatever. I give a thumbs-up.

A faint tingle washes over my face. Aha. I've got lips again. Fists clenched, I force myself to speak in a calm, even tone. "If the leprechauns have nothing whatsoever to do with the witches, why do you want them destroyed?"

"So we can get the girl," replies another random brownie, grinning at me.

Easy, Sarah. Hold it together.

"Will one of you please explain the entire situation? I'm having trouble understanding."

A brownie three rows deep pushes to the front. "Human girl goes into woods. She gets lost. Witches blame brownies for girl being gone. We want witches to stop hurting us."

I look at him/her. "How does this involve leprechauns at all?" Gah, it's like they're deliberately trying to drive me crazy.

"The leprechauns can find girl, but won't. They laugh at us."

Okay. Now it makes sense. "I think I'm finally getting it." I glance at Sophia. "Why would witches suspect brownies of kidnapping a child?"

"We no take children," yells about two-thirds of the brownies... sounding a bit too innocent.

I lean against my sister. "You don't? She's only ten."

"She bigger than other human," says a brownie.

A front-row brownie on the left jumps up and down. "She not children. She magic person."

"Leprechauns maybe take girl," says another brownie. "Not at first, but now they see witches hurt brownies, and keep her so more hurt happen."

"They have girl," yells a brownie in the back.

I'd sigh at the clouds, but the trees are in the way... so I sigh at the trees. "Please let my sister go and I'll try to help. She doesn't have enough magic, or the right kind of magic, to blow up leprechauns."

"We give you girl in trade for other girl," says one brownie, triggering the whole lot of them to start nodding and saying 'yes' repeatedly.

"Whoa. Hold on. Let's assume I find this other kid. What the heck are you going to do to her if I bring her here?"

"Send her back to village so witches stop. No hurt."

"Maybe *you* kill leprechaun?" asks the third brownie on the right in the front row. "You are creature of night."

I tilt my hand in a so-so gesture. "More a creature of dimness."

I'm still struggling with the notion of them existing at all, but something tells me slaughtering leprechauns is probably a lot worse than breaking mirrors for bad luck. Of course, if Eighties horror movies are any source of legit information, maybe leprechauns are evil bastards. I really don't want to think what the leprechaun from the movie would do to a lost child.

"Okay, I have one more question."

"Just one?" asks Sophia.

Right? Sigh. "You guys seem to be magically powerful. I mean, you managed to get a teenage girl and a tween to stop talking for five minutes."

"I don't talk too much," mumbles Sophia.

I fold my arms at her. "Really? When Nicole and Megan are over?"

"We don't talk *too* much."

"Heh. 'Too much' is relative." I pat her on the head. "Relax. It's normal at your age."

Sophia frowns. "I've heard you and Ash on the phone. You shouldn't say *anyone* talks too much."

Ooh. Little wiseass. I tickle her through the roots, making her squeak. She'd probably scream, but her thick winter coat protects her enough from my fingers. Instead, she squirms, gawking at me with a 'how could you take advantage of my helplessness' face.

The brownies exchange glances. Cripes, I think there are even more of them now.

"Anyway, you guys have powerful elder magic. What makes you think you need Sophia for anything?"

"Leprechauns elder magic, too. Girl not. No defenses." The brownie in the middle of the front row slaps a hand to his/her chest. "She make day to night. Girl have power to smash leprechauns."

If these critters think Sophia's going to go on a murder spree, they're clearly hash brownies. I face the throng and put on my most trustworthy smile. "Please let Sophia go, and I promise I'll help you with your witch problem."

Center Brownie peers up at me. "Creature of darkness—"

"Dimness," says the brownie next to them.

"Darkness." repeats Brownie One.

Brownie Two shakes their head. "Dimness."

"Darkness!"

Brownie Two gestures at me emphatically. "Dimness."

"Sare, will you smack me in the forehead?" asks Sophia—as the two brownies keep shouting back and forth 'darkness-dimness-darkness-dimness'.

"Why?"

"Because I'm tied to a tree and can't facepalm."

I rest my head against the trunk beside hers and whisper, "What's stopping me from kicking all their tiny asses and getting you out of here?"

"Don't!" whispers Sophia. "They're small, but super powerful."

"Creature of dim darkness!" yells Brownie One. "You go. Get human child from leprechauns. Bring here. We give this one to you as reward."

Grr. I whirl to glare at the little bugger. "You can't steal her from me and then call it a reward to let her go home."

"Just do it," says Sophia.

"What?" I spin to face her again. "I can't leave you stuck here."

She squirms. "Trust me, I'm not loving being tied to a tree either, but you'll never win an argument against brownies. As soon as you start winning, they stop making sense. Before you know it, the sun will be up and you'll..."

"I don't like this. You can't even move. How were they expecting you to help them like that?"

Sophia rolls her eyes. "Didn't you hear? I'm so magically powerful, I can blow up all the leprechauns from here."

"Right... I'm tempted to try the barbarian approach."

"No. They teleported me from London to Ireland. Their magic is serious."

"But apparently too weak to blow up leprechauns," I mutter.

"Don't tick them off! Please. Just... find the other kid, or grab a leprechaun." Sophia huffs. "I'll just hang here."

"Leprechauns." I shake my head.

"Yeah. Hurry before the sun comes up."

I look back at the brownies. "My sister doesn't have magic like you think she does, but since you won't simply let her go... I will help make the witches stop bothering you."

All the brownies nod, one so rapidly the little bugger falls over.

Another wearing a slightly more ornate outfit—the preschooler who got to play the 'flower' instead of merely a tree at the end-of-year play—approaches me. "I Kezbit. In charge. If witches stop, you will have human child as reward. If you bring other human child so we can give to witches, we trade you this human child. If you destroy leprechauns all so we can find human child, and give to witches, we give you this human child as reward."

"Right. I fix your witch problem, you let Sophia go."

"Agree." She or he extends a tiny hand.

Ugh. When did my life get this weird?

I shake. "Back soon."

30

DEEPER AND DEEPER SHE GOES

Dear diary,
I'm hunting leprechauns. No, seriously. I don't need a drug test. Wait, what's with the men in white coats? Hey! Stop! Let go of me.

Something tells me I'm not dreaming. My first night as a vampire, everything seemed far too outlandish to possibly be real. Back then, waking up in a morgue cooler naked had been 'extremely bizarre.' Oh, the innocence of my youth. Compared to taking a mercenary contract from brownies to exterminate the leprechaun nation, vampires sound completely sane.

So much for the denial excuse of 'I gotta be dreaming.'

You know how western movies sometimes do the 'this town ain't big enough for the two of us' thing? The brownie-leprechaun conflict sounds much the same. Only, it's 'this forest isn't big enough.' Before leaving my little sister rooted to a tree surrounded by a pack of weird little magical beasties, I at least managed to get a straight answer out of one regarding where to find the leprechauns. Klepto stayed with Sophia to keep her company—and deal with random nose itches.

Same forest, mile or two northwest.

Guess when you're two feet tall, a long-distance conflict is relative.

The woods are somewhat less dense in 'leprechaun territory.' It's anyone's guess if this is due to centuries of humans tromping around trying to catch one or if the brownies have used magic to overgrow their part of the forest as a defense. Brownies, I'd never heard of until tonight. Leprechauns are a little more well known, but it would be foolish of me to believe any folklore as truth until I see one in person. These guys could be amicable little dudes with beards and jolly green suits every bit as easily as some eldritch horrors from the deepest, darkest pits of awfulness.

For a while, I glide around in the treetops, trying to be as silent as possible since the only source of information available to me about these creatures is legend. Folklore says people constantly hunt leprechauns for treasure. If true, they'd likely have evolved to be wary and have good hearing.

Evolved. Pff. Yeah, way to go, Sarah. Apply science to magical creatures.

I sigh, hard... and cough up a little rock. Something metal clicks into my teeth. Ack. I spit it out into my hand. A deformed, tiny bullet. Oh, right. Jacob shot me in the back. I flick it aside and keep prowling. Every so often, I grab onto a branch and hover among the leaves, listening to the night.

Finally, I hear singing.

Not merely any singing... this sounds like an old man crooning an Irish shanty song played at double speed. I *know* I'm going to regret seeing the source of the singing, but Sophia needs me. Silent as a cat stalking up on an oblivious squirrel, I glide after the miniature minstrel, keeping myself about twenty feet off the ground. With any luck, Dalton was right about there not being many vampires in Ireland. If true, leprechauns wouldn't be used to 'predation' by silent flying humans. Owls are pretty damn quiet, too—but would they attack tiny people?

If anything, hearing a little man singing makes it more likely the sight waiting for me a short distance ahead in the trees is closer to the stereotypical depiction of a leprechaun and not some twisted horror.

Score one for vampire night vision.

This forest is *pitch* dark owing to the thick canopy and overcast night—but it's as clear as daylight to me, merely drab. Motion draws my attention to a small, humanoid figure strolling along brazen as anything. Not counting the hat, he's about the same height as the brownies, but has a normally proportioned head. I'd been expecting a bright green suit, pocket watch, derby... the whole nine. He *is* wearing a suit, but he doesn't look like the Notre Dame mascot. Considering the darkness, I'm mostly guessing at color, but I want to say it's tan or brown. He looks like someone hit a working class Victorian guy with a shrink ray. Pretty sure his hair and beard are ginger, though.

Wow. Leprechauns *are* real.

Maybe I am dreaming after all. Or, wait. No. Can't be. I made the mistake of drinking the blood of two mystics. Who knows what their bizarre essences are doing to me? Dammit. Not once has anything I tried to deny being real turned out to truly be a figment of my imagination. I'm not so lucky. Sophia's really been abducted by freakin' brownies, and I'm really following a leprechaun.

Chances are good he's going to run, turn invisible, or teleport away if he senses me coming. At least, the stories always make it sound impossible to catch them. I suppose considering human society regards them as myths, there might be some truth to the difficulty involved. Maybe they use magic to make people forget? Doing so sure works for me.

Is vampire telepathy 'magic' or something else?

Whatever.

I surge forward, swooping down at him from behind. The fabric of my top flutters, a faint sound, but enough for him to spin, raising his walking stick. He doesn't see me at first since he's expecting attack from the ground level. The little man looks up a split second before I grab him under the armpits as if collecting a runaway toddler, lifting him into the air as I land.

He screams in fright, then explodes in a furious shouting rant while walloping me about the head and shoulders with his walking stick. Gordon Freeman has nothing on a leprechaun. Fastest crowbar in the west has been dethroned. I can't say it *hurts* per se, but it's far from comfortable—kind of like being forced to listen to the U2 album they gave away on iTunes and automatically downloaded.

Were I human, I'd likely be dizzy, bleeding, and throwing him aside to make the walloping stop.

"Hey!" I shout. "Stop whacking me with your stick."

He doesn't, but switches to English. "Damn giant elf! What're ya doin' swoopin oot de air at me like dat? Oonhand me!"

"Stop whacking me with your stick!"

The leprechaun pauses his attack. "Is naht a steck. Eht's a shillelagh!" He bonks me over the head.

"Looks like a stick to me," I grumble.

Bonk. "Shillelagh!"

"Stick."

Bonk. "Shillelagh!"

"I'm not going back and forth with you."

Bonk. "Ya massive gowl. Call eht a steck oon mahr time' an' I'll lamp ya fierce." Bonk.

I shake him hard enough to make his hat fall off while shouting, "I don't want your damn gold. Just listen to me!"

His eyes widen in shock. "Ya dahn't want me gold?"

"No! Will you please stop hitting me with your stick?"

He frowns. Bonk. "Shillelagh!"

I furrow my brows. "Fine. Shillelagh."

Bonk.

"What was that for?" I yell, cringing.

"Ya dahn't mean et. Ya say 'shillelagh,' but yer thinkin' steck. There a bet o' difference between a steck and a shillelagh."

I open my mouth to say 'fine,' but he points the stick at me.

"Better mean et."

Whatever. A stick carried by a leprechaun is a shillelagh.

"Please stop hitting me with your shillelagh. I'm not after your gold."

He adjusts his suit vest. "Well, dat's a surprise. I donna think 'umans be fast anuff to catch me. Bot ya ded manage et… and you dahn't want me gold? Well, I owe you a favor den. Gotta ask ya though. What sort o' flute snags a leprechaun and dahn't want de gold?"

"Flute?"

"A right selly sahrt'a person." He points the shillelagh at me again. "But ya say ya dahn't want de gold already. Nae backtrackin', er ae'll right banjax ya wit' a curse da likes o' which ya never imagine."

"No, I didn't catch you for gold. Brownies have kidnapped my little sister."

"Oh, surely." He rolls his eyes. "Snaggin' a leprechaun is a right natural thing ta do when dat 'appens."

"It's complicated."

"I'm listenin'. Ya kin go 'ead an put me down now. We 'avin' a rapport."

I look him over. No obvious expressions to give away a lie, but he *is* a leprechaun. They'll do anything to protect their gold. He probably doesn't believe I'm not after it… or he wouldn't have threatened to 'banjax' me—whatever it means. "No offense, but I think you're trying to trick me. Hear me out first, then I'll put you down."

He folds his arms. Regards me for a moment, then bonks me over the head.

"Ow! What was that for?"

"Ya stell thinkin' o' me shillelagh as a steck."

Good grief. Is every magical creature under three feet tall annoying as hell?

"So, complicated. The brownies thought my sister could blow up your village. She can't. The only thing I want is to get my sister back from the brownies, alive and healthy. They won't let her go until I either kill all the leprechauns, which I am totally not interested in doing, or find this little girl who went missing in the forest." I proceed to explain the entire messy situation while holding him like a disgruntled Teddy Ruxpin who's got a shillelagh and isn't afraid to use it.

"Ahh. De child yer lookin' farh 'as been taken by de dark dryads."
He nods once.

"Say what?"

"Tree spirits."

"There's only three of them?"

Bonk. "Na, ya mog. Na say tree lek 'on, ta, tree, fahr'. Tree lek tree."
He points the shillelagh at a tree. "Wood spirits. Dere be dark ones an'
light ones. De dark ones 'ave the wee sprog."

I groan. "The brownies think you guys have her. The witches think
the brownies have her. The brownies are attacking you guys to make
the witches stop attacking them, and now you're telling me that some
other creature entirely has this kid?"

"Aye." He folds his arms.

"I'm guessing it's not good for the *dark* dryads to have her. Is she—
I mean, is it too late?"

"Maybe naht. See, dryads are all wimmin fahlk. Dey need 'uman
men to 'ave babies o deir own. De light dryads dahn't 'ave a problem
wit' et." He whistles as if watching a gruesome train wreck. "Dem dark
ones, though. Dey'll drahp a man dead as a stahn frahm lookin' at 'em.
Fierce oogly dings."

"Wait, they're medusas?"

"Na. Not lit'ral stahn. Na man go near one less'n 'e be blind." He
waves the shillelagh around randomly. "Dem dark ones. On a count o'
dem not findin' no 'human men, dey take dis girl an' make 'er one o
dem."

I look the leprechaun in the eye. "I swear to you I did not grab you
for your gold. If you're sincere about wanting to do me a favor, please
help me find this kid."

"Aye. Kin do. Y'ave me wahrd." He pedals his legs. "Ye kin put me
down now."

How did I go from being sucked into a magical portal in my
sister's closet to eyeball deep in 'mythological' creatures halfway
around the globe? Sigh. The hole just keeps getting deeper. I swear, if
we find this kid and she sends me on a fetch quest for the doll she
dropped in the woods...

Deep breaths, Sarah. I'm not in a video game.

I set the leprechaun on his feet. He picks up his hat, puts it on, and proceeds to walk away. A few steps later, he stops, looking back.

"Well, cahm ahn. What're ya waitin' fahr?" He resumes walking. "Follow meh."

Sure. Why not? This can't possibly get any weirder.

QUARRELING, QUARRELING

T he leprechaun moves pretty darn quick for a guy with such little legs.

Somehow, he doesn't appear to be racing along. His legs aren't blurring comically fast, but he's traveling at about the same speed as an ordinary human. I think I should just set my brain aside, stop expecting anything to make any sort of logical sense, and roll with what's going on—sorta like one does while watching a David Lynch movie.

"Mardle," says the leprechaun.

"I'm sorry?"

He laughs. "Tis me name. Mardle."

"Oh. Hi, Mardle. I'm Sarah."

"Pleased ta meet ya."

We walk for a bit in silence.

"You know where this girl is?"

"I do."

"Are we going there?"

"Na yet. Need ta 'ave a conference afore we start nudder war wit the dryads."

Sigh. Werewolves and vamps have a treaty, why not these guys? I should get a job at the UM—united myths.

A few minutes later, we pass between two trees and the forest in front of me abruptly changes into a tiny village. Trees are still everywhere—this isn't a human village with streets, courtyards, fountains, and parking meters. Reminds me a bit of hobbit homes, only the doors are in massive tree trunks rather than hills—and these guys are smaller than hobbits. No one bigger than a toddler could get into these houses in any semblance of comfort. Some thirty or forty leprechauns are in sight, some walking around, some talking, a few doing crafty things like carpentry or weaving.

All the leprechauns stop at once, staring at me like I've put ketchup on steak in a fancy restaurant. A few take it up a notch, giving Mardle the same kind of look my mother would give Sam if he tried to bring a wild skunk into the house as a pet.

In seconds, a swarm of tiny, angry men surround us, all shouting at once. Mardle holds his hands up in a 'hang on, slow down' gesture. I'm unsure if they realize what I am or if leprechauns get this bent out of shape if any human finds this place. My gut tells me we traversed a portal between those trees, or maybe a confusion enchantment to keep people from noticing a straight-up mini village. Hmm. My stomach didn't do a backflip, so it's probably a wall of confusion.

Good. I've had enough dimension hopping for one eternal lifetime.

The argument rages for a few minutes, then stops short when Mardle yells the same short phrase several times in a row. Stunned, the crowd stares at me in complete disbelief. Did he just tell them I'm pregnant with his child?

"What did you say to them?"

"Told 'em ya dahn't want me gold."

I blink. "They're *this* shocked about me not wanting your treasure?"

"Aye. Never 'appens." He grasps the lapels of his coat. "One moment ta explain."

The other leprechauns listen intently as Mardle rambles in some other language. Unlike the brownies, they all have recognizably unique faces… far closer to humans. Even Kezbit, the brownie… umm, king or queen, looked exactly like the others except for having a slightly more ornate outfit. It's like a factory stamped them out on an assembly line.

Hmm. I wonder if I could feed off them. Would eating too many brownies make me fat?

Okay, bad joke. Even my Dad would throw something at me for that one.

From looking at the others, no one individual stands out as being higher in station. They're all wearing 1800s-era suits, but no two are exactly matching in color. Their derby hats vary in size, generally having the same style. Somehow, their clothing is simultaneously well worn and pristine. And no, they aren't all gingers—only about a quarter.

Mardle finishes talking, looking around expectantly.

A leprechaun sporting a beard so long he probably steps on it sometimes points at me and barks at Mardle.

"What did he say?"

"'E wants ya to wipe out da brownies afore 'ey agree ta 'elp. We're a bit miffed at the unprovoked aggression."

"I can't attack the brownies. They have Sophia and they're too powerful."

"Don' believe 'em," yells a black-bearded one, in English. "Ya kin kill 'em but it moight take ya coupl'a trips."

"Huh?" I tilt my head. "A couple of trips? I'm not following."

Mardle laughs. "Aye. Ya squish one, t'others will teleport ya far off. E'ry time ya squish one, ya end up far away 'avin' ta keep goin' back."

"First, they be annoyin'," says a brown-haired leprechaun, who appears surprisingly young—like in his twenties. "If annoying don' work, they try embarassin'. An' once they git really angry, they be sendin' ya ta *dangerous* places, like da inside o' a volcanah."

I rub the bridge of my nose. "There had to be a hundred or more of them. I can't spend the next six months zooming all over the world killing them one at a time. If I don't get Sophia home in time for Christmas, my parents will kill me."

The leprechauns mumble amongst themselves, occasionally shrugging, scratching their heads, or picking their noses.

Grr. This is ridiculous. "Why are you guys fighting with the brownies? The dark dryads are going to hurt some little girl. Okay, I understand the brownies stupidly blame you for the problem. Somehow. I haven't taken enough LSD to understand brownie logic. They're wrong. They shouldn't have attacked you. Sorry if this sounds disrespectful, but a brownie-leprechaun war is both pointless and not my problem. There's a little girl out there in a lot of trouble. Help me find her. Once she's safe, you can go whack brownies over the head with your shillelaghs all you want."

Mardle looks up at me.

The leprechauns resume arguing with each other as if I've ceased to exist.

Sigh.

After a few minutes, their 'debate' fizzles out to silence when an elder-looking one approaches me. "The consensus be ya must choose a side. Brownies or us. We stand at an impasse. As long as one o' them wee infernal pests still haunts the woods, we cannot distract our efforts away from defense."

"Them or us!" shouts roughly three-quarters of the leprechauns.

"I can't kill the brownies." My claws didn't scratch the roots. Not sure they'd work any better on the brownies, even if they appeared squishier. "Some kid is being turned into a dark dryad. I'm sure it's not a pleasant process and is going to twist her into something dark and wretched. She's much too little to work customer service."

The leprechauns stare at me like I'm making up words.

"If you can't kell de brownies, den you'll fight us." Elder Leprechaun jabs his walking stick—I mean shillelagh—into the ground. "We may not be as dangerous as the wee bastards, but we'll not go down without de fight o' yer life."

"No! I don't want to attack you either," I yell. "The brownie-leprechaun war is pointless!"

The leprechauns break into a chant of, "Them or us!"

"Stop et nao!" yells Mardle, raising his hands to silence the crowd.

"Ey promised the lass a favor, so ey will 'elp. She ain' after no gold. Rare ta see a 'uman who nabs one o' us an' forfeit tha pot fer sake o' a strange wee lass she donna know from ae rock. You lot kin keep bickerin'. Ey got somethin' ta do."

I exhale, close to passing out from sheer relief. "Thank you!"

"Don' thank me yet, lass. *One* leprechaun ain' gonna be much 'elp against the dark dryads. We all go, an' we drive 'em right off na problem." He jabs the shillelagh at the group. "But they be a right stubborn lot."

"Umm. Okay. I should be able to figure something out. I'm a bit more capable than a normal person. Least we can do is go take a look, right?"

Mardle pats his hat down securely. "Aye. C'mon, lass. T'aint far."

He walks off. I look over the group again, but my pleading smile doesn't sway any of them. Most grumble about wanting brownie-mageddon. Right. Me going back there with intent to destroy them is an even dumber idea than Dalton firebombing a lair of vampires as a favor to an old flame who's *still* pissed at him. Guess love really does make people do dumb things. If I had no other choice to get Sophia away from them, sure... but I can't grab her and run off, leaving some other poor kid in a bad situation.

Sigh.

I keep accusing Sophia of being too nice.

Guess we have a lot in common.

DELICATE BALANCE

Mardle leads me out from the village into the woods, talking the whole time.

His accent is a bit strong, but not impossible to follow. According to him, this forest contains multiple portals connected to fey realms. It reminds me of the otherworld in Garrett Alder's closet. Speaking of him, I still wonder if the potion he wanted worked. A vampire changing his bloodline sounds like something highly likely to fail or end in disaster, but going from Beast to Fury isn't *too* drastic a change.

Anyway, both the dark and light dryads live primarily on the inside of these portals, safe from humans. It might be more accurate to say humans are safer from them in the case of the dark ones. Mardle's description of the 'nice' dryads makes them out to be quite lovely. They avoid people whenever possible except if they want to make more dryads. Their 'victims' often wake in the woods after believing they've had a nap.

Dark dryads, on the other hand, sound a touch more aggressive. Mardle says they'll try to kill humans whenever possible. The reason most people don't believe dryads exist is because the nice ones make them forget and the dark dryads don't let anyone leave alive.

I'm not too worried about death, at least at night, so his story doesn't rattle me too much.

The big problem the brownies have is the portal to the dark dryad grove is deep inside the part of the forest the leprechauns consider their home. As brownies are wickedly mischievous, the leprechauns have created magical barriers to block their passage. So, the brownies can't get to the place where the girl is unless the leprechauns let them by—not happening—or the leprechauns are wiped out.

Leprechaun annihilation may or may not occur, but it won't be me doing it.

"Wee blighters have been on us for tree whole days now," says Mardle.

"Only three days? Your people made it sound like the war's been long, brutal, and personal."

He shrugs. "We don't much care for brownies."

"One good thing… I guess the battles are short."

He whacks me in the shin.

"Ow." I hop a few times.

"Brownies could pull open tha portal fer ya. So kin we. 'Umans can't even see et."

"I'm gonna assume the dark dryads won't be interested in talking."

"Na. Maybe they talk if ye were a man. They 'ave na use fer women. Wee girls, they tek back an' corrupt. Yer too ol' a lass ta be useful ta dem."

"Wow, considering a girl 'old' at eighteen. Dark dryads are even more brutal than Hollywood."

"Quiet now. We're close."

I nod.

Mardle goes from strolling along to zipping from tree to tree. I follow suit, attempting to stay hidden as much as possible. After a few minutes of stealthy moving, he indicates a group of six gnarled, ancient trees quite different from any others in the area: sickly grey with weird, lumpy roots stretching over the ground like cancerous nerve cells. Their leaves are darker than they ought to be, nearly black, and somewhat wilted. Stranger still, a faint ghostly cloud hovers inside the ring the trees form.

"There 'tis. The dark sisters. Those trees er stuck between life an' death."

I can sympathize.

"The glowing cloud is the portal?"

Mardle blinks. "You kin see et?"

"Yeah. It's faint, but I can see it."

He squints suspiciously at me. "You didn't tell me ya's a mage."

"I'm not. My eyes are real sensitive."

"Hogwash."

"Honestly, they are super sensitive. I can see in the dark."

"And ya fly before." He rubs his beard. A little color drains from his cheeks. "You 'ave fangs?"

"Only when I need to."

Mardle swallows hard.

"I'm no threat to you or any of the other leprechauns. Yes, I figured out already it would probably be super easy to hurt all of you, but the brownies are wrong and I *really* don't like killing people. Or leprechauns."

He keeps staring at me, the gears inside his brain grinding on the realization he hadn't brought an ordinary human into his home village but a vampire who—probably—could've easily wiped them all out. Me not doing so, despite it being a far faster path to what I want (Sophia back) appears to calm his fears.

"P'raps we kin do somethin' just you an' me." He rubs his hands like a scheming weasel. "Dahn't feel bad 'bout hurtin' these beasties if ya 'ave ta."

"If they're torturing a little kid, I'm inclined to agree with you."

"Ye ready?"

"As much as possible."

"Follow me then." Mardle hoofs it for the creepy glowing mist.

I run after him toward the circle of twisted trees. He skids to a stop by a thick mass of roots forming a knee-high (to me) wall between the trunks, and holds out his hand. I take it, and we jump together over the barrier.

The glowing mist, and the tree circle, vanish before my feet hit the ground. All around us, the forest appears thicker, darker, and noticeably more sinister. Every tree in sight resembles the ones forming the gate, ancient, huge, and shaped in unnatural ways. Long, gnarled branches overhead all interconnect as though the nightmare trees all held hands to block off the sky.

Something tells me it's never daylight here.

Huge shadowy forms glide about in the distance, the pale white eye spots near the top of their 'heads' floating in the manner of will-o-wisps. They lack any true shape, merely a somewhat-head and a long trailing body of vaporous darkness. Considering my eyes are no longer capable of seeing shadows, it's obvious I'm looking at spirits of some kind. Fortunately, none of them appear too concerned with my presence.

"Whoa. This place would give Tim Burton bad dreams," I whisper.

"Eh?" Mardle peers up at me.

I wave him off. Not worth explaining. "Where?"

He scratches his head. "Not rightly sure."

The six-tree circle is a few paces behind us, so at least I don't feel trapped. If it really hits the fan, we have an escape. Every direction appears to be the same, gnarled trees stretching off endlessly. I listen, turning in place, opening my senses for any clue of which way to go. Hoping to avoid a fight if at all possible, I resist the urge to call out in search of the missing child. Also, no one's told me her name.

"Can you find her?" I whisper.

He shakes his head. "Me magic's all 'bout *avoidin'* people. Yer the hunter."

"Right..."

Grr. Frustrated, I huff. Next time I inhale, the air carries a faint human scent. I've been around my siblings, taekwondo class, and the dance studio often enough since my Transference to recognize the smell of child. Ooh. If I can smell her, she can't be too far away. Unless vampires are like sharks and can smell blood for miles.

Smelling blood—even if it is a pleasant sort of cotton candy smell—worries and angers me.

This place doesn't have any noticeable breeze, so it's damn near impossible to tell where she is by scent alone while standing still. I begin walking in a random direction, constantly sniffing to see if the smell gets any stronger. A weak, gasping breath tinged in pain comes from my right, giving me a more concrete idea of direction.

The giant shadow monsters still don't seem to care about me. None are particularly close, which is good. Compared to them, I'm about the same size as a leprechaun. If they're the lingering ghosts of some other creature, I don't want to meet a living one.

Drawn by a combination of impatience to get Sophia back, hope of getting the hell out of here before running into a dark dryad, and worry for this poor child, I move up to a run. In one of the long conversations I had with Aurélie, she spoke of ancient vampires who eschewed all trappings of society and preferred to live in the wilds like feral creatures. She believed them the origin of Beasts. Running in the woods makes me think of the story due to her telling me of how they lacked the ability to fly but could outrun the fastest horses. Those vamps would consider sneakers loud, clumsy, and slow. But they also had giant toenail claws and could climb walls and trees like monkeys.

Eww.

So weird. Having weaponized fingernails doesn't bother me. In fact, it's kinda cool. But the idea of the same claws sticking out of my toes is kinda disgusting. Makes no sense, right? Anyway, I don't need to worry about sneakers slowing me down or making me clumsy and loud compared to those 'nature' vamps. I can fly.

A weak grunt in the otherwise silent distance makes me picture a little kid trying to lift a heavy object. She sounds out of it... unsurprising if she's been without food for a few days. I speed up, slaloming the otherworldly trees, which get larger and thicker the farther I go. Not a great sign. Probably means the kid's at the center of the woods, in the oldest part.

The emptiness is kinda surprising me. Other than the shadows, Mardle and I appear to be the only living—okay, can't really say 'living' literally—things here other than plants. *Not* running into tons of dark dryads or other monsters defending their territory should be a relief, but it makes me suspect I'm in for a nasty surprise.

Finally, I catch sight of something moving.

Maybe a quarter mile ahead, a small figure writhes, seemingly stuck to the side of an absolutely massive tree. Amid all the grey and dark green, two little dots of neon pink stand out: kid sneakers. The scent of candy-like blood is stronger here. I could zoom in my eyesight the way Glim showed me, but no point when it's easier to simply fly-sprint straight to her.

I slam on the proverbial brakes within six feet of the huge tree, hovering. It's fatter at the top and base like an apple core, the roots on the ground and branches overhead curving away from the gargantuan trunk in such a way as to create the illusion of a giant torus-ring of open space around the 'heart' tree, the trunk of which is easily forty feet in diameter.

A little girl hangs semi-crucified by thorny vines on the side facing me. She's maybe seven or eight, dressed in a raspberry-colored winter coat, teal tights, and bright pink sneakers. The girl's head lolls forward, a dense wall of brown hair concealing her face. Her coat sleeves have been peeled open from the wrist end, exposing her skinny arms almost to the elbows. Thorny black roots wrap around each arm, burrowing into her, visible like swollen veins under her skin. Similar roots have punctured her coat and pierced into her legs, all coated in a slow seep of blood.

"*Mamaí*," whispers the child, barely conscious.

She struggles to lift her head. Two thin black roots spread up from her neck into her cheeks, separating into numerous thinner strands crisscrossing her face in narrow venous lines and making her cry bloody tears. Something thin moves under the skin of her throat.

Seeing this poor child rips my heart straight out of my chest and stomps on it. I'm too horrified and shocked to do anything but stare at her.

"*Cabhair liom...*" She struggles halfheartedly at the roots holding her to the tree. "*Tá mé ag iarraidh a dhul abhaile.*"

"I'm sorry... I can't understand you."

The girl cringes, no doubt in a great amount of pain. "Help me... I want to go home."

I zip closer, studying the vines holding her up. Looks like most of her weight is on the roots going down the neck of her coat, probably burrowing into her shoulders and back. Unimaginable... she's hanging on the thorny strands burrowed *inside* her.

"Oh... my." I cover my mouth. Nothing, no gory sight I've ever seen since becoming aware of supernatural crap, has prepared me for witnessing roots moving *under* a kid's skin. Despite being a vampire, the scent and sight of her blood nauseates me. "You're gonna be okay. My name's Sarah. Don't be afraid of me."

"Addy Parker," whispers the girl. "I'm scared. It hurts everywhere."

"Ye better hurry," whispers Mardle, behind me. "The dark ones are makin' 'er into one o' dem. Poor wee lass will be all made o' wood in' another day ahr two."

I sprout claws.

The poor kid doesn't even flinch at the sight.

In her position, my thoughts would be 'go ahead and just kill me.' Somehow, this kid *doesn't* have a fatalistic glint in her eye. She's not hoping I end her suffering; she's merely not afraid of me. I reach up and place my claws under one of the thorn vines burrowing into her right forearm. Since my attempt to cut the last batch of magical roots didn't go so well, it's best to make a small test slice first rather than slashing the load-bearing ones and having the rest tear loose from her.

Here goes...

I rip my hand forward, having a surprisingly easy time severing the horrible thorny tendril. A spray of black fluid gushes from the strand still attached to the tree. Addy gasps in pain, as though I slashed her actual flesh. Before I can even process her reaction, the air fills with shrieks and screams of rage.

A dozen or more lumps swell outward from the trunk of the giant tree, growing rapidly into creatures closely resembling slender human women, or rather, nude wooden statues brought to life. Their 'skin' is the same shade of grey as the rest of the trees, similar to sun-bleached driftwood. Where a normal person would have hair, they sprout moss. A collection of brambles sits atop their heads, part way between hair and elaborate crowns, some having branchy 'horns' as wide as their arm span. While their faces appear mostly human, dark wooden lips peel back to expose thin, pointed piranha teeth dripping with black fluid similar to the ichor seeping from the vine I severed.

More emerge from trees surrounding the 'mother' trunk.

There is no possible way I'm going to be able to delicately get this child down in a hurry without causing serious internal damage. Ripping her off the tree is going to kill her, and I really don't want to turn a little kid into a vampire.

At the emergence of the dark dryads, Addy tries to scream in terror, but she's so weak she makes a noise more like a tire losing air.

Frustrated, horrified, and angry, I swipe my claws at the nearest wooden face, walloping it hard enough to send the bitch flying head over ass and leaving a couple of hatchet gouges on her cheek.

Ow.

I think my hand broke.

A dryad above me, her legs still embedded in the mother tree, grabs in my direction despite being like ten feet away. Her fingers lance outward, elongating and braiding together into a whipping thorny vine. I dive out of the way, totally cheating with vampiric reflexes. Her attack passes over me and whips another dryad in the chest. Serves her right for sneaking up behind me. Vine strikes oaken boob with a *crack* as loud as Jacob's little handgun, but doesn't appear to inflict any damage.

A flash of yellow light detonates a short distance to my right, but there's no time to look as three more dryads dive at me, jumping off the mother tree into free fall. I dodge by flying. Three heavy *thuds* strike the ground behind me—but a vine-whip gets me around the leg, yanking me to a halt.

Another whip nails me in the side, but I avoid the one trying to wrap around my neck. Growling, I do a kick flip, yanking on my trapped leg hard enough to drag the dryad on the other end of the vine into a stumbling charge—and stomp-kick her in the face with my other foot. She flies back into the other two, knocking them to the ground in a pile of crackling kindling.

Motion behind me.

I spin, raking my claws down the chest of a dryad. The attack is modestly more effective than I expected using claws on solid wood could possibly be. Quarter-inch-deep gouges leak black sap. She grabs the wound, branchy fingers clattering, and shrieks in agony.

Whistling in the air warns me of an incoming vine. I duck, spinning into a slash across the abdomen of the dryad trying to blindside me. These bitches are damn tough, but not particularly fast. I go full on Neo mode, bending under some whipping vines, jumping over others, and squeezing in a claw slash or kick whenever possible while fighting 'slow-motion' enemies.

Against two or three of these things, I wouldn't be terribly worried. Sure, it would take me forever to kill one—like cutting down a tree using a pocket knife—but my speed is sufficient to stay well away from their reach.

However, I have a problem.

Fifty or sixty problems to be exact. With *so many* dryads coming after me, it's impossible to dodge everything. See, there's a key concept to avoiding being smacked in the face, and it's having somewhere clear to go. Far more often than I'd like, every inch of usable space in my vicinity is full of ouch, and the harder I push to get closer to the little girl on the tree, the more punishment I receive.

These bitches are pushing me back, swarming me like I tried to go shopping on Black Friday during the height of Beanie Babies. Every time I try to get around them or fly over them, a vine—or fifteen—grabs me by some random body part and pulls me down. In not even two full minutes, I look like I got into a fight with a weed-whacker and lost. My clothes aren't exactly shredded as bad as a vampire-on-vampire fight, but I'm a bloody mess.

Every so often, I catch a glimpse of Addy in the distance, helpless, in agony, and trying to call out for help. Seeing her ignites a spike of rage, and my next kick splits a dryad's head in half. Her body stops all motion in an instant, becoming dead wood. The others don't seem particularly upset by this, or even notice. Could be, I merely knocked her out. Considering how difficult it is for the dark ones to reproduce, they ought to be furious with me if I really killed one.

I keep pushing, trying to fight my way past the wooden army, but soon find myself using all my time to break thorn vines off my arms, legs, and chest. The damn dryads are trying to mummify me in roots. Fighting does *not* seem to be too effective, so I try luring them away from the tree, shredding the grabbing thorns off my body and flying around in a circle. Roots and branches burst up from the ground, more—or maybe the same—dryads keep erupting up in front of me, shrieking and grabbing for my face. I'm really damn glad to be a vampire, and not only for the speed and toughness. They'd totally have killed a normal human me in seconds. No, mostly, I'm glad for being exposed to the knowledge and sights undeath has hit me with already. Otherwise, these wicked, twisted perversions of women with their needle fish teeth and hollow black eyes would have put me straight into a mental hospital.

Especially the way they keep springing up out of the ground in front of me no matter where I go.

It's like being in a video game running on a crappy computer where it can't render all of the environment at once, and I'm only seeing a little bit of the impenetrable wall around the mother tree at a time. No matter how fast I fly, there's more damn dryads always in the way.

Another vine grabs my ankle, not quite yanking me to an immediate stop, though I am towing 300 pounds of wooden bitch—and I think my ankle is dislocated. They pile on, dragging me to the ground. Thousands of tiny thorns dig into my skin. Vines squeeze my legs together and immobilize my arms. A few even go around my neck.

Gah!

Ignoring the sensation of thorns tearing my skin, I wrench myself around hard enough to snap some vines and get my right arm loose. The dryads are too slow to react to my accelerated speed, giving me the chance to slice my way free and fly backward. They don't pop up to intercept me if I fly *away* from the big tree—but I can't leave Addy there.

It would be kinder of me to shoot her in the head.

Mardle appears in a flicker of golden light between me and the dryads. "Go! Back ta the gateway! Der be too many!" He faces the oncoming dryads and releases a magical blast of intense light.

"Ack!" I yell, recoiling as if someone stuffed a police-issue Maglite in my face and turned it on.

The dryads flinch, trying to shield their faces behind their branchy fingers. Most of them petrify, going from pale grey to chalk white and shifting into unmoving wooden statues. I'm about to yell at him for not using this magic earlier, but the effect is extremely short-lived. Their coloration begins returning in mere seconds.

Mardle yells, "Go! I've got an idea!"

"I can't leave her!" I shout, and start to charge at the dryads again.

He whirls at me, and snaps his fingers.

The mass of dark dryads in front of me instantly becomes the six-tree ring. Grr. I catch myself with flight in mid leap before going through the portal... until Mardle crashes into me from behind and pushes us both into the glowing mist.

We land in a heap, once again in the normal forest.

Without the threat of an attacking army of vile, twisted forest spirits, I don't bother moving, remaining sprawled on my chest, stuck between wanting to cry as if Addy is already dead and throwing a temper tantrum out of frustration. My usual reaction to failure is to go home and sulk for a while, but my failure has never meant the death of a child before.

Hundreds of tiny thorn wounds close one by one.

Feels like acupuncture.

Except for the dislocated ankle, which hurts a bit more for about five minutes.

"We should ask de aid o' de dryads," says Mardle.

"What?" I push myself up to kneel. "They just tried to kill me."

He again snaps his fingers at me; my ripped and bloody clothes become pristine. "Na them dryads. Da oother ones."

I really want a machine gun so I can go back in there and play *Tom Clancy's 'Splinter' Cell.* A big enough gun ought to make those dark dryads into toothpicks. Of course, knowing my luck, I'd hit the girl. Ooh, wait. Flamethrower! Hang on. My outfit's not ruined.

"Hey. You fixed my clothes."

"A dank ya' would be nice."

"Can you get those vines out of her?"

Mardle taps his foot, giving me a stern look.

Sigh. Stubborn. "Thank you for fixing my clothes."

He grins. "Ye welcome. An' I tried. Dahn't work."

"Where can I get a flamethrower?"

"Why'd ya wanna do a damn fool thing like that?"

I point at the creepy tree circle. "Dryads are made of wood. Do the math."

"No." He holds his hands up, shaking his head. "Ya burn 'em, and they'll kill the child fer sure. Wi'out all me leprechaun friends, der ain't a way ta get her back but them wantin' us to."

"Why didn't you tell me this before?"

He taps his fingertips together, flashing a cheesy smile. "Never been tha' close. 'Ad ta see it meself fahr I knew. Trus' me. De light dryads be tha only way we kin' 'elp tha wee lass wi'out da rest o' de leprechauns. Thar be a delicate balance 'ere among different creatures."

"Right…" I stand.

"It's koind o' loike yer family gatherin's 'round the 'olidays. One wee error an' all unholy heck breaks loose."

I blink. "You know my Uncle Hank?"

"Na. Most 'umans er like dat. Follow. Time be shart."

I can't help myself but snicker.

"Oy, ye makin' fun o' me height again?" Mardle holds up his shillelagh in bonking position.

"No… sounded like you said 'shart.'"

"Ay did say shart." He narrows one eye, widening the other. "Why's et funneh?"

"It's not." Cough. Snicker. "I just got hit in the head a bunch of times."

Bonk. "One mahr. Now c'mon."

Grumbling, I rub my forehead and trudge after him.

A BARGAIN SLIGHTLY AWKWARD

Mardle hops on my back so we can fly.

The little guy might be magically fast, but he's only a bit quicker than an ordinary human running. Judging from the noises coming out of him, he's rather enjoying flying, even if he does have to keep one hand on his hat and point the way using the shillelagh. Great. Between him and Sophia, I've got a new job: promoted from katana scabbard to hoverbike. Our trip across the forest doesn't take too long, maybe eight minutes, before we find a small clearing containing a ring of wildflowers. I wouldn't have even noticed them if not for a subtle cloud of magical glow inside the circle.

"Is that a faerie circle?"

"Na. Too big. G'won in."

I shrug one shoulder and fly straight into the glowing patch. Fortunately, the 'light dryads' don't live in a world of perpetual sun. The forest on the other side of the portal is more or less identical to the natural one, except for having more green moss. I don't pick up the scent of any humans, only an overabundance of wet earth, plant matter, and various flowers on bushes everywhere.

Whispery conversation emanates from the trees a fair way off on my left. Might as well check it out. We fly for a minute or two before I spot a bunch of women ahead, sitting around a grove of lush trees and soaking up moonlight. Pretty sure they aren't human. My first clue is their emerald green skin. Second clue is their glowing green eyes. White hair isn't definitive proof of inhumanity since I've seen plenty of normal girls who like to dye their hair snowy blonde—case in point: Mandy Carlin. Also odd is how they all appear to be the same age—mid-twenties. No kids, no elders, not even a single soccer mom. Oh, they're also all naked.

Gonna go out on a limb here and assume they're vegans, too.

I mean, can't get much closer to nature than being half tree, right? Or wait, would eating a veggie burger be like cannibalism to them? Never mind. No time to ponder such a pointless question.

The dryads all look toward me at the same time, going wide-eyed and cringing in a spot-on impression of Sophia accidentally watching a horror movie too intense for her. Meaning, she's watching a scary movie not starring Muppets.

Crap. I bet they can sense me being undead.

"I just want to talk! You have my word I will not harm anyone."

The dryads start running off in random directions.

Mardle shouts in a foreign language. Not sure if it's Irish or Leprechaunish. I'm also not sure if Leprechaunish is a word.

A few dryads stop running, hesitating to watch me suspiciously. With my most innocent smile, I approach and land at a distance close enough to talk without being so close they'll fear me as a threat.

"Please, I've come here to ask for your help. A little girl's life is at stake."

They mostly make sad faces at me.

"It is too late," says one. "We cannot restore you to life."

"Thanks for your sympathy, but I'm not talking about myself. An actual little kid. The dark dryads have her and they're torturing her." I explain what happened at the other grove, everything I saw, and how wonderfully my attempt to fight them went.

Over the course of a few minutes, the dryads exchange looks. Got a feeling they're having a telepathic communication or something similar to it. I'm unable to listen in, and yeah, I tried. While their thoughts are on a different wavelength, my mind powers *do* pick up traces of emotion. They're afraid at first, then cautiously sad, then spend a while radiating a mood like Sierra when she's on her way to the mall to get a new PlayStation game.

Now I've got *two* little girls attached to trees to deal with. Standing here watching a bunch of impossibly beautiful green women make odd faces at each other isn't helping. I'm about ready to yell at them to hurry it up when they all face me.

Three approach.

Okay, guess they've decided to believe me honest about not wanting to hurt them.

They're also surprisingly tall. Must be originally from Norway. My head only comes up to their shoulders. Yeah, I know I'm on the low end of average size and have an overly young face, but it's not too often I legit feel like a twelve-year-old by height next to another woman.

"We will help," says the dryad in the middle. "We ask you to help us as well."

Naturally. Massive amounts of willpower allow me not to roll my eyes.

Left Dryad smiles. "We will give you two wellspring seeds, which you can take and offer the dark ones in trade for the child they have stolen."

"For this, you will bring us a group of human men," says Right Dryad.

Ugh. I can't sacrifice a couple dudes to save one kid. "Umm… what's going to happen to these men?"

The three women in front of me smile, the rest all giggle.

"Use your wildest imagination," says Center Dryad. "They will not be harmed… but may be tired."

I blush. "Oh… you're going to…"

They all giggle.

"How long will you keep them here?"

Right Dryad grins. "A few hours. They cannot stay here."

"To part with a wellspring seed, we will need to make more."

"Umm, you're going to give away your babies so I can save the human girl?"

Center Dryad rests a hand on my shoulder. Ooh. Tingly. "Not entirely. A wellspring seed is not our young, but a vessel which can become such given the proper infusion of energy." She sighs. "While it pains us to think of a seed being tainted by the dark ones, it is far, far less a tragedy than a human's life being infected by their corruption."

"Balance," whispers Mardle. "The dark and light dryads do not seek the others' destruction."

None of this makes sense. But hey, I'm a vampire with a multipurpose stealth attack kitten. The dryads want men to have some, umm, 'vigorous fun' with. Oh hell. I gotta get this kid off the damn evil mother tree.

"Okay. I'm going to guess you won't trust me to bring you these guys after you let me use the wellspring seeds to stop the dark dryads from killing her? She's in a lot of pain and looks close to dead."

They make sad faces at each other.

"You are a creature of darkness," says Left Dryad.

"I'm more dimness than darkness." Sigh. "Right. Thought so. No one makes a fetch quest and gives the reward out before the deed is done."

"What is a fetch quest?" asks Right Dryad.

"I'm making a video game joke. Be back soon."

Another dryad runs out of the distant woods, zooming up to us. She's carrying two pale, whitish-green objects about the size of large potatoes, halfway between fat pumpkin seeds and acorns for shape.

"Whoa..." I pause. "You're going to let me have the seeds now?"

Center Dryad takes the giant seeds from the runner in both hands, then faces me. "The child you describe will not survive long once she is disentangled from the Dark Mother. They will most certainly agree to your demand of an exchange for two seeds. Not only are you giving them two in trade for one, a dryad grown from these seeds will be stronger and healthier than a corrupted human."

Stunned, I wordlessly accept the offering. Guess I'm committed to dragging a bunch of men out into the woods now.

"Bring the child to us as fast as you are able. We shall tend to her." Center Dryad steps back, clasping her hands in front of herself. "When you return with the men, the child will be healthy enough to go with you."

Reading between the lines, it sounds like she's saying they intend to hold the kid prisoner until I make good on my part of the deal. These dryads don't look likely to torture her at least. And... it's hard to argue the offer of magical healing. Who better to undo the effects of dark dryad's corruption than light dryads? After getting a close look at Addy, it's easy for me to believe these dryads' story she'll die anyway. Medical science is awesome and all, but I don't think they can fix 'thorn vines growing into the body.'

And wow, I thought for sure they'd insist I get the men before they parted with these seeds. They really are kind. I'm finding it impossible not to trust them.

"Thank you! We'll be back as soon as possible."

The dryads bow their heads in acknowledgement.

It's difficult to think of a six-pound nugget of wood as a baby, yet it basically is. These women regard them in reverence, but no way would they give away their children. At least, I hope not. The seeds don't give off any sense of intelligence or sentient thought. Not sure I'd feel right with myself taking a baby light dryad and giving her to the dark ones to corrupt. It would be like transplanting a normal kid away from home so they grow up liking country music.

Some evil is just too unspeakable.

CHILD FOR CHILD

Seeds clutched close to my chest, I fly scary fast across the forest.

Mardle started off sitting on my back, but my sudden acceleration made him lose his grip and tumble down over my butt, sliding all the way to my sneaker. He curses me out in not-English, then teleports onto my back again—and proceeds to bonk me.

"Wahrn me next time!"

"Sorry. In a hurry. Need to get this done before the sun comes up. Sophia's not going to spend a whole day tied to a tree."

"Oy what?" Mardle scratches his beard. "Didn't tink brownies tried ta corrupt small girls."

"You're thinking of Girl Scouts… they turn them into aggressive cookie merchants."

He doesn't say anything.

"They're not doing anything to my sister worse than holding her prisoner until I do their bidding."

Mardle goes off on a rant about how irritating brownies are. Clumsy curses, jinxes, making machines fail, going into towns or villages and tripping people, making them drop things, locking people out of their houses naked, stealing food, and so on. Leprechauns, also being highly magical creatures, are immune to the worst of it. Brownies also resist most of the magic leprechauns throw at them. The 'war' between them essentially consisted of a bunch of two-foot-tall people chasing each other around, brownies stealing hats and running away from the leprechauns trying to bonk them.

Pure insanity.

I don't know whether to laugh at the crazy scene he's describing or scream in frustration at being caught up in such an unbelievably weird mess.

Fortunately, our arrival at the dark tree ring spares me having to make the decision.

We fly right into it, reappearing in the gloomy, overgrown forest of all-consuming dread and suffering. A sense of foreboding doom hasn't hung over me this heavy since I had a paper due for school in three days without even starting it.

Every direction still looks the same, so it isn't my memory failing me. Screw it, I'm in a hurry.

"Addy? Where are you?" I shout.

A weak moan comes from behind me.

I fly around the tree ring and cruise toward her. Already, dark dryads emerge in response to me yelling, whipping vines at me high and low. Their wooden bodies creak as they reach their arms out from the trees, some in the high branches, others at ground level. One or two at a time, it's fairly easy for me to duck, swerve, or pop up to get past the thorny tendrils attempting to ensnare me. Cutting a dive too close forces Mardle to jump off my back to avoid being whipped in the face, but I grab him before he hits the ground.

He yelps, dangling from my fingertips, glaring at me like a cat who really *hates* being picked up.

By the time we reach the Dark Mother, a wall of evil dryads has gathered, easily seventy or more of them. The child doesn't look any worse than before, thankfully, though they've repaired the one thorn I severed.

The lot of them raise their arms, conjuring whipping tendrils studded in thorns.

"Stop!" I yell, slowing to a hover in front of the 'wall,' far enough away to avoid being grabbed. "I've come to offer you a trade."

None of them show the slightest sign of slowing down their attack.

I hold the two seeds up. "You know what these are?"

All the dark dryads freeze, staring at me with their hollow shadow-filled eyes. Some flash greedy smiles, black liquid dripping past their teeth and down their chins.

"Yeah, thought so. I've got two of them, and I'll give them both to you in exchange for Addy."

A smaller group steps forward from the wall, creeping closer, emitting raspy noises amongst themselves, a language so alien to human ears it's indiscernible from wind hissing through the cracked boards of a rotting cabin.

Addy struggles to lift her head and look at me. Blood wells out of small holes in her cheeks where the roots puncture in. Seeing a hint of hope in her eyes hurts more than Petra stabbing a piece of rebar into my back.

I cautiously hold my ground, ready for a trick. "Two wellspring seeds are yours in exchange for the child."

The dark dryad nearest me reaches out a hand.

"Let her down first."

A soft creak behind me gives away their ambush.

Ugh. Dad. Dryads made of wood and leaves… am*bush*. I'm going to slap him for making me think like him.

Twenty thorny tendrils burst out at me all at once.

I launch myself straight up, evading all but two. The painful grip of a spike-studded vine pins my legs together at the shins, jerks me to a halt, and swings me downward. Before I crash flat on my chest, I toss the seeds to Mardle. Aside from two years in peanut soccer, I didn't really do the sports thing growing up. And it shows. But… vampiric reflexes, strength, and a fast little leprechaun jumping make up for zero experience.

Twelve pounds of wellspring seed hurled by superhuman arms is enough to swat Mardle out of the air and knock him into a tumbleweed roll.

The dryads smack me face-first into the dirt. More vines grab me, but I don't bother shredding them... yet. Others go after the leprechaun. He teleports around in random hops, laughing and mocking the dryads for being slow. The ones by me lose interest in doing more than holding me down, their attention focused on the seeds as intensely as Ashley spotting someone across the mall carrying a unicorn plush.

Mardle feigns being afraid as a pack of dark dryads close in around him near a tree. He teleports behind them a fraction of a second before whips hit the trunk—then conjures a brilliant flash of white light, petrifying them momentarily.

"You'll never catch him," I yell. "Let Addy go, and you can have the seeds. Hurt her, and I'm coming back here with a flamethrower and a fifty-gallon drum of weed killer."

The dark dryads cease chasing Mardle. Somehow, I don't think my threat bothered them at all. They're giving up because they know they'll never catch him. Vines recede from me, so I stand.

Addy cries out in pain.

I spin toward her.

She convulses. Pulsating black thorn vines slide out of her body, slick with blood. Shit! They're just gonna drop her.

I dive over the wall of wooden women, swooping up to the tree seconds before the last of the vines lose their grip on the inside of her torso. She lurches forward into my grasp, her arms stretched up over her head, still held up by vines extruding out of her skin. Afraid of hurting her, I don't try to pull her down any faster than the horrible thorns retreat on their own. Finally, she's completely free; her limp arms flop down, no strength left in her tiny body. Expecting more trickery, I glide into the air with her, ready for a flying sprint.

Seeing us gaining altitude, clear of the Dark Mother, Mardle tosses the seeds at the dryad who first reached out to take them from me. The wooden fiends swarm after them like a pack of starving cats. Not waiting around for them to try grabbing me again, I fly low and fast. Mardle appears on top of me in a magical flash.

"Yer off a bit." He points the shillelagh over my left shoulder, about ten o'clock.

Addy emits a weak moan. "Ow..."

The smell of her blood is alarmingly strong. Just like the light dryads said, these cruel wretches didn't do anything about the holes they left in her. "You're gonna be fine. Don't fall asleep."

"Are we flying?"

"Yes."

"Are you an angel? Did I die?"

"No, and no."

"I think you're an angel," says Addy in a whispery voice—right before she passes out.

ONE NIGHT IN THE WOODS

I t's not even scary flying close to my top speed through the forest while I'm carrying an unconscious, bleeding little girl and have a screaming leprechaun clinging to my leg.

Hitting a tree at 140 MPH would sting, but I'll recover. In Addy's case, it might actually be a mercy. I'm not one of those girls who needs a GPS app and six stops for directions to find a place four blocks from home, but my sense of direction also isn't exactly the greatest. Somehow, be it sheer luck, determination, or some previously unknown supernatural power of vampirism, I find the dryad's flower circle right away without getting disoriented.

The screaming leprechaun may have also helped. Some of those howls did kinda sound like 'go that way ya daft fool.'

Picture a bunch of small birds hanging out in a park, just doing their bird thing, when all of a sudden, some jackass on a Harley comes out of nowhere. The light dryads do a perfect impression of the way those birds would scatter into an explosion of feathers, except this is more a bunch of bare green butts than feathers.

I'm the jackass on the Harley.

Only, replace loud noise with whatever energy I have as an undead.

I stop so abruptly, Mardle goes flying off my leg, wailing, and vanishes into the bushes. Cradling the girl, I land in the middle of the now-empty grove, surrounded by the rustling of a dozen naked green-skinned women running for their immortal lives. Captain Kirk would be in heaven here.

"It's me! Addy needs help!" I shout.

Beautiful faces surrounded in snow white hair pop out of the woods around us. Glowing bright green eyes widen. Upon realizing it's only me and not some undead harvester monster or whatever come to reap their souls, they come running over and mob around me. I feel like I showed up at Sophia's dance school with a husky puppy in my arms—only the dryads aren't squealing.

Three of them collect Addy from me, gasping in horror at the sight of her.

"Bring her to the spring, quickly!" says the woman I recognize as Center Dryad from earlier.

The dryads carrying the child, plus four others, rush off with her into the woods—so fast they blur. I look down at the blood on my top. Even though it smells like cotton candy, it's not the least bit appealing. The reality it came from such a small child hits me hard. On top of her passing out in my arms on the way here, it's overwhelming.

I sink to my knees, fighting not to give in to tears.

Diplomatic solution or not, if Addy dies, I'm legit going to the nearest military base and forcing someone to show me how to use a flamethrower. The absurdity of me genuinely being able to do it offers an emotional pillar to which I can cling, avoiding the sweeping tide of grief threatening to drag me into a sea of dark thoughts.

"The child will be fine," says Center Dryad. "She did not have much time left, but she had enough time."

I look up. "How much?"

"Another six hours and she would've become a dark dryad sapling."

Pretty sure she would have bled to death a lot sooner than six hours after they let her go. A few deep breaths I don't really need later,

I stand. Screw it. I needed them. Maybe not for oxygen, but they help me feel calmer. "You can really stop her from dying?"

The woman rests her hand on my shoulder again. Electric tingles from her touch spread down my arm. "Yes. It will take a little time. At this moment, my sisters are immersing her in the wellspring and infusing her with life energy to purge the corruption our warped cousins have inflicted."

Hope she doesn't mean a literal pool of water. It's freakin' December. Brr!

"Okay, umm…"

"Niatha," says the dryad. "I am the eldest of my sisters."

"Cool. Me, too."

She tilts her head, looking about as confused as Bree Swanson taking a physics final. "You do not seem to possess many years. Certainly there are others far more ancient."

"Oh." I grimace-smile. "Not vampires. I mean my actual sisters. I have two and I'm the oldest." I point both thumbs back to the right. "Anyway. Let me go do my part of the deal."

Niatha smiles.

"Umm. I'm kinda not from around here. Where is the closest town?"

She points. "Once you return to the outer world, travel a short distance east of the forest's edge."

"All right. Thank you for helping me save Addy's life. I'll be back soon." I start to turn away but catch myself. "How much time do I have before the sun comes up?"

"Almost three hours."

Whew. More than I thought. Guess time flies when you're getting your ass kicked by evil tree bitches.

"I'll be waitin' roight 'ere," says Mardle.

"Yeah. Probably a good idea for a leprechaun *not* to walk into a human town."

He grips the lapels of his little suit jacket. "Aye."

Okay, I can do this. One more step in this insane series of diversions and I can get Sophia away from the brownies. Wonder if the people who came up with the pre-Girl Scouts knew how devious and powerful *actual* brownies are… and how they use their powers of cuteness as a defense.

Maybe they did.

I fly back to the flower circle and cross to the 'outer world' as Niatha called it. Guess the dryads mostly live in the 'inner world.' No point getting myself lost in the woods. I fly straight up for a look around and pull my phone out of my pocket. Since it's rather difficult to navigate by the position of the sun at night, the compass app has been coming in really handy. Yeah, I know ancient sailors navigated by stars, but it's quite a bit trickier and involves a bunch of weird tools like sextants or something.

The only reason I even know the word sextant is movies.

Another bizarre thing is how small the forest below me seems comparatively to the land around it full of open fields. I'm almost certain the time it took me to fly between the dark dryad portal and the light dryad portal would've covered the entire patch of woods down there three times over. Either some serious elder magic is at work, or reality is fake and I'm a character in a video game with glitchy zone boundaries.

Whatever.

It's easy to spot the lights of a town not far to the east. Seeing traces of modernity—electric lights, cars, and so on—feels weird after dealing with brownies, leprechauns, and dryads. It's like the time we went to watch *Lord of the Rings* in the actual theater. Got so into it, walking out of the theater back into the real world afterward seemed strange. I kept waiting to see people walking around carrying swords and riding horses.

So, yeah. Easy job ahead of me. All I have to do is find a bunch of guys interested in random sex with impossibly beautiful—albeit green-skinned—women. Most people assume guys are all horny bastards who'd think nothing of hooking up with a woman they'll see once and never again. And sure, while there are loads of men like that, there are some who aren't. Like if I'd run into a pack of, umm, satyrs, and their price for helping me was to round up a bunch of women for sex, most people would find it evil.

Yeah, it's a double standard. Kinda like how if a high school teacher seduces a girl student, he's—rightfully—demonized and the girl's treated like a victim. But if it's a boy student and a woman teacher, a scary number of people are like 'way to go, kid.'

Grr.

I don't like having to do this, but Sophia's in trouble. And her being in trouble indirectly puts the Aurora Aurea mystics in mortal danger. Still, I can't *force* guys to go have sex with dryads. Well, I literally can. My powers are capable of it, but it's not something I'm totally okay with. Better get on with it before I think too much, chicken out, and cause another problem. Niath and her dryads seem nice, but they'd definitely keep Abby as their 'guest' until my part of this deal is fulfilled. If they don't release her, the witches don't stop attacking the brownies, and Sophia's going to spend a long time stuck to a tree.

Or, I'll be in a continuous state of returning to Ireland from wherever the little goobers teleport me each time I kill one. My luck, I'll end up stuck inside a pyramid in Egypt, up to my neck in beetles and snakes. By the time I dig out of there, Sophia would be grown up.

I'm starting not to like brownies.

Gonna eat a few when I get home—baked goods I mean—purely out of spite.

I land in a dark patch of field beside a road not far from the edge of a small town. Honestly, bringing a couple guys to 'feed' dryads isn't terribly different from me taking a blood meal forcibly. Supernatural creature doing what it needs to do to survive, and the normal person walks away largely unaffected, if a little tired.

Still, to make myself feel better, I resolve to mentally probe prospective victims first to check their responsiveness to the idea of casual sex with random forest spirits. I'm not going to force any guy to do it against his will, even if they won't remember it. Given only a few hours remain until sunrise, there aren't too many people outside. Sounds of activity draw me to a tavern, surprisingly active given the time. I head in, overcome by more than a little awkwardness as I've never 'gone to a bar' before. Still feels like something I'm too young for.

Oddly, no one gives me weird looks for seeming underage.

They're giving me weird looks because I have blood smeared all over me. Oops. Forgot to ask Mardle to clean my top. Oh well, nothing a little light mental domination won't fix. If I can walk across Woodinville stark naked and make people remember me dressed, I can hide a little blood. Wouldn't be the first time this girl had to conceal an inopportune bloodstain. Though tying a sweatshirt around my waist as an extra skirt isn't gonna work here.

Fortunately, I'm a vampire.

I'll take 'things I never imagined I'd say' for $200, Alex.

Okay, a bar at almost five in the morning. Good bet anyone here—other than me and the employees—has a fairly free schedule and probably a handful of personal problems. The clock nearly gives me an anxiety attack, but I'm still used to the schedule from back home. Sunrise has been happening around seven in the morning in Washington. It's due at 8:40 a.m. here. So, I have more time than expected.

Yay for obnoxious amounts of darkness in Europe.

It's strange more vampires don't live in Ireland. Maybe they're all in London. Or one of those Nordic countries where they get a couple months with no sun at all. Does staying awake for months at a time drive vampires insane? Meh. I don't want to find out.

Right, mission start.

I walk around casually eavesdropping and probing into men's thoughts by inserting the notion of a random supermodel walking up and offering to sleep with them to see how they'd react. I skip two guys who are married but would happily say yes. Skip another three who are married and would decline. The next two guys I check aren't interested in women. Skip. Next guy's reaction is to laugh and wonder who set him up for a joke. He wants to go with her but is afraid he's being pranked. Aww. He's not ugly; he's average with a side order of nerdy chubbiness. One down. I give him a mental compulsion to get up and follow me when I go out the door.

My next victim is a smooth talker trying to hook up with one of the few women here. He's only looking for sex while lying to her about being open to a real relationship. Sigh. You're coming with me.

Eventually, out of everyone in here, only five men fit within my self-imposed parameters for not feeling like a creep. Since I'm at a bar, might as well grab a drink. Tangling with those dark dryads kinda wore me out. The least-inebriated person in here is the bartender. A mild mental prod gets him to ask the lone waitress to keep an eye on the bar while he goes into the back room to check something. I follow him, pouncing as soon as the door shuts behind us. Most likely due to me being in a place like this and thinking about alcohol, his blood tastes like the wine coolers I had at Tiffany's house. Yes, I realize he's a big, bearded bartender in a back country Irish tavern—and anyone here asking for a wine cooler would likely get their asses kicked. Don't laugh. It's the only alcohol I've had. Beer smelled like the end result of someone boiling sweaty socks. I attempted to be the good girl and not drink before twenty-one, but they got me to try wine coolers. Hey, if I'm going to break the rules, it might as well taste good.

And this big bartender doesn't need to know my brain turned him into a foo-foo drink.

Feeding done, I make my way out into the barroom, then the front door. As soon as I go outside, my mental commands activate and the men I've selected for the dryads all get up at once and follow me. Hmm. It's a mile or two to the woods. Walking there is going to take a while. Back into their brains I go. A guy who had a 'yeah sure why not' reaction to the imaginary supermodel owns a Jeep-like vehicle more like something one would see roaming around the African savannah. It's on the older side and looks like it might've seen literal combat, but it's big enough for all of us—and it can drive right up to the edge of the trees.

I 'encourage' the guys to hop in, and cram myself into the space between the two front seats. Not comfortable, but I'm small enough to fit and this position lets me steer the driver. The other three guys fill the back seat. Squatting here beats a strange dude's lap or clinging to the roof—which I don't recommend. Did it once and the ride ended in flames.

Before long, the driver, Niall, gets us as close to the forest as possible in a vehicle. I mentally prod the men to get out of the Jeep-thing and insert another command to follow me and discard all memories from this point forward. It takes us longer to walk from the forest edge to the dryad portal than it did to drive from town to the woods.

I step through—and the guys vanish.

Damn.

I back up.

They're all standing there looking dumbfounded.

Okay, guess I've got proof normal people can't traverse the gateway between 'outer world' and inner. Hmm. Now what? Maybe it's simple. I make them all hold hands, grab Niall by the hand, and pull them into the gateway.

Success!

Another short walk brings me to the grove where the dryads lounge around casually. They glance over at me and, damn. The way they're looking at us, it's like I just showed up at a prison cafeteria with filet mignon and lobster.

"I'm back." I grin. "Did someone order Five Guys?"

The dryads rush over, ignoring my joke.

As soon as the men see them, they stop moving and stare transfixed. Wow, my derp hammer has nothing on these dryads. Sure, a lot of men think with their groin when they see a beautiful woman, but these dudes look like they'd legit walk straight off the edge of a skyscraper. They're not even thinking with the 'small brain.' No thought whatsoever is going on here at all.

The crowd of dryads hurry over and escort the men hastily off, deeper into the woods out of sight. Niatha approaches me with a fidgety eagerness reminiscent of how Sierra gets on the ride home from buying a new video game. I get the distinct feeling she wants to settle affairs with me and go join them as fast as possible.

So, yeah. There it is. I've forced guys to have sex with magical forest nymphs in exchange for a kid's life and getting Sophia back. My life is going to be an endless series of morally grey choices from this point forward, isn't it? Maybe I could rationalize it by saying I only forced them to follow me here. The dryads' charm is doing everything else. But I'm well aware what the end result of leading them here would be.

"You have my thanks, Sarah." Niatha smiles at me, then looks back over her shoulder at the woods toward a different spot than where the men went.

Two dryads emerge from the thick foliage, carrying Addy. She's no longer deathly pale—well, any more so than natural for an Irish girl. Her long, thick hair is damp, but her clothes remain dry. Her winter coat's been mended, the sleeves no longer ripped open to the elbows. Same for her leggings. There's no sign she'd ever been attacked by gruesomely disturbing thorns. At least none visible to the eye.

She says something in Irish to the dryads, making them smile sadly.

They set her on her feet in front of me.

"You *are* real," whispers Addy, wide-eyed in awe.

"So they say." I crouch in front of her. "I'm going to take you home to your family."

"Please."

I brush a hand over her head, moving her hair off her face, and stare into her eyes. My mind floods with memories of being lost in the woods. She'd gotten a little adventurous, strayed off too far, and become separated from her grandmother, father, and brothers while out hunting for mushrooms. Her family had seemingly vanished in an instant. Weeds and vines sprang to life and grabbed her. This kid is *not* going to remember the sensation of sharp vines piercing her skin and burrowing into her body. Unfortunately, I can't erase memories without seeing—and feeling—them. The pain of hanging on thorn vines is going to haunt me for a long damn time. Living wooden threads squirming around inside is such a disturbing sensation, I find myself trembling. She was in so much of a stupor she doesn't remember me sprouting claws or even fighting the dark dryads. The past day is little more than a painful, foggy fever dream.

By the time the last vestiges of such a horrible experience are eradicated from this eight-year-old's head, I'm a complete emotional mess. I can't believe anything in existence could be so evil as to subject an innocent child to such unearthly pain. What those dark dryads did to her is even worse than mandatory participation in grade school talent shows.

But yeah, seeing and feeling what she went through is enough to get me to scoop her into a hug and squeeze her like a kitten I plucked unhurt off a busy highway.

Mardle snaps his fingers and the blood vanishes out of my clothes.

"Why are *you* crying?" asks Addy. "Are we lost? Is something bad gonna happen?"

"No. Your parents are worried about you being lost and alone. I'm crying 'cause I'm happy you're okay." Behold the first time Sarah Wright tells a convincing lie. Okay, fooling a little girl isn't exactly impressive—but I suck at lying.

Addy smiles. "I didn't get lost. Bad spirits took me."

"Umm..." Didn't I erase that?

"Grandma's going to be mad, but not at me." Addy takes my hand. "You kinda have bad spirit energy, but you're not a bad spirit. What are you?"

Sigh. "I'm just some random teenage girl in the wrong place when the flaming toilet seat fell out of the sky."

"What?" Addy tilts her head, then laughs, her dark brown eyes full of happiness. "Don't be silly."

"Can you keep a secret?" I whisper.

She nods.

"I'm a vampire, but a nice vampire."

"Oh. Okay." She taps the tip of her sneaker into the dirt. "Can you please take me home now?"

Whoa. No reaction at all? "You're not at all nervous being with me?"

"No. Umm, something bad happened even if I can't 'member it. I kinda 'member you carrying me and flying. And you were crying. You can't be a mean vampire or you wouldn't have helped me." She scrunches up her nose. "Grandma said there aren't s'posed ta be any vampires in Ireland. The barghests eat them."

"Let me guess… giant black dogs with glowing eyes?"

Addy nods. "Yeah. It's bad luck to see one. They warn of death an' if they scratch, it never heals. Ever."

"Your grandmother is right. There aren't any vampires in Ireland. I'm only visiting. C'mon."

WITCH WAY TO GO

Returning to the leprechaun village isn't too long a trip, so we walk.

Addy's kinda worn out from her ordeal even if she's mostly forgotten the details. I carry her, Mardle walking alongside us. A short while later, the tiny town appears out of nowhere when we pass the enchantment protecting it. Multiple leprechauns come running, shillelaghs at the ready, until they recognize me.

"Wow." Addy looks up at me. "Leprechauns!"

I set her on her feet beside me, but keep holding her hand. The little guys gather around us, greeting her as though she were some high court noble princess or some such thing. She adores it, playing right along. A smaller group, and Mardle, pull me off to the side.

"So, you've managed to recover the human girl?" asks one, frowning.

The other two grumble.

They're annoyed because they lost any leverage they had over me. All the leprechauns at once—at least according to Mardle—could have held the dark dryads at bay effectively while I plucked Addy off the Dark Mother tree. Since they no longer have a little girl's life to dangle over my head in exchange for help destroying brownies, the little guys appear a bit miffed. Also, they're making faces at Mardle the same way I imagine Amish people do right before banishing someone from the village for showing too much ankle in public or smuggling a cell phone into the community. Considering the leprechauns were willing to let her die if I didn't wipe out the brownies, they're being awfully polite and friendly to her.

"Yes. Addy's safe." I fold my arms. "I'm also going to stop the brownies from attacking you."

"Why?" blurts one with a white beard, shocked.

"Wait, you *want* the war to continue?" I tilt my head.

"Na. Na. Na!" He flails his arms. "Why would you 'elp us when ya dahn't get nothin' out o' et?"

"Oh, I dunno. War is stupid. And this is a particularly stupid war."

They eye me suspiciously.

"Because it's the right thing to do?"

Their suspicion deepens.

I can't exactly read their thoughts, but enough emotion comes through for me to figure out they suspect me of attempting to somehow trick them into owing me a big favor. These little dudes simply *can't* comprehend the idea of doing something because it's right or feels good. Everything has to have a transaction. Favor for favor.

"I'm going to calm the brownies anyway. They have my sister, remember? If I stop the war, I get my sister back." I let my arms fall at my sides. "And it's the right thing to do."

"Ahh!" the trio chorus.

The 'transaction' of Sophia being returned to me in exchange for stopping the war makes sense to them. No longer defensive about how I'm trying to get one over on them, they erupt in cheers about the soon-to-end brownie war. Most of them start dancing, arm-in-arm, spinning in circles. This gets Addy laughing, which makes me smile. She really needed a dose of joy.

Mardle emits a squeal of delight, dances for a bit, then hurries back to me, tapping on my leg until I look down at him. He holds a green velvet pouch up. "'Ere ya go. Take 'et."

I accept the seemingly empty pouch, and peek inside—at shiny gold coins. "Gah! Are you serious? I can't take this from you. It's too much."

He waves me off when I try to hand it back. "Tis but a small nibble. A token o' me gratitude fer puttin' an end ta the brownie problem."

"Are you sure?"

"Indeed." He grabs his lapels, rocking heel to toe. "I've plenty. Enjoy 'et. Ye ought'a be gettin' goin'. Be daylight in a tick."

"Good point." Since everyone here seems taken with overacting genteel customs, I curtsey to Mardle. "Thank you for helping me."

"Bah. Nothin' compared ta ye stealin' me entire fortune. Sides…" He bumps his derby to tilt forward on his head, then winks. "'Ad a wee bit o' fun."

I shake hands with him, collect Addy, and head off to the brownie camp.

As soon as we spot brownies, Addy gasps and clings, seeming terrified of them.

"What's wrong?" I whisper.

She rambles in Irish, too fast for me to tell where one word ends and the next starts. The child looks around frantically for a moment, then pulls the drawstring out from the base of her winter coat. She ties one end around my left wrist, the other around her right wrist while muttering. As soon as she cinches the second knot, using her teeth to help, she calms.

"What's all that about?" I ask.

"Brownies!" she whispers. "I'm only eight!"

"Yeah. Seven to ten… gotta be eleven to get into the Girl Scouts."

Addy rolls her eyes. "No. Real brownies. They steal kids." She waves her arm, making the thin cord dance about. "This will stop them from taking me."

Oh, hmm. Wonder if this is where 'kid leashes' came from?

"If you say so. Cord's a bit flimsy. Even you could probably snap it."

"They can't make me get lost or separate us. It's a spell." She smiles. "You're too big for them to steal."

Since she's calmed down, I keep walking with her into the camp. The brownies all stop in their tracks, staring at us. Imagine a new 'must have' doll comes out on the market two months before Christmas. The brownies fixate on Addy like a pack of jealous kindergarteners whose classmate brought one of these ultra-rare and hard to find dolls to show-and-tell after no one else got one. Their creepy too-cute eyes brim with desire. Oh, holy crap. Addy's right. Any one of these little goobers look like they'd grab her if they could. No wonder the witches blamed them for a missing kid.

For some reason, they aren't looking at Sophia the same way. Could be, she's too old to count as a 'little kid' to them, or the brownies think of her more as a powerful magic user rather than a child. Speaking of Sophia, she's still hanging on the tree in a root cocoon, looking rather bored.

"No!" shouts three brownies, running up to us. "Take girl away from here now! The witches will know she is here."

"I'm going to take her home right away. The witches will stop bothering you. I'm here for my sister."

"Make witches stop first!" shout the brownies.

"I'm going to do that next. You're on the way."

"No!" they shout. "Witches first!"

"Bringing her home is going to stop—"

My surroundings change in an instant.

Addy and I are standing on a paved street in a small town. The cord connecting our wrists glows like Wonder Woman's lasso for a few seconds and dims.

"Eep!" She gawks at it. "They tried to take me!"

"Didn't they demand you *not* be there?" I scratch my head.

"Yeah, but..." She grabs my hand. "They can't help it. Stealing kids is what they do. I'm double chocolate cake and they're like a bunch of pregnant ladies. If they didn't try to keep me, the string wouldn't glow."

I chuckle—for a second. "Umm, what do brownies do when they take a kid? Hope they're not really going to eat you like cake."

She offers a nervous shrug. "No idea. Grandma says kids taken by brownies don't come home again. I think they get turned into brownies, too."

I cringe, thinking of the dark dryads. Yeah, fits the theme around here.

"Okay, now I'm scared," whispers Addy.

"What happened?"

Addy points. "This is the street I live on. The brownies know where my house is."

"Oh. We've been teleported—and no flying through a void of blackness thing like when the mystics grabbed Sophia and me. I should be freaking out."

"Brownies are scary," whispers Addy. "They only go out at night, but they can't get me when I'm in bed."

"Gotta love the 'blanket of defense.'"

She smiles, then whispers, "It's true. Old laws. Most elder fey can't get past an item of protection like a blanket, or cross the threshold of a house when the door is closed."

"Really?"

"Yeah. Unless you do something to deserve revenge, they can't just walk in." Addy walks off the road to the sidewalk, following it to the third house. She knocks, barely making any noise. No one inside notices. She knocks again a moment later, still nothing.

"I got this." I hammer on the door like a pissed off cop—stronger than mortal Sarah, but not enough to break anything.

A man upstairs erupts in a fit of shouting. Addy blushes and gasps. Okay, I'm not going to ask her what he's saying. His yelling soon sets a woman to shouting who sounds too young to be her grandmother. Lights come on inside. Three, maybe four adults based on tromping, come down a flight of stairs into the room behind the door.

It whips open inward, stirring up almost enough wind force to suck us into the house. A tall guy with a mop of disheveled curly black hair stares down at me, one eye wider than the other. He's about to lay into me for bothering them at such an early hour—but spots Addy.

"Papa!" she yells, leaping into a hug.

The nylon cord around my wrist drags me into the house as the guy gathers her up and spins, erupting in emotional cheering. I could snap the cord pretty easily, but no need yet. Superhuman agility lets me avoid wiping out, hurting Addy, or being thrown into the wall.

Three women watching from the base of the stairs—one older, one mom's age, one early twenties—also erupt in joyous shouting. I'm going to assume they're grandma, mom, and older sis, or maybe her mother's sibling. Grandma notices the cord and grabs hold of the father, bringing an end to his wildly swinging Addy around.

"Brownies? Ahh, I knew it." Grandma unties the cord from my wrist, then undoes it from Addy's arm. "Don't need this in here."

"Yes, we saw brownies, but they didn't have her. She used the cord when we got close to where they live. I know there are witches throwing energy into the forest to attack the brownies."

"What do you know of witches?" asks Grandma.

The young woman stares at me. She has a feeling I'm more than an ordinary human, and senses darkness. Okay, I am a vampire. Some darkness can't be helped, so I don't take it as an insult.

Addy's mother is too busy squeezing her and crying to pay any attention to me whatsoever.

"I know some witches are tossing curses at the brownies either as punishment for Addy's disappearance or to get her back... but the brownies had nothing to do with it. Dark dryads took her."

Grandma's cheeks go as pale as white granite. "The withered ones..."

"Yeah. I found her on the Dark Mother."

The young woman gasps, covering her mouth in both hands. Tears brim in her eyes. Ack. She obviously understands what happened to Addy.

Young voices upstairs call out in Irish. Three boys in pajamas, aged roughly six to twelve, appear at the top of the stairs. I can't understand them, but 'what's going on; why is everyone awake' is somewhat universal. Upon seeing Addy, they rush downstairs to join the cheering.

Whoa. Big family.

I look back and forth between the young woman and grandma. Addy knew about brownies, enchanted the string. These two aren't calling me crazy for talking about brownies and dryads. Aha. "So, could you please stop throwing magic at the brownies? I'd really like them to give me my sister back."

Grandma regards me for a moment. "Well, I suppose. Are you sure they had nothing to do with takin' her?"

"They've got your wee sister?" asks the younger woman.

"They definitely looked at her like they wanted to steal her, but... no. Brownies didn't have Addy. They do, however, have my sister. Sophia's got a little magic, so they thought she could blow up the leprechauns."

Everyone looks at me like I've got five heads.

"I'm still somewhat confused by what they said. Either the brownies thought the leprechauns had Addy, or they knew the dryads did and needed the leprechauns out of the way to get there. Talking to them was one of the most infuriating things I've ever done. They wanted to get Addy back so they could return her to you and make whatever 'the witches' were doing to them stop."

Grandma shakes her head. "They'd not have given 'er back. Maybe they said so. Maybe they even believed they could... but soon as they looked at 'er, they'd 'ave kept 'er."

I'm inclined to agree. They certainly seemed to try taking her when they punted us to the village. "Yeah."

"All right. We'll have enough to do helping her recover. *On* the Dark Mother, you say?" Grandma swoons. "Goddess give me strength."

The parents and brothers bring Addy upstairs. She waves bye to me over her father's shoulder. I wave back to her, smiling.

"She's okay. The other dryads cleansed her body of the dark ones' corruption"—wow, I really feel like a character in Skyrim talking like this—"and I made sure she didn't remember that horrible tree."

Grandma blinks. "You altered her memories?"

"Yeah. She's way too small to remember anything so horrible. Hell, I wish I could erase it from *my* head."

"You survived being close to the Dark Mother." Grandma leans slightly back, eyeing me. "You're no mortal girl."

"Darn." I fake snap my fingers. "You got me."

The young woman stares at me for a long moment. "You are… how did you get inside the house? We didn't invite you in?"

Hah. "Old wives' tale. Just like the one claiming everyone like me is bad."

"Thank you for bringing my granddaughter home alive," says Grandma.

"You're welcome. Apologies if it's a little rude of me, but I've got to be going."

"Aye. Sun'll be up shortly," says the younger woman.

"Yeah. And the brownies still have my sister. Need to get her back before the little goobers get too attached to her."

The women nod. Despite their gratitude, they're both obviously relieved to have 'the vampire' leaving the house as fast as possible. They graciously show me to the door, thank me again, and go back inside.

"Great. Now where the hell am I?"

COSMIC ENCOURAGEMENT

Considering Addy and her family went mushroom picking in those woods, it can't be far.

I zoom into the air, circling for a view. Sure enough, the forest is only about three miles north of here, not a long flight. From the air over the trees, the only place I truly recognize is the approximate location of the light dryad's circle, as I'd flown straight up from that point earlier. The brownie camp is southwest of it, but this forest has some weird internal distance distortion stuff going on.

Rather than waste hours confusing myself, I dive into the trees near the dryad circle and make my way to the brownie camp within the forest. Sophia's *still* on the damn tree. Klepto's clinging to the roots around her chest, licking her nose/face as necessary to deal with random itches. My little sister has epic amounts of patience. She's been stuck there for hours unable to move and appears quite calm.

At least she's bundled in her winter coat and not freezing. Maybe she even fell asleep standing up. It is, after all, *way* past her bedtime.

I land in front of her.

"Sare!" She squirms. "Do something! I really gotta pee!"

"We're going home now... or at least back to a hotel." I look around at the crowd of brownies filling in behind me. "The human girl is once again with her family. The witches have given me their word they will stop attacking you. The leprechauns will not retaliate against you unless you attack them again. Everything is back to normal."

Kezbit, the brownie in the slightly fancier outfit, wriggles out of the crowd and walks up to me. "We feel the witch magic stop. Deal is deal."

"My sister is still mummified in roots."

"Yes, yes," mutters Kezbit. "I am deciding if you stealing the other child from us broke agreement."

"Addy being taken was the cause of your entire problem. If you had her, the witches would attack again. Besides, I *couldn't* steal her from you because she's not yours. You would've had to steal her from me first... and you couldn't do so because she protected herself using the string."

The brownies rumble angrily, but it's the sort of 'dammit, she's right on a technicality' anger my Mom gets from opposing counsel sometimes in court—and experiences herself quite often as well. Though, if you ask me, I'm correct on way more than a technicality here.

"Fine!" shouts Kezbit, flinging his or her arms up.

The roots cocooning Sophia slacken and fall to the ground in a wreath of brambles. As fast as my vampiric self can move, I reach out and grab her hand. I don't have a cord handy to tie around our wrists, nor any idea how to go about enchanting one. Hopefully, the string linking Addy to me had been equivalent to holding hands.

"Oof," mumbles Sophia, stumbling into me. "My legs feel funny."

"Probably because you've been standing so long."

"No, I was hanging."

"You okay?"

"Yeah. Except for not being able to move, it was kinda comfy." Sophia gives me a 'still gotta pee really bad' stare.

I look her over. Nothing appears to be wrong. "You're surprisingly calm."

"I wasn't really scared. Brownies aren't dangerous if you're nice to them."

The brownies watch us walk off. They're not looking at Sophia with the same fierceness of greed as Addy, but a few seem tempted to grab her. Deciding not to take chances, I scoop Sophia up and fly us into the air, out of the forest. Klepto's snuggled inside her coat, only her head peeking out the neck opening. My sister doesn't have her helmet and I left my climbing harness behind, but neither is too big a problem. So we go a little slower.

"I'm tempted to handcuff myself to you until we get out of Europe."

She laughs. "Won't help. Magic stuff keeps grabbing me. It won't exactly obey the laws of physics."

Sigh. "So I've arranged the end of a brownie-leprechaun war."

"You did." Sophia squirms from having to go so bad.

"At least the negotiations were short."

"Boo." Sophia moans. "Okay, Dad."

I laugh. "We are going home."

"Wait!" she yells. "We still have to stop the spirit. I had a lot of time to think while stuck to the tree. What if stuff keeps happening to me because we're trying to leave?"

"Seriously? The brownies grabbed you after we decided to deal with the ghost."

She shrugs. "I dunno. Magic works weird. The timing could be off."

"You think the mystics hexed you to stay here until you helped?"

"No, not really. More like the universe wants me to do it. I messed up letting him out of the soul jar even if it felt like the right thing to do. I understand I'm too nice."

"Hah. Okay. You're right. We'll try going after the ghost one more time, but Christmas is coming up and Mom is going to kill me if we're not home in time. Speaking of time…"

Sophia wails when I go into a sudden dive, heading for the same town where I found five men for the dryads. The instant I spot a house with someone emerging from their front door, I swoop in to land behind them, drop Sophia on her feet, and grab the man, shoving him into the wall beside the door and covering his mouth.

He starts to scream, but goes limp as soon as I'm in his head. Sophia stands there doing the pee dance while I program this guy to unlock the door for us, then forget we exist. He's on his way downtown to open his little grocery store for the morning, and won't be back home before dark. Excellent. No need to give him a compulsion to ignore our presence in his house. We'll be gone by the time he returns.

I drop the connection to his thoughts.

Like an automaton, he unlocks the front door and walks to his car, ignoring us. Sophia looks freaked out, but follows me inside. It's not the mind control or the flying she's unnerved by. I'm sure she doesn't like 'stealing someone's house.' The instant we're inside, my breath catches in my throat. It's stuffy in here and stinks like someone used to smoke a crapload, like serious 'light a cig with the previous one chain smoking' kind of stink. It's old smoke, and I don't need vampiric heightened senses of smell to pick it up—but having amplified senses turns it from a background nuisance to horrible. Yellowed wallpaper and trim confirm this house has seen a *lot* of nicotine. Fortunately, nothing too recent. Guess the current resident doesn't smoke.

"I'll be in the basement. Try not to do too much damage."

Sophia scoffs at me, but still runs off in search of a toilet.

I re-lock the front door and start my search for the stairs, locating them a few minutes later behind a door I initially mistook for a hall closet. The basement is small, dusty as hell, and filled with a mixture of antique furniture and disassembled steel store shelves. Two small windows are a potential problem, but uncontrolled weeds outside kinda block them, and they're really damn dirty. Still, I take a few minutes to reposition old curtains for additional security, then walk over to a sofa from 1910 I plan to use as a bed. The fabric reeks of cigarette smoke even more than the house upstairs. Ugh. Talk about the worst smell in the world.

Know how much I hate the smell of old cigarettes?

I strip to my underwear and wrap myself in another curtain purely to keep the stink from soaking into my clothes. Bad enough it'll be in my hair.

CONSCIOUSNESS RETURNS WITH THE BURDEN OF A THOUSAND SOULS hanging heavy upon my chest.

Oh, wait. It's only Klepto.

She's curled up on top of me in a cute little grey 'fur donut.' This kitten is so damn small she's honestly about the size of a large donut. And damn. Sorry, Mom. We're not going to be able to get home for Christmas unless this cat moves. I don't want to disturb her.

A smell like Pine Sol hangs in the air. The whirring of a washing machine running comes from upstairs along with quiet scratching. What the heck? I *don't* hear the man who lives here anywhere, or anyone heavy enough to be an adult moving around. Hmm.

"Mew," says Klepto. She stands, stretches, and jumps to the floor.

Aha! I am free!

Since I *must* shower the funk of old cigarette out of my hair and no one is in the house but me and Sophia, I decide to carry my clothes upstairs and get dressed after cleaning up. Four kids plus two parents in the same house divided by only two bathrooms equals underwear no longer being embarrassing. It's a good thing I decided not to get dressed before leaving the basement, since my clothes are not on the floor where I left them.

I glance down at myself.

Underwear's gone too.

"Wow."

I'm not even sure how to react. What creature of ancient myth did I piss off now?

"Oh, wait." I point at Klepto. "You had something to do with this." Tribble.

"Why did you steal my underwear?"

She sits up on her back legs and makes a series of paw motions I utterly fail to comprehend.

Sophia had to put her up to doing it, so I'll ask her. I grab the curtain blanket, wrap myself in it, and go upstairs, grumbling at being surrounded in the stink of musty cigarette. The couch I slept on must've spent a century or longer in a bar… or the parents of the guy who lives here smoked a carton a day while sitting on it.

Upon opening the door at the top of the basement stairs, a standing wall of stink slaps me in the face so hard my eyes tear up. It's not 'stink' per se, but a collection of artificial smells and cleaning products, pungent enough to be instantly eye-watering. Coughing, I stagger into the hall, waving a hand in front of my face. I find Sophia in the kitchen wearing a man's tee shirt for a dress, down on all fours, scrubbing the floor like some kind of barefooted Dickensian waif servant. About the only break in the image is a lack of filthiness. She's squeaky clean—as is the rest of the house.

"What are you doing?" I croak, still not fully awake.

"Cleaning," chirps Sophia. "Since we're using the man's house and I kinda helped myself to some food… cleaning for him makes it feel less like stealing and more of a trade."

"Think you're taking it a little too far scrubbing the floors."

"The man lives alone. I don't think he understands floor scrubbing is a thing people can do. The dirt in this linoleum is older than I am." She points at where she hasn't scrubbed yet—dark yellow—then where she has—white… ish.

"Hah. Okay, whatever. I'm going to take a shower."

"Bathroom's down there." She points.

"Oh. Why did you have the kitten steal my underwear off me while I slept?"

"So I could wash them. We've been wearing the same stuff for days. It's disgusting. They're in the machine now. I'll grab you a T-shirt to borrow. There are no girl's clothes in the house."

"Okay. Thanks."

I stagger down the hall past a tiny washer-dryer combo and find the bathroom, my curtain wrap trailing behind me. I'm well into a nice, relaxing shower before I do the math about there being a washer and dryer in the house, upstairs, on the same water line as the bathroom.

Unfortunately, I figure this out about half a second before the washing machine's second cycle kicks in and sucks up the majority of the hot water.

Yeah, the neighbors are probably going to call the police.

Girls don't scream like this unless they're being murdered, step barefoot in cold vomit at two in the morning while on the way to the bathroom, or fall headfirst into an Arctic lake—like I just did. The time Sam left a realistic fake tarantula on Sophia's bed came close too, but I have bigger lungs than her.

My vampiric nature compensates in maybe thirty seconds, taking the paralyzing effect away from the ice blast coming out of the spigot.

Rapid thumping approaches the door. Sophia barges in, gawking at me. "What happened?"

"W-w-washing machine ate the hot water."

She slouches, relieved. "Oh. Whew."

I resume cleaning my hair, the icy water now feeling neutral in temperature to me. Granted, it means my body is also the same temp, even colder than the morgue cooler. No sooner do I settle back into the routine than the washing machine stops sucking up the hot water.

This girl is on fire.

Well, not literally.

I do manage not to scream at least—however, some F-bombs fall. Carpet bombing in fact. So this is how microwave entrees feel. From the freezer to the oven.

Sophia walks back in and deposits a T-shirt on the sink for me, then leaves.

I rush the last of my shower, dry off, pull the shirt on, then check myself in the mirror. Okay, this shirt will work as long as I don't move. It's basically car insurance: if I do anything with it, I'm no longer covered. Bending forward or back at even a five degree angle is going to reveal parts unknown to the world. My luck. I couldn't pick a larger man to home invade.

Towel time.

I make a temporary skirt from a dry towel and go to the living room. At least *this* couch doesn't stink like cigarettes.

Sophia putters around cleaning. She's both guilty for us using the man's home as well as taking food, plus she's nervous. My sister's one of those people who needs to keep themselves occupied whenever they're overly anxious. Sitting still doing nothing is the absolute devil for her when she's wound up about something. I'm still impressed she tolerated the brownie camp so well, being unable to move for so long. Ninety percent chance she caught a nap.

Once the dryer's done with our clothes, we change. There's something so nice about putting clothes on right out of the dryer. Like a warm hug. My sister throws the two borrowed T-shirts plus the towels we used in the washer and runs another cycle. It's a little wasteful on detergent and such, but she doesn't want to leave any trace of our presence. I can respect that. This poor man is going to think faeries invaded his house and cleaned it from top to bottom.

Finally, she flops on the sofa beside me. Despite her outward calm, she clings tight while we're channel surfing to find something to watch. We settle on a cartoon. It's not in English, but amusing enough visually—and there's nothing else on. So, we sit there for a little more than an hour until it's dark out. I take the opportunity to send the parents, friends, and Hunter updates via text. No, I'm not telling them about brownies and leprechauns in any forum where the NSA is going to see it. I'm sure Mom is climbing the walls in frustration at me using couched language like 'our vacation is taking some unexpected swerves, but everything's fine and we'll be coming home soon.'

Dad, of course, gets the hint about things happening I can't properly explain. He asks me if I wore a headband. It's tempting to say 'of course,' but doing so would be lying to Dad, so I tell him I didn't have one.

Sophia shuts off the TV. "It's dark out. Can we get food somewhere? I don't want to steal more from this man."

"Sure." I stand, stretch, and reflexively yawn.

She yawns in response while putting her coat on. "Do you still need to yawn, or did you do it to make me yawn?"

I purposefully yawn at her.

Naturally, she yawns again—and playfully punches me in the arm. We head outside.

Since my purse is back with the mystics at the bookstore, I have no money on me. Compelling some random mom-aged woman on the street to pretend to be our mother long enough to take us to a little place for food doesn't bother me much. It's less embarrassing than pretending to be homeless kids begging for food or money.

Sophia and 'Mom' remain at the table while I ambush a goth girl a year or two older than me in the bathroom. The girl's fast, and nearly gets me with a knife before I can dive into her head for the initial derpification. Her blood tastes like blueberry pie, probably a result of her having blue hair. No, I'm not tasting the dye. It's mental. I see blue, think blueberry.

After Sophia and I eat—I did not make the woman waste money on real food for me—it's time to erase us from her memory. Once she thinks she merely popped into this place for a bite on a completely random whim, Sophia and I slip away while she's still in a fog. An alley behind the restaurant offers a concealed takeoff location. I scoop Sophia up in my arms, holding her sideways before jumping into the air.

While my body tries to be as lifelike as possible thanks to my bloodline, certain vampiric truths remain. One such truth is I don't get tired. This comes in quite handy for the nearly two-hour flight across the ocean back to England. Sophia's skinny as heck, but no way could a normal person hold a sixty-something pound girl this long at all, never mind while flying.

She asks me what happened after I left her at the brownie camp. I share the story for the most part... leaving out the bit about the thorns digging *into* Addy's body. Telling Sophia they wanted to turn the girl into a dark dryad on top of even a watered down description of them might give her nightmares. No damn way am I going to mention the burrowing. Doing so would send her straight to therapy.

"I never expected anything like this could possibly happen." I glance down at the dark ocean racing along beneath us. "Stuff's getting super crazy."

"If you say you should've pretended to be dead and not come home, I'm gonna be mad at you. There will be crying."

I chuckle, despite a tear in my eye. "Isn't that a movie?"

"I don't think so. Dad said something about a movie called *There Will be Boredom*, but I've never seen it."

"Oh. Who'd watch a movie with boredom in the title?"

She laughs. "It isn't, silly. Dad's making fun of some movie he fell asleep to."

"Oh. Duh. Right."

"I have magic and a teleporting kitten. Totally awesome. Stop being sad. No take-backsies."

"Okay." I squeeze her a little tighter.

"So were you really gonna get a flamethrower? *Can* you get a flamethrower?"

"Yeah. Pretty sure. Just a little mind control in the right places. If I wanted to, I could probably get a tank or a fighter plane. Couldn't do much with them, but... yeah. Scary, huh?"

She nods.

Before too long, we're over land again. It's not too difficult to find London from this altitude, especially at night. Once the vast swath of civilization and all its electric lights come into view, Sophia summons the little blue magic ball.

"We haven't even landed yet. Don't you want to stretch your legs and rest a bit?"

"Rest? You're doing all the work." She cradles the orb in both hands, waiting for the white spot to stop spinning around. "Besides, the ghost isn't going to stop trying to kill people because I got tangled up with brownies."

"True."

"You didn't groan."

"Should I have?" I glance at her.

"Yeah. They wrapped me up in roots? Tangled?"

"Ahh." I laugh.

"Ooh. Got him." Sophia holds the tracker spell up.

Since she's in front of me, rather than riding on my back, I can see the 'compass' directly. It's fairly easy to follow as all I need to do is turn until the tiny white dot rotates onto the side of the sphere facing forward.

We follow the direction her spell indicates for a little more than ten minutes, flying at maybe half my speed. The dot shifts downward as we approach the Thames, pointing toward a bridge. I risk descending a bit, hoping the night sky will keep us hidden.

"There! He's chasing a white car." Sophia points.

She appears to be indicating a Volvo wagon. The car isn't driving unusually fast or in an erratic manner. A faintly glowing haze zooms along over the road behind it, gaining ground. I squint, zooming my vision in on the car. The middle-aged woman driving doesn't look at all familiar, but the white-haired girl in the passenger seat does— Mandy Carlin, the youngest and presumably least powerful of the mystics.

"Damn. He's gotta be trying to make them crash."

"Yeah. Hurry!" says Sophia.

I swing left, flying in even closer, right above the road. People generally don't look up unless a noise or flash of some kind grabs their attention. Hopefully, if I stay above the street lights, we'll be invisible behind the glare.

Sophia drops the tracking spell since we can see the ghost. She starts making weird faces and pointing her arms at the apparition. Not much happens other than a gurgle emanating from her stomach.

Mandy's car—assuming it's her mother driving—leaves the bridge without incident. The ghost hovers close behind them, but doesn't appear to do anything yet. Traffic here isn't moving fast enough for a fatal wreck. Unless the spirit is planning some weird chain reaction involving pigeons and a busload of circus performers, I'm sure he's got something specific in mind and is merely waiting for the Carlins to get to the right spot.

A short while later, they follow a road out of the city proper, heading toward the countryside east of the city, accelerating up to about sixty. Two spots of bright light get my attention in the distance: an oncoming big rig. Uh oh. There's a problem. I can practically feel the delight waft off the ghost.

"If you can do something, do it quick," I say. "He's going to make them hit the semi."

Sophia gasps. She thrusts her arms out. Pale yellow light surrounds her fingers. Similar light flickers around the ghost of Fletcher Maltby. For an instant, the vaporous form implodes in on itself, compressing to a spot the diameter of a tennis ball. He snaps back to full size seconds later, emitting a horrible screech, and abruptly veers off the road, racing out over fields. Wow, I think my sister basically tazed a ghost.

Hoping he's given up on the car, I chase him, having to fly faster than I'm comfortable going while carrying Sophia to keep up with him. She doesn't complain, despite having to flinch away from the wind in her face.

Fletcher re-enters London, bee-lining for a small, gothic graveyard fairly close to the city outskirts.

"He's in a graveyard... not good."

"Go after him!" mumbles Sophia into my shoulder.

DEAL WITH THE DEVIL'S THIRD
COUSIN TWICE REMOVED

G raveyards—especially ones dating back to the 1700s—give me the creeps.

I don't know exactly how old this one is, but it *looks* pretty ancient. European cities are weird. You can find buildings from the 1300s standing next to modern ones. Wonder if some vampires around here look at places like Westminster Abbey and think 'oh, I remember when they built that.'

Slightly more epic than Dad making the same comment about the Denny's in Woodinville.

We land on a narrow stone path in the midst of multiple tiny mausoleums at the graveyard's center, the spot where the ghost disappeared. Sophia stumbles a few steps on the ice before she finds her balance.

I am impressed.

My littlest sister isn't freaking out, crying, and begging me to get her out of this scary graveyard. We're surrounded by old stone, gargoyles, ivy, crumbling tombstones—some of which are taller than me—and darkness. Well, *she's* surrounded by darkness. I can see. Normal me would've taken one look at this place and run the other way. Sophia *should* be scared out of her mind. I think she's too fixated on finding the ghost to really comprehend where we are or what it looks like. Or maybe she can't see where we are too well.

"Fletcher Maltby," says Sophia—then stops, blushes, and looks up at me. "Should I call him Mr. Maltby?"

"Not sure rules of etiquette apply once someone's dead. If the magic they taught you requires using the ghost's full name, you better do it."

"Okay," she whispers, then faces one of the mausoleums. "Fletcher Maltby, I need to talk to you."

"Are you sure he's in there? I didn't think people who died on the gallows ended up in private tombs."

"It's not *his* tomb. He's hiding in there." She clutches at the air and makes a pulling gesture as if dragging someone forward by their shirt.

A transparent—mostly human—figure glides toward us out of the wall, flailing his arms as if attempting to grab onto nonexistent random objects in order to resist her dragging him into view. His head is slightly oversized, atop a distorted, stretched neck ringed in black bruise from the killing noose. Sunken dark eyes and elongated limbs further lend an otherworldly, ghoulish quality to his presence. I didn't get a great look at him when he escaped the jar, but he seemed far less human then. Guess he's piecing himself back together.

Sophia steps off the stone path into grass to avoid ice, and edges closer to him. "Please stop running away from me. I don't want to hurt you."

"You're the one who released me!" Fletcher points at her, his voice faint and echoing. "Why do you pursue me?"

"Do you understand why I let you out?"

He hovers there in silence for a few seconds. A sudden change in his appearance makes me jump back. The man's face goes blank—no eyes or nose—with an inhumanly large mouth leaking blood. His pallid skin stretches tight to the skull with a leathery creaking, bony chest visible under the tattered remains of the threadbare prison garment he died in. Fast, rapid breaths force his ribs outward, stretching the skin covering them to a grotesque degree. His hands enlarge even more, ink black wraith claws extending. His body contorts in agony and shudders, face twisted in as much a mask of unbearable soul-destroying pain as blank skin can convey.

I can sympathize. Same thing happens to me whenever the radio plays Kid Rock.

Whoa. I put a hand on Sophia's shoulder, ready to drag her away from the ghost. "Careful."

"He's not trying to scare us. I made him think of the jar." Sophia squeezes my hand. Yeah, she's frightened, but hiding it well. "It was evil and cruel of them to put your spirit in the jar. I let you out because trapping ghosts is wrong. You were in pain."

"I was…" Fletcher's more human face returns for only seconds before the monstrous version returns, syrupy half-congealed blood glooping over his teeth. "They will pay!"

"No." Sophia shakes her head. "The people you are trying to hurt didn't put you in the soul jar."

He surges toward her, stopping with his face inches from hers. "They didn't release me either!"

Sophia jumps back, color draining out of her cheeks. "True, but, they have no idea how awful it is to be trapped inside a soul jar. The mystics treated you like a ghost battery, not a person."

"They will suffer," rasps Fletcher, flickering back and forth between his two appearances.

"Being cruel because they didn't know any better isn't enough reason to kill them. The more evil you do now, the longer it will take for you to find rest," says Sophia. "You really need to let go of Fletcher Maltby. You've been him for a super long time. Don't you want to go back to the Cauldron?"

He hisses, darting forward, thrusting his face up to hers. "Not until they pay for what they've done."

"Ugh. You're not listening." Sophia face-palms. "These mystics didn't even know who you were until you started trying to hurt them. You've already killed people." She shivers. "I think it's my fault. You told me you wouldn't hurt anyone and begged me to let you out. But you lied."

"It's not your fault," I whisper, squeezing her shoulder. "You were lied to. Anything he did after you let him out is on him."

Fletcher's presence diminishes somewhat. The monstrous apparition fades into his human form, albeit still elongated and distorted. "Justice…"

"No. Justice happened already. You killed people when you were alive. The police caught you, and you got hanged. You should have gone back to the Cauldron. Mystics like 300 years ago did something evil when they trapped your ghost. But those mystics are all dead now. And the universe has already punished them for what they did to you."

"Yeah. They've probably reincarnated three times in a row as door-to-door salesmen… or maybe over and over again as farm animals— or maybe Cleveland Browns fans."

Fletcher glances at me, confused.

"Being a chicken in a factory farm cage is worse than a soul jar," says Sophia.

I hold a hand up to Fletcher. "Don't get her started."

He leans back. "She's vegan?"

"No. But I don't have to be a vegetarian to think it's cruel to mistreat animals." She sets her hands on her hips. "The mystics you're hurting don't deserve to die because they joined the same order the people who *did* hurt you once belonged to. And, really, you killed people. You did deserve *some* punishment, but no way a soul jar."

"You were a serial killer," I say. "You killed people in life and you've murdered seven mystics as a ghost. My kid sister can, and probably should, straight up destroy you, but she's so damn sweet, she's *still* trying to help you. Just… please go to the Cauldron so we can return home?"

"Their entire order bears the stain," rasps Fletcher.

I elbow Sophia in the arm. "Hit him with the same stare you used on Mom when she said you could keep Klepto."

"You used to be trapped in a soul jar. Now, you're trapped by your anger. There's no reason for you to hate these mystics. As long as you exist here in the outer world, you'll be consumed by anger and keep torturing yourself. The only person hurting you, is you." Sophia whips out her big-eyed pleading stare. "The anger and hurt will never stop until you return to the Cauldron. I want to help you, but I can't let you keep hurting people. It'll make me cry, but if you won't stop being a butthead, I have to do something mean."

Fletcher reaches out, tracing two fingers down Sophia's cheek. "You would... shed tears over one such as me?"

"I would." She raises her hands, concentrating.

A speck of whitish-blue light appears in the air not far behind Fletcher. In seconds, it grows to a spinning energy pinwheel, then further widens into a line of searing bright glow around a dark opening.

"Seriously," I say. "After what you did, anyone else in her position wouldn't have even tried talking to you and gone straight to the whole exploding ectoplasm thing."

"It isn't all his fault. The soul jar made his mind cave in, changing him into a manifestation of anger and vengeance, occluding his true personality." Sophia glances sideways at me. "What's 'occluding' mean?"

"Hiding. I'm guessing you just quoted Asher?"

"No. Mr. Bailey."

"Who?" I ask.

"Callum... one of the mystics back home." She grunts, widening the doorway. "There's only one way for you to escape the pain that's not gonna make me cry. Please go where you should've been able to go after they killed you."

Fletcher turns toward the portal. "No one has ever said they would weep over me. I—you are right. My thoughts are scattered, formless. Wrath and anguish taint my every breath. Blessed escape."

I indicate the portal like a game show hostess. "Right there. All expenses paid."

"You have my thanks, child. I would say I regret the deaths of those in this year, but I find my emotions out of reach. You are truly a unique soul." He stares at her for a long moment, then faces the portal, which inhales him in a startlingly fast blur.

"Whoa." I blink. "Like a scrunchie sucked up by a vacuum cleaner."

"Mew," says Klepto.

Sophia emits a faint snarl, pushing her hands together. The portal shrinks in on itself and vanishes.

"Ding," I say.

"Huh?" Sophia scrunches her nose up at me.

"You just made level."

"Dork."

"Seriously, you beat the big bad and you're only ten, so he's gotta be worth at least reaching level two."

"Such. A. Dork."

"Says the girl who loves D&D."

Sophia sighs at the sky. "Can we go home now?"

"Not quite."

"Why not?" She gasps.

"It's way too late to catch a flight. We can go to the airport so I can make someone honor the tickets we already have but didn't use. Although, getting a refund or reissue of airline tickets might be too difficult even for vampiric mind control."

"Seriously?"

"No. I'm making a sarcastic joke." I take her hand.

Sophia starts to say something, then looks around. Two seconds later, she jumps into me, trembling.

"What?"

"We're in a super creepy graveyard!"

I chuckle, picking her up. "Just noticed?"

"Ack! Go! Please!" wails Sophia, clinging to me. "I don't wanna be here."

"Soph… you have two ways to deal with anything haunting this place. Destroy or send home. Why are you scared?"

"Fear doesn't make sense!" She squeezes me. "Please, can we go?"

"Okay." I scoop her up. "I want to go home, too."

We glide into the air.

"Sare?" Sophia peers up at me, not even bothering to try keeping her windblown hair out of her face.

"Yeah?"

"I'm gonna have a nightmare about that creepy face he made. Can I sleep with you tonight?"

I chuckle. "I don't want to leap through a portal and find the sun up back home. We'll probably be in a hotel room sharing a bed anyway."

"Oh... right." She flashes a cheesy smile. "Okay."

VOID GATES FOR DUMMIES

O nly one person sees me drop out of the sky and land in front of the bookstore.

He doesn't remember. Part of me wonders if I should go back to the small town and erase myself from Addy and her family's memory… but who'd believe an eight-year-old talking about vampires? They'd assume she made it up or played pretend. Grandma, I'm sure, knows better than to discuss such things openly. She obviously knows of brownies and dark dryads and those aren't considered 'real' by society.

Alas, the bookstore's locked.

"Grr." I hold my hand out like a surgeon waiting for a tool. "Kitten."

"Huh?" asks Sophia.

"I need the kitten."

Klepto leaps from her shoulder to my hand. "Mew?"

"Mind getting the door?"

"Mew."

She faces the bookstore and a faint *click* comes from the lock.

"Thanks." I set her back on Sophia's shoulder.

We head inside, cross the deserted store, and head down to the

330 | AN INTRODUCTION TO PARANORMAL DIPLOMACY

ritual room. The place is empty of people. My purse sits conspicuously on one of the tables next to Sophia's helmet, a large envelope stuffed halfway into it. I grab the message, slice it open with a claw, and pull the letter out, reading it aloud so my sister can follow along.

"Sarah and Sophia,

"On behalf of the Aurora Aurea, I thank you for your great assistance in dealing with Fletcher Maltby. In the wake of the spirit's assault on us, members of The Serene Lodge have renewed their attacks, attempting to take advantage of the situation. We have, however, sensed the spirit's passing. It will take us time to gather our defenses against the Lodge and rebuild. For the time being, we have gone into hiding. Look under the blue book.

"Warmest regards and thanks,

"Asher Jones."

"They left!?" Sophia flails. "He said they'd send us back."

I sling my purse over one shoulder. "Blue book? Can they be any more vague? There are thousands of books in this place."

"Umm. Is that it?" She points at a huge tome as big as a man's torso, eight inches thick, sitting flat on the table not far from where we stand.

The massive book is bound in rich sapphire leather engraved in gold filigree. No other book in this room is even a third the size.

"Certainly the most obvious 'blue book' in sight." I grab the ridiculous thing and lift it. Pre-vampire me couldn't have done so.

Sophia swipes a few loose papers out from under it.

I set the book down and peer over Sophia's shoulder at a page of handwriting and lots of sketches. Looks like someone got drunk and tried to combine trigonometry with astrology. "He left you his math notebook full of doodles?"

"No. I think this is a spell." She reads over both pages, then re-reads them. "The note at the top says this will open the doorway back to my closet. I need to use the magic on a doorway. It's going to connect the door to my closet for a minute."

"Oh wow. Can you seriously open a gateway back home?"

"Umm. No idea. Might as well try. Worst thing I could do is fail."

"Worst thing you could do is cause a dimensional pinhole and suck the entire universe through a space-time inversion before spitting it back inside-out."

She blinks at me. "I'm telling Mom."

"What?"

"You're experimenting with drugs."

I laugh.

"Give me a few minutes." She walks out of the ritual room to the nearest storage closet, and sits cross-legged on the floor.

Well, if it saves us having to spend another night here and deal with an airport, why not?

She reads over the pages for a bit, then gets up to collect a couple candles, a hunk of chalk, and three bowls containing different colored powders. Like some kind of warped version of Mom cooking from a recipe she's never seen before, Sophia draws symbols on the floor using chalk, glancing back and forth at the page in her hand. She makes a few corrections, then sets up the candles—lighting them with a snap of her fingers—and begins dribbling small amounts of the colored powders on the floor, creating more symbols.

Okay, tween girls often mess around with occult stuff like Ouija boards and witchcraft, but it's *so* creepy watching Sophia do it. She's about as anti-goth as is possible to get. Blonde, blue-eyed, bright, smiling all the time, super sweet. My brain wants to picture her pulling tiny internal organs from bats or rodents out of jars while giggling and... just no.

Finally, she stands, returns all the bowls to where she got them, and runs back to stand by the circle she made. Hands out, she focuses. All the powders begin glowing their respective colors, blue, yellow, and orange. The candle flames stretch to four inches tall. A blurry duplicate of the chalk writing appears, floating a half inch above the real one. Or is it the real one floating and the illusion is on the floor?

Gah, my eyes. Looking at it is making me dizzy.

A moment later, she lowers her arms. "Okay. The portal's open."

"So what now?"

She swallows—not a good sign—and grasps the doorknob. "We open the door."

Sophia twists the knob and pulls the closet door aside, revealing an infinite void like the one in her room before we landed in London. Good sign.

"Hey, you did—"

A squishy black tentacle whips out of the darkness, grabbing me around the head with a loud, wet, *slap!* Feels like I've been struck in the face by a slab of raw fish. The sucker-studded appendage gives me a few test squeezes as if it's not sure what it grabbed. Great. I'm the piece of paper in a hat being drawn by an intra-dimensional giant squid.

"Eep!" yelps Sophia.

The slimy thing wrapped around my head yanks away, leaving me partially coated in ectoplasm. It's probably snot, but I'm going to call it ectoplasm so I don't throw up. An instant after the tentacle vanishes, the void barfs out a torrent of lukewarm slime, covering us both. The door slams closed on its own, loud as a gunshot.

"Uhh, that's definitely not right." Sophia wipes her face. "There shouldn't be any tentacles involved with teleportation. Sorry, I stink at this."

"Forget it... we'll go home the normal way." I scrape goop out of my eyes, slinging it to the floor.

"I could try again."

"Nah. You need more practice before attempting intercontinental gateways. We should consider this a win because whatever grabbed me *didn't* come out into the world. Try starting off a little smaller than England-to-Washington, like opening a door from home to school."

She blinks. "Ooh! Awesome idea. If I got it to work, I could sleep a whole extra half hour."

THE LONG WAY HOME

I sit on the end of the bed in our hotel room, wrapped armpit to knees in a towel.

Did you know void tentacle slime is as sticky as road tar? I didn't used to know. I do now. Okay, slight overstatement. It's not *quite* as sticky as road tar. We both still have hair and eyebrows. Sophia's attempt to use magic to de-slime our clothing had somewhat disastrous results. Fortunately, in her case, the winter coat absorbed ninety percent of the damage. It exploded. As did my entire outfit.

Imagine how much it hurts to have duct tape stuck to skin and ripped off real fast. Now expand the sensation over your entire body. I did learn something new about being a vampire, at least. Those thin hairs on my arms? Yeah, they grow back pretty quick.

Sophia succeeded in giving me an illusion of clothing, which made going to a nearby store less embarrassing than traipsing around in my underwear. I bought—no mind trickery, honest—us new outfits and a replacement coat for Sophia, along with a small carry-on bag and some extra underwear for both of us. I may be undead, but wearing the same ones every day is still ack.

Fortunately, the remainder of the sticky residue washed out in the shower under hot water.

Sophia's taking a bath now.

I'm doing something slightly less relaxing—calling the 'rents.

"What is going on over there?" yells Mom by way of answering. "Your last texts aren't making any sense."

Good. She's shouting. Means she's not too worried or upset.

"It's nothing too interesting. Had to use the card again for some clothes. Someone who didn't know what they were doing hit a giant mud puddle and covered us in slime."

"Sorry!" yells Sophia from the bathroom.

"I'm not sure what to say," says Mom, her voice half sigh.

"The exciting part's over. We've really gotten into the *spirit* of things here. But we're done. Gonna be on a plane tomorrow afternoon. I bumped into this really *charming* guy at the airport. We're taking off at ten-to-four, pretty much right around sunset. Got a nonstop flight, about ten or eleven hours in the air, and we should land at Sea-Tac around nine. I can, uhh, figure out some way to fly home or you could pick us up if you want."

"All right. We'll do that. Everyone's eager to see you and I'm sure you wouldn't mind the break from air travel."

"Sounds good. Okay, see you tomorrow."

"Night, hon," adds Dad.

"Oh, and please tell Sophia I don't want her opening any more ancient soul traps without asking permission first."

"Sure thing, Mom."

We hang up, and I flop back on the bed. I might spend the whole night like this. Hotel towels are kinda comfortable.

I WAKE UP RECLINED ON THE BED EXACTLY AS I'D BEEN BEFORE sunrise.

I'm above the bedspread, head propped up on pillows to watch television, still wearing a towel. Sophia spent most of the night tucked in under all the blankets, snuggled against me, asleep. Two things have changed since I blacked out at sunrise.

One: Sophia is no longer asleep. She's up, dressed except for shoes, and sitting on the bed next to me watching television.

Two: a woman in a cleaning service uniform stands near the bed, gazing into space, her mouth wide open.

I'm going to assume the hotel doesn't employ robots to clean rooms, and this one happened to run out of power in the middle of singing an aria. Something unusual must have occurred.

"Umm..." I sit up. "What happened? Why is there a catatonic hotel employee in our room?"

Sophia looks over. "She walked in, saw you sleeping, and started screaming."

"Damn. I'm not getting worse, am I?"

"No. Same as always. But you do sleep like the dead."

"Hah." I poke her in the side. "So, umm... you petrified her?"

"No. She's on pause. I stopped the flow of time around her."

I rake two hands through my hair. Argh. Well, if she's frozen in time, she's not seeing anything. I hop off the bed, drop the towel, and hastily dress. New jeans, pretty much the same style as my old ones, and an emerald green babydoll top. Guess I had dryad on the brain.

"Okay, unpause."

Sophia flicks her gaze to the woman—who resumes screaming, but trails off to silence, staring at me. Thanks to the heavy-duty curtains here, I'm online. I start to go into her head to erase the sight of me as corpselike, but the woman's already disregarding it since I appear totally normal now. She's convinced she's working too much overtime and imagining things.

Well, saves me some work.

"Sorry. I didn't realize you were still in the room." She retreats for the door.

"It's fine. We're checking out now. Do your thing if you want. We'll be out of your way in a minute." I smile at her and grab my sneakers.

Our flight takes off at 3:50 p.m., right around sunset. It's presently 2:39 p.m. and too bright out for me to go online. Fortunately, I don't really need to. Sophia puts her shoes on and we leave the room. I don't need to deal with the checkout desk since the hotel isn't going to screw me over for staying in the room past eleven in the morning. They may try to charge for a second night, but it's a comped room not associated to any credit card traceable to me or my family.

A convenient shuttle service gives us a ride to the airport. The hotel's basically at the edge of the airport property so it's not like we've got too far to go. Still, riding is nicer than walking. The day's clear but gloomy, pretty much perfect weather for me. Since we've got time, we stop at a salad place in the airport for Sophia to eat. She hasn't had food all day. It's painfully overpriced, but we are the demographic they're trying to exploit—people about to hop on a plane who don't have the time necessary to go elsewhere, and need food.

I order a salad with grilled chicken, mostly to feed Klepto. Kitty eats her fill, and I finish the rest, even though doing so condemns me to needing to use the airplane bathroom before the flight ends. Ordinary food does *not* stay inside me for nine hours.

Klepto teleports past the security checkpoint to avoid the x-ray machine or anyone questioning why an un-crated animal is in the airport. She hides behind some trash cans adjacent to a bathroom while waiting for us to get through the passenger line. I'm a little nervous how the security guy's going to react to a pouch of gold coins in my handbag, but he doesn't bat an eyelash. Hmm. The pouch appears to be empty from the outside, so maybe machines can't see the coins in it. Good thing I spat out Jonathan's bullet. Wouldn't want to set off the metal detector.

Klepto teleports into Sophia's arms once we're away from the security station. Soon, we take seats in the waiting area by the terminal from which our flight will roll out. The room is saturated in orange thanks to huge windows overlooking the runways letting the imminent sunset in. Giant airplanes fascinate me less than most people since I've grown up with a mother who worked for Boeing. I've toured the plant, seen them being put together and even gotten to play with the controls of a partially built 737 when I was really little.

At 3:28 p.m., the sun decides to be a bitch and give a last dying gasp before it sets in like a half hour. A bright orange flood turns up the temperature to about 350. Or at least, it feels like it. I do my best to shield my bare forearms under my loose top and try to flip my hair around in front of my face. C'mon cloud. Move back in front of the sun. Ouch. Stop it.

A man sitting behind me in the adjoined row of seats grumbles.

"Now what?" asks a woman who sounds on the older side.

"Signs are bloody everywhere, but some tosser is still smoking in here," says the guy.

"That's not a cigarette, Albert. It's probably coming from the kitchen. Someone burned chicken."

Ugh! I get up and walk over to stand behind a giant, round column, putting it between me and the window. Feels like I've walked out of the Nevada desert in August to air-conditioning. A few wisps of smoke trail after me, but thankfully no one seems to notice.

Minutes later, a voice comes over the PA, calling boarding for our flight. Sophia runs over to me, but we have to wait for the first-class people to get on before they call coach. Yeah, I technically stole these tickets, but no need to overdo it. Coach is fine. Klepto stops moving, pretending to be Sophia's emotional-support-plushie to get past the woman checking tickets.

As soon as my butt hits the seat, I recline, and let out a groan of relief.

I swear to the Flying Spaghetti Monster, if someone else kidnaps Sophia before we get home, I am going to kill them.

A STRANGE, UNCHARTED FUTURE

Parents are the strangest creatures known to humanity.

Once we'd gotten in Mom's Yukon after leaving the plane, Mom, Dad, and the Littles heard the full story I couldn't say over the phone or send via text. No one got gory details about what happened to poor Addy, only hearing she'd been 'entangled' to the tree. The Littles don't need to hear it and *I* don't want to remember it either.

Sophia and I have been home for a couple days and Dad is *still* laughing about Klepto attacking Jacob Winton's balls. You'd think a guy wouldn't find a story about tiny claws and another guy's sensitive areas so funny, but apparently, he does. Mom ran the gamut of emotion from screaming to laughing maniacally (in denial at the existence of brownies and leprechauns). I think she had some trouble processing everything since she started yelling at Sophia as if abduction had been her fault. She chilled and apologized soon after, admitting it had, indeed, been the stress of worrying about us so much for several days.

And like most unexplainable, bizarre, otherworldly, or totally strange things to happen in my life ever since I became a vampire, being magically abducted to London to deal with a pissed off ghost got filed away as another day. Months ago, Mom flipped out over me using mind control to encourage shoppers to buy Girl Scout cookies because Sophia cried at people ignoring her. Now, werewolves, brownies, leprechauns, and dryads stir only slightly more of a reaction than asking 'what's for dinner?'

Ashley and Michelle came over the day after our return and hung out like tweens into the wee hours, demanding all the details. I spent the following evening at Hunter's, at least until he needed to go to sleep. Telling him about the strange fey creatures got him wondering what other legends might have more truth to them than people think. And yes, Ashley dragged me to the mall for some last-minute shopping.

Oh yeah. Today's Christmas Eve.

I haven't gotten out of bed yet.

It's almost four. The whole house smells like cinnamon and apple pie. I'm taking advantage of my family's new habit of assuming I'm in need of extra vampire sleep if I don't go upstairs by three. I woke up thinking about the nightmare I had around Thanksgiving where I'd been a ghost haunting my living room watching the Littles have a horrible Christmas, not wanting their gifts. It's totally unrelated to me being a vampire, but we open gifts tonight instead of in the morning. Somehow, none of my siblings inherited my extreme anticipatory anxiety, or maybe it didn't show itself since my parents decided to move gift-opening to Christmas Eve in order for me to sleep long before they could be anxious about what Santa brought them.

Speaking of Santa, Sam figured the truth out shockingly early, at only seven. Sierra still believed in Santa after Sam stopped, but the boy never ruined it for her. Sophia held out the longest before she surrendered to a more adult perspective (only last year). But, yanno... if brownies and leprechauns are out there, maybe some manner of person-slash-creature exists similar to the Santa legend. Obviously, he's not exactly the same as we think as gifts do not transubstantiate out of thin air all over the world.

But who knows?

Even though it had been a nightmare, the emotion of me dreaming about my family dealing with losing me is heavy enough to pin me to the bed. Bah. I'm being a dumbass again. No reason for me to get maudlin about anything.

Right. Upstairs I go.

After I change.

I fling off the oversized tee I slept in—*gawd* I missed these while stuck in Europe—and throw on the over-the-top Christmas tree and candy cane nightgown traditionally worn by yours truly for the presents-opening ceremony. Pre-vampire me would actually sleep in it the night before, and spend all of today and Christmas Day wearing it—except for when family showed up to have dinner. Official holiday dinner requires nice clothes.

Everyone's up and in an energetic mood. Mom's happier than she's been in weeks. Dad's declared the next five days a work-free zone for him. The day goes by in an awesome blur of family time, board games, and of course, an Eighties movie. Even though we've all seen it before, Dad puts on *Labyrinth*. Probably due to the recent talk of magical creatures.

Klepto gets the zoomies and chases Blix around the house for half the movie. It's hilarious watching the imp try to escape a kitten who keeps teleporting in front of him. More amazing than what happened to us in London, neither one of them takes out the Christmas tree. For sure, I expected complete destruction.

After the movie, Dad puts the DVD back on the shelf, then stands there tapping a finger to his chin. "Hmm."

"What?" asks Mom.

"I think I've forgotten something." He looks at us kids. "Feels like there's something we need to do tonight, but I can't remember it."

Sam and Sierra laugh.

"Oh well, guess it's bedtime." Dad halfheartedly shrugs, letting his arms flap against his sides.

Sam sits there, calmly looking at him.

Sierra smirks.

Sophia's quiet for a few seconds, then flails. "Dad! It can't be bedtime, yet."

I know she's not at all upset, but she's acting to cover for Sam and Sierra outgrowing panic at the idea of not getting to open presents tonight. They're wise to Dad's wily ways and realize he's kidding.

"Aha!" Dad snaps his fingers. "You're right. You three need to take a bath before bed."

Sierra folds her arms.

"It's Christmas Eve, Dad," says Sam. "I believe you are forgetting the redistribution of wealth and the ceremonial unboxing."

Mom covers her mouth to hold in a laugh.

"Hah!" Dad pretends to 'remember' and snaps his fingers. "You're absolutely right. Time to open presents!"

The Littles cheer and scramble over to the tree, sliding to a halt on their knees. Oh, hell. Adulting is for losers. I run after them and flop on the floor. Amid the crinkle of wrapping paper and the sappy Christmas music Mom insists on playing in the background, the kids pounce on the gifts arranged under the tree. At least Sierra's calmed down enough in her 'old age' of eleven to look at the name on a box before tearing the paper.

Gawd, she made Sophia cry so bad one year for opening half her stuff. Wasn't trying to be mean though. As soon as she realized a gift belonged to Sophia or Sam, she handed it over.

Sam basks in an assortment of loot: model kits, a few video games, action figures, a toy lightsaber, and so on. Sierra also gets some video games—and a surprisingly heavy, long box. At first, I assume Dad's being weird and gave her a pool cue... but when she gets the thing open, she gasps and extracts a small sword from a shroud of white tissue paper.

"Jonathan..." Mom blinks, obviously caught off guard. "Did you give our daughter a real blade?"

"Cool!" whispers Sophia, wide-eyed in awe. She pulls the sword an inch or so out of the scabbard. "Umm, yeah. It's sharp."

"Be careful, sweetie!" Mom gawks at Dad. "You seriously gave her a sword."

"Yep." Dad gestures at Sierra. "Look under the tissue paper."

Sierra gingerly sets the sword on the rug beside her, then

rummages the box, holding up an envelope. She opens it, reads the contents, and squeals in delight. "Lessons!"

"Wait, sword lessons?" Mom looks back and forth between Sierra and Dad. "They really have those?"

"Yeah." Dad braces for impact, catching a flying hug from Sierra. "Oof. They do. Downtown. It's mostly for film actors, stunt performers, and theater people... but the guy said it's genuine skill. She'll need pads and such. And no, they don't swing sharp blades at each other in the school. Strictly wooden or padded PVC."

Mom fake-wipes sweat from her forehead, then gives Dad a 'she'll be bored of it in three months' look.

I'm not so sure.

Sophia scores a haul of pink stuff, a couple dolls, some plushies, jewelry, and such.

"Wow, you are *such* a stereotype," says Sierra. "But... you do love that stuff."

Sophia gathers about nine new plushies in a group hug, grinning at the parents. "Thank you!"

As far as my gifts go, they consist mostly of clothing and a few cute figurines from Mom. The Littles combined efforts and got me a Steam gift card so I can choose a video game or two. Aww. Oh, and Dad hands me a flat, smallish box.

Curious, I slice off the wrapping paper with a claw. Looks like the kind of box a necklace might come in. Excited, I pull the lid off and open the tissue paper inside. Sigh. He gave me a red Rambo-style headband.

"You mentioned you didn't have one." Dad grins.

As soon as I hold it up, giving him a 'really?' smirk, everyone bursts into laughter. Oh heck, why not? I start to put it on to be silly, but Dad grasps my arm.

"Don't put it on unless butts need to be kicked. Respect the headband," says my father in an overacted, solemn tone.

Again, everyone laughs.

He pulls something out of his robe pocket. "Here. Might as well have this, too. Needed the box for the headband."

Dad hands me a wad of tissue paper. I unfurl it to reveal a gold necklace with a pendant depicting a cute chibi vampire girl. Aww.

"Dad..." I hug him. "Thank you."

He pats me on the back.

"Oh, hey." Sam pulls a small, flat box out from under the tree, examines it, then stands. "This is for you guys." He runs it over to the 'rents.

Mom and Dad exchange a confused look, shrug, and take the box.

"From Sarah," says Dad.

Mom smiles at me.

He holds the box while she lifts the lid off. They look over the contents and gasp at me.

"Sarah..." Mom gawks for a little while before she remembers how words work. "A seven-day stay in Iceland? *With* airfare?"

"How the heck did you afford this?" asks Dad, gobsmacked.

"A lot of pizza deliveries," mutters Sam.

I wink. "Nah. I have a few tricks."

Mom waves the tickets and vacation voucher at me. "You stole this?"

"No. I kinda got a, umm... *gold* card."

Most people might think it difficult to convert leprechaun gold coins to modern cash, but most people don't rub elbows with Aurélie Merlier. She has connections and set me up with a guy. Yours truly has a bank account. Though, it's a little different. There's some trick to the way vampires manage their finances so they can avoid scrutiny and detection for existing so long. It's got something to do with corporate law, but it's over my head. Aurélie's going to explain it to me soon. So, yeah, the pouch appeared to be empty from the outside, but held a decent amount of coins. At Aurélie's suggestion, I only converted a handful of them into modern money. Gold holds value more reliably than digital numbers in a computer somewhere—and won't disappear if society disintegrates.

"A gold card..." Mom shakes her head.

"Not a credit thing. I'm making a leprechaun joke."

They both make 'ohh' faces at me.

"Straight up. It's legit. Really paid for. No mind tricks." I grin. "Merry Christmas, you guys."

Little footsteps thunder overhead upstairs.

"Did we have another one while I wasn't looking?" asks Dad.

Mom '*pffs*.'

Ronan runs downstairs in his pajamas. He rushes over to Sam, excitedly telling him about the new PlayStation 4 he got for Christmas. Sam, somewhat out of character for him, cheers excitedly.

"Where the heck did he come from?" asks Mom.

Sierra, Sophia, and I say, "Mirror," at the same time. The boys keep cheering. Ronan invites Sam over to play video games, but it's a bit late, and Christmas Eve, so a sleepover is kinda out of the question. They plan on tomorrow after dinner. Sierra is bizarrely responsible and *doesn't* start waving her sword around despite adoring it. She does, however, get her hands on an empty wrapping paper tube and goes full samurai. Sophia's in girly-girl heaven, swimming in plushies and pink stuff.

The joy in the air is so powerful I almost forget entirely about being a vampire.

Yeah, the stupidity attack I had in London, wondering if I made the right decision to stay with my family? Pff. Yeah. Absolutely the right thing. I'd do it again ten times. The future is going to be weird, but I'm going to make it work—no matter who I have to ki—mind control.

"Oh." Sierra pauses walloping the sofa arm. "I hate to be the bearer of dread, but we're not safe yet."

The room goes quiet. Everyone—myself included—stares at her. What the hell happened now? Did brownies follow me home? What sort of demon did Sam conjure up? Having an imp around is sort of a magnet for other paranormal stuff. Crap, don't tell me I missed an LA vampire out for revenge.

"Mew?" asks Klepto, eyes wide.

Sierra shivers. "Grandma Sheridan called. Uncle Hank decided to be here tomorrow for Christmas dinner."

"Ugh! You scared me," yells Sophia.

Sam shrugs.

Dad snickers.

I exhale out my nose, shaking my head at her.

Mom points at me and makes a 'you know what you must do' face.

"Uncle Hank's not gonna be a problem." An innocent grin curls my lips. "I got this."

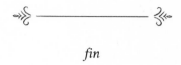

fin

ACKNOWLEDGMENTS

Thank you for reading *An Introduction to Paranormal Diplomacy!*

Additional thanks to Lee Sheridan for editing and Alexandria Thompson for the cover design. Sarah's story will continue in book ten...

ABOUT THE AUTHOR

Originally from South Amboy NJ, Matthew has been creating science fiction and fantasy worlds for most of his reasoning life. Since 1996, he has developed the "Divergent Fates" world, in which *Division Zero, Virtual Immortality, The Awakened Series, The Harmony Paradox, and the Daughter of Mars series* take place. Along with being an editor at Curiosity Quills press, he has worked in IT and technical support.

Matthew is an avid gamer, a recovered WoW addict, Gamemaster for two custom RPG systems, and a fan of anime, British humour, and intellectual science fiction that questions the nature of reality, life, and what happens after it.

He is also fond of cats.

Visit me online at:
Facebook: https://www.facebook.com/MatthewSCoxAuthor
Amazon: https://www.amazon.com/author/mscox
Pinterest: https://www.pinterest.com/matthewcox10420/
Goodreads: https://www.goodreads.com/author/show/7712730.Matthew_S_Cox
Email: mcox2112@gmail.com

- Prophet's Journey

Divergent Fates Anthology

(Fiction Novels - Adult)

The Roadhouse Chronicles Series

- One More Run
- The Redeemed
- Dead Man's Number

Faded Skies series

- Heir Ascendant
- Ascendant Unrest
- Ascendant Revolution

Temporal Armistice Series

- Nascent Shadow
- The Shadow Collector
- The Gate to Oblivion

Vampire Innocent series

- A Nighttime of Forever
- A Beginner's Guide to Fangs
- The Artist of Ruin
- The Last Family Road Trip
- The Phantom Oracle
- How Not to Summon Demons
- Ordinary Problems of a College Vampire
- A Vampire's Guide to Surviving Holidays

- An Introduction to Paranormal Diplomacy

Standalones

- Wayfarer: AV494
- Axillon99
- Chiaroscuro: The Mouse and the Candle
- The Spirits of Six Minstrel Run
- Sophie's Light
- The Far Side of Promise anthology
- Operation: Chimera (with Tony Healey)
- The Dysfunctional Conspiracy (with Christopher Veltmann)
- Of Myth and Shadow
- The Girl Who Found the Sun

Winter Solstice series (with J.R. Rain)

- Convergence
- Containment
- Catalyst

Alexis Silver series (with J.R. Rain)

- Silver Light
- Deep Silver
- Silver Quarrel

Samantha Moon Origins series (with J.R. Rain)

- New Moon Rising
- Moon Mourning

Vampire For Hire series (with J.R. Rain)

- Moon Master
- Dead Moon
- Lost Moon

Maddy Wimsey series (with J.R. Rain)

- The Devil's Eye
- The Drifting Gloom
- Dark Mercy

Samantha Moon Case Files series (with J.R. Rain)

- Blood Moon

Immortal Operative series (with J.R. Rain)

- Broken Ice

Young Adult Novels

The Eldritch Heart Series

- The Eldritch Heart
- The Cursed Crown

Evergreen Series

- Evergreen
- The World That Remains
- The Lucky Ones
- Nuclear Summer

Standalones

- Caller 107
- The Summer the World Ended
- Nine Candles of Deepest Black
- The Forest Beyond the Earth
- Out of Sight

Middle Grade Novels

The Adventures of Ubergirl series

- My Dad is a Mad Scientist
- Aliens Ate My Homework
- The End of all Halloweens

Tales of Widowswood series

- Emma and the Banderwigh
- Emma and the Silk Thieves
- Emma and the Silverbell Faeries
- Emma and the Elixir of Madness
- Emma and the Weeping Spirit

Standalones

- Citadel: The Concordant Sequence
- The Cursed Codex
- The Menagerie of Jenkins Bailey

Made in the USA
Middletown, DE
31 January 2020